Books by Jackie Kessler

HELL'S BELLES

THE ROAD TO HELL

Published by Kensington Publishing Corporation

THE ROAD TO HELL

JACKIE KESSLER

ZEBRA BOOKS
KENSINGTON PUBLISHING CORP.
http://www.kensingtonbooks.com

ZEBRA BOOKS are published by

Kensington Publishing Corp.
850 Third Avenue
New York, NY 10022

ISBN-13: 978-0-8217-8103-6
ISBN-10: 0-8217-8103-0

First Zebra Trade Paperback Printing: November 2007
10 9 8 7 6 5 4 3 2 1

Printed in the United States of America

This book is for Brett, my very own White Knight
(with just a hint of demon).
I love you.

Acknowledgments

Lots of people made this book possible, and they all deserve to win the lottery. Or, at least, own a private island or two.

To the Kensington team—John Scognamiglio, Magee King, Maureen Cuddy, and the whole Zebra gang—and to my agent, Ethan Ellenberg: you made everything possible.

To everyone at Backspace and to my writing group: You people rule. As always.

To the following people, who are invested in all things Hell: Jaci Burton, Cathy Clamp, Elaine Cunningham, MaryJanice Davidson, Ty Drago, Lila Dubois, Zinnia Hope, Brian Howe, Caitlin Kittredge, Joe Konrath, Richelle Mead, Diane Nudelman, Rainfeather Pearl, and Michelle Rowen.

Without the following people, Hell would only be a state of mind:
Renee Barr: Love your inner demon, baby!
Heather Brewer: Words cannot describe how seriously you rock. Seriously.
Stevie Guttman: L.A. is a different sort of Hell completely.

Most of all, to my mom and dad, who absolutely promised to skip the nookie scenes; to my wonderful boys, Ryan and Mason, who won't be allowed to read the Hell books until they're at least thirty-five; and to Brett, as always—it's all good, love.

Thank you all.

PART ONE

JESSE AND THE ANGEL

Prologue

On the Precipice

Whoever said you see your life flash before your eyes when you die was full of crap. You don't see your entire life. Just the most important parts.

Or, in my case, just the most recent parts.

As I die now, feeling strong arms holding me tight, hearing a voice whisper that it's okay, my mind plays back the events that set me on the road to Hell, good intentions and all. Faces flash behind my closed eyes, almost too fast to follow—the incubus's fang-filled grin, the Erinyes hissing with reptilian fury, the angel crying fat, salty tears. My love, my White Knight, a name on his lips that isn't mine.

Nice to know there's a "rewind" button that comes with life. If only there were an "erase" button for the really sucky parts . . .

Darkness pulls me down, my heart slows, stops . . . and once again, I'm in Spice.

Chapter 1

Spice

"**I**'m from Death Valley."

"Really?" I smiled as I poured champagne into two long-stemmed flutes. *Death Valley*. Heh. People had such a sense of humor when it came to naming things. Take Slaughterville, Oklahoma, or my personal favorite: Hell, Michigan. There's also Paradise, Pennsylvania, but I don't hold that against them; they also have the spiffy town of Intercourse.

Handing a glass to the dark-haired man seated across from me, I said, "I've never heard of anyone actually being from Death Valley before. Scorpions and vultures, sure. People, not so much."

He grinned, and a blush crept up his cheeks until it stained his big ears. Bless me, he was so endearing—he embarrassed easily and he was free with his money. What more could a girl ask for?

"Actually," he said, "I just work there. I'm a park ranger."

Ooh, a do-gooder. The last ranger I'd met had been of the bow-and-arrow variety, many years ago. Different beastie altogether. That ranger, a Royal Forester by trade, had been all too happy to bloody those he'd been sworn to protect in between bouts of raping women. Charming fellow. Sexy, in a pond scum sort of way. Remembering forest and frost and picking twigs out of his beard before our last romp in the crisp snow, I sank back onto the black leather sofa, feeling a smile stretch across my face.

Those had been good times.

"A ranger," I said to my latest client, rolling the word on my tongue. I tucked my legs beneath my body as I inclined on my left elbow, making sure my boobs almost, but not quite, spilled out from my low-cut red gown. Why give something away when Ranger here would be all too happy to pay me? I flashed him my best Utterly Smitten smile. "I'd love to hear more about what you do."

His blush deepened. "I guess that depends on what day it is. Sometimes I'm a tour guide. Sometimes I'm a naturalist. And then there's times I have to be a cop."

Ah. No wonder I'd taken a shine to him. Thinking of my own cop—who would actually be home tonight the same time I was, huzzah!—I asked, "Is there really that much trouble in the desert?"

"Well, not so much as like in the cities. But we get our share." The redness faded from his ears and cheeks as he spoke, and something hard and proud flickered in his brown eyes. Watching Ranger transform from a blushing boy into a seasoned man sent a delicious tingle up my spine. Yum.

Stop that, Jesse. Don't get all hot and bothered by the nice customer. A friendly chat, a little drink in the mega-expensive Champagne Room, a private dance or two, clothing optional. No more. "What kind of trouble?"

"We get our ravers, our smugglers, our scrappers. We even get our full-fledged homicidal maniacs."

Ooh, really? How cool was *that*? "What sort of maniacs? Serial killers?"

Okay, nipples, that's enough. Down, girls.

"Well, the Manson Family hid out in the Panamint Valley."

"That part of Death Valley?"

"It's part of the larger park, yeah."

"Sounds like it can be dangerous," I said, putting an extra purr in my voice.

He shrugged, but the flush returned to his cheeks. My

Ranger was modest. "I patrol in a Hummer, and I wear a bullet-proof vest. That's with the temperature soaring well past a hundred degrees. And my M16, of course. I wouldn't go anywhere without it."

Broiling hot sun combined with assault weapons. Sweet.

"Tell me more," I said, taking a tiny sip of champagne. I hated the stuff—it was so light and airy that even angels would have bitched about it—but my current Tall, Dark, and Handsome had ordered it as soon as we'd entered the Champagne Room. Maybe he thought it was obligatory. "Why'd you become a ranger?"

"I'm third generation. My parents both were rangers, and my grandpa before them. I love being part of the park service. And I love our mission."

"Mission?"

He took a deep breath, then said in a practiced singsong: "'To conserve the scenery and the natural and historic objects and the wild life therein and to provide for the enjoyment of the same in such manner and by such means as will leave them unimpaired for the enjoyment of future generations.'" He grinned at me before taking a deep swig of champagne. "National Park Service Organic Act, 1916."

"Impressive." Me, I preferred the Orgasmic Act of the here and now. "It's good that you're doing something you really believe in."

"What about you, Jezebel? Why'd you become a stripper?"

"Oh, I needed a career change," I said, toying with my drink. "I love dancing on stage, feeling the music moving through me. And I like taking off my clothes," I added with a wink. "So I decided to become an exotic dancer."

He said nothing for a moment as he stared at my face, a goofy smile on his lips. Based on how he was making with the soulful looks, Ranger seemed more turned on by my large green eyes than by my breasts doing their own rendition of "June Is Bustin' Out All Over." Crap, I'd guessed wrong; I'd been sure he was a boob man. There'd been a time when I automatically knew what Hook worked for each client—long hair, dangerous curves, narrow ankles, you name it. Now all I had to go by was my gut. Clearly, that dandy hunch factor wasn't as fine-tuned as my sex drive.

Mental note: Work on the whole women's intuition thing.

Finally Ranger said, "You're about the most beautiful woman I've ever seen."

Ooh. Flattery. Right up there with chocolate. "You're a sweetie."

"No, I mean it. Your eyes, your smile . . . God, your tits . . ."

Hah, I'd been right. Smiling, I took another sip of champagne.

He broke away from my eyes to slowly look me over, eating me with his gaze. He ogled the swells of my breasts, the curve of my hip, the V of my crotch. As he feasted on the image of my flesh, I swallowed my drink, knowing that all I was to him was eye candy, a snapshot of sexual gratification. Nothing more.

Über cool.

I grinned at him, my lipstick shining in the softly lit room— enticing, advertising the things I could do to him with my mouth. That's right, sweetie. You want to taste the alcohol on my lips, want to pepper my flesh with your kisses . . .

As Chris Rock once said, there's no sex in the Champagne Room. But that didn't mean I couldn't *think* about there being sex in the Champagne Room.

In the background, the music from the hidden speakers switched to Patti LaBelle's "Lady Marmalade." Excellent tune, sultry vocals. I let my shoulders move with the beat, felt my skin humming from the sound of the piano keys.

"Say," Ranger said, his voice husky, "would you mind dancing for me now?"

"Love to." I placed my glass on the side table, then rose to my feet. With my stiletto-clad foot, I nudged his legs apart. Standing between his knees, I leaned forward, shoulders back, until my rack was inches away from his sweating face. I ran my hands over my twin mounds until they nipped out, straining against the material of my gown.

He groaned, then parted his lips as if he were dying to give suck. "Oh, Jezebel . . . you're killing me . . ."

Heh. Not even close. I don't do that anymore.

"I'm supposed to start in the middle of the song, charge you for a full. But I like you." I raised my arms high and shimmied, getting all jiggly and wiggly. "I'll just consider this a warm-up. No extra charge."

Ranger said something like "Argghluh" and proceeded to drool.

Winking, I teased him with a teeny nip slip. Peek-a-boob.

"Jezebel," he breathed, "would you mind if I . . . um . . . touched myself while you dance?"

"Sweetie," I said, lowering myself into his lap, "I'd be honored."

One thing about a guy coming while you're giving him a lap dance: it's damn sticky.

I dashed to the women's room as fast as my five-inch heels would allow me. It was one thing to give the nod to Ranger doing the hand-over-fist thing with his salami; getting his jizz on my gown was something else entirely. I'd assumed he'd have enough control to hold back until I'd stripped down to my G-string. But no—as soon as I popped my tits out of my dress, blastoff. Blech.

Not that I particularly minded being covered in bodily fluids. But I drew the line at cum dripping off my work clothes. A gal's got to have some standards. And technically, it's a no-no for customers to touch themselves, or us, even in the privacy of the Champagne Room. If any of the bouncers—or, gah, the floor manager—saw the lewinsky drying on my dress, Ranger would be banned from the club. Forcibly. Premature ejaculation aside, Ranger was a decent guy; I didn't want him to get roughed up.

Besides, the poor dear had been so embarrassed that he'd emptied his billfold to make up for it. A five-hundred-dollar tip goes a long way to forgiving such a faux pas.

I rounded the corner and saw the women's room at the end of the hall. One of the other dancers kept a supply of oxi-something in one of the bathroom cabinets for just such a stainage emergency. If I had another gown in my locker, I simply would have shucked the dress off, poured another one over my body, and not looked back. Problem was, all my clean gowns were currently balled up in the hamper at Paul's apartment, doing their dirty clothing impersonation. Mental note: Do laundry.

Mental note, part two: Learn how to do laundry.

Yanking open the door to the bathroom, I was greeted with a stink foul enough to curl my hair. Yow, someone recently visited the fudge factory. Waving a hand in front of my nose, I beelined it to the sink—the one farthest from the rows of toilet stalls—and was about to turn on the water when I heard a soft groan.

Breathing through my mouth, I saw Circe seated in the far corner of the room, at the end of the huge vanity table. The raven-haired beauty was staring intently at her reflection in the wall mirror, clutching something to her chest. I glimpsed her pale face and dark eyes in the mirror, but it was the hugely muscled man looming behind her that grabbed my attention.

Dressed in a sleeveless tank and biker shorts that left nothing to the imagination, he stood behind her, massaging her shoulders. Leonardo da Vinci would have creamed his pants to have this guy model for him. His body was perfectly proportioned, perfectly sculpted, and he radiated confidence almost to the point of arrogance. Slurp! Score one for Circe. After her shift was over, I'd have to corner her and get all the juicy details about her latest love. Last I'd heard, she'd fallen hard for some skinny blond guy. Guess that was yesterday's news.

Mister Gorgeous bent over and whispered something in Circe's ear. She sucked in a hitching breath, then let out a soft moan, closed her eyes.

Humph. Maybe there was no sex in the Champagne Room, but it looked like the ladies' room was up for grabs. I must have missed that memo.

I opened my mouth to ask Circe how she could even think about foreplay with the smell in the bathroom as overpowering as it was, when I realized three things. One, Circe was crying. Two, Mister Gorgeous cast no reflection. And three, there was a dull red glow around Circe. This wasn't a freshly fucked glow, either. It pulsed around her like a dying heart—slow, sickly, erratic.

Shit.

I didn't know which was worse—that the aura around my pal meant she was perilously close to dying, or that there was a demon giving my pal a backrub. Of course, the latter explained the former.

Okay, Jesse. Play dumb. Most mortals can't see the nefarious. Ignore the obscenely huge—and hello, very turned on—demonic entity. Hmm. Actually, there was one place where he wasn't so huge. Must be the infernal equivalent of steroids.

"Circe? You okay?"

"Ignore her," Mister Gorgeous said, casting me a long look. "She couldn't possibly understand the pain he's caused you. He doesn't love you."

Circe said, "He doesn't love me." Her voice cracked, shattered into a thousand pieces.

"Who doesn't?" Right, keep your voice steady. Don't look at Mister Gorgeous. You don't see him, la la la . . .

"Larry." Circe said his name with a sob.

Pasting a smile on my face, I did something very brave, and completely stupid. I walked over to her, sat in the chair next to her, within spitting distance of the hulking demon. Pay no attention to the evil creature behind the curtain. The stench emanating from him was strong enough to make my eyes water. Now I recognized it for what it was: brimstone.

I said, "Larry? You mean the skinny blond guy? Sweetie, you can do better than him."

"You gave him your heart," the demon said. "He chewed it up and spat it at your feet. Show him how much he hurt you, how you can't live without his love."

Circe's breath was coming in hitches. I reached over to pat her hand, and that's when I saw the bottle of prescription pills she was holding in a death grip by her chest. "Whatcha got there?"

"He doesn't love me," she said again. "I gave him my heart, and he chewed it up and spat it at my feet."

Uh oh. Cyrano de Bergerac, infernal style. Very bad news. "Sweetie, there are other guys out there."

"I can't live without his love." Her voice faded as if someone had turned the volume way down, and something went dead in her eyes. She unscrewed the bottle cap. In a tiny voice, she said, "I'll show him."

I grabbed her arm, but she wrenched it away. Shit, she was strong. Massaging my sore hand, I darted a glance over her shoulder. Yup, the demon still had his hands clamped onto her shoulders. Not quite possession, but definitely influencing her actions.

The cheating bastard.

"Show him you still have your pride," Mister Gorgeous said. "Swallow the pills. All of them."

"I still have my pride," she said, her voice a monotone. She opened the bottle.

I touched her elbow. "Circe, listen to me. Unrequited love is a bitch, but it's not worth dying over. Come on, girl, this is stupid."

She spilled some blue pills into her palm.

Fuck. Okay, let's try some shock therapy. I slapped her, hard. The crack echoed in the room.

Blinking, she turned away from the mirror to look at me. My handprint stained her cheek an angry red. "Jesse . . . ?"

"Forget about the skinny blond asshole," I said. "He's not worth it."

"She doesn't understand how he hurt you," Mister Gorgeous said.

Circe echoed, "He hurt me . . ."

"Sweetie, he has no idea what he's missing out on. You're a sexy, funny, wonderful girl. And if he doesn't want a part of that, he's an imbecile."

She looked down at the bottle, at the pills in her hand. "You think so?"

"Probably impotent too."

That brought a faint smile to her lips. "Yeah?"

I said, "I read it somewhere, in one of those business maga-

zines, that it's been proven that the higher the level of imbecileness, the higher the likelihood of impotence."

"'Imbecileness'?"

"What, it's a word."

Her smile slipped. "I really love him. Why doesn't he want
me?"

"Because he's an imbecile. I thought we covered this. It's
not even his fault. Imbecileness runs rampant in the male sex.
Comes with all the testosterone."

"Think so?"

"Yup." I held out my hand. "Care if I hold your pharmaceu-
ticals for you?"

In her ear, the demon roared: "Swallow the pills!"

Circe frowned, turned her head. "You hear something?"

"Just the hum of the fluorescents. Know what you need?"

She shook her head.

"A glass of wine and a good vibrator."

Circe barked out a surprised laugh. "Jesse!"

"I'm telling you, it's a surefire cure-all for everything that
ails you, from a broken heart to the common cold."

"I thought that was chicken soup."

"I have never heard of pleasuring yourself with chicken
soup," I said. "But I'm willing to give it a shot." I made a
gimme gesture. "Fork it over."

With a sigh, she plopped the bottle into my hand, then the
loose pills.

Behind her, Mister Gorgeous said nothing, radiated pure
rage. Gleep.

"Come on, sweetie," I said, doing my best not to eye the invisible demon. "Let's cut out early. First round's on me."

Circe stood, looking vulnerable and beautiful, like a sculp-
ture of flowers. "You sure?"

"Absolutely. Let's tell Jerry to move us off the stage lineup,
then we'll tip out." The DJ was a real prick about dancers
missing their rotation; I'd have to slip him an extra twenty to
mollify him.

"Okay." She smiled at me. "Thanks, Jesse. I . . . Jesus, I don't know what I was thinking. Suicide's a sin."

"I keep forgetting you're so damn religious."

"I'll find Joey, tell him we're cutting out. Meet you back here to change?"

No freaking way was I staying in a bathroom with an angry demon. I started to get up when I felt a crushing weight press down on my shoulder, my neck. The demon squeezed, and suddenly I couldn't breathe.

I wanted to shriek at the top of my lungs. What I said in a hoarse whisper was, "You bet."

Circe took a deep breath, straightened her spine, and sauntered out of the women's room.

As soon as the door closed, something tangled in my hair and yanked my head back. I dropped the bottle and the pills spilled from my hand, bounced on the tile floor. Over the nauseating odor of sulfur, the ripe stink of my fear clung to my nostrils. Blood roared in my ears, pounded in my head, and my heart jackhammered like it wanted to break free from my chest. My arms were leaden, dead things; my feet were rooted on the floor. I couldn't run, even if the demon released me.

But as I stared up into his face, I had a sinking suspicion that the last thing Mister Gorgeous wanted to do was let me go.

"I know you," he said, his face twisting into a leer. "You're the slut from the Courtyard."

Even through my overwhelming fear, I heard the capital C in Courtyard . . . and I placed him.

Tell us, is it true that all Seducers are pox-infested carriers of disease?

Oh boy. Oh boy, oh boy, oh boy. Mister Gorgeous was a demon of Pride—and he had a personal grudge against me. Granted, most creatures of Arrogance had a chip on their shoulders when it came to one of my kind . . . former kind. Pride and Lust rarely work well together, unless there's seriously strong drink involved. But he had a reason to despise me: I'd embarrassed him in front of his buddies. To one of the Arrogant, there's no worse crime.

Licking my lips, I tried for the Dumb Blonde approach, ignoring the fact that my hair was a curly black. "Never saw you before." I even spoke with the right balance of Pants-Pissing Terror and Indignant New Yorker. Maybe he'd think I was just one of those rare mortals who were able to see the supernatural. "Let me go."

"You're lying. You smell of sex, slut."

"Last customer got too happy, got his splooge on me."

"That's not a lie." His grip on my scalp tightened, and I felt clumps of hair tearing at the roots. Between the shriek of agony atop my head and the flare of pain from biting my lip to keep from screaming, I was one raw nerve. "But you do know me," he said. "Oh yes, slut. And I know you."

Fuck.

He grinned, and my breath strangled in my throat. Icy fingers tripped up my spine, reached out to grip my heart. The demon bent down until his mouth was inches away from mine. "Once a fifth-level succubus, now a flesh puppet with a soul. How appropriate. The only thing lower than your type of trash is humans."

"My soul," I said through clenched teeth. "It's clean."

"You entice humans with thoughts of lust. Your work is in the name of Sin."

Yeah, well, old habits die hard. After four thousand years as a Seducer, what was I going to do, be a telemarketer? "Not Sin. Entertainment."

"A fine line."

"Maybe. Still a line. You can't claim me."

He growled, deep and low in his chest. "You talk tough for a mortal slut. You don't have your Fury friend with you to keep you safe this time."

My throat constricted as I remembered the softest brush of lips on my own. Just thinking of Meg brought angry tears to my eyes. "Don't need her protection."

"You think not?"

"You can't claim me for Hell. My soul's clean." Benefit of being only thirty days old in mortal years: that's not a lot of time to wreak havoc.

His eyes narrowed, and for a moment I glimpsed his true form swimming beneath his false human shell—charred black flesh, white holes for eyes, a maw crammed with razor-blade teeth. Then he pulled my head up until I was sitting up straight in the chair. He spun me around to face him, his hand still tangled in my hair.

"Old rules are bending, breaking."

"I got that," I said, far calmer than I had any right to be. "Seems the nefarious are encouraging mortals to kill themselves. What, business is too slow?"

"Business is booming." His dark gaze held me, explored me. "You mortals make excuses for your sins, think you can talk your way out of damnation. As if understanding why you commit certain actions allows you to forgive the action itself."

A demonic therapy session. Spare me. "The end doesn't exactly justify the means. I know that."

"The mortal coil is steeped in evil. Murder because of disrespect. Genocide because of disgust." He leered. "Lust because of entertainment."

My heart, already careening at marathon speed, started rocketing at a pace just short of cardiac arrest. Bless me, I hated being afraid. I really preferred causing fear—which is hard to do when you're short, cute, and human. Maybe I should start carrying a big gun. "You know what they say. The world's going to Hell in a handbasket."

"The trip is taking too long. No more sitting back, waiting for humans to die before collecting their souls for the Pit. We're encouraging them along."

I pushed aside my fear to sniff my disdain. Even an ex-demon has sin standards. "You assholes are cheating."

"Times are changing, slut." For a moment, his eyes closed in on themselves, faded to something old, worn. He released my hair. "We can't let the world be more evil than the Abyss."

I heard the implication behind his words, and I shivered. People think that the Devil is the King of Hell. They're wrong. The Devil—the nameless antithesis of the Almighty—has been around way, way longer than the celestials or the nefarious. The only thing keeping It from destroying all of humanity, and the world itself, is Hell. Torturing souls amuses the fuck out of the Devil.

At least, it used to.

Wrapping my arms around myself, I said, "So your King is changing the rules. Keeping things lively."

"You have no idea just how much has changed." He shook himself like a dog, regained his malefic ire as he smiled a shark's grin, all teeth and appetite. "And that means, slut, we can influence your actions more so than ever before. To put it in language even you could understand, we can seduce you."

Arrogant prick. "You really have to work on your pick-up lines."

"What's that pithy saying the mortals like to throw around? Oh, yes. 'The devil made me do it.' Quaint." His eyes gleamed. "And now, rather accurate."

I swallowed thickly. If the infernal really were going to be actively influencing people, encouraging them to live fast and die young, life was about to get much more interesting. Mental note: Start thinking pure thoughts.

Oh, puke, who was I kidding?

"I say with supreme confidence that I'll see you in Hell, slut. But you know," he added, "the Pit is a better place without you and your Fury friend."

I frowned, wondering what he meant by that. Of course Meg was in Hell. That's where the Furies hung their hats, like most creatures who weren't inherently Good. If not in Hell, where else could she be?

Stop. Don't think about her. She betrayed you, left you to die.

Her voice, like a kiss, in my mind: *We all do what we must.*

"Until next time, slut." Grinning like he'd eaten all the kids in a candy shop, the Arrogant disappeared in a puff of sulfur.

There's nothing worse than a demon with a grudge. And a little dick.

Chapter 2

Paul's Apartment

Three hours and eight hundred dollars later, I was chin-deep in a delicious bath, thinking very dirty thoughts as my body got squeaky clean. I'd actually netted more than a thousand today, but Circe's thirst had burned a hole in my wallet. The girl could drink like a parched fish. After our boozefest, I'd put her in a cab and paid the driver well, asking him to make sure she got into her apartment safe and sound.

This humanity crap was really crimping my style. Had to be the soul. Next thing you know, I'd be wearing a halo. Gah.

Paul's bathtub had all the necessary amenities: frothy bubbles that tickled my nose, and a handheld shower massager that tickled me in much more sensitive spots. Dotting the corners of the tub were pale tea candles, their wicks glowing the soft, deep yellow of an overripe mango on the verge of spoiling.

Yum.

I closed my eyes and inhaled deeply, taking in the faint scent of lavender. Whoever invented aromatherapy candles should have his own national holiday. Granted, lavender wasn't as soothing as a cup of hot tea, or slurping the marrow out of a femur, but it did fine in a pinch. (Not that I'd done any marrow slurping in quite a while, but hey—a gal can reminisce.)

The only thing missing was Paul Hamilton himself. He was

still at work, busy playing vice cop, instead of home with me, playing Cabin Boy and soaping my back. I sighed, petulantly splashed some water over the rim. Figured that the one day this week we were supposed to be home at the same time, he was running late.

Well, at least I had my spiffy water buddy, complete with three settings. Speaking of which . . .

Ummmmmm . . .

Just as I was turning the dial from "light spray/pulsing massage" up to "orgasmic," something outside the bathroom went *thump*.

I shut off the shower attachment and sat up with a frown, bubbles clinging to my nipples like effervescent pasties. After a moment, I heard someone moving down the front hall.

A huge grin broke across my face. My Cabin Boy returneth.

Pulling myself up, I stepped out of the tub. My skin immediately pebbled from the cool air; Paul kept the apartment set at sixty-eight, but I was used to hotter. Teeth chattering, I grabbed a towel and dried myself off fast enough to give myself friction burns. Even though I was planning on getting utterly soaked again (inside and out), no one liked lying in a wet spot.

Sufficiently less moist, I wrapped the damp white towel around my torso and tucked the end between my breasts. Style by way of muumuu. The mirror over the sink showed me not quite at my finest. Without makeup, my face was very much a second-glance sort of pretty: large green eyes, sharp nose and chin offset by full cheeks and cupid-bow lips, pale skin that made Goths burn with envy. Thick black hair framed my face with a million annoying curls. Fair skin, dark hair—a striking combination that added up to bleaching, tweezing, and cursing. On the plus side, my body was lithe and lean, with tits that didn't quit and strong, shapely legs. On the not-so-plus side, barefoot I stood at five-foot-four.

I really should have opted to look like a supermodel when I had myself magicked into a human. Twenty-twenty hindsight, and all of that.

A quick finger-comb proved that my hair was on strike. Fuck it. I'd pretend the tousled wet look from the 1980s was back in fashion. And Paul would be too busy locking lips with me to notice my scary hair.

Another thump, closer to the bathroom. Time to get lusty.

Thinking about whether I would start Paul off with a tongue bath or the real thing, I opened the bathroom door and padded down the hall to the living room. And froze.

Standing by the entertainment center, a woman turned to face me. Her long brown hair flowed over her shoulders and down her back, and a white toga draped around her curves like a frat boy's wet dream. Her blue eyes fixed on my green ones, and I felt the air whoosh out of my body.

Megaera.

Look at that, the Arrogant had been right: she really wasn't in Hell.

My heart sank down to my toes, pausing only to set my stomach aflutter. I wanted to laugh for joy; I wanted to hurl curses and assorted cutlery at her. I wanted to punch her teeth out until her mouth was bloody; I wanted to kiss her and crush her in a loving embrace. And I wanted it all to happen right now.

Bless me, how on Earth did mortals ever control their emotions? Screw that—how did they ever *understand* them?

Not knowing what to say, I just stared, taking in her appearance. Same old Meg. In the thousand-or-so years I'd been friends with her, I'd rarely seen her dress any differently. The ancient-Greek thing worked for her; she got a kick out of looking delicate. It was part of her warped sense of humor. My chest tightened as a memory flashed in my mind: Meg and me, roasting human drumsticks in the Lake of Fire, giggling like schoolgirls as we shared jokes about the Arrogant and Hell's elite.

And then I remembered the softest brush of her lips on my own as she kissed me and left me to die.

Now, standing before me in Paul's apartment, Meg grinned. There was nothing in that grin that spoke of friendship. It was a thing of madness—all hunger and anticipation.

The sight of that cold grin cut through my tangled mess of emotions. My breath catching in my throat, I stared at her again, stared *through* her shell and saw the flicker of an aura around her: red and thick, like freshly spilled blood.

In a strangled whisper, I said, "You're not Megaera."

The grin pulled into a leer, and her voice hit me like shattered glass. "I never said I was." Crimson pooled in her eyes, then leaked out of the corners and meandered down her face, staining her cheeks.

Oh shit.

My nostrils pinched from a sudden stench of rotten eggs and charred meat, emanating from not-Meg like rank perfume. Brimstone.

Apparently, tonight was Hell Night. Silly me, I'd thought that was just a collegiate fraternity thing.

As I stared into her bleeding eyes, my brain desperately signaled my legs to run like fuck, but my feet were glued to the floor. Helpless, I watched her form shift and blacken, sliding into an ebony caricature of flesh. The face wizened and cracked with age. Brown hair melted into black snakes that coiled in elaborate braids crowning her head. An enormous serpent undulated around her bony shoulders, flowing over her like a slithering ouroboros. The white tunic charred and lengthened until it was an obsidian gown of mourning. Behind her, massive bat-like wings slowly unfurled, engulfing the living room in shadow.

Swallowing thickly, I gazed upon Alecto, one of Meg's two sister Furies. I would have prayed fervently, except I didn't know which direction the prayers should go—up to Heaven or down to Hell. Mental note: Get religion.

Mental note, part two: First survive encounter with malefic entity.

All the bones in my legs melted into pudding, and I crashed to my knees before the Fury. Maybe she'd see it as a sign of respect. Or abject terror. Either worked.

"It seems your newfound soul has weighed down your tongue." She grinned wider, displaying fangs that looked sharp enough to rend steel. "Or perhaps you are just being rude."

I felt the blood drain from my face. Insulting a Fury was a surefire guarantee for a very short life expectancy, so I quashed my fear as best I could and opened my mouth to speak. While I was—had been—close with Meg, I'd had almost no interaction with Alecto. I opted to go the formal route.

"Greetings, Alecto Erinyes." My voice squeaked, but at least I didn't stammer. Yay, me.

The snake sliding across her shoulders moved down to duck its head beneath her left breast. "Your manners are appropriate for a human," the Fury said as the viper copped a reptilian feel. "But your timing needs work."

Eek. "My apologies, Erinyes. I'd mistaken you for another."

"Indeed." She raised a clawed hand to caress tendrils of serpents dangling by her ear. They darted out miniscule forked tongues and tasted her fingers. Beneath the mound of her breast, the larger snake flowed down and around, wrapping her waist in a scaled girdle. "You saw me as my sister. As I wished."

"Why?" The question was out of my mouth before I could call it back.

She leered, and her serpents paused in their finger-bath to hiss their scorn. "You, of all creatures, ask me why I parade as another?"

I bit my lip. Okay, she had a point. But it wasn't exactly my fault that I'd taken Caitlin Harris's form when I'd run away from Hell. Demons weren't trained to do the ethical thing. And really, the witch hadn't exactly complained at the time. (Then again, she'd been too busy experiencing the best orgasm of her life to bitch about me stealing her looks. And credit cards.)

"Besides," Alecto said, her bloody gaze crawling over me, "I thought borrowing one of my sister's outfits would be amusing."

Amusing, she said. I called it sadistic. My eyes began to water from the stink of spoiled eggs. Bless me, had there really been a time when I'd relished that smell?

She folded her arms over her chest, watching me for a moment. The silence between us was palpable, broken only by the sounds of scaled muscle unwrapping itself from her waist and sliding up her arm. Finally she spoke. "You will come with me, you who were Jezebel."

"Where?" My voice hardly cracked. Another point for me.

The blood in her eyes shone wetly. "Hell."

My heart slammed against my ribcage and suddenly I couldn't take a proper breath. Going to Hell as a mortal meant only one thing: torture. For the foreseeable future.

As I strangled with building terror, she stared at me, the blood streaming from her eyes as bright as a cherry's skin. Her claws tapped out a beat as she drummed her fingertips against her forearm. The serpent draped itself over her shoulders, tucked its head beneath the muscle of its body. The Fury waited.

My growing fear paused, allowing me to take a deep, shaky breath.

Waited?

Since when does one of the seven most powerful beings in all of creation wait for anything?

Answer: When she needs something. Desperately.

"Will you come with me?" she asked.

Asked?

"I don't know," I said, confidence overriding my survival instinct, "ever since they changed management, the food is terrible. And the portions are so tiny."

New York humor in the face of eternal damnation.

Her fingers froze on her arm. The snakes of her hair swayed and hissed; the enormous viper coiled around her neck arched its head up and stretched its maw wide, showing me all its pretty fangs. Gleep.

"You mock me?" Alecto sneered, her bloody gaze weighing me and finding me wanting. "You, a little human tempter girl?"

"Actually," I heard myself say, "I prefer to be called an exotic dancer."

Her wings snapped closed, the report as loud as gunfire. I

flinched, then stared down at the floor. Worrying my lip between my teeth, I braced myself for her violent response. I'd pushed my luck. There was a reason why even the Almighty supposedly tiptoed around the Furies. You never, never, *never* piss off an Erinyes. Period. Now she was going to annihilate me, send pieces of me flying through the planes until they rained down along the rim of Creation like organic confetti.

I hoped Paul wouldn't slip on my spleen when he came home from work.

I wished I could tell him goodbye.

"Your tongue will get you into trouble one of these days," Alecto said. "Perhaps I should just rip it out and crisp it over the Lake of Fire."

Gah.

"Now come along. Quietly."

A cold sweat broke over my skin. But even as the fear washed over me and through me, one thought kept me from merrily bidding *adieu* to my sanity: A Fury doesn't ask its prey to come along quietly. A Fury does whatever she damn well pleases.

And on the heels of that, a realization: Alecto was trying to psyche me out.

"Well?" Her voice steamed with impatience . . . and something I thought was uncertainty. "Are you coming?"

I raised my eyes to peer up at her through my bangs. She was drumming her fingers again, the clawed digits pounding her arm so hard they should have left trenches in her skin.

Holy fuck in Heaven, she was *nervous*.

Taking a deep breath, I said, "Sorry. I've already got plans for today."

Her eyes widened for a moment—perhaps when you're almost on par with God in terms of sheer power, you're not used to meeting resistance. Then those bleeding eyes narrowed dangerously.

"Come with me." Above her face, her hair tangled and untangled, the snakes writhing and reflecting their mistress's displeasure. "*Now*."

Hmmm. Still not dead. She must need me pretty badly.
"No."

In the longest pause of my mortal life, I waited with my
breath held. Beads of perspiration tickled my upper lip, making it itch. I fought the urge to wipe the sweat away. When one
played chicken with a malefic entity, one did not acknowledge
any physical discomfort short of decapitation.

After a small eternity, she spoke through clenched fangs.
"Return with me to Hell, you who were Jezebel, and I will take
you to your friend." She spat the last word. As a rule, denizens
of the Underworld weren't too keen on the concept of friendship. It was bad for their image.

I echoed, "My friend?"

"I will take you to Megaera."

The thought of Meg and I reconciling made my heart
dance a jig. Then I saw Alecto's fangs flash in a victorious grin,
and I realized she hadn't been offering a way for Meg and me
to kiss and make up. "Where is she?"

"If you choose to come with me to Hell, you will find out."

The Pit is a better place without you and your Fury friend. I
swallowed thickly, then whispered, "Is she okay?"

"No, tempter girl. She is far from okay. She is in grave torment." Alecto's eyes gleamed as she spoke, reflected her hunger
for violence. "If you come with me to Hell, I will take you to
her. Perhaps your presence would offer her some small comfort. She suffers because of you."

A pitiful sound escaped my mouth. Bless me, I didn't know
what to do. I couldn't go back to the Abyss . . . but I couldn't
leave Meg to suffer.

Alecto's eyes flared like supernovas, and I shielded my face.
Through the sound of her laughter, I heard her voice boom in
my mind:

**Never let it be said that I forced you to make this choice. I
give you a human's day to decide. Until tomorrow, Fury friend.**

The air shrieked as if ripping itself apart . . . and then I
heard nothing other than my own ragged breathing. When I
lowered my arm and opened my eyes, Alecto was gone. In her

place, scorched onto the living room floor, was the outline of a heart with a sword piercing it. The symbol of the Erinyes.

I wrapped my arms around myself as I shivered, staring at the smoking heart. This was the real reason why demons didn't have friends: once you cared about people, they could be used as collateral.

Chapter 3

Paul's Apartment

Okay. Deep breath, Jesse. Now is *so* not the time to panic.

Yeah, right.

I inhaled deeply, and sulfuric fumes scorched my nostrils. Grimacing, I squeezed my nose as if I could wring out the lingering odor of spoiled eggs. Why was it that my memory of brimstone was all warm and fuzzy, but in reality it made me sick? There really should be a support group for former demons that covered all this stuff.

Including how to handle it when Hell comes a-calling. Me and Michael Corleone: Every time we get out, they bring us back in.

Bless me, what were they doing to Meg?

No. I clenched my hands, my nails biting deeply into the soft flesh of my palms. Think about Meg after. First things first: Assess the damage.

Pulling my gaze away from the symbol burned into the floor, I glanced around the living room to see if anything else screamed "An Infernal Presence Was Here." The black leather sofa and matching armchairs sandwiched a glass, black-framed coffee table—Modern Chic as defined by Ikea. Against the opposite wall, the black entertainment center housed a television, a stereo, and roughly a million CDs and DVDs. Over the sofa, three Nagels hung suspended, dressing up the white walls with stylized half-naked women. I always thought Paul had a fine eye for art.

From the look of the room, anyone would think the only visitor here lately was the cleaning lady. As long as they didn't look down.

The hardwood floor was a smoking mess. Smack dab in the center, the pierced heart glowed faintly with dying red embers, giving it the illusion of winking. I gnawed my lower lip as I stared at the symbol. If Paul saw that when he came home, he'd . . .

Blinking, I realized I had no idea how he'd react. Just because we knew each other's bodies intimately and wanted to do the growing-old-and-gray thing together, that didn't mean I could read his mind. But given that the love of my life was a cop, I had a nagging suspicion he wouldn't just shrug off a symbol burned into his living room floor as the price one paid for living in New York City.

Throwing one last look at the ruined floor, I scurried into the tiny kitchen and grabbed the receiver from its cradle on the wall. Wireless phones: proof that magic was all around us, slumming as technology. I hit the star button, the number 1, and then the talk button.

A moment later, a warmth-inducing deep voice said, "Paul Hamilton."

"Heya, sweetie."

"Hey." I heard the smile in his voice, and it made my nipples ache. Bless me, he had such a sexy voice . . . and that smile, ooh . . . "I should be out of here in five, ten minutes." His words were punctuated by the clacking of fingers on a keyboard. That's my Cabin Boy—quite the multi-tasker. "Just have to finish up a bit more paperwork."

"That's okay," I said, grateful that he'd missed the Erinyes. That would have made for an uncomfortable moment, to say the least. *Paul, meet Alecto, Fury of Unceasing Anger. Mind the snakes—they bite. She's here to take me back to Hell. By the way, I used to be a succubus.*

"Say, I was thinking about bringing back some Chinese."

"Great," I said. "Listen, there's something wrong with the floor."

"Maybe some moo shu chicken, a couple egg rolls."

"Fine. About the floor—"

"Or maybe Szechuan wontons. I know you like them hot enough to melt your tongue."

"Sweetie, the floor's sort of messed up."

"Damn."

Biting my lip, I ventured, "But I'm sure it can be fixed . . ."

"I just erased my last two paragraphs. Stupid keyboard."

Huh?

"Look, Jess, I have to go. I keep screwing up the wording on this report. At this rate, I'm never getting out of here."

"But what about the floor?"

"Call George. I'm sure floors are part of the call-the-super list."

"Um, okay." I wondered whether George would consider erasing a smoking, charred glyph as overtime. "I'll do that." Now that I thought about it, did I really want Paul to get involved in Alecto's scheme, whatever it was? *Non, nyet, nein,* and fuck no. I shouldn't have called him at all. Okay, I'd have George help me hide the symbol. No symbol, no questions from Paul.

"Hon?"

"Yeah?"

"What's wrong with the floor?"

"Um. It's probably nothing. Just some scratches." In the pattern of a heart run through with a sword.

"Scratches can be fixed. Definitely call George. Star nine on speed dial. Let me go so I can finally get out of here and pick up dinner for us."

"Thanks, sweetie."

"Love you."

That never failed to make my toes curl. "Love you too." A ridiculous, lovestruck grin smeared across my face as I hung up the phone. It felt perfect.

Paul Hamilton loved me. No matter how bad my immediate future looked, for the moment, all was good.

That's the crappy thing about good moments. They never last.

Five minutes after I called George, the man himself stood in Paul's living room, scratching his head as he looked at the symbol. The super was one of those pear-shaped men that always look like they're wearing a girdle but really aren't. His paint-splattered overalls emphasized his curves in ways that would make Jessica Rabbit jealous. While his body wasn't exactly a paragon of manliness, his mocha skin looked delicious enough to slurp. Beneath a white baseball cap, he had mounds of black hair. I wondered if it was soft or wiry, how it would feel as I ran my fingers through it.

I shook my head. Bad former succubus. No lookee, and definitely no touchee.

But ooh, his hair was so black that it gleamed with blue highlights. Maybe he had blue-black hair all over that pear shape. Maybe he was more like a kiwi, furry outside and so succulent and juicy inside . . .

Argh. Mental head slap. I'm a human. I'm in love with Paul. And I'm definitely not going to think about having sex with a man who had more curves than me.

"Weirdest thing I seen since I been working here," George said, his accent a consonant-twisting combo of Brooklyn and Boston. "You say you found it like this?"

"Yeah."

"And it wasn't like this before you got in the bath?"

"No. I heard a noise, which is why I got out of the tub. And boom, there it was, right there on the floor." Minus the visit from one of the three Furies, of course.

"So someone snuck in, burned that into the floor, and snuck back out, all before you got out of the bath."

I did the Bambi Eyes thing. "Yes."

"Huh." His gaze slid to my cleavage. "You want, you can get dressed while I look at this closer."

Whoops. I glanced down at my towel. Between being a demon of sex for four thousand years and working as an exotic dancer here on the mortal coil, I was used to parading around barely dressed. Actually, I preferred it. I kept forgetting that most people felt uncomfortable when they were naked.

Mental note: Learn modesty.

Looking back at the scorch marks, he asked, "You know who did this?"

"Nope." Lying believably was one of those demon traits that I didn't lose when I became human. Maybe I should go into politics.

"Huh." He almost touched the mark, but he pulled his hand back. "Hey, this is still hot!"

"Fancy that. So can you paint over it?"

"Paint?" He shot me a look that said I was maybe as smart as a brain-dead louse. "You want me to paint over the wood floor?"

"Um. Of course not. I meant stain it."

"Stain."

A quick eye-roll on my part, then, "Look, I really need to either fix this or hide this. Can you do it?"

"Well," he said, rubbing his chin, "maybe. Been a while since I been able to really work with my hands."

Oooh. Wonder what those hands would feel like working on me . . .

Stop it, stop it, *stop it!* Focus, Jesse! "Terrific. So what, you could fix this in like five minutes, maybe?"

His mouth opened, closed. He shook his head. Maybe he was trying to figure out how to speak to me in small words. He took off his cap and wrung it between his hands. Finally he said, "See, I'm going to need a bunch of things. Paintbrush, tung oil, a cloth. Wire brush, maybe steel wool. And a pocket-knife. First I need to see how deep the burns go and grind away the burned wood. Then I got to use the wire brush on it, real careful so I don't got to do any sanding. Then I got to clean it all away with the paintbrush, dab on some oil, and see how it looks. Might have to smooth the whole thing down more with the steel wool."

He paused, either for breath or for dramatic effect. Then he said, "So no, five minutes ain't going to happen."

"Fine," I said. "Maybe ten?"

"Lady, you want to get rid of this in ten minutes? Cover it up with a rug."

"Oh," I said, brightening. "That's smart. Can you get me one of those?"

With a pained look on his face, he said, "You don't even live here, do you?"

I lifted my chin higher. "Of *course* I do."

The pained look melted into suspicion.

"Sort of," I amended. "Paul and I are in love."

"Love." He tugged his cap back over his hair, the rim shadowing his face . . . but not before I saw his dark eyes twinkle. "How sweet."

Something in his voice made me frown, but I couldn't put my finger on it. I tried to sneak a peek at his aura, but all I got for my effort was eyestrain. I couldn't read him. Crap. It figured that the spiffy magical ability I got along with my soul was defective. My talent was less dependable than a condom ten years past its expiration date.

He smirked at the charred heart on the floor. "And look, someone charbroiled their love for you. There's a whole lot of loving going on."

Unease bubbled in my stomach. Maybe I was crazy, but I thought the super lost his tough-guy accent. Clearing my throat, I asked, "So, can you help me?"

His smirk widened, and I noticed his teeth were stained from tobacco or coffee. "You really want my help?"

What I wanted was to give him a mad case of blue balls and then throw him out of the apartment; he was starting to seriously creep me out. But Paul would be home soon, and there was no way he could see the mess on the floor. Short of throwing my towel over it and distracting Paul with my womanly charms, I was out of ideas. So that meant I had to play nice with the super.

I turned on my Helpless Female smile, full strength. "Sweetie, I don't just want your help. I need it."

"Well now." He turned to look at me, his gaze lost beneath the bill of his white baseball cap. He reached out and touched my hand, held it, gave a squeeze. "If you need it, of course I'll give it to you."

Either the innuendo in his words or his unexpected touch made me gasp. Hidden beneath my towel, my sex began to tingle.

His finger rubbed against my palm. Shocks of pleasure rippled beneath his touch, worked their way up my arm. "You're sure you didn't see the one who did this to the floor?"

My voice breathy, I said, "Positive."

George chuckled, his voice rich and deep . . . and lush, almost thick enough to feel it dancing on my skin. With his free hand, he lifted the rim of his cap enough for me to see a soft red glow to his eyes.

"Babes," said the demon inside the man, "you're *such* a liar."

My breath caught in my throat. "Daun?"

George grinned in a very wicked way. "In the borrowed flesh."

Over the millennia, the incubus Daunuan had been the yin to my yang, the bump to my grind. Now that I was a human, his visit meant one of two things—he wanted sex, or he wanted something else along with the sex.

Before I could decide how to react to Daun's presence, he pulled me to George's body and clamped a hand on my bare shoulder. This close, I smelled the faintest hint of sulfur, but it was almost buried under the super's aftershave and sweat.

"Heya, sweetie," I said, trying to keep my voice steady and my sex drive in first gear. "This is a surprise."

Pressed against the super's torso, I was keenly aware that Daun was very, very happy to see me; his happiness jabbed me just above my belly.

"Been a while," Daun whispered into my neck. I felt the tiny hairs there stand on end, teased by his breath. "Missed you lots. When George here swung by, I had to tag along."

"How'd you manage that? He hang a sign up? 'Thrill me, chill me, possess me, baby'?"

"George has a bit of a coke habit. I didn't have to knock. He let me right in."

"Ah." Some mortals made it easy for demons to inhabit their bodies. Addicts of any sort were at the top of the list.

I felt him smile against my neck. " 'Ah'? Boring. Let's go for 'Oh.' "

His tongue trailed against the hollow of my throat. I groaned as a tingle worked its way through me, a soft humming in my belly and lower down. Bless me, how I'd missed his touch, his mouth, his—

The licks turned to kisses, and the tingle between my legs sparked into a full-blown electrical charge.

No, I thought, really wanting to howl a yippie-ki-yay. No, this was wrong.

What could be wrong? my body asked me. *A little friendly foreplay, maybe an orgasm or two. What's so bad about that?*

He's not Paul.

My body scolded me for getting a bout of morals at a distinctly inopportune time.

"Nice," I said, the word nowhere close to describing how Daun was making me feel. "But it's time to stop."

I tried to push him away, but Daun held me tight. The hand on my shoulder moved down to my back, where it began to knead and press. I melted against him as he massaged away my protests. *Stop*, I wanted to say again, but every move of his fingers rubbed away pieces of my willpower, and all I could do was moan. His mouth worked its way up my neck, my jaw, my ear. He hit a doozy of a spot, and I let out a delighted squeal they must have heard three floors down.

Nuzzling against me, he said, "You really want me to stop? Babes, just say the word."

My mouth opened, ostensibly to tell him to stop this right now, I refused to kanoodle with anyone who wasn't my true love. I'd never know what I would have actually said, because he crushed his lips on mine, and my brain short-circuited.

It didn't matter that his physical form was George's—the lust was all Daun's, and so were the moves. George's hand unwrapped my towel, but it was Daun's touch that pebbled my nipples, that made them ache for his mouth. No matter what shapes we'd worn over the millennia, Daun and I had always moved well together. Like now: his tongue rolled with mine as our saliva mingled; his hips rolled with mine as I bucked against him. One hand stayed on my back, pinning me, while the other fondled my breast, caressed its underswell, squeezed. I groaned, but his mouth ate the sound, swallowed it whole.

This was wrong, this was wrong, this was—

He broke the kiss to trail his tongue down my lips, my chin, my neck, down to the valley between my breasts. My breathing quickened as he cupped one full mound with his right hand, then slowly lapped his tongue over the curve of flesh.

It was wrong, but it felt so right.

His other hand released my back and slid between my legs. I groaned again, a mewling sound caught between a protest and a cheer. Daun took my swollen nipple into his mouth, encased it in wetness before he gave suck. And then his fingers slid between my labia, found my clit. *Pressed.*

I threw back my head and let out a cry of pure joy as my blood caught fire. He stroked me, relentless, insistent, and the blaze erupted into an inferno. Clutching his hair, I rocked my hips against him, faster, faster, my body moving with the force of the firestorm threatening to consume me. Cold air hit my nipple as he broke suction, but I was on fire, I *was* the fire, and cold air only coaxed me to burn hotter. Yes—oh, sweet Sin, yes . . .

Sizzling kisses, on my chest, my shoulder, my jaw. Nearly lost in my building climax, I almost didn't hear Daun whisper in my ear: "Call my name."

Ice water couldn't have been more effective at shocking me out of my lustopia.

My senses on hyperdrive, I pulled away from him, even as my body sang a lament for its stillborn orgasm. Shaking, I grabbed the towel from the floor and moved backward, my eyes locked on Daun's as if he were a snake poised to strike.

"Bastard," I panted. "Couldn't leave well enough alone?"

He shrugged, a bemused smile playing on his face. "I'm an incubus. What do you really expect?"

Wrapping the towel over myself until I was covered from armpit to knee, I said, "I expect you not to try to seduce me and steal my soul."

"Oh, but babes," he said, his eyes laughing, "do you know how rare it is for a succubus to actually have a soul?"

My teeth clenched, I said, "I'm not a succubus anymore."

"No?" He lifted his fingers, which glistened with my juices. He slowly licked them, his heated gaze on mine. "You still taste like a succubus."

I hugged myself, but I couldn't stop shivering. "Go away, Daun."

"What's the matter, Jezzie? Oh, sorry. *Jesse*." He flashed me a toothy smile. "I thought you needed my help. Remember?"

"I needed George. Not you."

Still grinning, he spread his arms wide. "But I *am* George."

"I said go away."

"Fine. Be that way. Don't ask for my help with the floor." He paused. "Or with the Erinyes."

My voice tight, I said, "What do you know about that?"

"Me? Why, I don't know anything. You don't need my help, remember?"

I closed my eyes, counted to ten. "You weren't such a schmuck when I was a demon."

He chuckled. "Actually, babes, I've always been this way. Once you got a soul, you lost your sense of humor. To say nothing of your sense of adventure. Or your sense of taste."

I opened my eyes to find him right on top of me, one hand to my left, propped against the wall unit behind me, the other stroking my cheek.

Still rimmed with red, George's brown eyes searched my face as if seeking answers. "You really love that flesh puppet with the big shoulders?"

Ignoring the husky male scent wafting from him, I said, "Yes."

Daun smiled, but there was no humor in it. "Like I said, no accounting for taste. I have *no* idea why your former Queen's still interested in you. You've gotten positively boring."

Maybe my heart didn't actually stop, but for a moment it was a close thing. The last time I'd seen Queen Lillith, she tried to kill me. If a cop hadn't taken down her host body, she probably would have succeeded. "She's back?"

"And badder than before. Completely healed too. Word is she's looking for payback."

All sorts of nasty images danced before my eyes like leprous ballerinas. "What's she planning?"

"Now that would be telling."

For a moment, I said nothing as I pictured shoving Daun into a ditch filled with starving pit bulls. "You really suck."

His smile spread into a feral grin. "I know. I'm good at it. You certainly weren't complaining. Wonder how your man would feel, knowing that his sexpot will always get wet for me?"

"Don't flatter yourself," I said coldly. "I'm with Paul."

He shrugged, his grin still in place. "For now. But there will come a day when you won't push me away, babes. And you'll call my name willingly." For a moment, red blazed in those brown eyes, a look that would have sent angels screaming for God to protect them. "And then you'll be mine. Body and soul."

Fuck.

"You're so cute when you're scared speechless," he said. "Later, babes."

The red in his eyes winked out, and George collapsed on top of me, knocking me to the floor. I grunted as I hit, and again as two hundred fifty pounds of dead weight landed on me.

Struggling to get George off of me, I cursed and screamed and kicked. None of that helped. He was out cold—side effect of a demon suddenly leaving its host body. With a snarl, I shoved him as hard as I could . . . and, to my surprise, he rolled off of me.

That's when I saw Paul standing over me, arching an eyebrow.

I smiled as sheepishly as possible. "This really isn't what it looks like."

Cinching the knot on my bathrobe, I walked back into the living room. Paul stood by the front door, where he was showing out a very confused superintendent. The poor man had woken up completely dazed, his eyes glassy and fearful, not knowing where he was. Stitched onto George's face had been a breathy combination of horror, embarrassment, and anxiety. I'd caught myself licking my lips, imagining what that fear would taste like on my tongue.

That's when I'd excused myself to go throw on a robe. Screw me on Salvation Day, when would I stop thinking like a succubus? I didn't want Hell in my life anymore. All I wanted was to be human, to spend my life with Paul, and to get a pair of killer shoes that cost less than Paul's monthly rent. Was that really so much to ask?

Daun's laughter echoed in my mind. *You still taste like a succubus.*

Shivering, I hugged my arms. *Go away, Daun.* I didn't know if we still shared the psychic connection between all creatures of Lust; maybe I was only talking to a phantom voice in my head. But just in case there still was something linking us, I said it again: *Just go away.*

And maybe it was only my memory that answered me: *You'll be mine. Body and soul.*

In your dreams, incubus.

No reply. Maybe I was only losing my mind. I could live with that.

I darted a look at the living room floor. The smoke and sulfuric fumes had dissipated, but the symbol of the Erinyes was still branded into the wood. Paul hadn't mentioned it yet; I assumed he was waiting until we were alone before he applied the third degree. While that could be fun under the right circumstances (handcuffs, bedposts, and a blindfold), I had a feeling Paul would be more inquisitive than amorous.

Crap. What to do?

What a one-time succubus did best.

Pasting on my game face, I sauntered over to the symbol. After checking to make sure Paul wasn't watching me, I planted my feet so that I stood in front of the brand, facing the front door. As Paul closed the door behind the super, I unknotted my belt and let the robe gape open.

Paul, half turning, caught my pose. Ahh, bless me, he was so gorgeous—his broad face, with sculpted cheeks and a strong jaw, spoke of strength; his small, expressive sea-green eyes spoke of poetry. And his fighter's nose, broken at least once in his life, spoke of violence. Yum. His light brown hair was growing out; it curled down around his ears and covered the nape of his neck, and a stray lock did the Superman dangle on his brow, just above his right eye.

Ah, love, you could rescue me any time you wanted . . .

"If I didn't know better," he said, "I'd swear you were trying to distract me from something."

I attempted to look innocent. Major eyelash batting ensued. "Who, me?"

Paul's mouth quirked into a bemused grin. "You know, other guys would be horribly suspicious if they came home to find their girlfriend wrapped in a towel, on her back, with the super on top of her."

"You forgot the part about the super being unconscious, and the girlfriend being pinned under his weight."

"The story sounds better without that part."

"Does the girlfriend look better without this part?" I let my robe drop to the floor, accidentally-on-purpose covering the symbol.

He chuckled as he strode over to me. "The girlfriend always looks amazing, with or without clothes." Closing the distance between us in three steps, Paul loomed over me for a moment and rained a magnificent smile on me before he wrapped me in his deliciously strong arms and lifted me off the floor. His mouth sealed itself to mine as he kissed me, kissed me, kissed me.

Unholy Hell, he gave *such* good kiss . . .

Just as I was about to melt into a puddle of ooze, he gently set me down and turned away to crouch down by my discarded robe. He lifted the material up with one finger and moved it aside, revealing the burned outline of the pierced heart.

Oh . . . crap.

Nibbling my lip, I waited while Paul assessed the damage to the floor. After a million years, he looked up at me. "So where are the scratches?"

I blinked, trying to decide if he was being funny. "What do you mean? Don't you see it?"

"See what?"

Frowning, I stalked up to the scarred floor and pointed. "Right there. In front of you."

He looked to where I pointed, which was directly at the charred outline. Squinting, he said, "I can sort of see something, but I think that's just from how the light's hitting it." He reached down, ran his hand over the burned surface. "Don't feel anything. If there are scratches, they're really minor."

I picked my jaw up from the floor, then said, "You mean you don't . . ."

Then I shut my mouth, clicking my teeth together. Either he was blind, which wasn't likely, or he couldn't see the glyph. Maybe only supernatural beings could see such marks. But I wasn't supernatural anymore. Okay, then maybe only those who were supposed to see them actually saw them. But that didn't explain why the super could see it. Then again, he'd been possessed by a demon. George probably could have ripped up the floor with his bare hands when Daun had been riding his body; seeing the symbol of the Erinyes was probably a cakewalk.

"So," Paul said, "George was up here, looking at the not-so-scratched floor, and then he just passed out?"

"Uh huh." As if I was really going to tell him about Daun's hands on my body, or Daun's taunting message about Lillith.

Paul stared at me for a moment, his eyes darkening like storms at sea.

Crap, his bullshit detector was going off. Mental note: Lying believably didn't count when talking to a cop. I said, "I think he may be doing drugs or something. His eyes looked red." No lie there.

A long pause before Paul spoke. "Must have shaken you up, have a guy collapse on you like that."

Actually, that, along with lying, was something I was very used to—lots of clients over the years had expired on top of me. (And below me. And next to me. The list goes on.) "It caught me off guard," I said, shrugging. "But I'm okay. It didn't really weird me out."

"Yeah, I can see that. And there's really nothing wrong with the floor. So what's upsetting you so much?"

Shit. Why'd Paul have to be so intuitive? Next time I find a soulmate, I want someone with the emotional intelligence of a salmon in spawning season. With a sigh, I lowered my head and rubbed the bridge of my nose, wondering what to say. *Well, sweetie, it's like this. In the past five hours, I've been threatened, propositioned, and nearly seduced by three of Hell's minions. It sort of set me on edge.*

I didn't think that would go over very well . . . not the least of which was the whole seduction part. Daun had gotten to me. I'd been ready to mount him and ride like the wind. I loved Paul—unholy Hell, I'd gotten a soul because of him—so how could I even consider fucking Daun? Stupid demon mojo. I almost wished that Daun would appear again so that I could kick him in the balls.

Strong hands pressed down on my shoulders, massaged away my tension. I closed my eyes, going with the movement. "Hon," Paul said, "you can talk to me."

His deep voice made me feel all squishy inside. Paul was the only one I knew who could turn everyday words into foreplay. "I know."

Paul's hands pressed harder. "This isn't about the floor or George, is it?"

"No," I said, then mentally threw myself off of a cliff into shark-infested waters. Stupid, stupid, stupid! "I just have a lot on my mind." Understatement of the day.

"Anything you want to talk about?"

I wished I could. I so dearly wanted to tell him the truth about me, about who I used to be. But that was a part of my life he could never know. It wasn't like I could prove I'd been a succubus, and on close terms with Lucifer Himself. All that confession would get me was a trip to a padded room, complete with a form-fitting white coat. And while restraints had their merits, white would never be my color. So I said, "It's just family stuff. Nothing important."

"One day, I'd really like to hear about your family."

"One day," I agreed, knowing I'd never go there.

His hands rubbed, rubbed. "You need a change of scenery, hon. Get dressed. We'll go out, grab some dinner."

"What about the Chinese food you brought home?"

"Leftovers waiting to happen. Come on, what do you say—dinner and a movie?"

I perked up. "Maybe dancing?" If I was possibly going to Hell tomorrow, damn straight I'd be dancing tonight.

He groaned. "Jess, I *hate* dancing."

Taking his hands from my shoulders, I led them down to my breasts. "If you take me dancing, I promise to do wicked things to you later." I rubbed my ass against his pelvis, feeling his growing agreement.

"You make a hell of an argument," he said, his voice husky. "How wicked?"

I grinned. "Very."

Chapter 4

New York City

"**D**ance Hall Daze."

"A pool hall."

I tugged Paul's arm, urging him to walk faster down the block. "Sweetie, you said you wanted to take me out, right? Out means dancing, not shooting pool."

"Out means out of the apartment. Out means getting you out of your funk."

Funk, he said. Hah. Funk nothing. I was a freaking basket case. Dinner itself had been very tasty—to think there'd been a time when I'd thought that "Chinese food" meant chopped-up Asians, sautéed over a medium flame—but I'd been too paranoid to really enjoy it. I couldn't stop myself from scanning the restaurant, wondering if Lillith or Daun were watching. One thing about eating hot and spicy food: that made it a royal bitch to smell brimstone nearby.

Daun I thought I could handle. Sort of. Okay, so now he was getting all evil and possessive (in more ways than one), but hey—he was an incubus. What did I really expect? Of course he was going to attempt to tempt me. And I could handle temptation, as long as I was on my guard. If it came down to it, Daun would never hurt me (unless we were in the middle of a particularly active bondage and discipline scenario). So I just had to practice saying no and meaning it. No problem.

Lillith, on the other hand, would cheerfully rip my spinal

cord out through my throat and wear it as a belt. She'd had it in for me ever since I could remember. To this day, I didn't know why she hated me so much. Some things weren't worth questioning, and this was one of them. To me, it was enough knowing that the former Queen of the Succubi despised me. Maybe Daun had been lying about her coming after me. He was a demon, so there was a good chance he'd been less than truthful. The thought cheered me somewhat.

And then there was Alecto, with her taunt about her sister. No matter how I tried to convince myself that I didn't care what was happening to Meg, I knew deep down that was Grade A bullshit. Worst of all, I kept wondering why Alecto wanted to take me back to the Pit in the first place. Had the King of Hell put out another contract on me? No—if that were the case, Alecto simply would have scooped me up with her serpents and bamfed us to the Abyss.

Never let it be said that I forced you to make this choice.

She wanted to take me back . . . but she also wanted the decision to be mine.

Bless me, what in Hell was going on?

"See that?" Paul's voice jolted me out of my thoughts. "You're still in a funk."

I squeezed his hand. "I promise I'll get out of my funk if we dance. Come on, we look too fine for a pool hall."

"You, maybe. Me, I look like a goober in this shirt."

"I think you look yummy." And he did. At my urging, Paul was garbed in a silver, long-sleeved woven mesh shirt that I'd bought him a few days ago. It was perfect for clubbing: it hugged his form, showing off his lean torso and broad shoulders to maximum advantage. Of course, it was also currently hidden beneath his leather jacket. He'd been only too happy to do the black jeans and black boots thing, but I'd had to coax him into the shirt.

"Terrific. I look like a yummy goober."

"I promise to slurp you up later," I said, already thinking about how my body would move to the music. Maybe dancing wasn't actually sex, but it was a close second. Feeling a beat throbbing through your body, moving in time to a melody that builds and builds . . . All that sweat, all that passion. "Come on, love. I want to dance."

Paul groaned. "You dance four days a week."

Lifting my arms, I did a shimmy-bop as I imagined a heavy bass thrumming around me, in me. "I take off my clothes four days a week," I said, "for guys I don't care about. Tonight, I want to dance with you."

He reached over and pulled me close. I gazed up at him, loving what I saw shining in his eyes as he looked at me. He said, "I'm not much of a dancer."

"Just follow my lead. It'll be fun, you'll see."

"Can't we just go to a bar, stand beneath the speakers?"

"Come on, sweetie," I said, pulling him along. "The night's young."

We trekked to East 23rd Street. It was brisk for early November, with winds that insisted on ruining my hairstyle. I clutched my black trench coat closed with one hand and the other twined in Paul's.

"How about an overpriced cup of bad coffee?"

"Paul . . ."

"Or maybe go to a dentist, get a root canal without Novocain. That's a lot more fun than dancing."

I opened my mouth to say something appropriately witty, but I closed it as we approached a newsstand at the corner of the street. My footsteps slowed, stopped. I felt something dark pass over my face, twisting my mouth into a scowl and narrowing my vision until all I saw were headlines screaming in their self-important bold all-capped letters.

THIRTEENTH VICTIM FOUND announced one; ARSON SUSPECTED IN BROOKLYN INFERNO insisted another. In a national daily, a headline swore that the murder rate in America was at AN ALL-TIME HIGH. Sandwiched between these tidbits were articles dedicated to the latest war, the latest man-made biological disaster, the latest fear gripping the world. Oh look, here's a story about how a five-year-old shot his grandmother because she wouldn't let him watch a television show.

We can't let the world be more evil than the Abyss.

Maybe it was too late for that. Maybe the humans would dance for the Devil and destroy themselves, no matter what Hell did.

You could go back, a voice whispered in my mind. *Leave the mortal coil behind and go with Daun. Hide in the halls of Pandemonium and screw your brains out in the Red Light District. The King of Hell would never know.*

No. I love Paul. I got a soul so I could be with him. Whatever's happening to the world, I'll stay by his side.

What about Meg?

My lips tingled, feeling the barest whisper of flesh as Meg kissed me and left me to die.

Stop that. Meg would be okay. She was an Erinyes.

"Jess?" Paul squeezed my hand. "You look sick. You okay?"

"Yeah," I said, sighing. "Just . . . sad."

He glanced at the papers, then pulled me away. "Come on. We're going dancing."

"Really?"

"If me making an idiot of myself on the dance floor will help cheer you up, then I'm all for it."

I loved my man.

I'm sorry, Meg. But I'm not saying goodbye to him. Not for Daun, and not for you.

I smiled grimly. Tomorrow I'd tell Alecto that I wasn't going back to the Underworld. Decision made. Time to celebrate.

We tromped along, heading toward the train station. Nine o'clock on a Thursday night, and New York City was getting ready to party. Groups of people strutted with us, around us, away from us, laughing and talking, contained in their own bubbles of energy. The streets hummed with cars and the distant thunder of the subways hidden below. Garbage peppered the scenery, poked between buildings and stores, littered the curb—here, overflowing cans and swollen trash bags; there, stray wads of used napkins and crushed cigarettes. The refuse, like the people in the streets, made the city more real, more awake. New York chortled with anticipation; New York reeked with life.

A Hell of a town, indeed.

Various peddler stands splattered the sidewalks, dotting the streets with leather purses and hot watches, with watercolor paintings of New York City, with bootleg CDs and DVDs. Ooh, lookee at all the jewelry!

"Uh oh," Paul said. "Jesse wants something."

"Jesse wants you," I said, staring at the most fabulous gold bracelet.

"Jesse's got me." He squeezed my hand. "Jesse's also speaking in third person."

"That happens when Jesse's depressed. Jewelry's a cure for depression."

"I thought that was chocolate."

"Jewelry trumps chocolate."

"So do shoes, and new clothes . . ."

"Be nice to me. I'm depressed."

Paul planted a sloppy kiss on my cheek. "I can tell. You've got waves of depression rolling off you."

To the peddler, I said, "I really like this one," pointing to the gold bracelet that had caught my eye.

The heavyset woman smiled, and her chins squished as she nodded. "It's a lovely piece. It's the links that make it special. Go on, pick it up, take a look."

Well, if she insisted. I carefully lifted the bracelet, ran my fingers over the chain. The craftsmanship was spectacular— the links had been masterfully wound together, giving it the illusion of being a braided golden rope.

"Pretty," Paul said. Gorgeous was closer to the mark.

"That design's very special," the peddler said. "See how thick the links are? Strong bonds, promising a strong life."

"I don't know," I said. "I have this tendency to lose jewelry . . ."

"Also a strong clasp."

"Yeah, but will it turn my wrist green?"

The woman smiled. "Not likely. It's eighteen-karat gold."

"How much?"

The woman tapped her chin as she looked at me, her eyes sparkling. Crap, I shouldn't have said how much I liked this piece. She named a price.

"Allow me." Paul pulled out his wallet.

I laughed softly, my breath misting in front of my face. "My White Knight in training."

"What, I'm not your Cabin Boy anymore?"

"You can moonlight as a White Knight."

"You're too kind." He winked at me as he handed money to the peddler.

Her eyebrow arched as Paul paid her, and with a rather knowing smile, she looked at Paul, then at me. "How long have you two been in love?"

"Forever and always," I said, blowing a kiss to Paul. He shrugged, a sheepish grin on his face.

"You two are good together," she said. "Here, allow me."

She wrapped the bracelet around my left wrist, then fastened the tiny links. When she finished, the golden rope was snug, but not too tight, and the clasp holding it in place was cleverly hidden. "It looks wonderful on you."

I kissed Paul and thanked the peddler, and then Paul and I started walking again to the train. Behind us, the woman called out, "Blessed be."

Heh. To me, a blessing still felt like a curse. But I appreciated the intent.

Winding our way through roughly a million people between the ages of twenty-one and forty, Paul and I finally arrived at the bar on the second floor of Dance Hall Daze. Me, I didn't want or need any alcohol beforehand; already I felt the draw of heavy synth as Soft Cell's "Tainted Love" blared from the speakers. But my man needed some liquid courage before his feet found their groove. So I waited patiently against the bar, my head bopping with the beat as Paul knocked back a vodka shot and ordered another.

The smells of booze and sweat filled the dance hall, mingling to form a heady, sexy scent. Above me, screens silently begged for attention, each mutely depicting a music video that had nothing to do with the song pounding on the dance floor.

People filled every crevice, clamoring to be heard over the music until their words merged with the melody and created a continuous buzz.

Bless me, how I loved to watch the humans dance. They celebrated life, practicing rituals of worship with their bodies as they moved and writhed and pranced. Dressed in their first impressions, they flashed smiles and offered promises of flesh as they gyrated. Some moved self-consciously, too wrapped up in their anxieties of the meat market to even think about letting themselves have a good time. Others lost themselves to the moment. Some flirted obviously. Others did so unintentionally. But all acknowledged the power of the music—the heavy backbeat that demanded attention, compelled movement.

I couldn't wait a moment longer. Grabbing Paul's arm, I pulled him onto the floor as I elbowed people out of my way. And then I hurled myself into the music—now the Bangles, telling us to "Walk Like An Egyptian." I let the song wash over me, through me, let it command my body as I danced. My only self-imposed restriction was to make sure I kept my clothes on. Sometimes it was tough to remember that I wasn't always a stripper.

Paul moved with me, his large feet glued to the floor as he worked against the beat. Heh, my White Knight was blissfully unaware of his tendency toward white man's overbite. I'd never tell.

"Cutting in."

I barely registered the words before some bimbo bumped me out of the way and wrapped her arms around Paul. Too surprised to react immediately, the music pounded in my head as I watched this blonde with legs up to her chin dance with a bemused-looking Paul. *My* Paul.

My now-I'm-happy-to-dance Paul Hamilton.

I shouted, "Hey!"

Paul either didn't hear me or didn't care. Not his fault; she was practically falling all over him. It was all he could do to untangle her body from his own . . . not that he was trying all that hard to do so.

Unholy ire bubbled in my veins. That nasty bitch! Let's see if that shit-eating grin would still be pasted on her face after I clawed her eyes out.

I took two steps toward them before someone clamped a hand onto my shoulder and spun me around. He was short, just a couple inches taller than me, but he radiated such presence that he seemed to loom over me. Like me, he wore all black. Like me, he had thick, curly hair, but his was short and sandy. Barrel-chested, bow-legged, he grinned down at me as if he'd just gotten a fabulous present.

"Dance with me." His voice made it clear he'd had at least thirty drinks too many.

The last thing I wanted to do was dance with some drunken slob. I had to go skin me a blonde. "Maybe later, sweetie," I said, shrugging out of his grip and turning away.

He snatched my hand and yanked me back to his side. Spinning, I lost my balance and crumpled against his torso.

"Come on, babes," he said, all traces of the drunken slob gone. "Just one dance."

Oh crap. "Daun?"

"In the flesh."

And he was, too—no human possession this time. The incubus Daunuan himself was on the mortal coil, dressed in mortal form. And that meant only one thing: he was on a soul collection. That didn't bode well.

I tried to pull away, but he held me tight. "You following me?"

"Heh. Believe it or not, I'm a working demon. That you're here's just a coincidence."

Uh huh. Sure it was.

Daun grinned. "I had to break in one of your replacements. So we came here, scouting for new blood for Downstairs."

"Replacement?" Before I'd run away from Hell, I'd lost my job in a burst of demonic outsourcing. "You're here with a fucking *angel*?"

"Yep."

"Who?"

"The flaxen sweetness dancing with your flesh puppet."

That stopped me cold. The blond bitch who'd bumped me out of the way was an angel? Holy fuck in Heaven. I tried to find her and Paul on the dance floor, but it was too crowded . . . and Daun was holding me too closely. He smelled of silk and sweat and sex.

"Since the King replaced all female Seducers with her breed, it's all been a huge buzzkill," he said with a dramatic sigh. "Sure, they look good enough to eat. But just try touching them. I'd get more action sucking on an iceberg. That'd be warmer, and at least it'd eventually melt. But not those holy snatches."

I wasn't exactly sympathetic—one of those holy snatches was making moves on my man. "Life's a bitch."

"And then you die, and go to Hell. And then the party starts." He looked at me, his eyes bright. "Babes, don't you miss my touch?"

"Lots," I admitted. "But I love Paul."

He snorted. "Who cares about love? We need more good old-fashioned lust. Sex with no strings. Naked desire, blatant action. That's what I'm talking about."

"Get yourself a blow-up doll."

"I prefer the real thing."

"Can't help you there."

"You can." He cupped my chin, and I felt power pulsing beneath his flesh, knocking against the human shell that hid his horns, his goat's legs, his tail. "There've been so many changes since you left. Hell's boring, babes. Without the real succubi, there's no sex any more. Just these frigid bitches with their holier-than-thou attitude and cold stares."

His hands encircled my waist as his power rippled down my body, slowly, wave after sensual wave. Nipples, down girls! Don't you dare burst through my bra!

"Come back to Hell." His breath puffed on my cheek, sweet and full of Sin. "Think of all the sex we'll have."

Now his power was stretching farther down my body, filling my belly, my groin, my thighs. Straining to control my body's reaction, I bit my lip, hard. "Daun, I can't."

"Jezebel," he purred, "you can."

"I'm not Jezebel any more."

"Sure you are. You just have a soul now." He trailed a finger down my jaw. "I wonder how it tastes."

Through clenched teeth, I said, "You'll never know."

Invisible fingers stroked my tits until I groaned. He said, "I love a challenge."

"Bastard."

"Flatterer." The ghostly fingers moved down my body until they brushed against my inner thighs. Wetness gushed against my panties, and I shivered in Daun's arms. My mouth opened wide as I gasped with pleasure, and Daun crushed his lips against mine.

No, pull away, pull away, pull—

His tongue found mine, and for an unknown amount of time, I was lost in his kiss. Then someone tore me away from him.

My head spun for a moment as I stumbled—my body wanted *more, now!* but my brain was sending out desperate *stop this shit!* signals. Then I regained my footing and turned to find Paul standing in front of me, one hand possessively on my arm, the other balled into a fist. I didn't have to see his face to sense his rage.

Looking up at him, Daun threw his hands up in a universal gesture of My Bad, So Sorry.

"Back off," Paul growled. "She's with me."

"Hey, Shoulders, you're the one who left her alone."

"She's not alone anymore."

"Yeah, I see that. Got tired of the blonde, came back for brunette, didn't you? Got to say, I don't blame you. Jezebel here's a fine dancer. Especially when she takes off her clothes." His false blue eyes sparkled with mirth. "Good kisser too. Wonder if she's a good lay. What do you think, Shoulders? Does she fuck better than she dances?"

Paul's hand left my arm as he started forward, murder in his eyes.

My heart pounding, I pulled him back. There were only a few times that a demon could attack a mortal, and self-defense was at the top of the list. Daun could rip out Paul's soul before

Paul landed a single punch. "Come on, love," I said, my voice a high-pitched squeak, "let's just go."

"Later, babes," Daun said to me, doffing an imaginary cap before he launched himself into the thick of the dancers.

Paul took a step after him.

"Paul," I said, trying to keep my desperation in check, "come on. You were right, this was a bad idea."

He whirled to face me. "A *bad idea*? Holy shit, Jesse—some girl cuts in on us, so that gives you the green light to kiss some asshole?"

"I'm sorry," I said, knowing it wasn't close to good enough, but what else could I say?

"What is he, one of your regulars at Spice? Or back at Belles? You kiss him a lot there too?"

This was so not the time for Paul to go all boyfriendish on me. "Love, please, I've never seen him before." Not in that form, anyway.

"Yeah, I could tell."

"Please," I said again, hating how easy it was for me to beg, "we can talk about this more, all night if you want. But please, let's just leave now."

Frustration and anger warred in his eyes, but he nodded curtly before leading me off the dance floor. Before we escaped, another guy reached out, grabbed my arm. I bit back a scream, then let out a ragged breath. Holy fuck in Heaven, my nerves were completely shot.

"It *is* you!" The kid was pimply faced and eager; if he really was twenty-one, I'd eat my boots. "I remember you from Belles! Jezebel, right?"

"Yeah," I said, casting a helpless look at Paul, whose face started to purple.

"Man, I loved you," the kid said, oblivious to the raging bull holding onto my hand. "I heard that place closed down. Where you dancing now?"

"She's not," Paul spat. "She just retired."

Chapter 5

New York City

Two blocks away from Paul's apartment, I finally broke the strained silence. "So I'm not dancing anymore, huh?"

Next to me, Paul said nothing, but his frown spoke volumes.

"Funny," I said. "And all along I thought that was my decision, not yours."

"It *is* your decision. Just like kissing strangers is your decision."

I blew out a frustrated sigh. "Look, that was a mistake, okay? I got lost in the moment."

"Uh huh."

"Hey, it's not like you were the walking wounded. Last I saw, you were all too happy to have the peroxide queen throwing herself all over you."

At least he had the decency to blush. That did little to offset the storms building in his eyes. "That was harmless, and you know it."

"Oh, so it's okay for some stranger to dry hump you on the dance floor, but an innocent kiss is off limits?"

That got him to halt in his tracks. "From where I was standing, there wasn't anything innocent about it. His tongue was halfway down your throat."

"Yeah, and her hands were on your ass. Why was that okay?"

"It wasn't. And that's why I pushed her away. Just in time to watch you kiss that guy."

"For the record," I said, "*he* kissed *me*. But that doesn't change the fact that you left me stranded while the blonde gobbled you with her hands."

"Jesus, this isn't about me!" His glare should have left me bleeding. "How'm I supposed to feel, knowing that my girlfriend is okay with kissing any schmuck off the street?"

"Bless me, it wasn't like that!"

"Oh, that's right. You know him from Spice, don't you?"

My anger froze. "No."

"Come off it, Jesse. He said he saw you with your clothes off. What was he, your Friday night special? Or maybe you knew him from your stint at Belles."

His words choked my breath. My hand fluttered to my throat, pulled at my collar as if that would give me the air I needed. "I couldn't help it."

"Right," Paul said. "You were totally helpless. He forced you to dance with him, to kiss him so deeply you were playing tonsil hockey."

"You don't understand! He wasn't just some asshole! He was—"

I clamped my mouth shut and turned away. I'd said too much, and nowhere near enough. Worrying my lip with my teeth, I started marching in the direction of Paul's building. Just a block away. Maybe we could just go upstairs, have angry sex, and forget all about what happened tonight with Daun.

Yes, forget about Daun and his promises, Alecto and her threats. And Meg, of course—forget about whatever torture she was undergoing, even now as I swore to myself that I didn't care.

That's the difference between humans and demons, I heard Meg laugh in my mind. *Demons don't lie to themselves.*

Paul matched my pace. "You know him." Something soft broke through his rage, blunting the edge from his voice. "Not from Spice. Not from Belles. From before."

"There was no 'before' Belles. I never danced before then."

"Before I met you. When you ran away."

I tried to imagine the conversation turning around—Paul would understand that what I did hadn't been my fault, and he would hug me and take me upstairs and love me. He wouldn't ask for explanations. He would leave my past where it belonged.

"You still haven't told me the truth about who you were," he said, "about why you ran."

Oh, no. Please no. I'm not ready for this.

"Jess. Talk to me."

"What's to tell?" I walked faster, pulling ahead of him. I couldn't bear to see his face, to watch his eyes judge me. "I used to fuck a lot of guys, I decided I needed a change, so I became an exotic dancer. The end."

I thought that would hurt him, get him to stop pressing me, but Paul was in full White Knight mode. He snaked his arm through mine, brought my desperate pace to a halt. "When you first started at Belles, you told me you were running from your family. You never told me who your pimp was, what he made you do with your johns. Because it wasn't just about fucking them, Jess. You did tell me that much."

I said nothing as I wished I could either disappear or drop dead on the spot.

"Was he your pimp?"

"No."

"But he's connected somehow. He part of your family?"

"I'm not going there, Paul. Drop it."

"No."

"Drop it!"

"Jess, I love you. And you say you love me."

His words hit me like blows. "I *do* love you."

"And I want to believe you. But we won't be anything more than lovers until you can be honest with me about who you were."

"I don't want to talk about this! Why can't you just leave it alone?"

"Because unless you trust me, we don't have a future together."

I bit my lip, frantic, not knowing what to say. Too many emotions to count tore through me, and I turned away.

"Jess, don't you trust me?"

"Yes," I whispered. "But it's not that simple."

"Yes it is, hon." He took my hand, held it tight. "It's complicated only if you make it that way."

"You'll never believe me."

"Try me."

So I lifted my face up to meet his gaze, and before I could stop myself, I said, "I wasn't just a whore. I was a demon."

After a minute of strained silence, Paul said, "You must have had to do some bad things in your time."

"You have no idea."

"No matter how bad it was, that didn't make you a bad person."

"I wasn't bad, Paul. I was evil."

"Stop that. You're not evil."

"Not anymore." I took a deep breath. "For more than four thousand years, I'd been a succubus."

"A . . ." He closed his mouth, looked at me. I couldn't read the expression on his face; it was like he'd flipped a switch.

"A succubus. A demon of Lust." Shivering, I hugged my elbows. "I didn't sleep with men to take their money. I took their souls, claimed them for Hell."

Paul said nothing. Very, very loudly.

I kept talking, partially to fill the silence—and partially because it felt like I could finally breathe again. "And I'd liked it. I mean, okay, it's not like I was exactly trained to do anything else. But I loved having sex. And every time, it was something different. A new lover to seduce, a new costume for me to dress in, a new challenge. But then He made the Announcement, and everything changed."

Paul watched me as if he thought I might leap in front of a Mack truck.

Even in the throes of my catharsis, I couldn't tell him what

King Lucifer had said . . . and how that had set everything in motion. So I skipped ahead. "Suddenly, I wasn't a succubus any longer. Now I was a Nightmare. After loving men for thousands of years, now I had to terrify them." I cast him a long glance. "I know about the dream you had before I met you. I know you saw Tracy come to you and love you. I know you saw her die."

Color drained out of his face, but whether that was from me mentioning his dead fiancée or from admitting that I'd been the cause of that nightmare, I couldn't tell.

"I couldn't do it," I said. "I couldn't dedicate my existence to scaring mortals. There was no purpose to it. No fulfillment. No . . . nothing. So I ran away. And Hell came after me. In Salem, a witch turned me into a human, and I got to South Station. There I grabbed a train to New York City."

Still saying nothing, Paul regarded me, his eyes blank.

"And then I met you."

I stopped talking. Wind blew around us, took my words and scattered them while I awaited judgment.

Paul said, "So you're a succubus."

Why was his voice so flat? "Used to be."

"And your family. That would make them what, succubuses?"

The pause between us grew before I said, "Succubi. Some of them."

"Some," he repeated. "What about your sister? She a succubus too?"

I stared at him, wondering if I'd misheard. "My . . . what?"

"Your sister." He watched me, gauging my reaction. "I mean, if you're a demon, wouldn't that make her a demon too?"

Something lodged in my throat. Swallowing thickly, I said, "I don't have a sister. Not in the flesh and blood sense."

"No?" He took a deep breath, shook his head. "I'm sorry. I shouldn't have pressed you. You're not ready to talk about your past. Come on, let's go upstairs, get out of the cold."

"Hang on a second," I said, my voice rising. "I don't have a sister."

"Okay."

"I don't!"

His eyes narrowed. "Then who was the dead ringer for you at your bedside when you were in the hospital?"

My head spinning, I said, "Hospital . . . ?"

He looked at me, long and hard.

Okay, so this is what it felt like to be on the verge of a nervous breakdown. "When was I in the hospital?"

Paul's eyes softened, stormy green muting to quiet seas. His voice so very tender, he said, "You don't remember?"

Afraid to speak, I shook my head.

"After everything that happened at Belles, you collapsed. I brought you to the hospital, and they ran tests. Exhaustion and malnutrition. You were there for a few days before they let you go."

"No," I said, memories winking on and off—now a gunshot echoing in my ears, now my blood splashing against Paul's face like spring rain—"that's wrong. I didn't collapse. I'd been shot. Here." I touched my heart.

"You weren't shot."

I felt my eyes widen, heard my words tumble out of my mouth: "I remember flying backward, hitting the ground—"

"Jess," Paul said, so very patiently, "if you'd been shot in the chest, you wouldn't be standing here now."

"But . . ."

Something sears through me, blindingly hot.

"If you'd been shot in the chest," he said again, "wouldn't you at least have a scar?"

"No," I whispered, "this isn't right."

Meg lowers her sword and approaches me. I stand my ground, although my legs feel like rubber. Wondering if oblivion hurts, I close my eyes and wait.

The softest brush of lips on my own. Then nothing.

"Jess . . ."

"This isn't right!" I screamed, my hands balled into fists. "I was a demon, I ran away, I became a mortal, I got shot, almost died! That *happened*!"

For a long moment, the whine of the November wind filled the gap between us. Then Paul spoke, and I felt my world begin to crumble. "Your sister said when you're under a lot of stress, sometimes your imagination runs a little wild." He smiled, but his eyed remained guarded. "I guess this qualifies. I'm sorry, hon. You weren't ready for this."

From the bottom of my soul, I shouted, "I don't have a sister!"

"I met her, Jess. You don't have to pretend anymore." He took my hand, kissed it. "Maybe you're twins, but you're still the pretty one."

Twins?

Understanding hit me like a freight train.

Caitlin.

"Bless me," I whispered, trying to remember my hospital stay and drawing only a blank, "what did Caitlin do?"

"Nothing," Paul said. "She told me a little about your life, about the tension between the two of you. About how you'd run away a long time ago."

I was losing my mind. "Paul . . ."

"Look, this is my fault. I shouldn't have mentioned her at all. But a *demon*, Jess? Come on, you have to admit, that's a little . . . out there."

"I knew you wouldn't believe me." A tremble danced along my arms, and the skin over my head felt too tight. "I have to go."

"Please don't."

Tearing my hand away, I shouted, "I just opened myself up to you, told you everything! And you think I'm crazy!" Then, lower: "And maybe I am. I don't have a sister. I don't. I never did. And I remember getting shot, I remember King Lucifer giving me a soul . . ."

"Jesse," Paul said, "Lucifer doesn't give out souls. He's the devil."

"No, He's not," I whispered. "I have to go."

"Where?"

"I don't know. Somewhere. I have to think."

I broke away from him, started walking down the block, away from his apartment—away from him.

"Jesse, wait!" He ran up to me, put something in my hand. Numbly, I looked down at the cell phone.

"Go do what you have to do. But please, call me, let me know when you're on the way back."

"Why do you care?" My voice was taut, ready to snap. "You think I'm crazy."

"I think you've got issues," he said, touching my cheek. "And I think you're majorly in denial about some important parts of your life. But I love you. And I worry about you. And I want to know when you're coming home to me."

He kissed me—far too tenderly to be passionate—and turned to walk back to his apartment.

I watched until he walked inside his building. Then I shoved away the hurt and pain Paul's words had caused me. Enough with the self-pity.

Time to kick a witch's ass.

I flipped open the cell phone and punched in a number I hadn't realized I'd known. Hitting "send," I bumped into a woman walking past me. I snarled at her, registering her red-rimmed eyes a second after I'd turned away.

Fear shot through me like lightning, and blood roared in my ears. Lillith had found me.

But no, it was just a mortal woman, her eyes bloodshot, her nose red—drunk. She glared at me, her brandy-breath strong enough to kill even the meanest of bacteria. Then she staggered away.

I let out a shaky breath. Satan spare me, I was getting paranoid.

Placing the phone to my ear, I heard the connection ring through. As I waited for someone to pick up, I started walking blindly, letting my feet take me to wherever. Other pedestrians avoided me as if I radiated poison. Good. The way I was feeling at the moment, I could have happily shoved them all in front of oncoming traffic.

In my ear, Caitlin Harris's voice: "Hello?"

"Heya, *sister*." I put as much scorn into my voice as humanly possible. It wasn't the murderous timbre the infernal had perfected over the millennia, but it came damn close.

A long pause, then: "Hi, Jesse." Maybe it was the connection, but for I moment I thought she sounded . . . what, relieved? Happy?

No, all I heard was a mocking pity. "Care to tell me what you did to me?"

"What do you mean?"

"Don't play that with me, Caitlin. Tell me what you did."

She had the balls to actually laugh at me. "Or what? You'll strip for me?"

"Look, you little bitch, I may not be a demon anymore, but I've still got connections. You don't want to fuck with me."

"Oh, but Jesse, after the lovely fuckover you gave me, wouldn't it be tit for tat?"

"Funny. You're a regular laugh riot."

"To be honest, I should thank you. That . . . whatever you did to me, wow, I hadn't had that many orgasms in ages. It was almost worth you stealing my credit cards and my money. Oh, right, and my looks."

"I know," I growled around my pounding head, "I wasn't a fucking girl scout."

"Nice image."

"Bless me, I'd been in dire straits. I was desperate, all right?"

"Let's not forget about that shieldstone. You have any idea how rare those are? You still have that, at least?"

I muttered, "I got mugged."

"Terrific. You might have been a hotshot succubus, but let me tell you, you don't know much about being a human."

"I'm learning quickly," I said. "I'm learning you can't trust anyone, for starters."

In an immediate reversal, she asked, "What happened? Are you okay?"

I looked around for the street sign telling me I'd stepped into the Twilight Zone. Nope. Just Third Avenue and 24th Street. "Why? Why do you care?"

She paused. "It's my good nature. Are you all right?"

"What's going on, Caitlin? What did you do to me?"

Static on the line. Then: "I gave you a gift. When I heard what happened to you, I came to see you. You were so pale, so cold. You'd almost died, might have still died. So I helped you. Healing's always been my best area. A little magic, and poof, healthy flesh again."

Did I remember seeing my own face hovering over me? Or was that a trick of my mind, a false memory? "You healed me as a gift?"

"Oh, no," she said with a laugh. "I did that because looking at you dying was like seeing myself on my deathbed. Purely selfish of me."

She might have been one of the strongest witches alive, but she was also a shitty liar.

"But I couldn't have you just waltz out of the hospital after being admitted with a gunshot wound to the chest. So I . . . changed things."

"Things," I repeated.

"Small things. Hospital records. Memories. That sort of stuff. You were officially admitted for exhaustion."

"And malnutrition," I said, rubbing the bridge of my nose, "yeah, Paul told me."

"You know, you really need to eat better. It's not all about what tastes good. You need proper nutrients, the four food groups, plenty of fruits and vegetables, milk—"

My headache began to dance a jig. "Caitlin . . ."

"Paul should do a better job of looking out for you."

"*Caitlin* . . ."

"Right. So, my gift. What were you going to do, awake and alive and human? You had no identity. You had nothing proving you were . . . well, whoever you said you were. Just Jesse, huh? Original. I suppose you were going for the Cher approach to surnames?"

I closed my eyes, started counting to ten. By five, Caitlin continued speaking. "Thanks to you drinking my potion and choosing my form to dress in, you were locked into looking exactly like me. So I decided to make you my twin sister."

My eyes snapped open. "You *decided*—?"

"Complete with wallet stuffed with credit cards, a bank account, and a Massachusetts State ID with the name Jesse Harris on it."

Admittedly, that was considerate of her.

Feeling the world shift beneath my feet, I grabbed onto a mailbox for balance. I hadn't remembered choosing to become Jesse Harris once I'd gained my soul. I'd gone from demon to mortal smoothly, like a street suddenly changing its name along the same path. And I'd never thought about that—about how I'd gotten credit cards with my name on them . . . or who was paying the bills.

Shit. I hated it when other entities mindfucked me. That this particular entity happened to be a human was just salt in the wound.

Caitlin said, "I didn't give you a checkbook, though."

My thoughts churning as I processed all the information, I said, "You couldn't manage a driver's license while you were at it?"

"Sorry. I don't drive."

Something she said nagged at me, but in the torrent of thoughts and emotions hitting me, I couldn't place it. "So . . . you're paying my bills and things? What are you, my sugar momma?"

"It's temporary."

"Why? Why're you being so nice?"

"I'm a nice person. A good witch, as Glinda once said to Dorothy."

"Bullshit. You tied yourself to me, gave me your name, for Hell's sake! Why would you do such a thing?"

"Let's just say I care about what happens to you."

Then I put my finger on what was bothering me. "Wait a second. Who told you I was in the hospital in the first place?"

I sensed her smile over the airwaves. "The Hecate knows much, Jesse."

Oh . . . fuck.

"Don't worry. She's not upset with you for what you did to me. Actually, She was rather amused by it. And you did protect me from that demon of Greed when it came looking for you. As far as She's concerned, you did right by me."

"Why did She tell you what happened?" I felt the blood drain from my face as I realized something far worse than the patron goddess of witchcraft telling one of Her worshipers about my hospital trip. "Why is the Hecate watching me?"

"She is the keeper of hidden knowledge and new beginnings," Caitlin said. "Nothing is hidden from Her."

"That is so not an answer."

"Do you like your new bracelet?"

Black dots winked on the edge of my vision. "How . . . ?"

"The design's called the Rope of Hecate. Very special. Supposedly, it ties its wearer to life. If I were you, I wouldn't get mugged again."

"What's going on, Caitlin?"

"Bye, Jesse. Blessed be."

I stared at the buzzing phone for a moment before I flipped it closed and stuffed it in my pocket. *Blessed be.* Just like the peddler had said to me earlier tonight. Friggin' witches. Mental note: Next time someone suggests I'm blessed, tell them where they should stuff their blessing.

On my wrist, my bracelet winked at me, a conspiracy of magic and gold. The Rope of Hecate. The goddess of witchcraft, apparently, was watching me so closely that she wanted to help me accessorize.

My fingers danced over the fine links of the thick rope. I should take it off, toss it into the closest trash can. Smash it against a wall. Hurl it into the street and watch its metamorphosis from jewelry to fashion roadkill.

But it really was a lovely piece of work.

The Hecate wants me to have the bracelet for a reason, I decided, admiring how it looked on my wrist. And who was I to piss off a goddess?

Nothing is hidden from Her.

Why was the Hecate interested in me? Why did Alecto want me to return with her to Hell? How long would Lillith nurse her grudge before she came after me?

Paul, why didn't you believe me?

Normally, when things got too tough for me to deal with, I coped by fucking my brains out. But since I wasn't about to go marching back to Paul yet, I decided to do the next best thing.

I was going to get absolutely shit-faced.

Chapter 6

The Bar Fly

Whoever said you can't drink away your troubles was a liar.

Sitting at the bar of the aptly named The Bar Fly, I was working my way through the bastard series of drink-to-get-completely-fucked-up drinks. I'd kicked it off with a Suffering Bastard (gin, rum, lime juice, bitters, ginger ale) followed immediately by a Dying Bastard (ditto, plus brandy). Now the bartender, a sweetie named Guy (as in, "Hey, Guy, get me another, will you?"), was cooking up a Dead Bastard (Dying Bastard, plus bourbon). I think Guy and the other bartender had a bet going whether I'd pass out on the stool.

That, of course, wasn't going to happen. The stool was so small, I'd collapse to the ground and do my passing out there, crumpled like a used tissue.

The Bar Fly was one of those hole-in-the-wall sort of places that you either heard about or discovered by accident. For me, it had been serendipity. When I'd hung up the phone with Caitlin, I found myself standing in front of a magic shop. Figured. It looked like a place that fleeced the unsuspecting consumer—breakaway links, rabbits and hats, smoke and mirrors. Trickery. Illusions that people paid to see, knowing all the while they were being fooled. Stupid shit for stupid humans. But what had caught my attention was the huge fly's head on an awning over the second floor.

No words; just the insect. Maybe it was a tribute to Beelzebub. Or Vincent Price.

My curiosity had gotten the better of me, so I went upstairs to find the smallest pub in the known universe. Heavy in wood grain—both as decoration and as alcohol—and so dimly lit that they either were late with their electric bill or were being trendy, the place was surprisingly busy. Maybe sixty other patrons were squashed in, hanging by the bar or slumming over at the private tables. I'd pressed my way to the bar and snatched the first empty seat.

One thing about being short: you can squeeze between other people like a greased ferret.

"Here you go," Guy said, handing me an ice-heavy glass. Our fingers touched briefly. The booze must have been working its magic on me, because I didn't even consider the possibility of sleeping with him. Not that I would have kicked him out of bed if I found him there—he was cute in the too-many-muscles sort of way. Kind of like an action figure. The ones with karate-chop action.

Hmm. I wondered what he'd do if I pressed the right button . . .

"I think this should be it for you," Guy said.

Crap. Another White friggin' Knight. Why was I constantly around guys who did right by rote? Guy and his "give me the car keys" smile; Paul and his "take my cell phone please" righteousness.

"I don't know. I still remember my name." I barely slurred. Points for me.

"Remembering your name is good," Guy said. "What is it?"

"Jesse."

"See, Jesse, it's like this. I wouldn't be able to live with myself, knowing that I let you get completely smashed, with no one to take you home."

"Sweetie," I said, perking up, "is that an offer?"

He smiled warmly. "More like a concerned bartender not wanting to have a customer go to the hospital with alcohol poisoning."

I slumped back down. Fabulous. I just got shot down by

Action Figure Guy. My life sucked. "You know, it feels like I could go one past the Dead drink. Maybe you've got a Burn In Hell Bastard?"

"Jesse, I think the bar's closed for you after the one you've got now. Unless you switch to soda. That's six fifty."

I handed him a twenty and told him to keep the change. If Caitlin was paying for my life, I could afford to be generous. Lifting the glass, I saluted him before I took a swig. My taste buds were pretty numb by now, but I thought Guy might have overdone the ginger ale.

Blessed White Knights. Give me the bad boys. At least they knew how to have a good time.

I sipped my Dead Bastard. The fine hairs in my nostrils had long since burned to a crisp from the acrid stench of booze and smoke, so I drank without benefit of smell. Or, apparently, taste. No problem—I still felt the warmth roll down my throat, setting my blood to a quiet simmer.

Now if only I could forget my name, I'd be a happy former malefic entity.

"Jesse Harris?"

Crap on toast. I hunched over, hoping that I'd misheard.

A woman sidled up to me, turned to face me. I felt something ugly cross my features as I recognized the blonde from Dance Hall Daze.

"You have got to be shitting me," I said, staring at her wholesome blue eyes, her spun-gold tresses, her flawless skin. She had the nerve to be wearing a white clinging dress that charitably could be called a scrap—and she made it look good. Her legs started approximately at her chin and ended in white strappy stilettos so high heeled that my feet hurt just looking at them. She was the most beautiful woman I'd ever seen.

Of course she was beautiful. She was an angel. They don't do fugly in Heaven.

Bitch. I wanted to barf all over her sky-high Manolo Blahniks, but then I would have lost all the lovely alcohol I'd consumed. Not worth it.

For a moment, I considered the possibility that this was Lillith, getting ready to do some serious ass kicking. But no—

even for someone as vain and power-hungry as my former Queen, there are limits. Dressing like a cherub would have been out of the question. Even she had standards.

"It's official," I said. "This day just can't get any worse."

"Jesse Harris," the angel said, pronouncing my name like it was a prayer, "I need to apologize to you."

I took a long swallow of my drink, heard the ice cubes rattle like broken teeth. "For what? Being a walking Barbie doll?"

"For flirting with your man. My Lord Daunuan told me to distract him."

Lord Daunuan? Hooboy. "Your lord is a little satyr with a big dick," I said.

"My Lord outranks me, so I had to obey." Her brow crinkled prettily. "I didn't know what else to do. I think I may have upset you."

"No, you think?" I knocked back my Dead Bastard and slammed the glass on the counter. "Piece of advice, sweetie. You want to succeed at being a Seducer, don't apologize for being a bitch."

One thing about the human constitution: the combination of fear, stress, and alcohol is murderous on the bladder. I leapt off my stool and fled to the ladies' room, leaving the celestial creature floundering behind me.

In the bathroom, I maneuvered around the gaggle of women clustered by the mirrors over the sinks and sequestered myself in a stall. I did my business quickly, my head buzzing from booze. But I was in no rush to leave; the last thing I wanted was to see the angel again.

So I sat, and as my butt molded itself to the toilet seat, I stared at the graffiti penned onto the walls. Ballpoint poems. Some witty sayings about love; more about sex. A handful of assertions regarding certain men's abilities in bed. Meaningless scribbles from bathroom scribes. I tried to focus on the words, but the memory of Daun's chuckles played in my head, his lusty voice stealing my attention.

Come back to Hell.

I frowned as I considered his words. Could I do it? Go back to the Pit, rid myself of my mortal shell and human soul, and just get jiggy with it?

No-brainer. Of course I could. Having lots of sex was as natural to me as breathing was to humans. When I was in my groove, I made bunnies look like prudes.

But going back to Hell meant two things. One, saying goodbye to Paul. No matter how upset I was with him for using his cop wiles to get me to confess my infernal past (and then not believing me), I loved him. I'd chosen a human soul so that I could be with him. I wasn't about to walk away from that, not even for rough-and-tumble sex.

Two, the reason I ran away from the Abyss in the first place was still there, squatting on the throne of Abaddon. The King of Hell had already passed judgment on me, stripped me of my role, my purpose. Sitting on the can, I shivered, remembering the feel of His words in my mind.

You are too soft.

A stab of pain wrenched me away from the memory. I glanced at my hand, unclenched my fist. Bloody crescent outlines formed a dashed path to the meat of my thumb.

I couldn't go back to Hell, not with Him presiding over all the damned. I refused to spend eternity as a Nightmare. And I would sooner get tarred in angel feathers than acknowledge Him as my sovereign ruler.

It could be that after time, Meg's voice said, the memory still painfully fresh, *you'll embrace your new role.*

Never.

Come back to Hell, Daun's voice chortled. *Think of all the sex we'll have.*

Screw you and your desires, Daun. I'm not giving up my life, or my soul, for you.

Meg whispered, *We all do what we must.*

And screw you, too, Meg. You were supposed to be my best friend. You chose duty over friendship. You broke my heart, and you left me for dead.

My, aren't we just wallowing in self-pity today?

Get out of my head, Meg.

I'm not Meg. I'm you, Jesse.

Great, now I was talking to myself.

It's called a conscience, Jesse. It happens to mortals. Nothing to freak about.

Fuck this.

I tore off a wad of toilet paper and did the blotting thing, even though I'd already dripped dry. Panties up, skirt down. I flushed, wishing my own worries could get sucked down the drain as well.

Wish in one hand, shit in the other. See which one filled up first.

I exited the stall and sauntered to the sink, pausing to frown at the tall blond angel standing by the door. A quick glance told me we momentarily had the ladies' room to ourselves. Talk about a miracle. I turned to the mirror, reached into my purse to grab my lipstick. "Can't you take a hint? I don't want to talk to you."

Her silence was far stronger than any words. Despite myself, I looked at her reflection in the mirror. Her face held such suffering, such unmitigated sorrow. Her big blue eyes looked lost.

No. I wouldn't feel sorry for the scab who'd stolen my job. I lifted my chin, filled my voice with scorn. "What? You can't really be that upset over groping my guy, can you?"

"I . . ." She looked up, perhaps looking for a sign from Heaven. "I have no desire to be a Seducer. All I ever wanted was to sing with the Seraphim. And now that will never be."

"You don't want it?" I barked out a laugh. "How could you not want to be a succubus?"

"Why would I desire such a thing?"

"You get to have sex. Lots of sex. Who wouldn't want that?"

"I've never engaged in intercourse," she said, her voice so very proper.

"Who said anything about intercourse? I'm talking about good ol' fucking."

She flinched, as if the profanity stung her.

"Bless me," I said, staring at her reflection, "you mean you're a virgin?"

Eyes large and wounded, she nodded.

"Man, the King of Hell is forcing virgins to be temptresses? That's just evil. Nicely done." I shook my head, appreciating the irony. "And here I'd thought we were being replaced by others who could do the job better."

"An angel could never be better at sex than a succubus."

Brownie points, huh? Sorry, I wasn't buying any—she was strictly angel food cake, and I was more of the devilish variety. "Well, good luck getting your celestial cherry popped." I touched up my lipstick, slashing crimson over my mouth. "First time's going to hurt like a bitch. Unless you rode a lot of horses in Heaven. How about it, Cherub? You ride on your high horse up there in the Sky?"

"I don't know what you mean," she said, her voice soft, filled with embarrassment.

"Horses. Come on, the bouncing." I blew out a sigh. "For fuck's sake, you do have hymens, don't you? Or are you not built that way?"

"I don't know. I never asked."

Something in her voice sliced a hook in my heart and tugged. Glancing over my shoulder at her, I watched her rub her arms, which did nothing to hide her shivering.

"You're afraid," I said, disbelief overriding my contempt. "How could you be afraid of having sex?"

"I wasn't meant to be a succubus," she whispered. Fat tears rolled down the angel's cheeks, and I thought I saw stardust in the salty liquid.

Bless me, I made her cry.

I should be throwing her an evil look right about now, taunting her and sipping her pain. Instead I said, "Look, what I said before, just forget it. Sex is fabulous. Try it. You'll like it."

"I hate this thing I'm supposed to be," she said, wiping away her tears. "All I ever wanted was to sing with the Seraphim. But that dream has been ripped away from me. There's no way out for me. I'm trapped."

Crap.

"Come on," I said, dropping my lipstick into my purse. This sympathy shit was going to kill me.

She sniffled. "Where?"

"We're going out. I'm going to show you that loving isn't anything to be frightened of."

"Are you . . ." She darted her eyes about, as if nervous that others were overhearing. "Are you making a pass at me?"

I couldn't help it: I snickered. "Sweetie, you're definitely not my type. I don't do angels."

"Then what . . . ?"

"I'm going to take you to a place where you can see lust at work without any Sin being committed." I smiled, already picturing the stage, the sound, the audience. "We're going to my day job. It's a strip club called Spice."

Chapter 7

Spice

"Hey, Jezzie! Thought you had tonight off."

I grinned up at Joey, the world's nicest bouncer. He was also fiercely protective of his "little sister" dancers and had been known to show customers how to fly out the door when they got too grabby. "Heya, sweetie. My friend here isn't too happy with her current job. She may be thinking about a new line of work. Thought I'd show her around, let her see what the action's like."

I turned to the angel. "Joey here's one of the last of the good guys. He worked with me at a previous club, then after it closed, he and a few others from the old place landed jobs here along with me."

"Spice is more posh than Belles ever was," Joey said. "More dancers. More customers."

"More expensive drinks that are more watered down," I said with a wink.

Joey grinned, holding his hand out to the blonde. She reluctantly took it and let him pump her arm in a hello. "Any friend of Jezzie's is a friend of mine."

"Thank you," she murmured, staring up at his face. Something lit in her eyes, and she turned on her smile. "You have a very strong grip. Do you work out?"

The man had the proportions of a pro weight lifter; even magic couldn't have given him that sort of body without any help. "Wasting your time practicing on him," I said to the angel. "He plays for the other team."

She glanced at me, her mouth set in a frown. Even that was pretty. Bitch. "Other team?"

Obviously, the cherub's shoe size was larger than her IQ. "He's gay."

She deflated so completely that I could have folded her into a box.

"But if I wasn't," Joey said, kissing her hand, "I'd be begging you for your phone number."

Either his words or his smooch seemed to perk her up. "Really?"

"Come on in, ladies," he said, avoiding her question. "Welcome to Spice."

He stepped aside and opened the huge black door for us. Even though the sound from within the club was muted from where we stood, vibrations from the blasting rock music pounded out a backbeat, coaxing my heart to thump in time. I felt a grin spread across my face, heard my breathing quicken from anticipation.

Honey, I'm home.

Bless me, I loved my job. True, I didn't get to have sex with my clients. But I got something almost as good: the look in their eyes that told me just how desperately they wanted to hear me cry out their names as I let them fuck me.

There's no greater turn-on than knowing that everyone in the room wants you.

As I sauntered past Joey, I offered him a ten. He plucked it from my hand and tucked it away with a soft "Thanks." Even though I didn't have to tip the doorman—whether I was on shift or not—I liked to keep my posse happy. The doorman, specifically, was the customer's first contact with the club; a happy bouncer was more likely to mention my name to clients who asked which dancers were worth their while. And those clients tended to search me out for private dances in the VIP lounge or the Champagne Room. So a tip was more like investing in my career. And like any businesswoman, I appreciated a good return on investment.

Especially when it stuffed twenties down my G-string.

Over the muffled rock music, I heard the angel's stilettos clicking behind me as we walked down the short, dark hallway that separated the action from public view. Couldn't have little old ladies shaking their liver-spotted fingers at us for flaunting mostly nude dancers where anyone could see them. Not for their lack of trying; once I'd caught a blue-haired grandmother peeking inside, her nose pressed against the stained black glass of the front door, trying to kickstart her heart by viewing—gasp—lusty men fawning over scantily clad women.

"What's that smell?" the cherub asked.

I inhaled deeply, taking in the orange scent of the floor cleaner. Beneath that, the faintest whiffs of tobacco and alcohol clung, fighting against the citrus tang. The ghosts of colognes and perfumes rode the air, tickling my nose with hints of J'adore, Eternity, and Dolce & Gabbana.

"Lust," I said with a grin, "wrapped up in negligees and five-dollar bills."

"Oh. I thought it was Swiffer."

I opened the thick door that separated us from the club proper. The heavy synth of The Eurythmics' "Sweet Dreams" rippled through my body, making my head bop along and my hips roll with the beat as I walked. Beneath that, an undercurrent of conversation and laughter from the men in the audience floated—sucking me in if I stopped to listen, washing past me like audible flotsam if I ignored it. On the main stage, aglow from yellow and red spotlights, a woman shimmied. Stripped down to her lacy green thong, she jiggled her small tits in time to the music, moved her arms over her body in quick jerks. Even though Kelly wasn't the best dancer at Spice, she had her avid following—based on the bills tucked into the garter on her thigh, some of her harem were here tonight. Maybe it was her Irish coloring that did it for the guys: mounds of orange-red hair, skin milky pale. Or maybe it was her blowjob lips and bedroom eyes.

Throughout the showroom, clustered in threes around small round tables, men sat in red plush chairs, grins on their faces, happiness in their pants. Maybe thirty customers were scattered around the room, talking to or about the dancers who left precious little to the imagination. A number of the house girls were working the floor—some flashy in their spandex gowns and rhinestone earrings, others more elegant in their cocktail dresses and pearls. All wore enough makeup that they'd need to shovel it off. Hair was up, down, pinned back, curled, teased, glued with hairspray—you name it. Clashing perfumes battled above the eye-watering mix of booze and sweat that permeated the room.

And sex, of course—beneath everything else was the spice of sex. The sex of Spice.

Yum.

I breathed in the excitement of the crowd, the intentions of the dancers. My nipples hardened, both acknowledging the air conditioning chugging at full throttle and reacting to the various smiles and remarks from customers waving and motioning to me as I led the angel to the bar. Kelly wasn't the only one with a harem.

A grin stretched across my face. Men dripping with desire and trembling with unspoken passion . . . the promise of sex, even if that promise wouldn't be kept—ah, bliss! I blew kisses at my regulars, put an extra wiggle in my step as I sashayed to the back of the room.

Jezebel's here, avid fans. Let the lusting commence.

At the bar, I smiled at the lovely man who offered me his seat, then stared at his friend until he vacated for the angel. "Thanks, boys," I said, my voice husky with amusement. They seemed to think it was from wanting them: one man preened and flashed his capped teeth, and the other hemmed and hawed and made a big show of staring at the stage.

Capped Teeth asked me, "Can I buy you a drink?"

I winked. "Thanks anyway. But I'm here to show my friend a good time." I draped an arm over the angel's shoulders, letting my fingers brush lightly over her left boob. Already sitting ramrod straight, her spine stiffened even more, nearly popping my shoulder from its socket. She looked like she wanted to find a rock, crawl under it, and die.

Heh.

"Oh. Oh!" Capped Teeth seemed to get the hint. Muttering something about comfortable shoes, he led his buddy to an empty table on the showroom floor.

"Hi, Jezebel. Thought you had tonight off."

I pivoted in my seat to face the bartender. "Heya, sweetie. My friend here's never seen a gentlemen's club from the inside, so I couldn't resist bringing her here. Hey, Angel, say hi to Andrew."

The angel slunk down in her seat, mumbled something that could have been a hello.

Andrew dropped me a wink. "Seems nervous. Honey, can I get you a shot, help you loosen up?"

She blinked her celestial blue eyes at him. "A shot?"

"J.D.," I told Andrew. "And make it a double."

"She going to audition?" he asked as he poured the whiskey into a shot glass.

Ooh, look at that. I'd never seen an angel blush before. Pretty, if you're into the whole crimson sunset sort of thing.

"Audition?" she squeaked.

"Doubtful," I said to Andrew, slapping a twenty on the counter. "She's too uptight. I want her to see how the other half lives."

Chuckling, Andrew set the glass down in front of the blonde and palmed the cash. "Change?"

"Keep it." As far as I was concerned, Caitlin was buying the drinks tonight.

Andrew grinned his thanks, then vamoosed to fill orders from impatient waitresses.

"I still don't understand why you've brought me here." She sat as if her panties had been starched. "If you wished to embarrass me, consider your mission accomplished."

"Bless me, will you relax?" I motioned to the drink. "Knock that back and settle down. We're here for you to observe."

"Knock . . . ?"

With extreme patience, I said, "Drink that quickly."

"I don't drink alcohol."

I took a deep breath, counted to three. "Of course you don't."

"It's not appropriate."

"For a cherub stitching silver along the clouds? Nope. But you're not in Heaven anymore." I kept my voice low, but I didn't have to worry; even though men surrounded us, they were thoroughly engrossed by Kelly's stage show, or by the handful of dancers offering lap dances and Champagne Room fantasies. I jabbed a finger at the angel. "You're slumming with the damned and the demons now. So get off your high horse, because sweetie, you're never going to be a Seducer if you think you're above your clients."

"But I don't want to be a Seducer," she said, her voice pleading. As heart-stoppingly beautiful as she was, the petulant whine in her voice turned her ugly, made her more real. And the fear in her voice was far more than real—it was almost orgasmic.

Stop that. Bad former succubus. Focus on getting the angel past her fear of sex. Do your good deed for the millennium.

Sex with no strings, Daun chortled in my mind. *Naked desire, blatant action.*

No. That was the wrong approach for this. Angels didn't understand sex or lust.

But they did understand the concept of love.

Leaning over until we were nose to nose, I said, "You planning on running?"

She swallowed. "No."

"Rebelling?"

Her fear kicked up a notch as she stammered, "Damn me, no!"

"Well then," I said, "stop bitching and start opening yourself up to the possibilities."

Tears in her eyes, she asked, "What possibilities?"

"That lust isn't all that bad." Hoping that none of my former brethren were watching, I kissed the angel's soft, soft lips.

Her mouth was supple, yielding, and I nudged my tongue between her lips—just a flick, a hint of something wicked. She gasped, then pulled away.

I licked my lips slowly, making an *ummm* sound. "You taste like peppermint and gold."

"Why did you . . ." Her voice died, overcome by her blushes. But I saw something besides confusion and embarrassment in her eyes, something dark, something stretching its jaws wide.

I could reach her.

Über cool.

"Feel that?" I asked, my voice low, one conspirator to another. "That tingle in your breasts, that touch of heat in your crotch?" The widening of her eyes told me I'd hit the description right on the head. Of course I had—maybe I wasn't a Seducer anymore, but I still knew how to kiss with power, magic or no magic. "That's lust."

Her eyes shone with unshed tears. "How do you know what I'm feeling?"

"Your nipples are erect." Pointing with my chin, I motioned toward the two bumps on her boobs that pushed against her white scrap of clothing. Until that moment, I'd wondered if angels had the anatomy of Barbie dolls—breasts without nipples, a slit with no clit. "That's not just from the air conditioning."

She glanced down at her chest. "Oh," she said, sounding small. Sounding betrayed.

. . . the softest brush of her lips on my own as she kisses me and leaves me to die . . .

"My kiss made your body react," I said, killing the memory of Meg's farewell. "A reaction to an action. Did it feel good?"

A pause, then the barest whisper: "Yes."

"It should. Whether mortals or entities, we want to be desired, to be loved. We use our bodies to express that love. There's nothing to be afraid of."

She clenched her teeth, flashing her pearly whites. "This isn't love."

"It's lust," I said. "Lust is your body wanting another's touch, wanting to be loved. You liked my kiss. Imagine what it will be like when you kiss a client, when you inspire their bodies to come alive in your hands, to hear their voices beg you to love them . . ."

"But lust isn't love!" She crossed her arms, hiding her body's salute to hormones. "Lust is just the flesh. God is love."

I had my doubts about that, but I kept mum. When she didn't continue, I prompted, "So?"

"So how can I love God when my body . . . *lusts* flesh?"

Mental note: Angels have a God complex, and not in the all-powerful, all-knowing way.

"Look." I pointed to the men in the audience. "See how they're watching the dancer? See how their bodies feign indifference even with hunger burning in their eyes? They want her. What's more, they want her to love them. And when she looks at them, when she smiles or winks or jiggles at them, they think, just for a moment, that it's just for them—and they ride that feeling, that desire to be loved."

"It's not love."

"Maybe not. But it's the illusion of love."

"God is not an illusion."

I was going to say that God was eternal and life was fleeting, so maybe humans only had time for the illusion instead of the real thing. Then I thought I'd sound like an ass. Bless me, I hated philosophy, even if I was trying to discuss it while sitting in a strip club.

The song finished, and Kelly cupped her tits and wiggled as the audience applauded. The DJ asked the gentlemen to show Kelly their love, and some did—about ten men flocked to the tip rail, waving money, waiting in line to stuff their bills between her boobs and hope to cop a feel.

The angel asked, "Do those men intend to fornicate with her?"

"Sweetie, they can intend all they want," I said with a wry smile. "But the only action they're going to get will be their hands on their rods—and that's not allowed here."

She frowned. "Then why are they paying her?"

"They're tipping her because they liked how she danced. They liked how she made them feel." Leaning over, I whispered in her ear, "They liked that she made them feel wanted, loved." I darted my tongue out and licked her lobe to emphasize my point.

She let out a startled squawk that turned into a moan as I kissed her neck, just once—just enough to feel the fine hairs of her neck tickle my lips.

"Feel the heat pulsing between your legs," I said, gently nibbling her earlobe. "Feel the anticipation building inside you, dancing along your limbs like thousands of tiny shocks. This is lust. It's not frightening. It's living. It's being alive."

"It's wrong," she groaned. "It's not love."

"If it was wrong," I said, kissing her neck again, "why did God build your body so that it experiences physical pleasure?"

"God made me an angel."

"Yes." I sat back, stared into her wide, terrified eyes. "And then He saw fit to let you be a succubus."

"Gentlemen," the DJ announced, "please say hello to the angel of Spice!" Next to me, the blond cherub's eyes almost popped out of her skull. Applause rippled through the audience even before the DJ continued, "Everyone, show your love to Faith!"

Kelly wiggled her way backstage as Faith strutted forward, the spotlights highlighting the huge, feathery wings strapped to her shoulders and the creamy robe molded to her body. White-gold hair cascaded down her back like a platinum waterfall. A guitar strummed, a quick, playful tune, and she bopped her hips to the melody. George Michael's voice blared from the speakers, singing the opening lyrics to her theme song, "Faith." She taunted the audience by running her hands down her breasts, her belly, her thighs. Her legs spread wide, she pumped her hips, proving that some angels wanted to be fucked.

Even back at Belles, Faith always did have a wicked sense of humor.

"Watch her," I said to the cherub, who was staring, transfixed, at Faith. "See how she lets the music ride her body, how she lets it seduce her."

The angel's voice breathy, she said, "She's touching her breasts . . ."

"She's showing the audience that she loves her body. She's giving thanks to God for the vessel He gave her. Her dance," I said, "is like worshiping God."

Gak. I hadn't said the G-word this much in centuries. If I'd still been an infernal creature, I would've had to surrender my union card.

The angel frowned prettily. Even her pout wrinkles were gorgeous. Bitch.

On stage, Faith flounced in time to the funky guitar riff, shaking her sweet bippy and jiggling her boobs. "Loving your body, celebrating your body, is like worshiping God. And sex," I said, drawing out the word, "is like sharing that worship with another."

"Sex isn't love," the angel said, clearly unconvinced.

"Sex expresses love. And lust leads to sex."

She stared long and hard at me. "Is that why you like it so much? Because sex . . . is like worshiping God?"

I liked sex because it was fucking amazing. "Sweetie, with the right partner, sex can be almost holy." Not that I'd know *holy* if it bit me on my ass, but whatever.

Silence stretched between us even as music and men's brassy talk filled the air. I watched the angel watch Faith dance, saw something flit across the angel's eyes. The gears were turning.

Sweet.

Opening my purse, I dug out my wallet and produced a ten. "I'll be right back."

"Where are you going?"

"I'm off to show the dancer a little love, greenback style."

Turning my walk into something dirty, I sauntered over to the tip rail. I felt the gazes of lusty men on my back, my rack, my legs, crawling over me and into me as if seeking buried treasure.

Sometimes, it was really nice to be nothing more than an object of sexual desire.

Money in hand, I draped myself over the brass rail, kicking one leg up behind me while I waited. The music switched over to "I Want Your Sex." It must have been Faith's first show of the night; she always kicked off her performances with a three-song tribute to George Michael. The menfolk never seemed to mind—they were too busy wondering whether Faith's body was as soft as the feathers strapped to her back.

Faith ditched her robe and wings, revealing a lacy white bra and matching G-string. Shimmying in time to the music, she bounced her way to the tip rail. If she was surprised to see me, she hid it masterfully.

I blew her a kiss, held out the folded ten. The spotlight illuminated my movements, temporarily making me part of her show. As Faith offered me her cleavage, I fought back an urge to climb up next to her and strip off my dress.

Slowly tucking the bill between her breasts, I was careful not to touch the exposed tops of her mounds. No groping the dancers. If our customers couldn't do it, I shouldn't do it. She winked at me, then dropped to the floor to crawl over to the next patron, standing to my right. Look at that—based on the line by the rail, I'd started a trend.

Heading back to the bar, I watched the angel pick up her shot glass and sniff the contents. Making a face, she put the drink back on the counter. That she was curious about it at all was a victory. I'd have her ready to spread her legs in no time.

So I wasn't a succubus any longer. I would always belong to Lust. And that was gospel I was happy to preach.

Chapter 8

New York City

After midnight on a chilly November Friday along the streets of Manhattan: wind howled like a werewolf in heat, kicking up litter and swirling the tails of my trenchcoat around my legs. My heels clicked on the sidewalk, but those steps were swallowed by gales, silenced in the blustery whine that stung my ears and whipped my hair around my face. Car exhaust and the dank, cloying pressure of impending rain dampened the ever-present odor—now just the lightest hint of a smell—of too many people and too much sewage in too little a space. Graffiti and billboards alike were shrouded in darkness, their promises and enticements illegible. Store windows slept; no stars shone in the nighttime sky.

Perfect weather for a drunken walk home.

My arms out for balance, I tottered in my high heels, singing Chumbawamba's "Tubthumping" at the top of my lungs, not giving a shit who heard.

Behind me, the angel said, "You're sort of staggering. Maybe we should get a taxi."

That wasn't how the song went. Taxis were nowhere in the lyrics. "He drinks a . . . wait a second. How's this part go? He drinks a something drink."

"You're drunk, aren't you?"

"He drinks a cider drink. Or a vodka drink. Or a bourbon

drink. Fuck, I think I lost the words. What's that song with bourbon in it?"

"And this is why the Cherubim don't drink alcohol."

"Come on, you have to know the one I mean. One bour-bonnnnnnnn . . . one something, one beeeeeeeeer." I grabbed the angel's hand, swung it wildly in a two-person wave. "Come on, sing with me!"

She wrenched her hand free. Anger flickered in her eyes, a sudden flash of lightning. "I can't. Only the Seraphim can sing."

"Bullshit. I'm singing, and I'm no angel. Hey, I know that song." I took a deep breath, then belted out, "I'm no angel . . ."

"You're right," she said, her voice crisper than the midnight air. "You're no angel. You're not even a demon. You're just a drunken human."

"I'm just one demon," I tell Meg. *"What sort of damage could one demon do?"*

"You could inspire a revolt in the Pit. You could incite the mortals on Earth."

"I'm not the type to inspire anything other than lascivious thoughts."

"You'd be surprised. And you know too much to be allowed to roam free."

"I know just as much as all the nefarious."

"The others aren't considering what you are. The others are complaining, moping, taking out their frustration and rage on the damned. But none of them are contemplating the possibility of other options."

"Millions of demons," I say, *"including the elite and the various Kings, and none of them have any thoughts of . . . questioning the new status quo?"*

"None."

None, I thought now, icy fingers creeping up my spine. Why had I been the only creature to balk at the King of Hell's absurd declarations? My tongue thick from alcohol and fear, I whispered, "What am I?"

"You heard me," the angel sniffed. "You're nothing more than a one-time demon, drunken to the point of idiocy. You're just one human."

Alecto's voice, whispering: *Fury friend*.

"Jesse Harris?"

Why did she want me to go back to Hell?

"Jesse Harris, are you all right?"

The angel's voice grabbed me, pulled me away from the memories threatening to drag me under. Gasping, I stared at the tall blonde who radiated otherworldly beauty and celestial coldness, desperate to ask her why Daun taunted me with possibilities, why Alecto mocked me with secrets, but the only word that came out was: "Why?"

"You've gone pale. Are you going to vomit?"

Alecto, impatient, nervous: *Are you coming?*

Since when does a Fury ask—

I will take you to Megaera.

Oh, bless me, Meg, what are they doing to you?

Until tomorrow, Fury friend.

"Humans tend to vomit when they consume too much alcohol," the angel said.

Shivering, I wrapped my arms around myself. Yes, I was human. King Lucifer had given me a choice, had given me a soul . . . My lips tingled, remembering the feel of His kiss, remembered telling Him . . .

"You will always be my King, Sire."

"No, Jezebel," Lucifer says. *"But you may call Me sire, if you wish."*

My stomach heaved. I staggered to the curb, doubled over, and retched. Violent waves of sickness burst from my mouth, stinking of alcohol and acid. My knees buckled and I collapsed to the ground, panting.

I didn't realize the angel had been holding my hair away from my face until she released it. Tangled curls plastered themselves against my wet cheeks, fell heavily in front of my watering eyes. Without speaking, the angel handed me a tissue. I stared at its white crumpled form, wondering if His wings once had been just as fair, just as fragile.

Lucifer the Light Bringer.

Sire.

"Your nose," the angel said.

Numbly, I wiped away runners of snot. When I finished, I opened my hand, watched the wind snatch the used tissue and carry it away—refuse dotted with bodily waste, memories of something that never was.

"Everything used to make sense," I said, tracking the tissue's flight until it disappeared from view. "I knew my role. I knew my place. I knew what I was."

A cold, beautiful hand touched my cheek. I turned to face the cherub, to see her eyes brimming with something softer than pity.

Sympathy.

"I understand." Her voice hummed like a bumblebee serenading a flower. "I, too, had my place. I was one of the Cherubim, and I watched over the mortals and shined the light of God upon them."

"I loved them all," I said, remembering tangled sheets, sweaty bodies, hungry kisses.

"Whoever they were," she agreed, "whatever they'd been."

"I made them feel loved, and then I took them to Hell."

"I helped them see the light, helped them walk the righteous path that leads to Heaven."

"And then everything changed."

She nodded sadly. "Everything."

"Everything used to make sense," I said again, clenching my fist. "Now the only thing I understand is that I love Paul, really love him. All I want is to spend my life with him."

"That is a good want."

"And now they have my friend, want me to go back to something I can't be. Why can't they leave me alone?" My words echoed in my ears as I shouted, "Why won't Hell let me go?"

The angel, if she had an answer, kept it to herself.

"And maybe I should go back," I said numbly. "I'm screwing up with Paul. Maybe I should leave him before it gets worse."

"Screwing up how?"

"He wants me to stop dancing." I opened my fist, let my hand go limp, defeated. "More than that. He wants me to be something I'm not."

"Is that what he said?"

I bit my lip. "He said he wants me to stop dancing."

"And?"

I saw Paul, his sea-green eyes troubled, his kissable lips pressed into a thin line . . . "And that I should do what I need to do."

"And?"

. . . Paul's hand, outstretched to me as he says he wants me to come home to him . . . "And that he loves me."

"He *loves* you, Jesse Harris. He cares for you. Doesn't everything else pale? Aren't the possibilities of how to share that love endless?"

I sighed. "Not counting the no dancing thing . . ."

"To love another is to sacrifice a piece of yourself."

A cold wind blew across my heart. "You're saying I should stop dancing?" Stop basking in the spotlight, stop peeling off my clothes in time to music as it seduces my skin?

Stop being me?

"If love were easy," the angel said, "then no one would hate."

Shit.

My head pounded out a beat that made my teeth vibrate. Self-pity, meet hangover.

Double shit.

"Come on." The angel tugged at my sleeve. "Let's get you a taxi."

"**Y**ou really didn't have to take me home."

Waiting patiently as I rummaged through my purse for the key to Paul's apartment, the angel shrugged. "I wanted to make sure you got home safely. You were rather inebriated."

I shot her a look. "I spewed my inebriation all over Park Avenue South."

"You didn't seem to be in the best of shape."

"Well, I'm home now. You can skedaddle to wherever it is you hang your halo." Bless it all, where was the fucking key?

"I don't have one, you know."

I glanced at her, wondering if she was talking about a key. "What?"

"A halo. Only the Seraphim are granted such an honor."

Interesting, in the who-really-cares sense. "And here I thought it was a fashion statement."

"Angels are awarded halos the day they earn the right to a name." Her blue eyes lit with the passion known by televangelists and Bible thumpers, and her pale skin seemed to glow. Maybe that was just the harsh fluorescent lighting in the hallway. "On that blessed day, they are elevated to the level of the Seraphim, and all of Heaven rejoices."

"Hold the phone. You don't have a name?"

"None of the Cherubim do. Only the Seraphim," she said with a sigh. "And the Archangels, of course."

Man, that sucked. An eternity of "Hey, you with the feathers, come here" would leech away anyone's sense of humor. "Guess you weren't just being standoffish. My mistake."

She cocked her head to the side in a way that suggested she was thinking a Very Big Thought. "Do all demons have names?"

"Sure. Tons of them. Most of the infernal collect names the way a gigolo collects notches on his belt."

That seemed to give her pause. She pursed her lips, and her brow crinkled prettily. Maybe she didn't get the analogy. Or maybe she was constipated.

"So," I said, "what do I call you? Barbie?"

"I think Angel will suffice." She smiled warmly, making me think nauseatingly lovely thoughts about birds singing and bunnies twitching their cute noses. "Actually, it's sort of pretty."

Oy. I rolled my eyes, then continued looking for my key. "Well, Angel, thanks for doing the whole guardian stint. I'm all set, so go fly away."

"Are you sure? Perhaps I should wait until you are inside."

"I'm fine." I tried the doorknob, hoping it would be unlocked. Nope. I racked my brain to see if I had any lock-picking skills just collecting dust, waiting for me to hone them. My brain suggested something about sliding a credit card into the doorjamb, but I dismissed that as nonsense. Like I'd risk get-

ting splinters in such a valuable piece of plastic. I'd sooner seduce a leper than ruin my AmEx.

I jiggled the knob again, then let out a startled "Whoa!" as
the door swung open and I stumbled over the threshold, then
fell against Paul. As I regained my footing, I noted his baggy
pajama pants still somehow molded around his package, making me appreciate the easy-access fly slot. But the tenseness of
his bare shoulders, the set of his square jaw, made it all too
clear that sex was the last thing on his mind.

"Thought you were going to call when you were on your
way home." His voice could have frozen the Lake of Fire.

My mouth opened, closed. Finally, I opened it again and
said, "I totally forgot."

A pause that stretched uncomfortably, then he asked, "So
where'd you go that you had such a good time?"

"A pub called The Bar Fly, then a quick dash over to the
club . . ."

My voice died as his stormy green gaze pierced me like fishhooks. "You were at Spice?"

"Um, yeah. But not to dance," I said quickly, watching
emotions crash across his eyes like waves breaking. "My, um,
my friend was interested in what it's like to be a dancer, and . . ."
I motioned helplessly to the hallway so Paul could see Angel,
could see that I'd been trying to help her out.

"Your friend," he said, each word like a punch, "seems to
have disappeared."

I whirled around to see the hallway completely empty.
Either Angel had exited stage left, or she hopped on the inter-
planear express and bamfed herself away. I squeaked out,
"Oh."

"This wouldn't be the same friend that you kissed earlier,
would it?"

"What? No. No!" I said, realizing what he was implying. I
turned to face him, to throw his accusation in his face, but I
couldn't find the words. He just stared at me, his face like
stone.

How could silence be so deafening?

"I'm sorry I forgot to call," I said, my voice rising, filling that ugly gap yawning between us. "Bless me, it's not like I accidentally murdered your puppy. I just forgot!"

"I can't believe you went to Spice," he said through clenched teeth, "after what we talked about before."

My heart slamming against my ribcage, I snarled at him, "One, we didn't talk about Spice before. You'd arbitrarily decided that I wasn't going to dance anymore. That's not a *talk*. And two, you also said that it was my decision to make."

"Right. Just like it's your decision to kiss whoever you want, or to not call me when I asked you to call."

"It's not like that! And you're the one who didn't believe me when I told you who I was, what I was!"

"Don't change the subject." His voice was quiet, level, even as his eyes screamed at me. "You kissed some guy who you say you know, but you won't tell me who he is, and he makes it clear he's seen you butt naked. And then you walk away from me, don't call me, and go off to Spice. Give me a fucking break, Jesse—what'm I supposed to think? How'm I supposed to trust you?"

"You didn't believe me before, when I told you what I was," I said, tears stinging my eyes. "Seems like I'm not the only one with trust issues."

We stared at each other, the air between us charged with a tension that bordered on hatred. After all I'd done for him—after I'd chosen to live for him—how could he treat me like this?

"You want me to trust you? Fine. Stop stripping."

Grinding my teeth, I said, "I'll do that when you stop being a cop."

"When hell freezes."

A bare second after that, a smoky vapor shot out of his eyes, his ears, his mouth, surrounding him like a black nebula. I blinked and it was gone.

No. No, no, no.

That had to be me projecting my anger and despair. I hadn't seen what I'd just seen. A trick of the light, I told myself, that was all.

But I knew in my heart, in my soul, that I was fooling myself.

"I'm going to sleep on the couch."

For a moment, his words didn't make any sense, and then I realized he was still talking about our fight. Our stupid, human fight. "But aren't we not supposed to go to sleep angry? That's one of the rules. This is the part where we're supposed to kiss and make up."

"Jesse, the way I'm feeling right now, I don't want to touch you."

My breath hitched. The demons of Pride with their instruments of torture couldn't have hurt me more. What he was saying wasn't real.

What I saw wasn't real.

"Please," I whispered, reaching up to touch his cheek, "let's go to bed."

He pushed my hand away.

"Come on, Paul, I'll make you feel good, I'll show you how much I love you—"

"Sex isn't going to fix this, Jesse." His voice was as soft as decay. "I need space tonight."

Biting my lip, I looked down at my feet as the tears spilled down my face. "Want me to leave?" I asked, dreading the answer.

The silence between us grew until I wanted to scream. Finally he said, "It's late. I don't want you walking out there alone."

"Then . . ." I took a deep breath. "Then shouldn't I at least take the couch? It's your apartment."

"Take the bed. I'll be quiet in the morning so as not to wake you."

Always the White Knight.

I heard his footfalls padding away, down the hall, and then I heard the bathroom fan turn on before a door closed, cutting off the sound. It was as final as a guillotine's blade hitting home.

Paul hated me.

All of this—falling in love, getting a soul—was for nothing.

But even worse than all of that, worse than balking the will of Hell, the black ring of his aura meant only one thing. I sank down to my knees and sobbed, my head pounding in time to my wails.

Paul Hamilton was going to die.

PART TWO

THE FURY AND THE DEMON

Chapter 9

Paul's Apartment

A hint of eggs . . . frying, maybe . . . Breakfast?

The press of lips against mine . . . a tongue prying my mouth open to dance over my teeth.

Paul.

With an *ummm* sounding in my throat, I surrendered myself to that kiss, let that tongue slice me, attack me. Not soft and loving . . . something hard. Something raw.

Desire.

Paul . . . love, I knew you'd forgive me . . .

I tried to open my eyes, but they were caked with old makeup and restless sleep, and they preferred to remain firmly shut. Besides, the kiss worked better with my eyes closed.

My mouth locked against his as my tongue joined in the action. His cologne filled my nose—a spicy, primal scent that screamed *male*. Eau d'Aphrodisiac. My back arched, pushing my breasts against the silk of his shirt, offering them like fruit from a tree, ready to be plucked, sucked, squeezed. A delicious tingle of wetness down low, followed by a growing warmth between my legs. As my body woke up—very, very happily—my brain was still wrapping its mental arms around the concept of no longer being asleep. And something else.

The hungry kiss . . . the cologne . . .

. . . were wrong.

Paul?

Stop that, my body told my brain. *Sex! Sex! Let's have sex!*

My brain told my body to go fuck itself, and commanded me to wake up. Now.

I tried to say something, but that's tough to do when you're already speaking in tongues. So I broke the kiss, forced open my eyes.

"Hey babes," Daun said. "Miss me?"

Oh fuck.

All the sweet warmth pulsing through my body instantly coated with ice. I scrambled backward and up, stopping when I felt the cool wood of the headboard pressing against my back. Daun's amber gaze lingered over my bare breasts, traveled down to my pubic hair. In my effort to backpedal away, I'd kicked off the comforter.

Mental note: Wear pajamas.

"Missed you," Daun said to my crotch. "Been thinking about you all night."

"I'm flattered."

"You been thinking about my offer?" His heated gaze rested on my face, and I squirmed as I felt his power, his presence, caress my jaw. "You ready to come back with me, get the orgy started?"

"I . . ." Black dots swam in my vision, so I closed my eyes. Marginally better—now the black dots were purple, and sort of lit up the backs of my eyelids. I wasn't in any shape to fend off a horny demon.

Especially when I wasn't completely sure I wanted him to leave. "I don't know."

A pause, then: "You don't know? I'm offering you the best sex of your existence, and you don't know? What's there to think about?"

"Hell's sort of a one-way trip now that I've got a soul."

"Please, that thing? A few months with me, you'll be back down to demon standard. If it could happen to your old Queen, it could happen to you."

Maybe. But Lillith had been the First Woman (the pre-Eve model), not to mention cursed by God. Those things had helped her morph into the first mortal demon. All I had were my good looks and charming personality. "The King wouldn't exactly welcome me back with open arms."

"The King's got other issues on His plate right now. He's making waves, and a number of the old gods are grumbling. He'll be too busy to notice one former Seducer returning to the fold." Daun paused, and I heard the smile unfurl across his face. "You and me, and lots of sex. What do you say?"

Thinking of Paul, I said, "No."

"No," Daun repeated, as if he didn't understand the word. Then he let out a throaty chuckle that was the stuff of sadistic villains. "Jezebel. You really think that love will save you, don't you?"

My eyes opened with a will of their own. Daun still wore a human costume—round face, curly brown hair, no horns—but beneath the shell of flesh, his power swelled, rippling through his form. Raw sexual desire, sensuality dripping like honey, thick and clinging and oh, so very sweet . . . All I needed to do was open wide, and he would fill me, thrill me, take me to places I've never imagined . . .

I clamped my teeth down on my bottom lip. With the pain came the clear thought: *No.*

His power reared back, settled down. And waited.

Oh, fuck me, that had been so close. It would have been so easy to just let his magic roll through me, drown me in a sea of mindless passion.

"Yes, *love*," Daun said, as if nothing had passed between us. "You and your flesh puppet with the shoulders, you have such an adorable routine going. You're just too cute. I watch you, you know. It's better than listening to pundits argue politics." He leaned in close, wrapped in the smell of sex and brimstone. "I watch you play at this love thing. And babes, you give me such a laugh."

All the blood in my body pooled in my ankles as his words hit me. "A demonic voyeur," I heard myself say. "My, my."

"Come on," he said, his voice a low purr. "Forget about your meat pie. I'll give you something much better to stick your fingers in." His teeth flashed as his grin stretched impossibly wide.

Shivering, I grabbed the comforter and wrapped it around my body. "I said no."

"No? Why? Because of your meat pie? That mortal piece of flesh?" The grin slipped, leaving his mouth a horrific snarl. "You think you love him, Jezzie? You think he loves you? Where is he now?"

"At work."

"Did he wake you with a kiss, like always? Did he stare into your sleepy green eyes and tell you he loves you? Did you smile at him and tell him the same?"

My eyes widened as Daun threw the morning ritual in my face. He had it down pat—before Paul would slip away to work, he'd do the whole demonic Sleeping Beauty thing, and then, my kiss fresh on his lips, he'd go off to save the world and I'd go back to sleep.

Daun really had been watching us.

Shit.

"Did he fuck you last night?" he asked, his eyes shining. "Fuck you good and slow, getting your sweet spot and licking your candy from his lips? Or did he tell you that he doesn't trust you?"

A soft keening sound escaped from my mouth before I whispered, "Stop."

"Did he tell you he couldn't bear to touch you?"

I turned away as my eyes brimmed. "Please. Stop."

"Love sucks, Jezebel. It's complicated and stupid. It plays head games with your heart and heart games with your head. Walk away from it, babes. Come back to the Pit. Together," he said, "we can raise Hell. The fun way."

Bless me, I hated feeling so lost. "I . . . I don't know."

"You think about it. As your man makes you feel like shit for being who and what you are, you think long and hard."

Something thick lodged in my throat, and I swallowed it down, tasting rotten plums and old pennies.

"Oh, one more thing."

My eyes burning with unshed tears, I looked up at him.

"That heart on the floor in the other room? It's glowing." An ugly smile played on his face. "You might want to think faster. Because Jezebel, I guarantee, whatever it is the Erinyes wants with you, sex is nowhere on the list."

Fuck.

"When you finally see the dark, all you have to do is call my name. Bye, babes." Daun dropped me a wink, and he vanished in a puff of sulfur.

I scrubbed away my tears with the back of my hand. I'd have time for self-pity over what happened with Paul later. Maybe. For now, I had to think about my immediate future. Worrying my lip between my teeth, I wondered what to do.

Option A: Tell Alecto and Daun to fuck off. But that meant leaving Meg to rot. And no matter how angry and confused I was over how she could have chosen duty over friendship, I loved her still. So Option A meant spending the rest of my life wondering what torment Meg was suffering. Leave the life-long guilt to others; me, I seriously meant to avoid it. Guilt was murder on the complexion.

Option B: Agree to go to Hell with Alecto—for whatever reason she wanted me to go in the first place. Find out the truth about Meg. Subject myself to unknown torture, evil, and overall misery for the foreseeable future, and probably longer. Meh. Pass.

Option C: Agree to go to Hell with Daun. On the plus side, sex. On the negative side . . .

Hello, negative side?

Well, a voice whispered, still sounding obnoxiously like Meg, *you'd have to leave Paul.*

But I love him.

You think he loves you? In my mind, Daun chuckled. *You think about it. As your man makes you feel like shit for being who and what you are, you think long and hard.*

Why was I fighting Daun's advances? Other than the eternal damnation thing, that is. And even that wasn't a guarantee—like Daun said, Lillith had become a mortal demon.

Why not me?

I brought a handful of the bed sheet up to my nose and

sniffed. I wanted to smell Paul on the cotton, wanted to feel his presence next to me. But all I smelled was fabric softener.

Was Paul thinking about me right now? Was he still angry? Did he forgive me?

I wished I could hear his voice.

Did he still love me?

Reaching over to the nightstand, I picked up the cordless phone and pressed the speed-dial combo to connect me to Paul's police station. Even if he was furious with me, I needed to speak to him, to tell him that I was sorry.

And if he was really still that angry with me and told me to go to Hell, maybe I'd take him up on his offer.

No luck. The desk sergeant politely told me that Paul wasn't available, but he'd let Paul know that I called. I told the sergeant to have a pleasant day as I silently hoped he'd succumb to a bout of diarrhea at an inopportune time. Then I called Paul's cell phone. Voicemail. Well, at least I got to hear his voice.

Mental note: Be more specific when making wishes.

"Hi," I said after the little beep. "Um. I just wanted you to know that I'm thinking about you. And. Um. I'm sorry about last night. Um, I'll be home. For a bit. Hope you'll call me. Love you. Bye."

A silver-tongued devil I most clearly was not.

Where was he? Wasn't it early in the day for him to be saving the world? Didn't he usually wait until after lunch for heroics?

Maybe he was on another call. Maybe he left me a note.

A quick circuit around the apartment proved that Paul had other things on his mind this morning besides leaving me a note. Granted, I hadn't really expected one; the only reason he hadn't tossed me on my ass last night (and not in the fun-filled sexual way) was because he had a do-gooder streak in him roughly the size of Alaska.

He's just busy, I told myself. He'll call.

Uh huh, Meg's voice whispered in my mind. Once she'd played at being my conscience. Now it seemed like my brain had decided to keep her voice around for such occasions. *Sure he will.*

He will.

He's ignoring you, Jezzie. That's what humans do when they're angry. They ignore each other. They hurt each other.

Don't start about the hurt. You hurt me, and you're not even human.

I told you before. I'm not Meg, Jezzie. I'm you. And this isn't about Meg anyway. This is about you, and Paul . . . and whether you're still willing to sacrifice everything for him.

I love him.

Comforting. Except he doesn't trust you. Bets on how long a relationship without trust can last?

Hot tears burned trails down my cheeks as I padded naked around the apartment, lost. The charred outline of the pierced heart pulsed on the floor, with the mid-morning sunlight beaming through the living room window like a spotlight from Heaven. The glow was insidious, subtle—a hint of red winking among the black, the spark of embers in a dying campfire.

Daun had been right. Alecto was coming for me today— and soon.

Crap.

I had to figure out what to do.

I caught the hint of my reflection off the small window in the dining room—bed head that would have given hairstylists a case of the nerves, smudges beneath my eyes that looked like bruises, my eyes large and shocked, framed in yesterday's makeup.

No wonder Paul hadn't woken me this morning. One look at me probably was enough to make him want to call in a priest and book the next available exorcism.

Being human sucked. Emotions sucked. Love really, really sucked.

Full circle to self-pity.

Hating my life, I forced myself to climb into the shower. My world was unraveling, but real life didn't allow time-outs when shit happened. My afternoon shift at Spice kicked off at noon. Maybe I was utterly miserable, but that was no excuse to give up a few hours of flashing my boobs and inspiring a lot of wet dreams. Some people smiled even when they were sad; me, I'd strip down to my G-string and bask in the aura of sexual desire, even though the one man in the world I wanted couldn't bear the thought of touching me.

Sex isn't going to fix this, Jesse.

I did the shave-soap-shampoo thing as Paul's judgment played in my mind, again and again. By the time I rinsed off my conditioner, my despair and self-loathing had given way to a bubbling anger.

How'm I supposed to trust you?

Rage filled me, hotter than the scalding spray of water that washed me clean. Who was he, with his holier-than-thou attitude?

I need space.

Well, fuck Paul Hamilton six ways to Salvation. I'd give him all the space he needed. White space, complete with debris.

I finished my shower and toweled dry. Then, with my hair wrapped in terrycloth and my body covered in a thick robe, I stormed out of the bathroom.

And let out a screech when Angel appeared in my path.

"I'm sorry to startle you," she said, all innocence.

"Holy fuck in Heaven," I shouted, one hand over my heart, "doesn't anyone believe in knocking anymore?"

"I wished to speak with you."

"Fine. Speak. But I'm on a tight schedule." I pushed past her into the bedroom.

"I'm sorry. I didn't realize you were busy."

"Yeah, well, I have to get dressed, do my makeup, wreck Paul's apartment, pack up, find a place to live, and then get to work. So if you don't mind, make it fast."

Silence for a few precious minutes, which I used to finish rubbing my hair dry. My black curls rejoiced in their shiny cleanliness, bouncing and springing as I ran my fingers through them. There were times when I dearly missed having powers— I'd never, not in a hundred years, learn how to style my hair properly.

"Er, why do you want to wreck your lover's home?"

"Because he pissed me off."

"Oh. And the packing?"

"He says he needs space. What do you want, Angel?"

She paused, perhaps absorbing what I'd told her. I barreled past her and went back into the bathroom, tossing my towel to the floor. Paul could let the maid get it. The mirror had unfogged enough for me to start applying my makeup, so I pulled my cosmetics bag out from its resting place in the second drawer beneath the sink. I slammed the drawer shut, feeling extremely satisfied by the echoing bang. Yes, a little wanton destruction would put the spring back in my step.

"I think it is a mistake for you to ruin your lover's home just because you are angry."

I cast a glance over my shoulder and up at the cherub. Bless me, did she have to be so tall? "Really? Why's that?"

"Isn't the answer obvious?"

"The man wants space," I said, turning back to face the mirror and apply my eyeliner. "I'm thinking a mallet through the living room wall would accommodate that nicely. Humans put too much emphasis on walls anyway."

"You have a mallet?"

"Hmm. Good point. Maybe a baseball bat will do. Paul's got one of those under his bed."

"But this will ruin any chance at you and he making amends."

"I don't want to make amends. I want to make a mess. A spectacular, unholy mess."

"That doesn't seem very beneficial."

"No, but it'll be very therapeutic." I reached for the eye shadow. "I'll blow off steam while I blow up his stuff. Maybe I'll yank his Nagels off the walls and hurl them out the window. If I get lucky, maybe I can smite a few passersby."

"You don't mean that."

"Nothing like a good smiting to kick off the day. Why should God get to have all the fun?"

My blasphemy must have stunned her to silence. Good. I concentrated on layering my lids with sparkling green powder, then I took out my mascara wand and began pumping out my lashes to biblical proportions.

"I've been told destruction is hard work."

Her words caught me so off-guard that my hand slipped. "Oh, crap." Grumbling, I reached for my eyelash comb. Bless me, there were times when I really missed being able to magic myself up a perfect face.

"You're pretty enough without any cosmetics, you know."

This from a woman who was so gorgeous that supermodels would gleefully commit hari-kari. "You're all heart."

My left eye was absolutely stunning—the liquid liner had gone on smoothly, the green shadow transformed my eye into a sparkling emerald, and the mascara hadn't dreamed of clumping. But the right eye was officially a fucking disaster, and my eyelash comb was barely making a dent through all the makeup globs pasting my upper lashes into a follicle pancake. Muttering, I ransacked my bag for the eye-makeup remover.

As I tissued away the clumped mascara, I glanced at the angel's reflection. "Why'd you ask about destruction?"

"Just curious about how difficult it is to do a good job. Um. Evil job."

"Actually, destroying things is easy. It's when you get creative that it takes work."

"And I assume you're very . . . creative?"

"Sweetie," I preened, "when it comes to destruction, I am an artiste."

"Well then, shouldn't you have waited to shower until after you destroyed everything?"

"Why?"

"Won't you get all sweaty and filthy when you . . . give your lover space?"

Bless me, the blonde had a point. "Fine. I'll shower again."

"Weren't you the one who said you were on a tight schedule?"

Fuck.

"Of course, if you decided to rearrange some things, maybe you'd still be able to fit everything in . . ."

"Fine, fine," I said with a disgusted sigh. "I got it. No trashing the place."

Her smile radiated good deeds. "I knew you'd make the right choice."

"Don't you dare start rubbing off on me."

Her celestial blues clouded over. "'Rubbing off' . . . ?"

At least she was still stupid. That brought a smile to my lips. "Never mind. So what's so urgent that you had to pop in unannounced?"

She frowned at me, tilting her head to the side as she considered me. Whatever. I finished my eye makeup as she debated whether to answer my question. I was on my lip liner when she finally said, "I wanted to thank you. For our talk last night."

"Oh?" I smirked at her reflection. "Is that what they're calling it these days? And here I thought it was still referred to as 'making out.'"

Heh. Lookee. I made the angel blush.

"Not that. The explanation. You made it all so clear. It really made sense when you said that sex could be almost holy." Her lips quirked into a smile. No matter how much color I added, my face would never look half as sensual as hers did at this moment—lips parted in an expression of simple delight, blue eyes sparkling with an inner light.

That bitch.

"That's my new purpose," she said. "To give my clients a touch of the Presence, to let them experience something holy. To let them experience God."

Right before she whisked them down to Hell. But far be it from me to quash her religious fervor. "No problem."

"So now I must return the favor."

I stared at her reflection before I tossed my makeup into my case and zipped it closed. "You must, huh? Explain."

"You helped me when I needed it. Now I must help you."

"Really?" A celestial-turned-infernal entity, in my debt? Ooh, possibilities. "So how'm I supposed to cash in on this unexpected windfall?"

She smiled, displaying her pearly whites. "Think of me as your guardian angel, Jesse Harris. I'll be watching you." With that, she blinked out of existence.

Bless me, Angel and Daun would be a perfect freaking match. What was it about otherworldly beings watching me these days?

And why did they keep accosting me in or near the bathroom?

Chapter 10

Paul's Apartment

I opened my dresser drawers and pawed through my clothing. Later, at Spice, I'd be covered in temporary wrappings, like a living birthday gift. Until then, I'd be content in a green turtleneck, jeans, and low-heeled boots. The bra and matching panties I picked were puritanical: opaque and full coverage. The red satin of the material, though, would have been worn by Puritans subsequently burned at the stake for witchcraft. Paul liked this particular set of lingerie—he said it was the perfect combination of "wicked innocence."

Paul.

I need space.

My lip curled into a snarl. That angel-groping White-Knight-wannabe I'm-so-fucking-righteous Paul Hamilton.

No, stop that. Snarling messes up the lip liner.

I glanced at the clock radio on the nightstand. My shift at the club didn't start for a couple more hours. Plenty of time to stuff my belongings into a suitcase and find a temporary place to hang my hat.

And shower again, if necessary.

I reached under the bed and emerged with Paul's Louisville Slugger. The wood felt comfortable in my hands. Natural. I hefted it, brought it down into the meat of my palm, where it hit with a satisfying *thwock!*

I nodded grimly. Perfect.

Even though I wasn't hungry, I decided to make something to eat. I'd need my full strength when I introduced the baseball bat to the living room walls.

Stomping down the hall, bat in tow, I was about to turn the corner to enter the miniscule kitchen when the fine hairs at the base of my neck stood on end.

I wasn't alone.

The leather chair in the living room, its huge back to me, slowly spun around.

Biting my lip, I raised the bat high over my shoulder, ready to knock whatever was waiting for me into the next level of existence via grand slam. Not that the Slugger would do me much good if it were Lillith turning around—her weakness was iron, not wood. But getting her stomach mashed into pulp would slow her down.

Wondering if I had time to race into the kitchen to grab a cast-iron frying pan, I watched the chair finish its spin, stopping when the person seated in it was fully visible. And then I felt my heart stop.

Sitting in the chair, the Fury Alecto smiled, white fangs gleaming against the jet of her charred flesh. The vipers of her hair rose in a reptilian beehive, hissing a hello.

On the floor in the living room, the glyph glowed a brutal crimson . . . then disappeared.

I was out of time. The bat slipped from my numb fingers.

"Don't worry," Alecto said. "You won't be needing that."

My voice a trapped scream, I said, "You told me I'd have a human's day to think about it."

"It's the next day, is it not?"

Mental note: Nefarious creatures don't operate in real time.

"So," she said, twisting a strand of snake around her pinkie, "have you made your choice, Fury friend?"

"Um. Working on it."

She stared at me, the blood from her eyes spilling over her cheeks like red wine. "You have had more than enough time to consider. Now make your choice. Return with me to Hell, now, and I will take you to Megaera. Or stay here and never know what has happened to my sister. Choose."

I thought about Meg—how she'd sneak me away from Apocalypse Drills, how we'd toast eyeballs over the smoldering bonfires in the Heartlands, how we'd mock the elite and whisper our secrets that we would never trust with anyone else.

How I loved her.

Love sucks, Daun reminded me. *It plays head games with your heart and heart games with your head.*

A month ago, Meg had made her choice. And now I made mine. I met Alecto's murderous gaze and said, "I'm staying."

The Fury's hair recoiled, the serpents tangling and hissing. Her face contorted into a mask of utter rage. "You will never see her again, you who were Jezebel."

I hated it when supernatural entities tried to strong-arm me into anything. Crossing my arms under my breasts, I said, "I made my choice, Erinyes."

Our gazes locked, the air between us thick with tension. After a small eternity, she hissed through her teeth, a sad, defeated sound. In a voice completely stripped of malefic ire, she said, "That's just great. I should have known the hard sell wouldn't work with you."

I blinked. "Excuse me?"

She ran a taloned hand over her eyes. The black snakes of her hair nipped at her clawed fingers, perhaps trying to cheer her up. Without looking at me, Alecto said, "Fine. Let's try the direct approach. You still care for my sister. I saw it in your face yesterday when you thought I was she. You still love Megaera."

"That's debatable," I said, my head spinning from the Fury's abrupt change in demeanor.

"Don't lie to me." She lowered her hand and raised her head until her bloody gaze met my own. "Your feelings are tattooed to your soul. I see the truth of things clearly. You still love my sister."

"So what if I do? I made my choice," I said, sounding far more confident than I felt.

"The wrong one. I need you to come with me, freely and of your own will."

My heartbeat quickened with anticipation. "Why?"

Her lips pulled up in a tight smile. "I need you to accompany me to Hell so that you can save Megaera."

After I picked my jaw up from the floor, I said, "Care to explain that?"

Alecto sighed—such a perfectly normal sound. Just an ancient burned woman with bleeding eyes and snakes for hair and the mother of all serpents for a stole. Other than the form itself, there was nothing overtly threatening about her. For now. She said, "When Megaera failed to bring you back to Hell, she subjected herself to the King's judgment. And He found her wanting."

"Maybe He missed that episode. Meg led me to my death. She did her job." Duty over friendship. I worked my jaw, grinding my teeth together hard enough that sparks should have flown from my mouth. Bless me, even a month later, the betrayal still burned.

"She was supposed to bring you back. That was her assignment. She failed."

The memory of Meg's voice, just before she kissed me and left me to die: *Will you return with me now?*

I told Alecto, "No, that's not right. Meg offered me a choice." The ghost of Meg's touch made my lips tingle, and I tasted mint and old parchment.

Her sister stared at me, blood seeping from her eyes. Alecto's hair writhed around her face, the serpents twining and untwining, pulsing with menace. "The choice was not hers to give. And now she suffers for making that decision."

Suffers.

I wrapped my arms around myself, shivering from the ice that crept up my spine. For a creature of the Pit to truly suffer, the punishment must be particularly horrid. Bile rose in my throat as an image came to me of one of Hell's more gruesome torments: Meg chained, spread-eagled and dripping in honey-eyed mead, her body draped over a badger's den. Her screams would not be loud enough to cover the sound of the animal digging its way up and out, burrowing through her flesh. Once the creature tore its way to the layer with the sweet liquid, Meg's wounds would slowly bind themselves together, the badger would be replaced, and the scene would play itself out again.

And again.

I whispered, "What is He doing to her?"

"I did not lie to you before. Return with me, now, and I will take you to her. Will you come with me?"

Again, a choice from an Erinyes.

"Why didn't you ask for my help yesterday? Why did you try to intimidate me into doing what you wanted?"

Her mouth tightened into a thin line. "I am unused to mortals saying no to me. And I have never before asked a human for help." She shrugged. "I am what I am, tempter girl. So the question is, are you truly a Fury friend? Will you come with me and save Megaera?"

Meg's face appeared in my mind. I saw her blue eyes sparkle with wicked thoughts, heard the sound of her joyous laugh.

Oh, Meg. You betrayed me, betrayed our friendship out of a loyalty to Hell. I should let you rot.

But bless it all, Alecto was right: I loved her still. More than a thousand years of friendship was too hard to ignore.

"She's your sister," I said, my throat dry. "Why don't you save her?"

"I am not allowed."

"Allowed?" I spat out a surprised laugh. "Who can tell *you* otherwise?"

The snakes of Alecto's hair rose up as one, their mouths dropping open in a collective hiss. The gargantuan serpent around her shoulders unwound its tail, rattled its threat. The Fury's face remained stoic, impassive, but her fingers drummed a beat on her chair's armrest. "She is being rightfully punished. Even I must follow rules, tempter girl. There is no way for me to free her. But you," Alecto said, her voice dropping low, "you escaped Hell."

Barely.

"You bucked the King's authority once before. You can do it again. Please," she said, the word clearly foreign to her tongue, "come back with me. Save my sister."

My heart thumped, the beat sounding far too loud to my ears as I considered her request.

I wanted to say yes. Whether it was to escape Paul's judgment or to find a way to help my old friend, I wanted to tell her yes, take me back. Take me away from this plane of despair and destruction, where people murder each other with words and actions, where humans are the demons of their world.

Take me home.

But I had too many questions, and no answers. Why was she asking for help instead of demanding it, forcing my hand? And why was Alecto convinced that I—a former fifth-level succubus and infernal runaway—could somehow free a being nearly as powerful as the Almighty?

"I'm an exotic dancer," I said, "not a hero."

"You're her friend."

Yes. But Hell didn't give a fig about friendship. Something stank to high Heaven, and it wasn't the brimstone. "Will you give me a spiffy talking sword, or something like that?"

Alecto's mouth pulled down into a scowl. "What?"

"Well," I chirped, "isn't that how it works? The intrepid heroine receives a talking sword, or some sort of magic item that will help her in her quest to save the world, retrieve the potion, or destroy the ring of power?"

The Erinyes growled, and her snakes hissed in reptilian harmony. "Do you joke?"

Some entities have no sense of humor.

"No dice," I said, lifting my chin high. "I'm not going. Nothing could hurt Meg, not unless she wanted to be hurt. You of all beings know that. She's a Fury."

A moment passed as she quivered with hatred. She spat, "Small wonder she left you to your fate." Then she poofed away in a burst of malefic sulfur.

I waved away the stink of rotten eggs, noting that this time, the Erinyes left the floor unscathed. Figured. When I wanted to trash the place, the nefarious entity cleaned up after herself.

Staring at the baseball bat on the floor, I debated taking my emotions out on the Nagels hanging on the wall. But the encounter with Alecto had left me uneasy, unsettled—and without an appetite for destruction. I sighed. Maybe chocolate would cheer me up.

Meg, wherever you are, you have to fend for yourself.

Because I would be damned if I ever returned to Hell.

Chapter 11

Spice/Paul's Apartment

"Jesus! Careful with that elbow, Jezzie. You almost poked my eye out."

"Sorry," I muttered, not tearing my gaze from the vanity mirror. My hair was being positively scary today. Must have been influenced by all of Alecto's snakes. Well, screw it. I'd be doing the Rocker Groupie thing in a few minutes; might as well go for big hair circa 1987. I took my brush and started teasing out my locks, adding about three inches to my height.

Paul certainly liked taller women, if the way he'd been fawning over Angel at the dance club was any indicator.

You're being silly, my stupid conscience said. *Angel had been flirting with him, not the other way around. And she did it only because Daun had told her to. That wasn't Paul's fault.*

Right. The White Knight could do no wrong.

Of course he could do wrong. He's only human.

Like you, Jesse.

I told my conscience to take a flying leap off the Empire State Building. Then I focused on fixing my hair.

Whoever had designed the dressing room at Spice must have had at least ten sisters: attached to the wall like a low-riding shelf, the vanity table wrapped around half the room, complete with individual chairs (the comfy plush kind, not the ones that fold in half the moment you sit your ass down) and a wall-mounted makeup mirror. Soft-light bulbs dotted the mirror frame; the counter was wide enough for the Avon lady to display her entire set of wares and still have room to fix a sandwich. Each chair had a number; each number matched one on the row of lockers that ran across the far end of the room. Up to thirty dancers at a time could do the makeover thing simultaneously and not get in each other's way.

Well, not unless they were liberal with their elbows.

Next to me, Faith clucked her tongue. "What's wrong, girl? You look madder than a bear with a canker sore."

"Paul's being an ass," I said. Okay, snarled. "Got into a fight last night. He's not returning my calls."

"Boo fucking hoo," Mimi said, off to my right. "Trouble in paradise. And here I thought your guy could do no wrong, the way you talk about him."

I shot Mimi a look that should have roasted her bottled-blond hair. She was one of those I'm-too-sexy types who acted like her farts were something that should be sold to the highest bidder. "Your sympathy's overwhelming."

"Just surprised that your boy toy's actually human. You make him out to be practically touched by God."

Where I come from, them's fighting words. I was about to suggest that she take her hairbrush and stick it up her ass when Faith asked me, "He get mad at you for going out without him last night?"

Casting one last glare at the peroxide queen, I said, "Something like that."

Mimi rolled her eyes. "Fucking pathetic."

That's it. If I couldn't murder Paul or even trash his apartment, I could at least gleefully slaughter Mimi and tap dance on her carcass. But before I could do more than picture myself decorating the dressing room with streamers of Mimi's small intestine, Candy let out a snort behind me.

"Guys can be possessive," she said as she tucked her boobs into a blue demi-bra. "They're stupid that way."

You'll be mine, Daun's voice whispered. *Body and soul.*

I closed my eyes and shuddered, my body remembering Daun's touch.

You still taste like a succubus.

Candy was still speaking, but her words were nothing more than static. Ghost fingers brushed against the curve of my breast, teased my nipple. Biting my lip, I told my body to stop that. Daun wasn't here now. And Daun wasn't my immediate problem. That honor belonged to—

You really love that flesh puppet with the big shoulders?

Yes. Except I also wanted to kill him. Slowly. And excruciatingly painfully.

Love was fucking complicated. I should never have turned my back on Lust.

And then there was Meg.

No. I wasn't thinking about her. She could rot, for all I cared.

You're lying to yourself.

Go away, Meg.

That's the difference between demons and humans, you know. Humans lie to themselves.

Shut up. You chose duty over me. Fine. Now it's my turn, and I choose life over a dead friendship.

I can see that.

Hear that, brain? I made my choice. So turn off the picture of Meg's face. Mute the sound of her giggles. Rip her out of my memory, like the way she ripped out my heart when she betrayed me.

Hello? Is this thing on?

Humans don't work like that, Jezzie, Jesse. Humans have a conscience. Humans dwell in the "what if."

Ah, crap.

Scowling, I shoved the voice away as I took my frustration out on my hair; in turn, my roots shrieked as they faced death by hairbrush.

"Shit. You didn't hear a damn thing I said, did you?"

Blinking, I looked at Candy's reflection. She stood behind me, hands on her hips, looking like an advertisement for liquid chocolate. Dark chocolate—there was no café au lait about her. From her tight cap of curls down to her stiletto-clad toes, she was an ebon goddess in electric-blue lace.

"Sorry," I said with a tiny shrug. "Lost in thought."

"Couldn't tell, thanks for the news flash." Candy shook her head. "You're eating yourself up over your man. Fuck that. You're about to go on stage in front of a room packed with lusty men."

"Not that packed for Friday lunch," Mimi said.

Candy pinned her with a glare. "So you don't need a crowbar to walk the aisles. Big fucking deal. Now do you mind? I'm in the middle of a pep talk here, and your smartass mouth is crimping my style."

Mimi snapped her mouth closed with an audible click, but I heard her mutter something suspiciously close to "runt."

Candy talked as she shimmied into her PVC shorts. "Now, as I was saying, there's a lot of men out there. Men with too much money and too little female attention. You want to get back at your man? Go out there, have a fucking killer set. Line your G-string with dead presidents."

"That'll get back at Paul how?" I asked.

She grinned at me, nearly blinding me from the flash of her teeth. "Honey, you'll be so busy counting your money, you'll be asking, 'Paul who?'"

Good point.

A rap on the door, then Joey's voice: "Jezzie, you're on."

"Thanks, sweetie," I called. I grabbed the bottle of hair spray and quickly cemented my tresses in place. Then I stood up, knotted my sleeveless black rocker tee at the waist, and adjusted my Daisy Dukes so that no ass cheeks peeked out. Then I blew my reflection a kiss.

Showtime.

I boogied down the hall, my heels clacking on the floor in time to the ending refrain of Prince's "Cream." Another dancer, Tori, headed my way, probably en route to the dressing room. As we approached each other, my pace slowed. She riveted me with red-rimmed eyes, her lips fixed in a knowing smile. My throat constricted, and suddenly I couldn't breathe.

Lillith smiled, opened her mouth—

—and sneezed.

Huh?

Tori sniffled, wiped her nose. "Fucking allergies," she muttered, walking past me. "Love your shirt, J."

"Thanks," I said, able to breathe again. My head felt swimmy, and my legs wobbled so much that I nearly wiped out. Pit swallow me, I was losing my mind. Get a hold of yourself, Jesse. Drooling men await.

By the time I arrived backstage, I had barely a minute to loosen up—I rolled my shoulders, rocked my head back and forth. Prince faded, and Kelly jiggled up to me, glistening from her time on stage, clutching fistfuls of money to her naked chest. We did the "Hey" thing, filling an entire conversation with one word:

ME: Hey. (Meaning, Hi, did you have a good set?)

HER: Hey. (Meaning, Yeah, pretty good, but you have to work it to see real tips.)

ME: [Eyebrow quirk.] (Guys're stingy today?)

HER: [Shrug.] (Tightwad losers, the lot of them.)

She dashed past me, and then from the DJ booth Jerry's voice filled the club. He called my stage name—my real name, the sum of who I was, and who I would ever be.

The temptress of Spice: Jezebel.

Hell yeah.

I stepped on stage, the first notes of AC/DC's "You Shook Me All Night Long" blending with the loud applause from the audience. My men, they like the Hard Rock Whore thing. Over the cheers, electric guitar strummed from the speakers, sassy, playful, hinting of wickedness. Grinning as the melody seeped into my skin, I sashayed forward, taking stock of the men seated in front of me, around me—watching me, wanting so desperately to touch me. Sweaty faces, hungry eyes.

Über cool.

The drums kicked in, working with the guitar to form a seductive rhythm. Hands on my thighs, I rolled my hips to the beat. My hands moved up my torso, tracing the outline of my breasts before they stretched up and up, ran through my hair as they reached for the sky. Brian Johnson's voice rang out, gravely and so damn sexy, and as he sang I danced—big movements, unabashed, inviting the audience to fuck me with their eyes.

The barest pause at the end of the song, then the pounding drum intro to ZZ Top's "Sleeping Bag" thumped out. Thrilling in the way the music battered my body, I untied the end of the rocker shirt before I peeled it over my head. Strutting to the stage's edge, I winked at the flustered businessman at Table 2 and let the garment fall into his lap. Not a good idea to throw away outfits, but today I didn't mind—the shirt had been Paul's.

Gyrating in the spotlight, I tore the shorts from my body, the Velcro making a satisfying ripping sound. Ah, fuck it. I tossed that out too, causing a minor fistfight by Table 3.

That's right, boys. Show me your love.

Stripped down to my black mesh bra and G-string, I sauntered to the brass stripper pole in the middle of the stage. Gripping it with both hands, I swung in time with the song, kicking up a leg and whipping my hair around in a frenzy. All to the beat: the music pulled me under, and I let it take me away.

Soon ZZ Top melted into Poison telling the audience to "Talk Dirty to Me." I ditched my bra. My breasts, all too happy to be free, jiggled as I danced, my nipples erect from the air conditioning and the avid stares of the customers. My shoulders rolled and my ass wiggled as I drank in the music, sipped the sound of Bret Michaels' throaty vocals.

Purr, baby.

Dropping to the floor, I crawled my way to the tip rail, my body undulating to the guitar lead. Tits-first, I said hello to all the lovely men with all their lovely money. Ones and fives slid next to my hip, thick fingers lingering on my thigh after they tucked the bills into my barely-there underwear. The new owner of my shorts offered me a twenty. Smiling over my shoulder, I showed him my ass, wiggling my intention. I felt his nervous fingers touch my flesh as he nudged the money beneath the strap of my G-string. Turning, I blew him a kiss, knowing that at that moment, he would have given me his soul to feel my mouth on his.

Yes, sweetie. I would suck you down, swallow you whole, make you explode with pleasure.

Flush with tips, I rose to my feet and pranced to the middle of the stage for the rest of the song, dancing for my posse. The music gave way to a crash of applause and whistles, and I basked in the attention, feeling their desire pour over me, thick and sticky as blood on my skin.

Grinning madly, I waved to all the yummy men. Who needed Paul Hamilton?

Before I picked up my discarded bra, I caught a glimpse of long blond hair, of legs that stretched from here to Omaha.

Seated at the bar, the angel raised a glass to me.

"**I** still don't understand what you're doing."

Fumbling in my purse, I said, "What I'm doing is standing outside of Paul's apartment as I look for my key."

"Yes," the cherub said, "but my concern is why you are here in the first place."

"I need to get my stuff." I'd been so busy not stressing after Alecto's return that I'd accidentally left my suitcases at the apartment. Now I needed to retrieve them before Paul came home. I didn't know where I was going next, but that didn't matter. I could do the hotel thing for a few days, maybe slum at Faith's for a couple while I figured things out.

Angel said, "I think what you need is some time to think before you do anything rash."

"What are you, my mother?"

"Demons don't have mothers."

"It's something the humans say. And I'm not a demon anymore." Crap, where was the key? "I don't suppose you could open the door for me."

"Of course I could. But I won't. Entering an abode without permission would be wrong."

"Yeah? Where was this sense of righteousness earlier, when you just zapped yourself inside and nearly scared me to death?"

"That was different," she said. "I needed to speak with you."

"Well, I need to get inside."

"Then you should use your key."

Bitch.

After some more fruitless rummaging, I upended my purse, scattering the contents onto the floor. Lipstick, tissues, loose change, more tissues, three sticks of gum, wallet, half a chocolate bar. Some funky stuff that I assumed was a purse's equivalent of belly button lint. But no key.

Crap.

"Maybe this is a sign," Angel said. "Perhaps you're not supposed to take your things and leave. Perhaps you're supposed to make amends with your man."

"Perhaps I should learn not to lose my flipping key." I leaned over and thudded my forehead against the door, the wood cool against my skin.

And from inside, I heard voices.

Oh, terrific. My soon-to-be-ex-lover was home. Maybe he'd be kind enough to let me in so I could tear him a new asshole before I kissed that ass goodbye. Maybe—

A woman's laughter peeled out, the sound as ripe as freshly plucked fruit.

Frowning, I pressed my ear against the door. Maybe I'd left the television on?

No, there was Paul's voice, muffled, yes, but his voice all the same.

My chest felt too tight, and something lodged in my throat. Swallowing thickly, I listened, hoping I was wrong, knowing I wasn't.

More laughter, followed by a feminine voice cooing. And now Paul, letting out a groan . . .

"Unlock this door," I said to Angel.

"Jesse Harris, that would be—"

"Unlock this fucking door," I said again, my voice a strangled growl. "Now."

Either my urgency or my demonic nature must have convinced the cherub not to screw around, because she replied, "It is done."

I threw open the door and stormed inside. And there, in the living room, on the cheap Ikea sofa that was falling apart but

Paul couldn't bear to part with, there was Paul himself, his button-up shirt unbuttoned and hanging off him like a dead thing, Paul's head thrown back but not so much that I didn't see his blissful smile, Paul's hard torso and chest and shoulders glistening with sweat and scratches from nails that weren't mine, Paul moaning in ecstasy, Paul with a woman straddling him.

Paul with some nasty skanky lily-assed cocksucking festering rotting piece of trash whore on top of him. Fucking his brains out.

Right. Now. In front of me.

She faced away from me as she rode my man. Her body moved sinuously, flowing like white water. She moved, he followed. Her ass rose, and Paul's crotch rose with her; down they came, her ass, his crotch, locked together like a Chinese finger trap. Naked, her flesh gleamed, pearls of sweat on her pale skin. His jeans and underwear puddled around his knees, forgotten. The musk of their sex filled the room, filled my nose until all I could smell was her body on his.

I must have made a sound. I must have, even with my blood roaring in my ears so I couldn't hear anything but the mad *boom! boom! boom!* of my heart about to explode in my chest. I must have made a sound, because she turned, looked over her bare shoulder at me.

And grinned.

Unholy Hell, that's *me*.

That's my face. My big green eyes, sparkling with mischief and delight. My mouth, set in a wide grin with a slight overbite. My round cheeks, my pointed chin. My black curly hair that hated to be tamed with a brush. That's my body on top of Paul's, my legs sandwiching him.

"Heya, Jesse," she said, that fucking smile still on her face.

My voice.

My twin sister.

Caitlin fucking Harris.

Something popped in my ears, and my vision narrowed to a red pinpoint until all I saw was her smile. Yes, focus on the smile. Keep those teeth in sight. Because I am so going to punch those fucking teeth right out of your fucking head, you little scum-sucking ho of a sister.

I took exactly two steps before the bolt of power slammed into me, threw me backward. Heat—sizzling through me, enveloping me in a magical inferno. I screamed as my insides cooked and my bones melted, screamed as the stink of burning meat assaulted my nostrils, screamed until the sound cut off with a grunt when my body crashed into the wall.

Pinned.

Can't move.

Unholy Hell, can't even think.

"Better," Caitlin said. "I do so love an audience. Succubi, both present and past. How nice."

Her gaze on mine, she moved her hips faster. Beneath her, Paul groaned. His arms reached up, circled her waist, lifted her up and pushed her down, impaling her on himself. And up. And down. With every lift up, she gasped in delight. With every stroke down, she purred his name.

And grinned at me.

Stuck on the wall, I hung like a smoking picture. I couldn't look away, couldn't even close my eyes.

Please. Stop.

Don't let me see this, hear this. Smell this.

Paul's groans gave way to harsh panting. His breathing increased, and with every thrust he grunted, a primal sound of male pleasure. "I," he said. "I. I'm—"

Black smoke, seeping from his eyes, his mouth.

"—going to—"

Blackness pulsing around him, through him, eating him alive.

"—come—"

No! He can't die, not like this, not like *this* . . .

I heard her next words as if she'd hissed them directly into my brain: "Say my name."

Oh.

Oh no. No no no.

Not Caitlin. Not Caitlin at all.

Beneath her, Paul hitched in a breath. Gasping, he called her name.

"Lillithhhhh—ah!"

The orgasm took him completely, his body jittering beneath hers. And she smiled, content, her eyes sparkling as she looked at me.

"There now," she said to him while she stared at me, "was that the best sex you've ever had, lover?"

"Yes," he whispered, then his arms dropped and his head lolled and his voice faded into a small hiss until the word leaked away.

"You know how to make a girl feel special." She grinned at me. "Now, how can I show my appreciation? Oh, I know."

No. Oh by all that's unholy, no.

She bent down and kissed his lips.

NO!

I screamed myself raw, but my mouth was frozen, and I didn't make a sound as she sucked out Paul's soul.

When she pulled away, the black aura around him winked out, leaving Paul's body empty, spent. Lillith turned to me, and as her form shifted into something else, she licked her lips. "Your man tastes like apples."

You bitch.

I swear to any god listening, to my King and my Sire, to the Almighty and the Nameless Evil. I swear I'll see you dead, you thieving whore.

Her body rippled, washed itself of my shape. "Jezebel, you've always had a flair for the dramatic. He's just a flesh puppet, after all. Well, was."

Cunt!

She chuckled, low and throaty. "Ah, love. It makes you mortals do the most interesting things. You want him so bad, Jezebel? Come and get him."

Lillith blew me a kiss, then disappeared.

Chapter 12

Paul's Apartment

As soon as Lillith vanished, my body collapsed to the floor. A sound like a twig snapping, then a blinding pain in my arm.

No, don't think about that. Don't think about how the room is tilting to the left, how I'm finding it difficult to breathe.

Don't think.

I scrambled to my feet, even though the room kept rotating and the floor tried to slip out from under me. Left arm cradled to my chest and my right arm out for balance, I tottered over to the sofa. And there I crashed to my knees.

Paul.

He could have been sleeping. A rebellious lock of sandy hair dangled over his left eye like a question mark. Eyes closed, his brown lashes feathered out, leading the eye down to his sculpted cheeks, dotted with stubble. The rugged look. His strong jaw was relaxed, his lips parted as if waiting for a kiss.

He wasn't breathing.

I heard a high-pitched sound, like a kitten calling for its mother. My throat tightened, and the mewling took on a panicked note.

Paul wasn't breathing.

My Paul.

You were going to be so very sorry you'd made me feel so bad. You were going to miss me, want only to kiss me, hold me, love me. You were—

You are—

Paul.

Reaching out, smoke wafting from my burned flesh, I touched Paul's cheek. Cold. My fingers left smudges of black on his skin. No, that's not right. He shouldn't be dirty. I tried to rub the spots away, but all that did was streak the soot on his face.

"Jesse Harris," a soft voice said. "Please, Jesse Harris. Let me."

A gentle hand touched mine, moved it away from Paul's face. I opened my mouth, tried to say that he shouldn't be dirty, but all that came out was another tiny mewl.

The soft voice said, "Be calm, Jesse Harris."

Warmth pulsed from the hand covering mine, and that warmth traveled up my body, wrapped me in a thick cocoon. A wave of comfort rolled over my chest, and I took a deep, shuddering breath. Then I sagged, my arms dangling, hands limp on the ground. I tried to lift my hand, to touch Paul again, but my arm wouldn't move.

"I have healed your arm and your burns," Angel said, removing her hand from mine. "But you need rest. Come, let me take you to your bed."

Swaying, nearly falling to the floor, I shook my head. "No." My voice cracked, turning the word into broken glass. "Heal him."

"I cannot. He is dead." She sighed, said, "There is no healing from death."

I wanted to scream, to insist that bless it all, she had to heal him. But my mouth didn't work properly, and the weight of a thousand despairs dragged me down. I slumped to the ground. Fighting the exhaustion claiming me, I gritted my teeth, forced myself to look the cherub in the eye. "You," I said, pushing the word out of my mouth. A breath, another word: "Owe." And again: "Me."

Angel frowned at me, then turned to look at Paul. Shaking her head, she rested her left hand on his bare chest. "I saw his soul," she said, her voice like spring rain. "It was clean. White, with streaks of gold and silver. Even the webs of red were pure. Any lust had long since been altered by love. It was beautiful."

Tears spilled down my cheeks. Of course it was beautiful. I hadn't seen it, but I'd felt it. Known it. Loved it. Paul's soul was a thing of symphonies, of swirling crescendos and magical progressions. His soul was music. And Lillith's theft severed that music in a violent finale.

"She had no cause to bring him to Hell," Angel said, her brow crinkling. "What she did was wrong."

"My fault." My love had gotten him killed.

"No, Jesse Harris." Steel glinted in Angel's blue eyes, knives slicing through the sky. "No matter her hatred for you, there are still rules. She overstepped."

"Old rules," I said, remembering what the Arrogant had told me just yesterday. "Bending. Breaking."

Angel nodded. "They are. The King of Hell has changed much. But some of the old rules remain. The innocent cannot go to the Abyss. That is still a rule, even if unwritten." She looked at Paul's empty form, something close to a sneer playing on her lips. "This isn't right."

Beneath her touch, the color leeched from Paul's skin, fading until his form was an alabaster shell.

I whispered: "Heal him?"

"I cannot," she said, sighing again. "I hoped that perhaps I could call back his soul. But it is linked to your former Queen, and thus trapped. It cannot return to the flesh, no matter how I beckon." Her shoulders slumped. "He is dead, Jesse Harris. All I can do is preserve his form. Without his soul, his body is dead. I am truly sorry for your loss." She started to remove her hand.

I summoned the last of my strength. "Stop!" The word hovered in the air, echoing, beseeching.

Angel paused, her fingertips brushing against the hair on Paul's exposed chest. "Jesse Harris, preserving him like this still leaves him a husk, devoid of life. I will not do such a thing. It is an anathema. You must rest now."

Warmth crept up my limbs again, and my eyelids drooped.

No.

My hand clenched into a fist so tight that it trembled. My teeth clamped down onto my lower lip until I bit through, spikes of pain shredding the warm blanket of sleep the angel wrapped around me.

Give me my rage.

Bracing myself with my hands, I pushed myself up with a snarl.

"Jesse . . ."

"They just crossed the line," I whispered, my fury burning away the last vestiges of sleep. I climbed to my feet. "They want me back in Hell so bad? They've got it."

"Please, you're not thinking clearly . . ."

I gnashed my teeth against my lip until I tasted blood. "Yes," I said. "Yes I am. You just keep your hand where it is. You keep him preserved." Then I took a deep breath, and with my blood on my lips, I called his name.

"Daunuan."

My stomach taut, my chest too tight, I braced myself. No costumes this time. No possessions, no human facades. I'd called him, and between my blood and his name on my lips, he'd come.

The demon Daunuan was coming.

Shadows pulled themselves from the corners, stretching, throwing themselves across the room and slowly devouring the light. The halogen lamp flickered, died. In the darkness my senses whirled, acute to the point of pain: the sound of my heart thumping a crazy beat, of my breath hissing through my teeth as I panted; the tang of blood on my mouth, in my nose—sharp, precise, cutting through the smell of my sweat, the cold stench of my rage.

A scream of wind—my hair whipping around my face, stinging my cheeks, attacking my eyes. A streak of color—red lightning, fire burning through midnight. And then a deafening boom.

I clamped my hands to my ears and doubled over, grimacing as the monstrous sound charged my flesh like electricity, then sunk into my skin, settled into my bones. The thunder echoed, faded, leaving behind the steady ringing of mourning bells in my ears.

The sudden, overpowering stink of rotten eggs brought tears to my eyes. I inhaled deeply, then exhaled quickly through my nose. And again. And again, until I was numb to the odor. Awash in brimstone, I lowered my hands and stood tall.

Darkness still enshrouded the room, but I didn't have to see Daunuan to feel the effect of his presence. He towered in front of me, radiating lust, turning the air itself into an aphrodisiac. Hints of his thick hair winked in the blackness, and his eyes, the same yellow as his hair, glowed like a demonic Cheshire cat's—trapped sunlight, cursed gold. The silhouette of his horns seared the darkness above his glowing eyes, hot coals in a sea of black. A flash of white as he grinned, his fangs glistening with unspoken intentions.

"Well, well," Daun said, his voice the deep purr of a sleepy mountain lion. "If it isn't my darling Jezebel." He rolled my name on his tongue, letting the *L* hover too long. I felt that tongue slide into my cleavage, lick the swell of one breast, then the other. Sweat popped on my brow as I forced myself to ignore his touch.

"And a succubus," he said, the smile all too clear in his voice. As he spoke, invisible fingers fondled me, rolled my nipples until they hardened in his grasp. I caught myself starting to pant from his attention, so I bit down on my lip, hard. "What interesting company you're keeping, babes. Last I saw, your friend here was making moves on your man."

"It's one of those strange bedfellows times," I said, my voice betraying none of my desire, or my barely checked terror. I couldn't let Daun get to me, not yet, not before he promised to help me. "Can you tone down the demonic darkness thing?"

"You're the one who summoned me, Jezzie. Mortals usually prefer all the trappings. You being a human now, I thought you'd want the whole enchilada." His tongue lapped my nipple, then his lips clamped down. I bit back a moan as he gave suck. "You're so quiet, babes. What's wrong? Am I scaring you?"

"No."

"Liar. I smell your fear, Jezzie. It's intoxicating." Fangs flashed again in a silent laugh. "And you should be scared. You didn't cast any circles of protection before you summoned me. There's so much I could be doing to you right now."

Oh fuck.

The invisible mouth offered one last kiss on my breast before it disappeared. Daun said, "I could send you to your knees."

A crushing force pressed on my shoulders, and I fell to my knees.

"I could force you to bow down before me."

A kick to my back sent me crashing to the floor. My hands and forearms slapped against the hard wood, took the brunt of the impact. Something stepped on the back of my head, nudged my forehead to the ground. The floorboards tattooed their pattern against my brow, and still the pressure on the back of my head increased, as if it meant to drive me through the floor.

Fuuuuuuuck.

"My Lord," the angel said, "is this really necessary?"

"Quiet. This is between me and Jezebel. My *summoner*."

Behind me, the cherub fell silent.

"Now then. I could be doing all sorts of things to you. But I'm not that into power games." Daun chuffed laughter, the disembodied sound galloping in the dark. "Forcing you to do anything takes the fun out of it."

Invisible hands lifted me up, placed me back on my feet. If not for those hands, I would have collapsed in a gibbering heap. Daun was right. In my exhaustion and anger, I'd forgotten the most important rule: When mortals consort with demons, they damn well better prepare themselves. Charms, circles, wands, a credit card—whatever afforded them protection, they'd better use it. Because without it, the infernal had free rein.

Too late to play it safe, I told myself, commanding my legs to stand firm.

Far too late.

"Lucky for you, I'm more into temptation than brute force," Daun said.

A ghostly finger stroked my crotch until heat flared between my legs. I bit back a gasp.

"See?" he said, chuckling. "Temptation. And after all our years together, I know how much you like to be surprised. The darkness stays, Jezzie. If you see what I'm doing, where's the surprise?"

My knees threatened to buckle as the strokes grew bolder. Stop, I told my body. Not now.

Not yet.

My body humphed its disappointment, but obeyed me. For now.

"Very impressive," I said, my voice husky. "But I didn't call you here for sex." Not quite a lie. Just not the whole truth.

The finger paused. "You summoned an incubus without any intention of fucking me? I don't know if I'm insulted or amused." The finger resumed its stroking, and something kissed the hollow of my throat, my jaw, my earlobe.

I swallowed thickly, trying to ignore the shocks of pleasure dancing on my skin. "I need your help."

The finger vanished.

In my ear, Daun whispered, "Maybe you're confusing me with the former angel. I don't do help."

"Daun . . ."

"You won't fuck me, you rub your love for your meat pie in my face, and then you have the gall to ask for my help? Not interested. Bye, babes."

I felt him move away from me, but I didn't panic until the yellow of his eyes and hair winked out. I shouted, "Please!"

In the darkness, he laughed softly. Coldly. "You need help so bad, Jezebel, I suggest you get your man to do it. Those big shoulders have to be good for something besides being a way station for your ankles."

"He can't," I said, fighting back tears. Bad enough I'd already begged. Crying right now would be very bad. Daun may have been a friend once, but he was first and foremost a demon. The nefarious feasted on mortal weakness, consumed it like candy. I was just a human, complete with emotions that threatened to drown me.

And a soul to offer to the highest bidder.

"Oh?" I heard the curiosity in Daun's voice, hoped it would override his anger with me. "You've got an itch he just won't scratch? The flesh puppet's got some values that are messing with your wicked desires?"

"Not exactly."

"Then what's stopping your man from helping his true love?"

"Him being newly dead."

I heard the gears turning in his head, and a moment later the darkness evaporated. Daun loomed over me, yellow eyes gleaming, long golden hair flowing over his shoulders. His body stood in sharp relief against the halogen light: his turquoise skin, peppered with flaxen curls, gleaming with sweat and the promise of sex; heavily muscled arms folded across his powerful chest; narrow waist leading down to a pelvis covered in a sandy brown pelt; strong thighs giving way to goat's legs and hooves. And a dick the size of a torpedo. Malefic standard to the max.

The mortal part of me recoiled. The demon I used to be wanted to throw myself on Daun and start humping.

He looked past me, his gaze fixed on the sofa, drinking in Paul's empty form. "Babes," he said, clearly impressed, "that's more like it."

"Not my handiwork."

Daun arched a golden brow at me, then jutted his chin toward the angel, whose hand rested on Paul's unmoving chest. The cherub blushed, avoided Daun's heated gaze.

"Not her, either," I said.

Eyes narrowed, Daun walked over to where Paul's body lay. He inhaled deeply, then snorted, his blue nostrils flaring. "*Her.*"

There was no question who he meant. Numbly, I nodded.

"She moved fast."

"Did you know?" I didn't really want the answer, but I had to ask. "Was this what she'd planned from the start?"

He looked at me, his eyes unreadable, a smile playing on his face. "There's no good answer, you know. If I say yes, I knew all along that your former Queen meant to seduce your man and steal his soul, then you'll hate me until the Lake of Fire freezes. And if I say no, I had no idea, your former Queen doesn't exactly confide in me, then you won't believe me."

"I'd believe you," I said.

But you wouldn't, Meg whispered. *You'd always wonder if he'd lied to you.*

That's not true.

In my mind, Meg laughed. *Just goes to show that humans are all too happy to lie to themselves.*

Shut up, Meg.

As if Daun could hear my conscience mocking me, he said, "I keep forgetting how much demons and humans have in common. You're lying to me now, but I don't think you know you're lying. You mortals are a complicated piece of work. I liked you better as a demon. Then you were deliciously one-track minded."

Shit. "I guess you're not telling, then."

His eyes sparkled with secrets. "Like I said before, babes, love sucks. Especially short-term, mortal love. And really, what other sort of love is there for humans?"

"Some love is stronger than that."

"Right, here's where the stripper breaks into a country song." He snorted laughter. "How's the joke go? Play the song backwards, and he'll come back to life."

Tears fought their way from my eyes, soldiered down my cheeks. I looked down at my feet so that Daun wouldn't see me cry.

"So what are you supposed to be doing?" he said to the cherub. "Turning him into a jar of meat preserves?"

Angel said, "My Lord, Jesse Harris requested this of me."

"Thought you were playing for the other team now. Or are you moonlighting as a guardian angel?"

"I owed her a favor," she said tersely. "All debts are now paid."

"Good. Owing anything to mortals can come back to bite you in the ass. But having the situation reversed almost always works out to your benefit. Speaking of which . . ." His voice broke off, and I felt his amber gaze on me. "Tell me, babes, what were you going to ask of me?"

I looked up at him, the tears doubling my vision, softening the lines of reality so that for a moment, I thought I saw sympathy in his yellow eyes. But no, that was the biggest lie of all. Daun was a demon, and demons didn't have feelings. "Why do you want to know?"

"Just curious," he said. "I can't bring him back to life, and I sure as shit won't challenge your former Queen. So I'm wondering what you needed my help with. Funeral arrangements, maybe?"

"Something like that." I took a deep breath, blew it out. My heart thumping madly, I said, "I need you to kill me."

Chapter 13

In The Arms of Don Juan

"**P**oor babes," Daun said. "You've lost your mind with grief."

"I'm perfectly sane." Considering that my lover had been first seduced and then murdered in front of my eyes, I was doing pretty well.

Daun didn't seem to agree. "Then you've got a fucked up sense of humor."

"I've never been more serious."

By the sofa, Angel said, "I agree with my Lord. You're insane."

Daun and I ignored her. He stared at me, his amber eyes unblinking. In his natural form, his face was all lines and sharp angles, revealing nothing soft. A smile unfurled, and even that was hard, cutting: a slash of mirth, a slice of humor. "You want me to kill you."

I lifted my chin. "Yes."

Something slammed against me, pushed me backward to the floor. My head connected with a *thud*, and for a moment stars burst across my vision like mental fireworks. Daun threw himself on me, straddling my hips and pinning my shoulders with his elbows. His shaft jammed against my stomach, and he rubbed himself against my belly. That would have been fine, except in the middle of getting his jollies on me, he wrapped his hands around my throat.

"This?" he said, his voice a deadly purr. "This is what you want?"

I squeaked out a no.

"Or maybe this?" He lifted one of his hands, the other still pressing into the soft flesh of my neck. As I watched, the nails on his fingertips stretched into razors that would have given Freddie Krueger the mother of all woodies. Eep.

Daun pressed one of those finger-razors against my cheek, the tip grazing my eyelashes. I didn't dare to breathe. Not that I had a lot of choice in the matter, what with Daun slowly choking the life out of me.

"Want me to slice off your nose to spite your face? Because that's what this is, Jezzie. Your bullshit pride."

I tried to speak, but his hand squeezed my windpipe. Grunting, I managed to whisper, "Not pride."

"No?" He removed his hand from my neck, and I gasped in a harsh, shuddering breath. Blood roared in my ears as I breathed, the air burning my throat. As much as I used to enjoy sexual asphyxiation when I was a succubus, it lacked a certain *je ne sais quoi* as a human. Probably due to the whole needing-to-breathe part.

Propping himself up on one hand so that he hovered over me, Daun pressed his other hand against my jaw, his razor-nail winking distance from my eye. "If not pride, then what? A death wish?"

I opened my mouth, but only a wheeze came out. Bless me, what was it about the malefic that they always had to go for the throat? I swallowed, working moisture into my abused esophagus. Finally I was able to speak. "No. It's the final straw."

He cocked his head to the side, his eyes narrowed, plotting. Considering my words. The razor-nails retracted, but he leaned down on me, pressing against my shoulders with his elbows, one of his fingers on my cheek, stroking. "Do tell."

Here we go. I had exactly one chance to convince Daun and the cherub to help me. I didn't want to think about what would happen if either of them refused. "I've had enough, Daun. I got out. I left Hell behind, got a soul, started over."

His fangs flashed—either a grin or a leer. "Been there, read the book. Don't bore me, babes." His tongue darted out, licked his lips.

Implied threat duly noted. "I was supposed to have a happy ending, ride off into the sunset, the whole shebang. But you guys won't leave me alone. And I've had enough."

"'You guys'?" His mouth twisted into a smirk. "I can't speak for anyone else. Me, I want you back for the sex."

"Not *her*," I said, not daring to speak Lillith's name aloud. "She took Paul, sucked out his soul."

"Ooh. Sucking face with a dead man. Shivers."

If I didn't need the demon so desperately, I would have taken Paul's baseball bat and smashed Daun's fangs out of his mouth. "She said if I wanted him so bad, I should come get him."

He darted his gaze to the angel. I couldn't see her reaction, but when Daun turned back to me, something flitted across his eyes. Bless me, why couldn't I read auras when I really needed to? He said, "She told you that?"

"Yes."

"Baiting you."

"Yes."

Angel cleared her throat. "His soul was clean, my Lord. She had no authority to claim him."

As Daun pondered that, I threw in, "And then there's Alecto . . ."

At the Fury's name, Daun hissed, and Angel murmured a prayer. Oops. Very few creatures blithely speak the name of an Erinyes. Being friends with Meg for so long must have burned away that automatic reaction of avoiding all things Fury. Yet another thing for me to hold against her.

Meg, you stupid thing, why did you submit to the King of Hell? What is He doing to you?

Angel's voice cut through my despair. "What on Earth does the Erinyes want with you?"

"Nothing on Earth." I told them about Alecto's visit, how she'd given me time to consider her request, how hours ago she'd practically begged me to return to the Abyss. When I finished, Daun shook his head as he chortled. "You gave the bitch the boot, eh? Good for you, Jezzie. You've got balls."

Now. Now, while his mood is good, and he's impressed with me.

"Boobs, not balls," I said. "And I've changed my mind. I'm going to Hell. I'm going to help Meg."

Daun's laughter shriveled and died.

"And I'm going to save Paul."

By the sofa, Angel muttered something under her breath.

"And then I'm going to march up to the King of Hell and tell Him to leave me and mine alone." Here we go. To Daun I said, "But to do this, I need you to seduce me and kill me, so you can lead my soul to Hell. And," I said to the angel, "I need you to do the Snow White thing to my body, so I'll be able to return when I'm done."

Daun glanced at the sofa, and I could feel him and the angel exchanging a look. You know it's got to be bad when a celestial and an infernal share the same thought.

"Definitely insane," Angel said.

The demon nodded. His eyes shone as he regarded me, his finger tracing a line over my jaw. Beneath him, I lay on my back, waiting for his reaction. I wished I could rip off my shirt and jiggle my tits to encourage him, but his elbows still pinned my shoulders.

"So," Daun said, rubbing his shaft against my belly, "I want to be sure I understand this. You want me to kill you so that I can take your soul to Hell?"

"Right."

"I'll seduce you, and you won't fight me? You'll kiss me willingly, let me fuck you? You'll surrender completely?"

"Yup."

"And all so that you can go to Hell?"

"Exactly."

He grinned, showing a mouthful of fangs that would have made any momma shark proud. "Sounds like a win-win to me."

"Jesse Harris, your plan makes no sense." I heard the

adorable pout on Angel's lips, even if I couldn't see it. Bitch. "Even if you were to go to Hell, how would you save your lover and your . . . friend? How would you return?"

On my left wrist, the Rope of Hecate rested. I felt its weight even as I felt Daun dry humping me. *The Hecate knows much*, Caitlin had said. *Nothing is hidden from Her*. Maybe the bracelet was just gold, and I was making a huge mistake. Maybe not. Was I willing to bet my soul on it?

My answer was lying dead on the sofa.

I said to Angel, "I have an idea about the return part."

"An *idea* . . . ?"

"As for the rest, I'll figure it out. Bless it all, this is something I have to do. Don't you get that? They've taken Paul. They've taken Meg. I mean to get them back. Which is why," I said to Daun, "I need you to promise me that when we're in Hell, you'll cut me loose. Swear that you'll sever the soul bond."

A bemused smile played on his lips. "And why would I do that?"

"Unless you're planning on helping me, it's going to be hard to make with the rescue mission if I'm tied to you."

"Hmm. I'll have to think about it. After all, we have time."

I glanced at the sofa, at Paul's arm dangling lifelessly. "No, we don't."

"*We* do. But him? You're right about that. He's slowly rotting. That's what happens when meat pie goes bad. It rots."

Bastard.

Daun's eyes sparkled with wicked thoughts. "Your decaying meat aside, if you want me to do you properly, it's going to take time. Incubi aren't about the wham, bam, thank you ma'am. It takes time to do it right."

I bit my lip, bringing a splash of pain and blood to my mouth. Bless me, he was right. I was still thinking like a succubus. Female Seducers had one chance to approach their clients, give them the ride of their life, then whisk their souls down to Hell. Quick (relatively speaking), fun, and, unless the client was into masochism, completely painless.

But the incubi worked differently. Every succubus fresh out

of Seduction 101 knows this. Like their female counterparts, the male Seducers had one chance to lure a mortal, trick her into offering him a kiss. But there the similarity ended. Once a human willingly kissed an incubus, game over—she was his, completely, in mind and body. And once she called his name while under his power, her soul was his as well.

From there, the incubus stretched his seduction to last for days, even weeks, giving his entranced lover undivided attention as he saved his own hunger for their final bout between the sheets. With every encounter, the human grew more dependent on the demon until she lived only to be loved by him. And every sexual act stripped her more and more of her energy, her very life force, until she was a shell of who she'd been. And only then, when the female was on the brink of death, her demon lover would come to her and love her and kill her.

Mars and Venus, Seducer-style.

It had nothing to do with a difference in technique. An incubus's sperm acts like a cancer in a mortal woman's body, ravaging her from the inside. It's immediate, effective, and incredibly brutal. The Marquis de Sade would have given his left nut to learn how to mimic even a tenth of the torture caused by an incubus's spunk. The male Seducers see their prolonged seductions as a gift to their clients—instead of ending such intense pleasure with unbearable suffering, they slowly leech a client's sustenance until she can't feel the agony of their consummation. Then, already beyond the ability to feel pain, the client dies with the incubus's cum scorching her thighs.

And then she goes to Hell.

I didn't have time for standard incubus operating procedure. But Daun, being who he was, would insist. Therefore, I had to piss him off enough to do what I wanted, but not enough so that he walked away completely. A finely honed skill. Luckily, I'd had a few millennia to practice.

"A talented demon like you can't bring me to orgasm in one sitting?" I smiled sweetly. "You must be getting old."

He leaned in close, stopping only when his mouth was inches from my own. "You think so little of me. Perhaps I should just leave you with your empty flesh puppet."

Shit.

"Ah, look at that. Such pain in your eyes. You wear it so very well." He grinned. "Fine. I'll do you in one session. I'll enjoy watching the agony eat you alive."

I felt the blood drain from my face. What's a little mind-numbing torture? I was getting what I wanted. Yay me.

"Do you really think he's going to do as you ask?" The angel's voice brimmed with disbelief. "That he's going to release your bond to him once you're in the Underworld? He's a demon, Jesse Harris. He won't help you. It's not in his nature."

The scorpion will always sting, King Lucifer said, His mournful voice replaying in my mind. *That's its nature.*

Daun chuckled. "Ye of little faith. Here, I'll even swear it on my name." A lazy smile playing on his face, he said, "I, Daunuan, do swear to release your soul when we are in Hell. Agreed?"

Too easy. But what other choice did I have? I wasn't exactly in the position to ask him to put it in writing. "Agreed."

He leaned down and kissed me, his saliva mingling with my own, the blood on my lip sealing the compact. The barest flick of his tongue on mine, then he pulled away. "Done."

One down. "What do you say, Angel? Will you help me?"

A pause before she answered. "I do not sanction this, Jesse Harris. What you wish to do is suicidal at best, and will probably damn you to an eternity in Hell."

"I like to live dangerously."

"This has nothing to do about living." She sighed, vexed. "But what your former Queen did was wrong. The rules are there for a reason. Your desire to save your lover is noble, Jesse Harris." Another pause, longer this time, before she said, "For this reason, I will aid you."

My eyes closed as I released a breath I hadn't known I'd been holding. This could work.

This *would* work.

"Well now, babes," Daun said, his breath hot on my neck, "shall we begin?"

He sat up, his hands locked onto my shoulders, his hips over mine. An impish grin lit his face as his gaze crawled over my prostrate form. "So many ways to start," he purred. "I'm giddy with anticipation. The things I'm going to do to you, Jesse Harris." He leaned down, whispered in my ear, "I'm going to show you what love really is." He punctuated that with a flick of his tongue on my lobe.

Hooboy.

At least I'd die with a big, fat smile on my lips.

Like Paul did.

"My Lord," the angel said, clearly uneasy, "perhaps you would care to use the bedroom? I believe that's the designated area for copulation."

"Here's good. Besides, I want you to watch." He winked at her. "Maybe learn a thing or two."

I didn't have to see the angel to feel her blush.

"Now." Daun's hand cupped my cheek, then trailed down my jaw, my neck, my chest. His fingers flowed around the swell of my left breast, pausing to gently squeeze the mound of flesh as if testing for ripeness. He slowly rubbed his thumb over my erect nipple, sending delicious shocks down to my groin. "Let's get these clothes off of you."

Beneath his hand, smoke wafted. The smell of burning cotton pricked my nostrils. "What're you—"

My shirt and bra burst into flame.

Fuck! I swatted madly at the fire, but before the heat touched my skin, the clothing flaked away. Cold air enveloped my exposed upper body, peppering my flesh with goosebumps. I didn't know if that was from the quick temperature change or from the momentary horror I'd felt when I thought I was going to burn alive.

Daun's eyes twinkled. "I keep forgetting how sexy you are when you're terrified."

"You know, sweetie," I said, my voice a high-pitched squeak, "this isn't exactly getting me in the mood."

"No? Fear used to get your sweet spots."

"That was when I didn't have to worry about spontaneous combustion."

"Hmm. Point taken. Let me kiss it, make it all better." He leaned down and took my nipple into his mouth. My breathing quickened as his tongue lapped at the nubbin of flesh, stroked it with wetness before he sucked. Groaning, I thrust my chest up, pushed myself deeper into his mouth. His fangs grazed the sensitive knob, and I gasped from the tiny flare of pain.

He broke suction to kiss the underswell of my breast. "You're about to combust again."

"Huh?"

My jeans caught fire. This time I felt the heat on me, in me, before the denim magicked away, taking my underwear and stockings with it.

"Don't you dare burn my boots," I said, my voice thick. "These are Jimmy Choos."

He paused. "I'm about to seduce you and kill you, and you're worried about your boots? I swear, for a creature four thousand years old, you are such a *girl* . . ."

"Girl, nothing. They cost me over seven hundred dollars."

"Fine," he said, "you take them off. I'm busy anyway." He attacked my other breast, and as I writhed beneath him, I slid my legs up and unzipped my boots, then kicked them off.

Mission accomplished. "I'm good."

"You are? Let's see."

Daun kissed down my belly, around the dark triangle of my pubic hair, spreading my legs apart to kiss my inner thigh. Eeee. If I had still been wearing panties, they would have been soaked.

"Yes," he whispered. "You're *very* good . . ."

My sex throbbed, demanded to be touched. I grabbed his hair and directed him up to my crotch. His tongue darted against my inner fold, searched for the magic spot—yes, there!

I bucked against him, my head rocking from side to side as a quivering wave of pleasure rolled over me, cresting . . .

. . . until I saw Angel watching, fascinated, as Daun ate me. Next to her, Paul's lifeless form sprawled, his chest unmoving beneath her hand.

Paul. My poor Paul. He's lying there dead, and here I am, about to experience the ultimate big-O orgasm.

The wave pulled back, rippled away into nothing, but I barely noticed as I stared at Paul's hand, dangling off the sofa. Paul, I swear to you, I'm not betraying you. I'm going to Hell to save you, love. What's happening now, that's just how I'm going to get there.

It means nothing to me.

Daun's kisses stopped. "Babes? What happened?"

I heard his words, but they washed over me as I silently told Paul again that screwing Daun meant nothing. I love you, Paul.

Please don't look.

"Oh," Daun said. "Never mind. I get it."

I turned back to face Daun, who was straddled over my hips, watching me. I said, "Get what?"

"You're distracted."

"Am not."

"No? You're crying."

I was? Shit. Dabbing at my leaking eyes, I said, "Sorry. I'm okay now."

"Uh huh."

"I am. Really. Have at it." I threw my arms wide, pasted a grin on my face. "Naked female lies waiting for sexual gratification."

Something unreadable flashed in his golden eyes. "You're a million miles away."

"I am not." I reached up to try and pull him down for a kiss, but he shrugged out of my grip. "Come on. I'm okay. Let me kiss you."

He laughed softly, but his eyes—unholy Hell, how could a demon have such expressive eyes? "Slow, babes. I keep forgetting you're a human, down to your cute little soul. Of course you're distracted. But I can fix that."

This was such bullshit. Just come on and let me kiss you, fill me with your magic and make with the soul-sucking. "I'm telling you, I'm okay."

"Sure you are." His smile took on a wicked edge. "You used to enjoy fantasies with me, help me fine-tune the role play. Let's see how good a role player I really am."

Uh oh. "Daun . . ."

"Shhh." He reached over, grazed his nail against my forehead.

My eyes rolled back, and I felt myself falling.

I open my eyes with a gasp. Shivering, I sit up, wrapping the comforter around me. Memories bombard me in kamikaze dives—pictures flash in my mind, snapshots of Circe attempting suicide, of Daun dancing with me, of the golden bracelet on my wrist, of Alecto's plea for Meg's rescue. Of Paul, my man, my Cabin Boy and White Knight, telling me things I didn't want to hear.

Of Lillith stealing his soul.

For a moment, I'm convinced it all happened, that Paul is dead and Meg is being tortured somewhere in the bowels of the Earth. My heart shrivels to a dead lump in my chest, and I can't breathe.

But then I hear Paul's gentle snores, like drunken bumblebees. I turn to look, and yes, there he is, fast asleep next to me. In the soft light of dawn peeking its way around the window shade, I can see Paul's face clearly—in sleep, his features are softened from their usual chiseled preciseness. His strong jaw is relaxed, his lips parted, begging for a kiss.

A huge grin breaks across my face. Of course Paul's next to me, sleeping—it's 6:30 in the morning, according to the clock on my nightstand. Where else would we be now, but in bed?

It was a dream. A stupid, freaking nightmare.

I let out a relieved breath, muffle a giggle between my fingers. That's it. I'm never eating chocolate before bed again. Not unless the chocolate is dripping down Paul's—

"Hon?" Paul's voice, thick with sleep. "What's wrong?"

Just hearing his voice sets my belly fluttering. "Nothing," I say, rolling on top of him to give him a full-body squeeze. The comforter drapes over my shoulders like a cape, and I realize that I'm naked (no real shock) and so is Paul.

That's different. Usually Paul sleeps in his tighty whities, even after a round of Extreme Copulation. He's also fully erect. Maybe he'd been dreaming about me. "I'm just glad to see you," I say, rubbing myself over him. "Feels like you're glad to see me too."

"Mmmm." He opens his eyes, blinks sleepily at me. His lips quirk in an adorable smile. "I'm always glad to see you."

"Flatterer." I reach down to stroke his cheek. The stubble is rough on my fingers, scrapes against the palm of my hand. My brain doesn't get that I'm fully awake, because it flashes an image of Paul in Lillith's arms, of his soul on her lips.

Stop that. It was a dream. It's over, it's done.

"Jess? What's wrong, hon? You look like you're about to cry."

I feel the tears in my eyes. Stupid body. Being human was so . . . leaky. "I'm okay. Just had a bad dream."

"Want to talk about it?"

"I thought I lost you. It's silly." I smile, force the tears away as I trace the outline of his jaw. "You're right here. Everything's okay now."

Something dances across his eyes, a thought too fast to follow. He nudges my black curls away from my eyes as he peers at my face, an odd smile on his lips. "You've never looked at me like this before."

"Like what?"

His hand strokes my cheek. "Like I'm your everything."

"That's like poetry. 'I'm your everything.' I like that." My smile stretches until it eats my face. "And it's true, you know. I'd do anything for you. I'd die for you."

"Oh, I know." He laughs—a soft, almost bitter sound of muted joy, completely out of place with the way he's smiling at me. "Would you give me a good-morning kiss to start my day right?"

Yum. "As my White Knight requests."

Before my lips touch his, he stops me, puts a finger over my mouth. "Babes, are you sure?"

I search his face, looking for the joke. Finally I say, "Of course I'm sure," wondering for a moment why Paul sounded like Daun.

"Well then." He removes his finger from my mouth. "Kiss me."

"If you insist." Smiling, I lean down and plant my lips on his . . .

. . . and I'm falling into his kiss, sucked into his mouth and swallowed whole. He opens wider, his tongue thrusting against mine. With that touch, electricity surges through me, crackling, transforming my blood into liquid fire.

Oh, yes—scorch me with passion.

Our lips fused together, he rolls me onto my back and straddles me, pinning my hands above my head. Then he moves down, licking my jaw, my neck, stopping to kiss the hollow of my throat before tracing lines along my collarbone with his saliva-slick lips.

My heartbeat quickens as he kisses his way down to my left breast. I feel his breath, hot and moist, on my nipple as he presses his lips around it in an *O*, teasing it for a moment just before he gives suck. Moaning, I arch my back, pushing myself farther into his mouth. I want to wrap my arms around him and thrust myself onto his shaft, but his hands still pin my arms.

"Fuck me," I tell him, my voice a throaty purr. "Please. Fuck me now."

"Soon, babes. First, a little fun. I want to make my succubus squeal."

He nips me, just the slightest graze of his teeth, and my nipple swells to the point of bursting. Then he changes sides, his mouth working on my right nipple until it's just as hard as the left. Writhing beneath him, I struggle to free my arms. I have to hold him, pull him to me and into me, but he won't let me go. I groan, rocking my head from side to side as the heat blossoming in my nipples spreads down to my crotch.

"Paul . . ."

"Shhh."

With his tongue he traces the outlines of my ribcage, then licks over my navel and the curve of my belly, pausing just above the top of my pubic hair. Releasing my hands, he spreads my legs wider, gently nudging with his fingers and sending goosebumps up my thighs. I reach down and tangle my fingers in his hair, then I steer him where I want to feel his kiss.

"Here, babes?"

His tongue darts out and licks me, lapping the wetness between my lips, plumbing me. I bite the inside of my cheek to keep from crying out as my body tenses from his attention. So close, sweetie, bless me you're so close . . .

"Ahh, yes. Right . . . here."

He finds that magic spot, and there he stays, sucking and wagging his tongue faster and faster until I think I'm going to die.

Oh . . . unholy Hell . . .

Something deep and wild tears through my flesh, and then I'm screaming as every part of me erupts, screaming from joy and unbridled passion.

Anything you want, love, I'll give you anything you want, be anyone you want, just please please please do that to me again, love me again, love me—

The orgasm peaks, then slowly ebbs. Aftershocks roll through me, bucking my hips and curling my toes. Paul kisses my sex after every jerk until my body lies still. Grinning like a lovestruck fool, I sigh, content, and my eyes slip closed.

"So," he says, his fingers stroking my thigh, "can a talented demon like me bring you to orgasm in one sitting?"

"Mmm. Bless me, yes . . ."

"Good girl. Call my name," he growls, shoving his fingers deep inside of me.

I squeal as I suddenly climax again, rocking me to the core as I shout his name to the deepest level of the Pit—*his* name, not Paul's, his true name: "Daunuan!"

Wave after wave of unadulterated pleasure breaks over me, crashing on my flesh, stinging my skin with bliss. Daunuan, my mind chimes, the name burning itself into my soul.

Daunuan.

"Now, Jezzie."

He pulls his hand out of me and mounts me, thrusts himself deep inside, deep to the breaking point, then slides out and back in, and again, pumping, faster, faster now, his hands gripping my shoulders and my heart slamming against my chest and my groin is on fire, on fire, oh bless me I'm on *fire* and he's smiling at me as he fucks me, fucks me raw and he says, "You're mine."

Yes . . .

He crushes his pelvis against mine and with a grunt, he explodes inside of me—

—and it burns it burns oh help me Sire it's burning me burning me *alive*—

My body jerks beneath him, bucks him off of me as my muscles try to break away from my bones and they're charring and my flesh is on fire and my heart is cooking in my chest and I'm screaming screaming screaming until my tongue blackens and flakes away—

Hands grasping my face, holding my head still. A voice, *his* voice, calling to me: "Jezebel! Jesse, hear me!"

And I do, even with the meat of my body broiling in the juice of my blood, I hear him.

"No pain, Jesse. There is no pain."

Like a circuit being flipped, the agony switches off. I feel the conflagration roaring through me, devouring me, but it's someone else's body.

Thank you, I try to say, but all that comes out is a groan.

"Jesse," he says. "Jezzie. It's okay. I'm here."

I'm sinking down, but his strong arms are holding me, keeping me safe. A finger slides across my brow.

"Sleep, babes. I'll wake you when it's over."

The last thing I feel is the press of his lips on mine, and then his kiss steals my breath and the world disappears.

Chapter 14

Across the Dimensions

From somewhere in the gray nothingness around me: "Jezebel."

The voice resonated within me, reverberated through my soul. I knew that voice—its rich timbre, its profound sadness. Lucifer the Light Bringer. I wanted to speak, to throw myself into His arms, to ask any of the thousands of questions bubbling inside. But I couldn't move. Wrapped in a cocoon of nothing, I floated.

He said: "Remember, the butcher may be tricked into turning piper."

Sire, I don't understand . . .

"Listen."

And I did, but instead of His voice, I heard Daun from far away, saying: "Almost got her . . ."

"Remember," Lucifer said. "Listen."

In the background, closer now, Daun's voice: "Hang on . . . yes, there she is."

My brow tingled, as if from the brush of the softest of lips, and then something nudged me, hooked me, reeled me in . . .

My eyelids fluttered, then opened. Everything around me was still gray, but I sensed colors just out of my field of vision. A damp thickness enveloped me like clothing soaked with sweat and semen; it clung to my limbs, my skin, weighing me down. It was sort of relaxing in a disconcerting way, like floating in a hot tub filled with congealed blood. Not that there was anything weird about bathing in blood . . . except there was. That sort of thing Just Wasn't Done. That sort of thing was Very Bad. Problem was, I distinctly recalled splashing through fountains of blood, gushing from severed jugulars. I remembered the *patter patter patter* of the thick liquid slapping against my skin, remembered the sweet aroma of fermenting copper.

Thus the disconcerting feeling.

I pondered, floating there in the gray skein, wondered what I was. Demon. Human. A demonic mortal with a soul, complete with the ability to love someone other than itself, intimate with the concept of sacrifice. I had existed without a soul for four thousand years. Now all that was left of me was a soul. But I still felt like *me*, whatever that meant—the me who seduced mortals with my body and took them down to Hell, the me who seduced mortals with my dance and took them for all their money. Me.

The former succubus, the one-time human.

Jezebel.

From somewhere above me, Angel's voice: "I don't understand. How could she have vanished?"

"Fuck if I know." That was Daun again, closer, just beyond the gray veil. "But I've got her now. Come on, Jezebel. Time to shed your skin."

Pressure against my lips, pushing against the cocoon around me. A ripping sound, then his tongue broke through, red as fire, and thrust into my mouth, found my own tongue, dueled with slashes of flame.

Ooh. Whatever I was, demon or human, the temperature in the hot tub just got kicked up a notch. Sweet . . .

As the kiss deepened, the gray skein molded itself to me, clung to me as if desperate for purchase in the growing storm of passion. Then the mouth attached to mine jerked up, taking me with it. I stretched, stretched, *stretched* until I reached the breaking point—then snapped like ethereal taffy, burst through the wet grayness, still locked in a fiery kiss.

There really should be a word that combines "whoa" and "yum."

The tongue drew back, the lips pulled away, and the kiss

ended with a quiet, anticlimactic *pft*. Unanchored, I swayed on my feet, eyes closed, feeling so light that angels would have traded in their wings to attach me to their backs. I sensed my limbs but didn't feel the weight of gravity pulling them down.

I felt like I could fly. Which was silly; humans can't fly.

"*Humans do fly,*" Megaera says to me before I run away from Hell. "*They use marvelous machines to do so. Airplanes and helicopters and gliders and parachutes and the like. But they do fly. They just had to learn how.*"

No, not like that. I felt like I could step onto air and drift away.

That's because you're dead, Jezzie.

Oh. Right.

More out of habit than anything else, I took a deep, cleansing breath. Released it. But that was it—no follow-up inhale, no automatic organic switches being flipped to tell my body, Lookit, you need to oxygenate me, pronto. After a month of breathing, not needing to was downright weird.

No worries there, Jezzie. You're going to Hell, and you're probably going to be destroyed. You won't have to fret about not breathing for very long.

Thank you very fucking much. Get out of here, Meg.

I told you before. I'm not Meg. I'm you.

A conscience with an identity crisis. Fine then. I'll call you Peaches.

I don't like Peaches. *Peaches is for a fat poodle with a stupid haircut. Peaches is for a stripper with more silicone than brain cells. Peaches is not for the conscience of a one-time succubus.*

Complain to the management and get the fuck out of here.

How about Elektra? I'd make a cool Elektra.

Scram.

Peaches scrammed. Look at that—a bright side to the afterlife.

I opened my eyes and saw the strangest thing: Daun, on his knees before me, a look on his face that flowed mercurially from horror to terror to complete adoration. Awed, I thought, staring dumbstruck at the demon who owned my soul. He's completely awed.

Of me.

Next to him, the cherub, too, was gazing at me like I'd just introduced her to the joys of cunnilingus. She covered her mouth with a delicate hand, as if trying to catch a gasp before it escaped.

I glanced over my shoulder, but I quickly confirmed what I'd already known—they were really staring like that at me, not at some magnificent god-type hovering behind me. Turning back to the stunned supernatural pair, I said, "What? Do I have something between my teeth?"

"You," Daun said, his voice breathy, "you're—"

"Never going to blend in Hell, looking like that," Angel said, her words cutting into Daun's like a celestial blade. "Your soul is clean. You'll stand out like—"

"Like an angel among the demons," Daun murmured, still looking at me in a very unDaunish way.

Before I could say there *were* angels among the demons, slumming as succubi, the blonde waggled her fingers. A wave of power washed over me, scrubbed me with magic. My body tingled, tensed . . . and changed. A cherry-red stain worked its way over my hands, my arms, my torso. On my head, my hair rippled, receded until I was bald as a lioness. Below, my pubic hair thickened and curled, then stretched out, spreading across my hips and down my ass and legs until it covered my lower limbs like a fungus. I felt my feet lengthen and harden, the toes mashing together and the heels pulling up. Staring at the ground, I saw hooves at the base of my legs, gleaming, solid. I didn't have to see my face to know that my eyes had transformed into those of a cat's—filled with a luminescent green and a slit for a pupil—that my lips were a leathery black, that my teeth had sharpened into fangs.

The human shape had painlessly given way to that of a scarlet satyr, minus the goat's tail and horns. My natural form. I stared at my hands, at how my claws extended, begging to rend flesh and pick out marrow from human bones.

Something swelled in my heart, but I couldn't tell if it was relief or sadness. Gah, these mortal feelings were killing me. *Did* kill me. Stupid feelings.

Bless me, if I was really dead, why was I still caught up in the human touchy-feely bullshit of emotion? Souls didn't have feelings—sure, they reacted to pain and pleasure, but they didn't waste time contemplating how things made them react. As far as I knew, they just . . . were. So why was I experiencing something akin to regret?

Whether demonic or mortal, philosophy still wasn't one of my strong points.

On my left wrist, the golden Rope of Hecate winked at me. The vivid red of my skin made the gold shine all the more brightly. That the jewelry was on my spirit form boded very well. Now all I had to do was get Angel to do one more teensy favor . . .

"There," the blonde said, sounding incredibly pleased. "Don't you look like a beautiful creature of the Pit?"

I blew her a kiss. "Isn't flattery a sin?"

She blushed.

"At least I'm rubbing off on you." I ran my hands up my torso, over my bare breasts, up over my head. "I'd forgotten what it feels like to be a demon."

"You wear it well," Angel said.

Next to her, Daun shuddered like a big, malefic hound shaking off water. "Spare me. No matter what plane of reality, women are all the same. You're all about the clothing. At least you didn't ask if this shape makes you look fat."

My eyes widened. "I look *fat?*"

"You look juicy," Angel said.

Gah! "Juicy in a squeezable way, or in like a bless me, that girl'd better do a juice fast for a few millennia way?"

Daun's mouth quirked into a smile. "Juicy in the I'd do you way."

I beamed. Daun always knew just what to say.

"Come on, babes. Let's get the party started."

Taking a last look at the trappings of my former life, a lump formed in my throat. On the ground, my naked body lay discarded. Empty. The gold bracelet on my corpse's wrist sparkled, giving the illusion of life. Bless me, my human body looked so delicate, like a porcelain sex doll. Humans die so easily—a snapped neck, a shattered spine, disease. A broken heart. Was that why their bodies could experience so much pleasure—to offset how fragile they really are, how they could be extinguished in a blink?

Angel had one hand pressed against my body's forehead; her other hand was on Paul's chest. I approached him, knelt by his side. When I tried to brush his hair away from his eyes, my fingers passed through his brow. Crap. The only entity I could touch now was Daun, because he was bound to my soul. To everything and everyone else, I was a whisper, a hint. Insignificant.

Mental note: Being a ghost sucked angel feathers.

I leaned down and kissed Paul, pretending I could feel his lips against mine. I'm saving you, love. I promise.

Then I rose and wrapped my arms around the angel, miming a hug. As she stammered out a good wish and (ick) a blessing, I whispered in her ear (literally *in*—I overshot and wound up with my mouth halfway inside her face), "When we're gone, move the bracelet from my wrist to his."

She opened her mouth, perhaps to protest, perhaps to agree, but I silenced her with a vaporous kiss. When I pulled back, I thought I tasted peppermint and gold on my lips.

"Farewell," she said, with all the enthusiasm of a doctor pronouncing a patient dead on the table.

Look at that, she was trying to cheer me up. I smiled brightly at her. "See you soon, Angel."

With one final look—at Paul, at my body, at the physical reminders of my life—I turned to Daun. "Okay, sweetie. Let's go to Hell."

"Babes," he said, caressing my cheek, "that's music to my ears."

Shifting between planes is sort of like diving into a swimming pool filled with K-Y Jelly—it doesn't hurt, but there's a moment of utter oozishness when your form exists in both dimensions. You're covered in the slippery goo of conflicting realities, and you reek of sex. (Actually, that last part is probably unique to Seducers. But whatever.)

"Here we go, babes." Daun led me by the hand, helped me step through to Hell, and the heat slapped me in the face. On a cold day, the Abyss hovered around 3,000 degrees. The sensitive hairs in my nostrils curled and flaked away; the fine hairs on my face, arms and belly shriveled. Sweat beaded on my brow and around my breasts, only to immediately evaporate. More than the feeling of the heat was its undeniable stink: an eye-watering blend of burning sewage and spoiling meat, layered on top of dirt and rot.

I grinned. Damn, I'd missed this place.

We'd emerged in a small room, dimly lit in shades of red— the light emanating through the earthen walls, straight from the Lake of Fire that surrounded Hell like the Belt Parkway surrounded Brooklyn. Around the smell of searing heat was the cloying, graveyard scent of fresh soil—and the tang of sex. We were in the mountain complex of Pandemonium, home to all the nefarious. More specifically, as my nose told me, we were in the Red Light District, which housed all creatures of Lust.

Except for a squalid sleeping mat on the loamy floor, the chamber was completely barren. Unless you were one of Hell's elite, you were privy only to the common rooms, which all lesser-ranked demons shared. No individuality allowed—personalization was frowned upon, in the if-you-disobey-you-get-your-liver-plucked-out sense.

"Home sweet home," Daun said, pulling me close. "Let's you and me celebrate."

He crushed my mouth to his, bruised my lips with a violent kiss. Down in the Abyss, my soul was as solid as his rod— which, based on how his rod was currently doing pushups on my belly, was solid indeed. I opened my mouth and rode his tongue, thrilling in how a simple kiss could make my entire body hum.

Stop, my brain shouted, flashing a desperate message to my body. *We're on a rescue mission! Nookie later!*

Then Daun's fingers slid down my back and rubbed against the rim of my ass, and my brain shorted out.

Just as I started melting against his body, something hooked into the scruff of my neck and yanked. I fell backward, then I was slammed face-first into the wall. Yeowch. Talons dug into the soft flesh on the back of my neck, shooting darts of pain up the base of my head.

Someone pressed against my back, pinned me to the hard-packed dirt of the wall. A purr of delight in my ear, and then a woman's lush voice:

"I knew you'd come," Lillith said.

Chapter 15

Pandemonium

Just as it registered that I was in very deep shit, Lillith yanked my head back and smashed it against the wall again. A burst of white exploded behind my eyes, and for a moment everything went a lovely, numbing gray. Then my forehead shrieked that getting my face mashed against solid rock hurts like a bastard, and the numbness decided to agree—it dissipated, replaced with spikes of agony driven into my head by an invisible mallet. Squashed against the wall, my face rubbed against the soil; dirt coated my tongue, slid down my throat, and my nostrils clogged with the stench of earth and decay. I squirmed, but Lillith's body pressed hard against my back, gluing me in place.

This was really, really bad.

No, forget *bad*. This *sucked*.

Behind me, Daun's voice rang out—cold, regal, almost like one of the Arrogant: "You have no business here, Lillith. Jezebel is mine."

Testosterone at its finest. You tell her, sweetie.

"Yes," Lillith chuckled, a sound like a spastic vibrator. "I see your little bond, incubus. Very clever. But my claim supersedes yours. Your bond means nothing to me."

Uh oh.

Daun snorted. "A Nightmare overruling the claim of a Seducer? I don't think so."

"I may be a *Nightmare*," she said, turning the word into a disease, "but I'm still the consort of King Asmodai. You watch your tone with me, incubus, or I'll have to teach you some manners."

She slowly pulled her talons out of my flesh, first one, then another, then the third and finally the last, and I bit down on my lip as my neck screeched to high Heaven, singing its pain like gospel. Fuuuuuuck, that hurt. Through the agony, I felt a rubbing pressure on my right shoulder. It took me a moment to understand what it was.

The bitch was cleaning her claws on me, wiping residues of me on my own body.

I snarled, rearing back to buck her off. Lillith pushed me down, then clouted my head against the wall again.

Wow, look at all the pretty stars.

"Settle down, Jezebel," she said, "or I'll get you a collar for your neck before I break it."

This is me, settling down. Maybe I'd just watch the stars and comets dancing along my field of vision . . .

Daun said, "Let her go, Lillith. Or should I summon Pan to moderate?"

If my neck and face hadn't felt like they'd just met the business end of a meat grinder, I would have cheered. No one willingly agrees to a god's intervention, not even a god aligned with one's own Sin. Gods have very, very warped senses of humor, especially by demonic standards. I'd met Pan a handful of times over the years. He's even more twisted than Daun.

"Oh yes, incubus," Lillith said. I could hear her grin stretching her mouth wide enough to deep-throat an elephant's cock. "Scurry along and get your satyr god. I'm sure he'll give Jezebel to me on a silver platter. That is, after he's done shoving his dick into every orifice on her body and severing her head from her neck so he can come in her skull."

Erk. She was insane and completely graphic. I was doomed.

"That's a chance I'm willing to take," Daun said, voice smooth as satin bedsheets. "Are you?"

A heated pause, and then: "Actually, you can give the satyr god a message from me."

I felt her shift, then something moved through her—I felt it as she pushed against me, tight as a virgin—a bubble, just beneath the surface, growing obscenely pregnant as it rose up and up, and with a cosmic birth cry, it erupted out. Over the stink of brimstone shot a flash of odor, heat lightning trapped in a forest. Then a *BOOM* that left my ears ringing.

And Daun was gone.

I wasn't sure how I knew this. I wasn't really a demon, so my psychic Seduction sense hadn't kicked back on, and I didn't actually see what had happened to Daun, what with Lillith doing the perp push to me against the wall. But something in the corner of my mind sort of dimmed, and I understood intuitively that Daun wasn't in the room any longer. He was . . . gone.

Icy tendrils wrapped around my heart, squeezed, freezing my blood. Daun was gone! The psycho bitch had blown him away, and it had nothing to do with fellatio. Shit!

Just as I was about to fling myself into full-fledged panic, I realized that however dim, Daun's presence still hovered in my mind, a hint of a kiss, a feeling as slippery as body lotion. At least he still existed. He may have been blasted into malefic confetti, but he hadn't been annihilated. Yay for our team.

"There now. Just us girls," Lillith said.

Oh, goodie.

"**I**'ve been waiting for this moment," Lillith whispered in my ear. Then she grabbed my shoulders, hefted me up, and threw me across the room. For about two seconds, I soared gracefully through the air as if I were flying. Then I crash-landed in an unceremonious heap on the ground, like demonic bird droppings.

Ow. Ow, ow, ow.

I slowly pulled myself up to my hands and knees, spitting the dirt from my mouth. My head still ringing from my beating and Daun's abrupt departure, I looked up and gazed upon the creature who had been my Queen for thousands of years.

For a diminutive person, she positively loomed. Her bare

flesh gleamed, a metallic sheen of bronze that captured all races—amalgamous, shifting, now the golden tones from Asia, now the deep mocha of Africa, now shifting again. Bordering her broad face, plaits of thick, wiry black hair dangled, the bones woven into its strands flashing like gemstones. Long lashes framed her large eyes, black as leaf rot. Her pug nose displayed her nostrils in full; her bee-stung lips would have driven Angelina Jolie insane with jealousy. The apples of her cheeks flushed like the fruit from the Tree of Knowledge. Her body was all curves and swells—large breasts that begged to be sucked, a round stomach and full hips that made her appear soft, powerful thighs that could crush a lover mounting her. Her thick swatch of pubic hair both hid and highlighted her mound, advertised her sex. Delicate hands; tiny feet. A fertility goddess carved of flesh; sexual aggression and dominance hidden in seductive packaging.

Lillith: the First Woman, original Bridezilla, and utter psycho bitch from Hell.

"You owe me, Jezebel," she said, her small fists glowing with power. "For what you did to me Above, you owe me."

Eek. Do the lying stunned thing later—she's about to blow.

I scrambled to my feet just as Lillith pointed at me. Whoops. I felt the magic blasting its way toward me before I actually saw it, and I summoned up reserves of energy I didn't know I had and leapt to the right. The bolt slammed into the wall with a mighty *THOOM*, sending dirt showers into the chamber.

She wound up for another malefic pitch. "For the way you stole my victory, you owe me."

"Hey, you were the one trying to kill me," I said, scanning the room for anything that could be used as a weapon. Shit. Whoever decided that the minor-level nefarious didn't merit their own interior decorators obviously had never been attacked by rampaging demon queens.

"There was a contract on your head, Jezebel," she said, taking aim. "There was nothing about that head having to be attached."

She let loose and I dove, barely avoiding getting singed. Mental note: Acquire sidekick to act as living shield.

Lillith slowly approached me, energy wafting from her hands, signaling her power. "Do you know how long it took me to heal, after you had that mortal shoot my host body?"

"Okay, one, I had nothing to do with that. And two, I'd say about thirty days."

"Bitch!" She blasted, and I rebounded off the wall in my effort to avoid getting zapped. "If I hadn't been healed, I'd still be recuperating, even now!"

"Good to have friends to help you," I said, wondering who she'd fucked to get to heal her wounds. Demons don't do healing; it's not in their makeup. So who could have, would have, helped her? A god with a grudge?

"Oh yes, Jezebel," she purred. "I have friends. Powerful friends. Friends who want you humiliated and tortured, even more than I do."

Who else despised me as much as she did?

Sneering, she said, "Do you have any idea how much it hurt? That fucking iron tore through me, shredded me. It ripped me apart!"

"I don't think it did too much for the human host either," I said, eying the door. Good news was that it was wide open. Bad news: Lillith was in the way.

"Stay still!" She made with the aiming again.

Crap, I didn't know how much ponging I could do before she wound up hitting home. When all else fails, stall. "What's your beef with me, anyway? You've hated me since the beginning."

Pointing at me, she said, "You weren't at the Beginning."

"You know," I said, "technically, neither were you . . ."

She snarled, and I threw myself to the right just before a burst of magic slammed into the wall exactly where I'd been crouching.

"Little slag! How is it that something as low as you could have His eye?"

Whoa. Time out from the showdown at the demonic OK Corral. Lillith was *jealous* of me? I racked my brain, but I had no idea who she could have been talking about. "Who? King Asmodai?"

She snorted with laughter. "Him? He'd fuck anything with legs. No. I mean the One who kissed you so sweetly before He left us."

It took me a moment, but then I got it. "King Lucifer?"

"Give the girl a kewpie doll." Her eyes shone—black, birdlike, hungry. "I saw you, the day of the Announcement. I saw Him speak to you, as if you were something worthy of His attention. I saw Him kiss you."

"It wasn't what it looked like . . ."

She took another pot shot that nearly scalped me. Mental note: That line never, ever works.

"For thousands of years, I've strutted before Him," she said as I pulled myself off the floor, "awaiting His pleasure. I've deposited my best catches at His feet. I dedicated my life to doing His work. But He never acknowledged my advances."

Hell hath no fury like a demon scorned. "Maybe you're not His type."

"I am every woman ever created!" Her hands alight with blue flame, she raged as her fists smoked like mini-bonfires. If I hadn't been jockeying for my continued existence, I would have fetched some marshmallows. She bellowed, "I am *everyone's* type!"

I pictured me and her, getting biblical. Blech. I'm happy to do the sapphic thing, but I'd sooner chew off my left arm than screw my former Queen.

"But *you*," she hissed, her eyes glinting with malice, "you with your common looks and your questionable prowess, you've always gotten praise from Him."

"Would it help if I told you I have no idea what you're talking about?"

She sniffed, looking down her nose at me. "Of course *you* wouldn't be able to glean His presence. Only the elite intuitively recognize one another, no matter what form they wear. You? You were just a fifth-level succubus. A bottom feeder. You wouldn't recognize majesty if it bent you backward and raped you."

As she soliloquized, I inched toward the door, all the while keeping eye contact. Don't mind me, I'm not interrupting your diatribe . . .

"He'd come to me, and every time I'd think that yes, now is the moment when I'll feel His lips upon mine, He would ask about you. About your client hit rate. About your status. About *you*," she said, spitting the word. "And now I understand why. You'd gotten to Him somehow, before me. You were one of His favored."

I blinked, too stunned to remember to be fearing for my life. Death. Whatever. "You think that King Lucifer and I . . . bless me, you think we were fucking?"

With a snarl that would terrify a rabid wolf, she wound up for another blow. I lunged to the right, aiming for the door—

Over the stink of ozone: rotten eggs. Then a solid *THUMP*, followed by a grunt.

I risked a glance over my shoulder. And saw Daun, straddling Lillith, an iron sword raised over his head. "Pan sends his regards, bitch."

Shrieking to rock the Firmament, Lillith attacked. All the hair on my body shot up as she threw her magic at Daun, sending him flying off of her and slamming into the wall. The sword clattered to the ground. I scrambled for it, but Lillith leveled another blast at me, one that sparked off my hooves as I leapt out of the way. Eep.

"Maybe you stole Him away from me," she said, her fists glowing with power, "but I already have the ear of our new lord and master."

"Good for you." Behind her, I saw Daun slowly pick himself up. He shook his head as if to clear it, and while the snarl on his face spoke of his rage, his eyes were unfocused. Whatever magic she'd hit him with, he was having trouble shaking it off. Crap.

Now my back was to the open door, but I couldn't abandon Daun. Stupid soul bond. Couldn't the loyalty thing have kicked in at a time when my survival wasn't at risk? To keep Lillith's attention away from Daun, I said, "Wonder what King Asmodai would say about your latest project?"

"Him? If it meant solidifying his own rule as King of Lust, he'd chain me down and send the King of Hell a written invitation to hump me."

Huh. Okay, she was probably spot on. While creatures of the Pit were all about possessing things (and people) they wanted, they'd also sell out anyone to increase their own power base.

"Our new dread ruler is all too happy to hear my suggestions," Lillith said, running her hands up her thighs, "to feel my hands upon His body as I work away the tension of ruling Hell."

"Sounds like you're His new fuckbunny," I said. "Congratulations."

Her lips pulled into a tight smile. "Not yet. But soon He'll give into temptation. Especially when I deliver to Him the broken form of the one who embarrassed Him in front of all the denizens of the Abyss."

Hooboy.

Moving silently, Daun reached for the sword. Go, demon ninja stealth. Grab the weapon and make like a guillotine.

Without breaking eye contact from me, Lillith said, "If you try it, incubus, it'll be the last thing you ever do."

He froze. Crap. Demon ninja bested by psycho bitch. Story at eleven.

Okay, Jesse. Think. You can't beat her with magic. So how can you beat her?

"You forget yourself, Lillith," Daun said, his voice smug, dripping with venom. "You can't hurt her. Her soul's clean."

I saw her smile stretch into a feral grin before she pivoted to face him. "I can't hurt the mortal Jesse Harris. But I have no qualms about destroying a human pretending to be a demon."

This was my chance, while her attention was split between me and Daun. I thought of how Lillith had undermined me for thousands of years, of how she had kept me at fifth level, all due to her petty jealousy. Biting my lip, I took a step forward. Then another.

I thought of how she took from me the one man I'd ever truly loved. My hands clenched into fists, I took a third step.

"A human pretending to be a demon?" Daun chuckled. "Takes one to know one, I suppose."

Another step as Lillith screamed, "I am no pretender! There's only one mortal who descended to demonhood, and that's me! I'll rip her spine out of her throat and feast on her liver!"

Another step. I cocked my arm way, way back.

"I'll skin her and use her hide as a pillow! I'll—"

That's when I tapped her on the shoulder. Interrupted mid-rant, she turned to face me, and I slammed my fist into her jaw.

She stumbled to one knee, and I was on her like a mongoose on a cobra. I pounced onto her back, wrapping my legs around her waist and tangling the fingers of my left hand into her hair. Howling loud enough to do a werewolf proud, I rammed my fist into Lillith's nose.

A crunch never sounded so sweet.

With a roar, Lillith slammed her back—and me—into a wall. No dice, bitch; you're not uprooting me from my perch. I pounded her upside the head, thwocking her good and hard, not giving her a chance to use her magic.

Snarling, she parried my blows, knocking my hands away from her eyes and ears. "Get the fuck off me!"

I dug in like a tick on a deer. "Think you can steal my man?" As I spoke, I struck my fists against her head and face, punctuating my words with jackhammer blows. "Think again" (thud) "you" (thud) "skanky" (thud-thud) "ho!" (thump!)

Lillith slammed me into the wall again. I grunted, feeling the effect of the blow vibrate up my back, my legs loosening around her waist. She reached up and grabbed my shoulders, then pivoted down like a hinge, throwing me off.

I crashed against the back wall, my rage filling me, fueling me so that I barely felt the impact. Springing to my hooves, I launched myself at her, my arm swinging forward. My fist connected with her nose again, mashing the cartilage and bone. She staggered back, her hands clasped to her face, screaming her pain.

"This is for fucking my man and taking his soul." My mouth pulling into a winning smile, I landed an uppercut clean on her jaw.

Lillith sprawled backward, careened into the wall and then slid bonelessly to the ground.

"Jezzie."

I darted my gaze to Daun, standing just behind me. Covered in dirt and soot, only hints of his blue flesh peeked out. Beneath the grime, sweat caressed his muscles, gleaming like body oil, and I found myself wanting to wipe him down from head to hoof. Bless me, only Daun could turn filth into eye candy.

His fangs flashing in a huge grin, he offered me the iron sword. "You want the honor of decapitating the bitch?"

I beamed. "You always know just what to say."

"Comes with a millennium of practice." As I took the hilt, our fingers touched, sending a shock of desire up my arm. Yum. He winked at me, then rubbed his pointer finger against his thumb. I felt that touch between my legs, against my clit, stroking me, swelling me bigger than his ego.

"Do the bitch," he said, his voice a low purr that resonated in my belly. "Then I'll do you."

Well, when he put it that way . . .

Sword in my hands, I marched up to my former Queen. Nudging the blade beneath her chin, I mused aloud, "Wonder what would happen if I sliced off your head with this spiffy iron sword? Think you'll sprout a new one?"

Groaning, Lillith said one word that was pure music to my ears: "Mercy."

Gloat later. For now, information. "Where's Paul?"

I sensed Daun's hiss rather than heard it—in my mind, the throbbing presence that I knew was the incubus stiffened, then folded in on itself like a deflating balloon.

No, don't think about Daun now. Watch Lillith.

She didn't answer me, but her eyes gleamed, and I could feel her already calculating, judging, plotting. Uh uh. Not this time. Smiling, I pressed the blade up, and the edge sliced into her neck. She let out a strangled cry, blood seeping out of the fresh cut and around the sword's edge, staining her skin.

Maybe I had a soul, but I was still a demon at heart. Slicing her felt damn good.

"I don't have to do it clean," I said, shoving the blade further into her neck. "I can saw your head off, one stroke at a time. Bet that would hurt worse than any bullet. A lot worse. Wonder how long you can scream before your voice gives out."

She said nothing, but her eyes were wide as teacups, and her lower lip quivered, shattering her illusion of stoicism. If I were really a demon instead of a soul wearing a demon's shell, I would have smelled her fear—it would have been tangy and rancid, like spoiled grapefruit.

Grinning as I imagined that smell in my nostrils, I said, "Where is Paul?"

"The Caverns." Her voice was raspy, harsh, sandpaper over vocal chords. "He's in the Endless Caverns."

Oh . . . crap.

My face must have given away how my heart had sunk to my knees, because Lillith said, "If you miss him so much, why don't you go find him? Otherwise he'll be wandering around in there forever. Lost," she added like an afterthought.

Yes, Paul would be lost, stranded in the temptations of the Caverns, a slave to his own desires. Trapped for all time. My vision blurred, doubled, and I blinked away my tears. In my hands, the sword trembled.

"Jezzie," Daun said from behind me, "now would be a good time to shut her up permanently."

I stared down at Lillith, the weapon in my hands growing heavier with every passing second. Do it, my mind screamed at me. You've wanted this for ages. She hurt you, she hunted you. She killed Paul and stole his soul. Lop off her head and wash your face in her blood as it spurts from her neck.

Around the hilt, my knuckles whitened as I squeezed my hands, tested the blade's weight.

And what happens then? In my mind, Peaches clucked her tongue. *She's still King Asmodai's pet. You really want him to come after you, drag you all the way to the Court in Abaddon, throw you at the King of Hell's feet?*

You really want Him to judge you again?

Peaches gave way to His voice, mocking, derisive: *You are too soft.*

No. Never that. Never again.

I removed the sword from beneath her jaw but kept it pointed at her breast, using both my hands to hold the blade steady. Fucking thing weighed a ton. "You know, I finally figured something out."

Lillith glared at me, her eyes sparking like obsidian chips, her nostrils flaring.

"You don't hate me because you think I was one of King Lucifer's favored. You don't even hate me because I embarrassed your new liege lord." Smiling coldly, I wiped the sword on her bare shoulder, smearing her blood on her bronze skin and relishing the look of hatred on her proud face. "You hate the fact that I defied Him, and you couldn't."

"You have no idea what you're talking about," she growled.

"The best you can ever hope for is to be His lapdog. He may pat you on the head, He may kick you in the corner. He may even fuck you. But you'll never be anything more than that." I sniffed, showing her just what I thought of her place in the new regime. "Just a lapdog, yapping at His feet."

"Big words for a mortal. A dead mortal." She lifted her chin, as if daring me to strike. "I think you don't have it in you to kill me. I think your soul has softened you even more than He said at the Announcement."

My lip curled in a sneer. Look at her, kneeling on the dirt floor. This is all she ever will be: a blowjob waiting to happen, a cocktease of power. Kill her.

But she looks so pathetic, with the grime on her knees and a pout on those sullen, swollen lips. Sweat beaded on my brow, began to drip down my temples.

Kill her!

In my hands, the sword wavered.

"Come on, Jezebel," Lillith purred. "I'm helpless before

you. Do you need me to make it easier? Here." She tilted her head to the side. "Go ahead. What are you waiting for?"

Gritting my teeth, I stared at her exposed neck. Do it.

Don't do it, Peaches said. *Do you really want to damn yourself for her? Is she really worth your soul?*

Lillith grinned. "I knew it." She raised her arms—

—and in my mind, I felt Daun reach out—

My arms drew back with a jerk, and I grunted as my hands swung forward, the sword blazing a path to Lillith's neck. I couldn't stop the movement, even if I really wanted to; Daun was in my mind, riding me, pushing my body to obey his silent command.

Lillith vanished in a puff of sulfur. A second later, the blade whistled past the space where her neck had been.

"Jezzie," Daun said after the smoke dissipated, "what the fuck just happened? Why didn't you slice her open, spill her insides all over the ground?"

"I couldn't." I dropped the sword, and it fell to the floor with an impotent clang. Groaning from embarrassment, I covered my face. "I just couldn't kill her."

"Why in Hell not?"

"I pitied her," I said, my voice muffled by my hands.

"What?"

Through my fingers I shouted, "I *pitied* her. Bless me, I'm such a lousy former malefic entity!"

A pause, and then I felt his hands press down on my shoulders. "Babes," Daun sighed, "this was a really, really bad time to go New Testament on me."

PART THREE

PAUL AND THE KING
OF HELL

Chapter 16

Hell

"**W**ell," Daun said, "that's that."

I lowered my hands to stare into his eyes, which were sparkling with mischief and wicked intent. There'd been a time when I relished that look. But now all it did was cause a knot to form in my stomach. "What's what?"

"If the bitch was actually telling the truth and your meat pie's in the Caverns, that's all she wrote. You can't go in there. And he can't get out." He shrugged, a lazy movement of his shoulders that belied the intense look in his eyes. "No rescue mission."

"Bullshit on that." I jabbed a finger at his chest, where it slid on sweat and dirt. "I'm getting him out."

"Oh really?" Daun arched an eyebrow. "How're you planning on doing that?"

"I'm going to march in there and get him." I waggled my wrist under his nose, showing the golden bracelet. "A Wiccan practically forced this little trinket on me. It's called the Rope of . . ." I paused, not wanting to call the Hecate's attention onto me. I didn't get to be more than four thousand years old by being completely stupid. "Of the patron of witchcraft. I figure She did it for a reason."

He frowned. "Witches suck."

"Yeah," I said, thinking of Caitlin and her secrets, Caitlin and her taunting hints of knowledge. *The Hecate knows much.*

"And some of them have no fashion sense. But they do know their shit when it comes to magic and their patron goddess. She must have wanted me to have it."

"What, you think the witch knew you'd want to pull an Orpheus?"

"Nothing about witches surprises me anymore."

"Fair enough."

"So I'll go into the Caverns, find Paul, give him the bracelet, and then he'll return Above." Saying it like that made it seem so simple. So what that I was overlooking the fact that I could wander about the Caverns for the better part of a millennium and never retrace my steps, let alone find Paul? Minor details.

They say the devil's in the details.

Shut up, Peaches.

"As much as I don't mind you being trapped in a different plane than your flesh puppet," Daun said, "there's a flaw in your plan."

Only one? Maybe my plan made more sense than I thought. "How's that?"

"You haven't said how you're getting out of the Caverns once you go in."

Oops. "Yeah, well, I'm working on that part."

"You take your time," he said. "You're not going to the Caverns any time soon."

"Pardon me?"

Daun grinned, licking his lips slowly, and my sex tingled in response. Stop that, body. "You and me, babes, we have a lot of catching up to do. We've got the entire District to paint red. And that's just the start."

He took my hand, rubbed his thumb over my palm. Goose-bumps tripped up my arm.

Yo, body, I said stop that.

Drawing circles over my wrist, just above where the Rope of Hecate lay, Daun chuckled. "There's going to be a whole lot of loving going on. We're going to desecrate every level of Hell, right up to the Court itself."

"Loving later," I said, trying to pull my hand out of his

grasp and failing miserably. Fine, he could hold my hand and write invisible tantric messages on my skin. No problem. "First rescuing. Specifically, first rescuing Paul, then Meg."

"Right." His heated gaze roamed over my body, leaving scorch marks in its wake. "As if I'm going to let you do that."

My throat constricted; if I were still breathing, I would have choked. "Excuse me?"

"You're mine, Jezzie." With his other hand, he traced the curves of my face, then let his touch drift down my neck and chest, stopping to caress my breast. I stifled a moan, pretended not to notice my nipple springing to attention. Fondling me, Daun said, "If you think I'm going to let you go, you're even crazier than the angel thought."

"You promised," I said through clenched teeth, absolutely not paying attention to how my groin was starting to pulse with need. "You swore on your name to let me go."

He slid his fingers over my chest, ran around my other boob in concentric circles until he was teasing my nipple. I bit my lip to keep my reaction in check. With a grin that would have scarred small children, Daun said, "You're right. But I never said I'd let you go right away."

Oh crap.

"Now," he said, his voice an eager hum, "let's get busy."

"Daun—"

But he was already at my breast, sucking my nipple, working my tit until all I could do was gasp. His hands flowed over me like water, raining pleasure after pleasure on my flesh as they washed over my skin. When his fingers drummed between my legs, I somehow regained enough sense to tangle him up in my arms and push him back. "Daun, stop."

Something dark flashed in his eyes. "You don't get to tell me to stop."

Oh. Oh boy, that's not good. "Sweetie—"

"Shut up, Jezzie."

My mouth clicked closed. No matter how I tried, I couldn't pry open my lips. I felt Daun in my mind, sliding around my thoughts, commanding my body to betray me. I slapped at that presence, tried to push it away, but the soul bond was too strong to fight and impossible to ignore; it spoke a language that my body had to obey.

Fighting back panic, I took a step away from him, imploring Daun with my eyes and hands to let me go.

He said, "Stop."

My hooves rooted to the ground, refused to move.

"Stand still, Jezzie."

My hands dropped to my sides. I stood like a life-sized doll for she-devils, my heart pounding so hard I thought it would break through my ribcage.

He lifted my chin in his hand, stared deep into my eyes; all I saw in his was my own wide-eyed reflection. "I could force myself on you. I could command you to be my slave, to beg for me to touch you. I could tell you to gouge out your eyeballs and eat them. And you'd have to do everything I say. You know this, don't you?"

I did. Oh bless me, I did.

A whimsical smile played on his lips. "I could command you to forget about your meat pie."

No. Please no.

I closed my eyes, wondering if the bond was strictly physical, or if it meant that Daun could erase my mind, make me think whatever he told me to think. I didn't want to find out the hard way.

Paul, I swear, no matter what, I'm coming for you.

He can't make me forget you.

"But what I said Above still stands." Daun's hand left my chin, trailed down my jaw and neck, traced a line over my shoulder. "I'm not into power games."

Could have fooled me, you evil fuck.

Now he was behind me, both his hands on my shoulders, pressing, rubbing, working their own sort of magic: Even though I was paralyzed by his command and by my own growing fear, my body was reacting to his touch. Warmth spread over my shoulders and neck, stretched down my back and across my breasts, licked its way down my belly and hips.

"You like this," he said—either a comment or a command, it didn't matter. Because I liked it.

Oh, sweet Sin, I *liked* it.

His hands moved deftly over me, and my hips begged to dance against his, to buck with every rolling press of his fingers. But no—he'd told me to stand still, so I couldn't move, not even to give in to the feeling building inside of me, churning through me as my groin tightened and bless me, now his hands were on my breasts, squeezing me, plucking me, tracing every curve, every oh he's reaching down, down over my belly, my mound, my oh my oh he's in me and *in me* and let me move let me move let me . . .

Air, hot and moist, tickling my earlobe as he whispered: "Yes, you like this, you want this more than anything. I can tell. I bet I can taste it."

His fingers slid out of me, and my body wailed for him to dive back in, the water was fine. If he sensed my ache, he ignored it. That rat bastard. I stood, waiting on his pleasure, almost vibrating from how he'd wound me up. He made an *ummmm* sound, then ran his wet fingers over my mouth. As he rubbed my lips, I caught the scent of my own juices, tart and pungent. My body screamed *Sex, now!* and if I hadn't been forced into being a living (well, dead) statue, I would have thrown myself on him and ridden him like a bronco.

I knew that I had to leave, to rescue Paul, to help Meg, but all I could think about was how I liked Daun's touch. How I wanted him, more than anything.

"You do still taste like a succubus, you know," Daun said, kissing my neck.

Oh, sweetie, let me fuck you, and I'll show you that I can still move like a succubus . . .

"I've missed you, Jezzie. I missed all the sweaty sex. There's no one in Hell like you. When she told me to tempt you back to Hell, how could I say no?" His mouth on mine, surprisingly gentle. Then he said, "Open your eyes, babes."

I did. His amber gaze locked on mine, hidden thoughts flashing behind his pupils. I wanted him now, right now. Just say the word, sweetie, and I'll pour myself over you, I'll swallow you down, I'll make you explode inside of me . . .

"If I gave you the choice, right now," he said, "would you stay with me? Answer me true."

My mouth opened, and I said, "No."

Argh! No! Wrong answer! Say you want to be with him always, you want to fuck him until the end of Creation!

But Daun had commanded me to answer true, so I had. Because as much as I wanted him in me, my heart (stupid dumb asinine human heart) had been stolen by another.

Daun's eyes narrowed. "Why not?"

The frost in his voice dampened the desire blazing through me, and with a gasp I felt my body's *On* switch get flipped to *Off*. I didn't know if Daun purposefully rescinded his command to want him, or if it was an accidental side effect of his anger. I didn't care; for the moment, I could think, even if I still couldn't move. "I have to bring Paul back. I can't leave him trapped in the Caverns."

He tilted his head, considering me. "Maybe I'd let you visit him in a couple centuries. He's not going anywhere."

"He's not supposed to be here at all," I countered. "Even the angel said that. His soul's clean."

"So's yours. Yet here you are."

"I'm here for him. I'm going to free him. I have to."

Rage stormed in his eyes, rippled over his face as he sneered. "Why? Because you *love* him?"

"Yes."

"What's love, anyway? It's just a fleeting, fickle thing. And it fucks you more than any dick out there ever could."

"Daun." I wanted to plead with my hands, but he hadn't given me permission to move other than to speak, so all I could do was beg with my voice. "I really love him. I didn't ask to. It just happened. And I can't just tuck it into a jar and put it on a shelf. Please try to understand. He's my everything."

My words hung in the air between us. He looked at me, his gaze heavy on my body, judgment waiting in his eyes. "Give me one reason why I shouldn't command you to forget love," he said, "to forget your man. One reason why I shouldn't command you to stay with me."

Staring at the incubus who had been my friend for thousands of years, who had helped me more than once and saved me from human horrors, I held my head high and answered him truthfully. "Because the only way for you to have me like that is for you to force me to stay, to use the power of the soul bond to make me forget him. And you said yourself, you're not into power games."

A pause that stretched into forever as he considered my reply, and then: "You're right, babes. I did say that." An ugly smile stretched across his face. "But demons lie."

Shit.

"I do so love that look you get when you think the world is ending. It's positively addictive." His eyes gleamed, glowed, and a wicked grin ate his face. My legs tried to move, to get me away, but all I could do was stand and watch as he spread his arms wide. "I don't need to play those games, Jezzie. Because I have power. Far more than you know."

A humming, deep, like the slow waking of hornets in winter. Then a ripping sound, followed by the crack of bones. Something rose behind Daun, unfolding, growing up and out, until he was surrounded in shadow. It split in two, stretched out behind him, huge, batlike, as blue as his flesh.

Wings.

I stared at those blue appendages, a tiny voice in my mind gibbering that this was impossible—Daun wasn't strong enough to have wings. Gods wore them like otherworldly accessories; angels sported them as a given. But for demons to have wings, they had to amass an incredible amount of power. Only the elite and the greatest rank of lesser demons could fly. Daun was—had been—a second-level Seducer. What was he now?

Pit swallow me, how strong was he?

He said, "It's the new me."

"You wear it well," I replied, my voice a smothered scream. "Looks like I missed a lot in the month I was gone."

"You have no idea." He clamped his hands onto my shoulders, dug in tight. "But you will. Come on, babes. Time for the grand tour."

A slap of brimstone, and then the Underworld shifted.

One thing about materializing in midair: it really fucks with your equilibrium.

My hooves dangled in the air, the hot winds over the Lake of Fire brushing against my most sensitive spots and searing my nostrils. For a split second, I felt Daun behind me, his hands hooked into my armpits and his cock pressed against my lower back. I had time to very distinctly think: Oh shit.

And then we fell.

Aaaaaaaaaah!

Before I could muster a proper gut-busting scream, Daun stopped our plummet, beating his wings against the stagnant air with powerful strokes, almost as if he were swimming. We hovered over the fulminating Lake, its orange-red surface dotted with specks of blue flame. From this height, a glassy sheen covered the fiery liquid like a birth cowl: strands of molten lava, caught in the Lake's updraft, quickly cooled to form delicate filaments, easily broken. Pretty, in a third-degree-burn sort of way.

Look at that. We weren't going to cannonball into the Lake of Fire after all. If I had still possessed all the standard human bodily functions, I would have shat myself.

Daun seemed to be enjoying the situation immensely. With every downward thrust of his leathery wings, he bucked his hips against my back. Hello, erection jamming into my spine. Normally, I'd be jockeying for a better position, but at the moment, suspended over the Lake of Fire, the last thing on my mind was sex.

Mental note: Avoid the Mile High Club.

If not for Daun's earlier command to stand still, I'd be scrabbling up his back right now and holding on for dear afterlife. I had this thing about flying: I hated it. Based on how my stomach was lurching, it hated me right back. And there was nothing I could do about it; I was Daun's prisoner.

Being dead sucked. I *so* wasn't going to do this again.

Even this high up, the smell of the Underworld filled the air—rotten eggs and acrid heat that was almost palpable; sewage and sweat and the tangy scent of fear. Problem was, it was *my* fear I smelled, which took the fun right out of it. Beneath us—way, way, way, way, *way* beneath us—the Lake churned. If I fell from this height, would I hit the bottom of the Lake?

Huh. Did the Lake even *have* a bottom?

Sounds drifted up from the Third Sphere, pulled me out of my thoughts of free falling: shrieks of the damned, vocal chords straining, voices filled with tears; laughter of their tormentors, burbling with mirth. The screams and the guffaws mingled, forming a cacophony of joyous misery. But as I listened to the music of the Underworld, I thought the chortles sounded forced, almost as desperate as the mortal pleas for mercy.

"Look, babes." Daun's deep voice reverberated in the air like thunder. "Hell, scurrying beneath your hooves. See how it's changed?"

"All I see from here is the Lake."

He clucked his tongue. "Then you're not looking hard enough."

We moved, cutting through the red-tinged air. Daun soared with confident strokes of his wings, as if he'd been created to ride the wind. All I can say for me is that I didn't vomit. The last time I'd flown anywhere was when Meg had taken me to the First Sphere, before the Announcement that had rocked the Abyss to its core.

She didn't drop you, Peaches whispered. *Neither will Daun.*

Yeah, but what if I weigh too much for him to hold?

Peaches sighed. *Daun's right, you know. Sometimes you're such a girl.*

Go fuck yourself.

Okay, a naughty girl. But still a girl.

As we flew, my fear slowly ebbed, replaced with a dawning horror. Daun was right: Hell had changed. Dramatically. "Where's the Wall?"

"The King destroyed it, about a week after you hoofed it to the mortal coil." I heard the rage in Daun's voice, felt the tension in his arms and stomach as he carried me. "Said we had no reason to hide our glory. *Glory*. Pfaugh!" He spat, and his loogey spiraled down, disappeared somewhere over Hell.

Me, I'd always thought the Great Wall that had surrounded the periphery of Hell was rather gratuitous. It's not like we really needed to defend ourselves against invaders. And let's face it: the damned weren't going anywhere. Other than the mortal intimidation factor, I hadn't seen any purpose to the Wall. But still, it had been ours—a colossal, defining characteristic of the Abyss.

And now it was gone—apparently in a blaze of glory. Somehow, I doubted the King was on a Bon Jovi kick.

All I could say was, "Wow." An incredible understatement, but it summed it up. "Just . . . wow."

"And that's not the worst of it," Daun said. "Look down at the boundaries."

Beneath us, I clearly made out the peripheral shape of the Pit: an extremely elongated oval, with a neck at the crest that served as the entrance to damnation. I didn't see the mighty Gates. Gone, I realized—without the Wall, there could be no Gates. My heart shriveled. I'd always liked those wrought iron fortifications, with the placard of welcome hanging over them, attached by severed hands. All creatures had been required to pull a stint as Gateskeeper on a rotating basis. When it had been my turn at the Gates, I would enjoy examining each new mortal entrant to the Pit, sniffing out each sin and confirming that yes, this person was damned. I loved tasting fear wafting from the souls of the truly evil, enjoyed sharing my brethren's infernal victory over another job well done.

All that, gone.

Outlined in the blue-threaded orange of the Lake of Fire, Hell sprawled, its heat-baked surface glowing with the colors of various Sins. Northwest was the powder blue of Sloth, its snake pits reduced to black dots along the rocky terrain. Bordering it to the east was the red glow of Wrath, home to Berserkers and those mortals who had dedicated their lives giving into their rages. From this height, I couldn't see the dismembered body parts that littered the ground, but the Mount of Prometheus—where the enraged were chained until they didn't have enough limbs to be bound to anything but the inside of a plastic bag—stretched up like the Earth giving Heaven the finger.

I squinted. Something looked off about the boundary between Sloth and Wrath, but I couldn't quite place it. Frowning, I scanned the rest of the Third Sphere, the plane of the damned and lowest level of Hell, trying to pinpoint what was different.

Just south of the Berserkers, the turquoise of Envy spread out long, coming to a wide base, where the bulk of its freezing waters were kept in cast-iron tubs that could fit a hundred humans apiece. Beneath Envy was the squat, yellow land of Covet with its towering cauldrons of boiling oil (in pots of gold, of course). To the west of Covet were the Heartlands of Lust, their dark blue boundaries housing legions of bonfire mounds. The Pridelands stretched northwest of Lust, swathed in royal purple, their enormous instruments of torture winking beneath me like millions of fishhooks laid out in neat rows. At the ass-end of Hell, appropriately enough, sprawled Gluttony in all its vomit-green finery.

Again, something nagged at me, like a tickle I couldn't scratch. Which, given how Daun hadn't allowed me to move yet, was spot on. "What's different?" I asked aloud, more to myself than to Daun.

"The boundaries," he said again. "Take a good look."

I stared at the section between Pride's purple and Lust's deep blue . . . and with a gasp, I saw it: the boundaries had blurred, bonding the lands of the Arrogant and the Seducers. The same for the boundary between Lust and Gluttony—the blue and olive green merged, softening the outlines of Sin.

"How could the boundaries blur?" I said, my head spinning. Most of the denizens of the Abyss despised those not of their own Sin. And that was being generous. The Envious and the Greedy had hated each other for a slight impossible to explain or understand, from the very beginning of the Underworld. Pride and Lust had a deep loathing for one another that was almost as old. The Lazy, when they could be bothered to actually think, hated everything that moved. And so on. The only things that kept infernal tempers in check were the unmistakable boundaries of Sin. All demons could traverse all parts of the Third Sphere safely to deposit their mortal catches; no matter how the nefarious detested one another, we all played for the same team—and there were rules to follow. Without a mortal client in tow, however, demons traversed the Lands of Sin at their own risk outside of their home base. From as far back as I could remember, it had been that way.

But now, with the boundaries softening, that could only lead to open conflict among the malefic. It was worse than throwing oil onto a raging fire.

"He's reshaping the Abyss," Daun said with a snort. "He says it's a kind of shock treatment."

"The King Himself is doing this?" I asked, stunned. I'd thought that maybe Hell was reshaping itself to reflect the mortal coil, with its ever-changing standards for Sin. "He's the one who said we were too soft, and this is His response—to soften the boundaries of Sin?"

"Yep."

I seriously wondered if the King of Hell was retarded.

Daun growled, "He's dicking around with everything. The Kings of Sin are clawing at themselves, this close to declaring a war of Sin and Land. And that's not even getting into all the changes in the elite."

My stomach lurched, but this time it had nothing to do with our flight. The elite of Hell *never* changed. Sort of like death and taxes were a given for the humans, the elite being permanent assholes of the Pit was a given for the lesser demonfolk. "What sort of changes?"

"Rosey's gone," Daun said, his voice low-pitched, sharing a secret. "Our sovereign ruler destroyed him a few days ago."

Rosier was—had been—the Prince of Lust, second only to King Asmodai. "Shit. What did he do to score oblivion?"

"He bragged to Naberius how he was going to drop you at His feet, to show Him and all of Hell that he could clean up His mess."

Eek. "Did he now."

"The King got word of it. He summoned Rosey to His side and boom, demon ash all over the Courtyard. It's how I earned my wings—there was a hole in the ranks, and Pan tapped me."

My eyes widened. "Bless me, Daun—are you one of the elite?"

"No. Not yet. But at the rate our Dread Lord is going, soon." He lowered his voice. "Rosey's not the only one He's destroyed. Just the most recent. He did it in front of the other Kings and principals, just before He etched the Great Rule onto the side of Abaddon."

"*The* Great Rule?" Before the Announcement, there had been ten. After I ran, Daun had told me the King had blasted them off the side of the infernal palace. "What Rule?"

"Look to the east, Jez."

I turned my head and saw the looming mountain fortress of Pandemonium, home to all demons and other nefarious entities—and, towering above it, the black palace of Abaddon, gleaming, a dark jewel at the pinnacle of the Underworld. Even from this distance, I could make out the six-word command, etched in the palace wall:

OBEY YOUR KING OR BE DESTROYED.

Staring at those words, I felt my stomach knot.

"There's a desperation in Hell that never used to be here before," Daun said, his voice whisper quiet. "Nothing you can easily place, but it's a feeling that's there all the same. The elite are paranoid, the Kings are itching for war. The place is rank with tension."

"And the fumes from the Lake of Fire."

"That's my babes," Daun said, "always quick to point out the obvious. You want down?"

"Please."

"So polite. Being human's screwed with your sensibilities."

We flew down at a stomach-flipping speed. Bless me, I didn't know how birds managed their swan dives without barfing all over their feathers. Down, down, the land of Lust blooming beneath us, spreading out like a fungus, the screams and stench of burning humans assaulting my senses. Daun zoomed us past the main Burning Grounds, flying us over the heads of demons and damned alike, all too lost in their own torments to notice two more entities soaring past.

As we approached the base of the Second Sphere, Daun slowed. The main path framed the bottom of the black mountain, leading up and in. Off to the left, another path veered around a crop of large boulders, leading to a hidden point beneath the ebon crag of Pandemonium.

"Here we are," he said, finally coming to a halt. "You can move now."

As my hooves touched the rocky soil, he shoved me away from him. Off balance, my legs tangled beneath me, and I stumbled to the ground. Demon fall down, go boom. Ash puffed around my face, and I spat dirt from my mouth. Nothing said Hell like a mouthful of barren soil.

"The Abyss is nowhere near as fun as it used to be," Daun said.

"I'm getting that." Propping myself up onto my elbows, I looked up at him. Staring down at me, Daun radiated sex, his long hair windswept, his arms folded over his broad chest. He could have been the cover model for demonic romance novels.

"You chose to run away from Hell," he said. "You chose to become a human for real, complete with a soul. You're so big on choice, Jezebel. Well, here's another choice. Either stay with me here and be a demon once more, be true to who you really are. Or go in there, into the Caverns, and try to find your poor lost love. But if you do that, you do it without my help."

"How can I choose?" I couldn't hide the bitterness from my voice, from my thoughts; it coated my tongue like vinegar. "You own me, Daun. You can tell me what to think. Anything I do, how can I know if that's really my choice?"

He chuckled. "Well, I guess that's a chance you have to

take. Now—either me, with all the hedonism that implies, or him, lost forever. Choose."

I already had. From the moment I'd called Daun's name in Paul's apartment, I'd made my choice.

Biting my lip before I spoke, I tried to think of the right words. Nothing came to me, so I told the truth—a former demon's last resort. "I love him, Daun. I have to go find him."

His body showed no reaction; his face remained impassive. But his eyes . . . bless me, his eyes blazed hotter than any of Lust's bonfires. "Fine."

How could a creature of Evil sound so hurt? So small? "Daun . . ."

He motioned with his hand, and his heavy presence vanished from my mind. "I've released you. No more soul bond. You're free. For whatever that'll get you."

"Thank you." I pulled myself up until I stood before him on wobbly legs. "I knew you would free me. You'd promised on your name."

A smile flitted across his lips, cold, mirthless. "Demons lie, Jezzie. You should remember that. Go on, try to find your flesh puppet. But I'm not fishing you out when you get lost." His smile slid off his face. "You go in the Caverns, babes, you're on your own."

I threw myself on him, wrapped him in my arms and planted a huge kiss on his cheek.

"I'll be back," I said, hoping I wasn't a liar.

"Uh huh," he said, shrugging out of my embrace. "Care to place a bet?"

"I already have."

"Bye, babes."

"See you on the other side." With that, I turned away from him and marched into the Endless Caverns.

Chapter 17

The Endless Caverns

There were lots of things that I missed about being a demon. My hair (whenever I had hair) had always been perfect, I'd never needed a bra no matter how well endowed I was, and my body had moved in ways that would make contortionists scream for mercy. But at the moment, the one thing I missed most about not having my infernal powers was being able to see in the dark.

Scratch that. Dark was what happened at night. This wasn't dark. This was absolute blackness.

Ouch. Yow! *Fuck!*

Absolute blackness with about a zillion sharp rocks.

Between my hooves and the thick pelt of hair swathing my lower limbs up to my pelvis, my feet and legs were well protected. But I was walking with my arms outstretched so that I wouldn't go face-first into anything nasty, so my hands and forearms wound up peppered with tiny lacerations from their accidental encounters with the rock-studded walls.

I had no idea how long I'd been wandering around, blind. Stepping into the maw of the Caverns felt like forever ago—with that single, decisive step, everything around me had disappeared. Including the entrance. Turning back was not an option. And so that meant moving forward.

Wherever that was.

I'd long since yelled myself hoarse; obviously, no one was

going to show up with a torch or a flashlight. Or the electric company. I'd even called Paul's name, knowing it was point-less, telling him that I was coming for him. Slowly. Blindly. Around me, the dank stench of the cave pressed into my flesh, weighed down my limbs. Whenever I opened my mouth, I tasted the humidity on my tongue. The only sounds I heard were my own hoof-falls and my curses whenever I sliced my hands against a jutting rock.

Trapped in the Endless Caverns, I realized just how help-less I was . . . and just how lost I was getting. I had no idea what I was doing. Other than stumbling around in the dark and bleeding, that is. That I had pretty well covered.

Mental note: Improve strategic planning skills.

After a short infinity of nothing but cave smell and cave rocks, I met the cave wall. As in, my path was completely blocked. Cursing a blue streak, I turned to retrace my steps, but I bumped into a barrier that hadn't been there before. Crap. I pivoted to the left and walked four steps . . . and smacked into yet another wall. Grumbling as I rubbed my sore arm, I stag-gered three steps backward and came to a full stop, my back against another rocky wall face.

Well, shit.

Flummoxed, I sat on the floor. Time to brainstorm.

I waited for insight.

Come on, insight.

Peaches? Any wisdom?

Yeah. Don't go to Hell.

Double shit.

Blowing out a sigh, I closed my eyes. Which changed noth-ing, as I couldn't see worth a damn anyway.

Sitting there, alone in the dark, I heard them: ghostly voices, whispers within the rocks, chittering like rats.

Another?

Another.

What's this one?

A lover.

Questing?

Indeed.

A demon?

Half-breed.

"Heya," I called out. "Can you hear me?"

She asks us?

She tasks us?

Gah. Rhymers. I hated Rhymers. Stupid little elves. They always made me feel like I was trapped in a greeting-card store. My nose plugged from the stink of festering orange juice. "I'm looking for a mortal named Paul Hamilton."

Take her?

Oh yes.

Take her.

Make her guess.

Where are we taking you?

Hands—all over me, grabbing my face, my shoulders, my waist, my legs.

"Hey!" I swatted at them, clawed them off, but still they came: small hands, vise-like, with tiny fingers that attached themselves to my flesh like suction cups. "Get off me!" Hands clamping over my breasts, my ass, my hooves, my wrists; fingers squirming over me, prying between my lips. "Quit it, you dumb cookie elves! Let go!"

Hands plugging my mouth, wrapping around my throat.

She screeches and screams.

But she doesn't guess.

Let's examine her dreams.

Let's hear her confess.

Hands hoisting me up, arms out, flat on my back, carrying me like a crucifix. Hands and disembodied voices everywhere, giggling, whispering, riddling in the bowels of Hell.

When is a demon not really a demon?

When it is really a mortal.

What will she see, what will she hear—

When she faces the flash and the portal?

I bucked, I kicked, I thrashed my head and snapped my fangs, but to no avail—the invisible hands of the Rhymers carried me away, deeper into the darkness.

When is a choice never a choice?

When there is nothing to choose.
Free it may be to one such as she—
But if it's free then there's nothing to lose.

Please. Block my ears. If I had to listen to any more of the demonic nursery rhymes, I would lose my mind.

To ignore their taunts, I focused on Shakira lyrics in Spanish, then in English, then in Spanglish. Halfway through "Suerte," the hands threw me forward. I crashed to the floor, only slightly gratified that the stones beneath me were smooth; it still hurt like a bitch when I landed.

"A light, my delight," boomed a voice, "give us a light."

Torches sprang to life around me, their sudden illumination stabbing me. Wincing, I shut my eyes, orange motes swimming behind my lids.

"She dresses so pretty. Hides her true form, more's the pity."

Biting my lip, I slowly opened my eyes. Gray swam around me, focused into a pattern of stone. Okay, that would be the floor. Get up, Jesse. I planted my stinging palms on the ground and hoisted myself up to my elbows. When I raised my head, I looked up at a hairy elf pointing a black weapon at me. No, not a weapon. A . . . camera?

He said, "Smile."

Flash!

A thousand suns burst before me. I jerked my head back, squeezed my eyes shut. Powder rained over me, settled onto my skin. In the wake of the dust, colors shot through my head—hot yellows blending with cool greens, swirling with bright oranges and haughty reds, a whirlpool of tinted light, dazzling me, drowning me.

"The portal, the portal," the elf chanted, his voice warped, tinny. "Let's make her immortal."

Hands lifted me, moved me as I swam through the colors, trying to break free from their weight. I shouted for them to stop—I needed to find Paul. My voice filled with pigment, colored my words.

"Need, indeed. Always about need. But let's see what she *wants*."

The hands set me down, held me upright, turned my head

forward and pried open my eyelids. Through the haze of streaming color, I saw a mirror.

"Reflect, but circumspect. A want is not a need."

In the mirror I saw a gray room of cold stone.

"Choose and lose. Let's see which you heed."

And in that room was a door, and I knew that behind that door was everything I'd ever wanted, everything I'd ever dreamed of, in the deepest, blackest pit of my heart. All I had to do was open the door . . .

The hands released me, and I stepped through the mirror.

My hooves clack against the stone floor like high heels on linoleum, tapping out a beat as I approach the plain wooden door. The air is thick against my body, as if I'm cutting my way through a cloud. I stretch my arm out, ready to push open the door, and I notice the golden bracelet snug against my wrist. It winks at me, an old friend sharing a secret. It clicks in my mind what that secret is, and just before I touch the bare wood I command myself to find Paul.

Find Paul. Bring him home.

My fingers touch the door.

Find Paul. Bring him—

The door swings open . . .

Find Paul—

. . . and the smell hits me, a combination of chocolate and sex, and then the sounds of running water and eager laughter and the *oohs* of caresses and soft moans of passionate touches stolen in the moonlight . . .

Find—

. . . and I walk through the door . . .

. . . and step into a pool of chocolate. It hugs me, forms a second skin around me as I wade into the liquid confection. Submerged up to my chin, I move my arms back and forth, kicking my feet until I'm floating in the blissful stickiness. Its rich scent seeps into my nose, delights my senses.

The bathing room, resplendent in obsidian and ruby, gleams from the heat of the chocolate pool, the walls slick with condensation. I walk the length of the pool, murmuring greetings to the creatures dotting its lip, all prostrating themselves as I pass them before continuing with their foreplay. Nymphs and satyrs, gods and demons dressed as humans, all tangled in intricate lover's knots, their bodies pulsing, their sounds of pleasure echoing in the large chamber—moans harmonizing with coos, sudden gasps a staccato in the air, their pants keeping time.

"Lady."

I smile up at Joey, who is bent over double, naked save for his black necktie, presenting me with a goblet of hot chocolate. I take the drink, my fingers lingering against his, enjoying the shudder that plays over his sweat-slick muscles. I thank him for the beverage, and he smiles his appreciation as he bows, his tuxedo tie hidden as he bobs his head in deference. One of the incubi grabs Joey's hand and leads him to the back of the room, already nibbling on his ear, stroking his shaft. Joey's groans blend with the music of sex, bodies slapping a backbeat.

Sex and chocolate. All is right with the world.

I take a small sip of my drink, humming my glee as the taste dances over my tongue, slides down my throat. Sinful without sin. Yum.

A demon in red approaches, knuckling his forehead in the manner of the truly old ones. "Is the temperature high enough, Lady?"

"It's fine, Zepar," I say, motioning with my free hand. "Go, have fun."

"Damnations, Lady." The Seducer bows, his red armor resplendent in the candlelight. "Until the Gathering." Touching his fist to his forehead, he backs out of the bathing room.

Mmmm. I'd nearly forgotten about the Gathering—a small appearance to the hordes of Hell before the Great Orgy. The thought brings a smile to my lips. Nothing like a lot of fucking to kick off the festivities.

"Lady," says Caitlin, her voice a caress, "you should come out and dry off. The Gathering begins in a half hour."

I pout, splashing the liquid chocolate. "You're too young to be my mother."

She smiles, used to the old jibe. "Old enough to keep you on schedule."

"You're right, you're right." I quaff the rest of my drink, then hand her the empty cup.

Caitlin inclines her head as she takes the goblet. "You should eat something. More than chocolate, I mean. You need the four food groups. Especially beef."

"I'm fine."

She frowns at me, as only a sister can, but all she says is, "A half hour, Lady." She bows as she exits the room. I don't try to stop her. Even after all this time in my entourage, she remains uncomfortable with nudity. I shake my head. Poor Caitlin.

Time to get dry. I swim across the pool, slowly ascend the stairs and step onto the tile floor. Three women approach, carrying huge white plumes stitched into elaborate fans. Dripping chocolate, I extend my arms. Candy, Circe, and Faith wave their fans, catching the air and directing it onto my wet body. The chocolate slowly dries, encasing my form in thick sweetness. When the chocolate is completely solid, I nod. The three dancers step back, melting into the other attendees writhing around the edge of the pool.

I stand, head thrown back, hands raised in supplication: a chocolate sacrifice. Daun approaches from the left and Angel from the right, each taking one of my candy-coated arms. They begin with soft nibbles, their saliva shining on my flesh, their teeth gently working through the shell until my fingers waggle free.

Slowly they work their way up my arms, eating me, releasing me, polishing my body with their lips and tongue. Daun sucks chocolate from my nipples, his growls of pleasure echoing my own. Angel kisses chocolate off my back, consuming it with love and adoration, and I quiver from her soft touches. They work their way down my form, Daun laving my front and Angel buffing my rear. My groin tightens with every feather kiss of Angel's, her delicate lips trailing down my buttocks, the backs of my thighs, sluicing the chocolate from my skin. Daun is more aggressive, slurping the candy from my flesh, my purrs goading him on. As Angel sucks my toes, Daun tongues my clit until my wetness fills his mouth, replacing sweetness with sweetness as an orgasm pulses through me.

Yes, my dears. Polish me with your reverence. Rain your adoration over me.

Love me.

Daun kisses my nub one last time, then stands back as the dancers move forward. Faith stands ready with my outfit. I step into the ruby garment, and she pulls it up, wraps it around me and cinches it tight—gauzy genie pants with a broad sash around the crotch and over my chest, with more of the diaphanous material swathing my arms and coming to a point over the backs of my hands. Beneath the opaque strip covering my genitals and breasts, my skin peeks out, shell pink against the crimson fabric. Clothing still feels odd to me, but I recognize its importance. Especially here, in my seat of power, I understand that flaunting something all the time is the quickest way for everyone to grow used to it, complacent. In Hell, complacent malefic entities meant bored malefic entities. And that meant a constant migraine for me. Power should be hinted at, displayed only when necessary.

And sex is one of the strongest kinds of power. Thus, I wear clothing when I'm not fucking.

Candy hands red slippers to Angel, who places them on my feet. Circe reaches up and pulls two long pins out of my hair. My black locks tumble free, crashing over my shoulders and down to the small of my back. As she fluffs the strands around my face, movement by the doorway catches my eye. A man, tall, human, watching me, his sea-green eyes sparkling, a smile crooking his lips. Sandy brown hair teases his ears and neck. His work shirt and jeans are completely out of place here in the bathing room—here in the Abyss.

I stare at him, wondering who he is.

"Lady," Alecto says from above. I tear my gaze away from

the stranger to look up at the Fury, her reptilian tresses undulating around her blackened face. "The hordes of Hell await your pleasure in the Courtyard."

A glance at the doorway tells me the stranger has disappeared. Something about him nags at me, a dream I can almost remember. Frowning, I try to place his face, his eyes.

"Lady?" Daun touches my shoulder. In my ear, he whispers, "Babes, what's wrong?"

"Nothing," I reply, my mind searching for the man's name. "It's nothing." I raise my arms, and magic washes over me, transporting me to the dais in the Courtyard. Around me, the legions of Hell crash to the ground, prostrating themselves until all I can see are multicolored backs and limbs intertwined, like a carpet of flesh on the floor of Abaddon. Their reverence fills me, thrills me, and it's with a smile on my lips that I address the denizens of the Underworld.

"My brethren." I let my voice ripple over them, my power touching them, caressing them with love. "I will not waste your time with pretty words and false threats. Know that I commend your work with the damned. With every shriek of agony, with every plea for mercy, the damned are that much closer to repentance. With every creative use of tortures that humans cannot begin to imagine, you continually entertain the Nameless One."

I pause, allowing the weight of my words to settle over the Courtyard. "Its gaze has been pulled from the mortal coil, is once again fastened here in the Abyss."

Murmurs through the Court. A few of the elite dare to glance at me before cutting their gazes back to the ground. I note those looks, remember those faces. Those are the ones to watch, to keep close or possibly to destroy.

"But we must continue in our work," I say, my voice reverberating, "lest the Nameless One grow bored. If Its touch falls again onto the mortal coil, humans will lead themselves to destruction. And then Hell will be no more."

By the back, over the bodies of millions of the nefarious, I see him again, leaning against the wall: sandy brown hair falling over his face, his arms crossed over his chest, his unbuttoned shirt flapping in the hot wind. Even from this distance, I see humor dancing in his stormy green eyes. He smiles at me—familiar, amused.

Why isn't he falling over himself to show me his adoration? Who is he?

Ignoring him, I continue my speech to the demons of Hell. "So I say to you all, be evil. Show your charges what it means to fear. Lavish them with pain. Play with them. Give them hope, only to extinguish it brutally."

The Berserkers among the multitude chortle their appreciation, their bodies thrumming with the urge to do violence. But what I say next murders their glee. "And when their spirits are broken and their Sin has been repented and their souls are again pure, release them. Let those redeemed find their way to the Sky, and make room for those more worthy of your attentions."

A buzzing among the infernal—angry whispers, quiet hisses. They still react poorly when they hear of Heaven, as if the place itself has any power over them. I bite back the urge to roll my eyes. Sometimes I forget that damned and demons alike can be such children. Even now, most of them don't understand that we're all on the same team.

So I cater to their nature, speak a language that even the simplest of them could understand. "Fill the Pit with the screams of the damned. Fill the air with the sounds of their cries. Rock the rim of Creation itself with your laughter."

I reach out, embracing the millions of creatures before me. "You are Hell. You define it, reshape it with your every move. Be true to yourselves and to your land. Be evil."

Grinning, I release my power, raining lust onto the demon hordes. "Let the Orgy begin!"

As soon as the words leave my lips, the infernal open their arms and their legs, and soon the Courtyard is filled with the grunts and thrusts of fornication.

I walk among them, watching their bodies writhe, listening to the sounds of their fucking, my fingers dancing over them as I pass by. With my touch, the nefarious grow more passionate—their strokes become frenzied, their pumping a tumult of wild abandon as they lose themselves in the joys of sex. From the gelatinous forms of the Gluttons and the Lazy to the taut shapes of the Proud, from the green-tinted desire of the Envious to the golden wants of the Greedy to the barely contained rage of the Berserkers, they all mimic the movements of the Seducers. Goading their brethren on, the succubi and incubi encourage the others to discover new pleasures of the flesh. In one fell swoop, the nefarious bond under one Sin: all creatures of the Pit, from the least of imps to the mightiest of gods, radiate Lust.

All but one.

I wind my way to him, my gaze fixed on his, ignoring the moans and cries of my brethren, my children. He winks in and out of sight as the revelers spill across my path, and I gently push them aside as I move forward, seeking his form, searching for his sea-green eyes. Someone grabs my hand and pulls me back; I stagger into Daun's arms. He kisses me, thrusts his tongue down my throat. I cup his balls, flicking the tip of his shaft before I shrug out of his embrace. Craning my neck, I see the stranger, still loitering by the far wall of the Courtyard, waiting beneath an arch.

Waiting for me.

I approach the arch, my brow furrowed, a frown on my lips. He looks, feels, so damn familiar that it's infuriating. An amused smile plays on his face as he watches me, and I'm torn between wanting to slash that smirk off his face and plant a serious kiss on those sensual lips.

Alone with him, the sounds of copulation fading to white noise, I ask, "Who are you?"

"A white knight, lost on the path." His deep voice fills me, kisses me until my nipples pebble and my core vibrates with need. I reach out to him, intending to pull him onto me, into me, but he steps backward into a gray room just beyond the archway. He asks, "Will you help me find the way?"

Aching to touch him, I walk beneath the arch, leaving the trappings of Hell behind me. My slippered feet whisper over the smooth stone floor as I step into the gray room. The man waits for me, poised beneath a large mirror as if ready to dive through.

Sweet Sin, I've never wanted anyone, anything, the way I want him right now.

A want is not a need.

From the archway behind me, I hear the sounds of Hell's orgy: the panting and gasping of demons screwing and reaching heights that God Himself never imagined; the laments of the damned, wallowing in their sorrow and fear, balanced on the cusp of personal salvation.

Standing before me, the stranger smiles. Worlds shine in his eyes.

"Jezzie."

Behind me, standing beneath the arch, Daun reaches out to me, beckoning. "Babes, come back. Hell's not the same without you."

Choose and lose.

"Help me find the way," the stranger says, then steps through the mirror.

"Jezebel," Daun says, my name a plea. "Jesse. Come back."

Let's see which you heed.

I'm sorry, Daun. A wordless cry on my lips, a name trumpeting in my heart, I dive through the mirror—

—**a**nd in a crash of silver, I burst through the frame.

My arms shielding my face from the spray of shattered glass, I fell to the stone floor and landed hard on my side, the name in my heart buffering my body's pain.

Paul.

With a grunt, I pulled myself up, shook my head to clear it from the sounds of Hell fucking, the smells of heat and sweat and sex. As I brushed the glass shards from my arms, my eyes stung with dust and unshed tears. I bit my lip to keep myself from sobbing.

I could have stayed, could have ruled the Abyss with firm

hands and open legs, could have amused the Devil Itself with sexual delights that would have inspired Anne Desclos to write new chapters in *Histoire d'O*.

My heart tightened, as if wringing the last drops of lasciviousness from my heart. How could I mourn something that never was?

It was real, Peaches whispered. *If you had chosen to stay in the mirror, it would have been real to you.*

But not truly real.

Does that matter? You wouldn't have known the difference, wouldn't have cared. If you'd chosen to stay in that reflection of Hell, you would have remained there forever.

Staring at a jagged piece of glass, I saw my face distorted, warped. Be evil, I'd told the denizens of the Abyss. Being lost in a reality of my own making was about as evil a punishment as I ever could have imagined. Ghostly hands ran up my body, invisible teeth nibbled chocolate from my flesh. Just a memory, I told myself. A yesterday that never was.

Off to the left, a groan. Dropping the broken glass, I turned to see a hairy elf crawling away from the ruins of the mirror, his camera a smoking heap on the ground. I stormed over to him, my hooves grinding the shards into powder. My mouth twisted into a snarl, I yanked the elf up by the scruff of his neck. He squawked, flailing in my grip. His greasy pelt slick in my grasp, he nearly slipped free. Then my talons found his flesh beneath the matted hair and dug in. He cried out, then hid his face in his furry paws.

My voice a growl, I said, "Where is he?"

"He?" The creature lowered his hands, blinked wide eyes. He looked about as innocent as a wolf in pigskin. "He? Who is he?"

"You know who I mean, you little shoemaker's nightmare." I leaned in close, until my nose touched his, flashing my fangs in a hungry grin. "Take me to Paul Hamilton. Now."

"He made his choice," he gasped, "there's naught you can do. He—"

"So help me, if you rhyme, I'll staple your lips shut." I motioned with my left hand, and a fiery red staple gun appeared in it. Testing its weight, I waved it in front of his face. "I'm having a really bad day here, so don't fuck with me."

He squeaked and tried to shrink inside of his pelt.

"Take me to Paul Hamilton, you little Santa Claus kiss-ass. Now!"

"Another mirror," he cried out. "Bring it now!"

Through the gray stone, dozens of tiny elves shimmered, stepping out of the wall. From the ground, a long, silver slab appeared, then lifted up about two feet off the floor. Beneath the mirror, a group of elves carried it over their heads. They approached me, barely up to my thighs, their red eyes gleaming—each looking like it was a toss-up between obeying the elf in my hand and dropping the mirror to take a chomp out of my legs. Without the cover of darkness, the Rhymers were sad, scrawny things, their nakedness obfuscated by their tangled pelts. They reeked of rotten oranges.

I pressed the staple gun to my prisoner's cheek. He squawked, "Set it down, set it down!"

Eyes bright, the Rhymers leaned the long mirror against the wall. Instead of reflecting the elves in its surface, it shone like jet: black, empty. Cold.

"Dandy," I said, shaking the elf. "Now what?"

"Say his name," he whined. "Say his name, and you'll see his desire."

I pictured Paul's handsome face, from his small, expressive eyes to his broken nose, to the way his lips quirked into a lopsided grin whenever something tickled him. Sculpted cheeks, strong jaw. Powerful neck. Wavy brown hair, curling around his ears, dangling over his eyes.

My Paul.

I'm coming for you, love.

Lifting my chin high, I said, "Paul Hamilton."

The mirror rippled, waves of white cresting its dark surface. Then it settled, focused, showed a gray room with a plain wooden door. Behind that door, Paul waited.

"Go in, if you dare," the elf said. "If you do, beware. It's his desire, his choice. The ending comes from his voice."

I pressed the staple gun against his mouth and pulled the trigger. *SNIKT!*

The elf screeched, his hands clawing at his bleeding, sealed mouth.

"I warned you, you little fuck." I dropped the thrashing creature to the ground. "Get out of here before I staple your balls together."

He took off in a sprint, leapt through the wall like a ghost that seriously had to find a bathroom.

"That goes for the rest of you too," I said to the elves. "Go annoy some marketers or something. And do it without talking."

Their eyes blazing malice, the Rhymers oozed through the stones, only the smell of putrid oranges marking where they'd been.

I looked at the mirror, wondered what Paul's greatest desire was. Wondered if I really wanted to know.

Discarding the stapler, I touched the golden bracelet on my wrist. Had Angel done what I'd asked?

One way to find out.

I stepped through the mirror, walked to the door, turned the handle.

My heart leapt when I saw Paul seated beneath a huge sycamore tree . . . then sank to my knees when I saw Paul wasn't alone.

Chapter 18

The Endless Caverns

Leaning back against the base of the huge tree, Paul might have been sleeping. His eyes were closed, his mouth relaxed into an easy smile. He wore the same work shirt and jeans he had in my desire, the same clothing he'd worn when Lillith had stolen his soul. Grass stained his cuffs, his shoes. If I hadn't been looking for the color of his soul, I would have missed it—whether because we were in his fantasy or because he didn't belong in Hell, his soul hid beneath his form, like a ripple just beneath the surface of a pool. But it was there all the same: white, resplendent with streamers of gold and silver, branches of rose extending from his heart.

My White Knight.

A breeze caught the tails of his shirt and flapped them around Paul and the woman snuggled against him. Resting her head on his exposed chest, she was a small thing, pale with short black hair, almost swimming in her yellow shirt. Her bare legs were tucked beneath her body, her arms wrapped around Paul's torso. When the wind died down, her hair fell away from her thin face, revealing a contented smile of her own.

Staring at that smile, my mind flashed on a photo I'd seen only once before on Paul's nightstand, a photo from before Paul had met me. In the picture, the woman's smile was captured for eternity—a good smile, full of the promise of youth and love.

Tracy, Paul's dead fiancée.

I rubbed the bridge of my nose. Crap. Why couldn't he have been trapped in a tower?

A nagging voice in my mind, sounding horrifically like Lillith's, asked me why Paul wasn't fantasizing about me.

No more than you did about him, Peaches said.

That's not fair. I did fantasize about him. He pulled me out of the dream, led me back to reality.

So maybe he needs you to do the same for him.

Huh. Keep talking sense like this, and maybe I will rename you Elektra.

Peaches made happy noises in my mind, while the Lillith voice barfed.

I approached the couple, my hoof-falls muffled by the springy grass. Around me, outdoor summertime smells danced in the air—clean sheets and hot dogs and sweat, bottled with humidity. The sunlight winked off the Rope of Hecate, turned my leathery skin the lush red of ripe strawberries. I easily recognized the benches around the trees as part of a park, and a glance past the tree line revealed a row of brownstones. New York City—specifically, Washington Square Park. One of Paul's favorite haunts.

Other people littered the grass and ground, laughing, talking, reading, inhaling city air and exhaling city dreams. A large number were gathered near a street performer strumming a guitar, singing the Beatles' tune "With A Little Help From My Friends." Paul and Tracy had taken refuge on the other side of the clearing, within easy earshot but not close enough to be trampled by other listeners.

Steps away from the dozing couple, I remembered that I was still in my natural form. As tempted as I was to keep it—man, wouldn't that scare the little tramp—I thought that Paul might not appreciate it if I made his former fiancée piss her pants. Assuming she was wearing pants; from this angle, all I could see was her long shirt and hints of her thighs. So I called up my power, let it transform me into the form that Paul knew best: the twin sister of Caitlin Harris. I clothed myself in a white sleeveless blouse (*sans* bra) and denim cutoffs (*sans* undies), with low-heeled sandals on my feet. My black curls I tied back with a scarf the same bright green as my eyes. A quick poof of cosmetics later, my costume was perfect.

I stared at the streamers of energy drifting from my finger-tips, watched them dissipate in the summer air. Bless me, how I'd missed my magic. It was tempting to stay in the dream, if only it meant I could work my demon mojo once more.

You did before, you know. Back in the Caverns, before you stepped into Paul's desire. You created the staple gun. Wonder what that means.

Not now, Peaches. I've got to win back my love.

If you've got your power back, you could just zap her into oblivion.

Yeah. But Paul wouldn't like that. And that's cheating.

The old rules are bending. And it's not cheating, especially since technically, he's dead.

But not damned. I won't fuck with him that way. He'd never forgive me.

Weren't you breaking up with him?

Not until after some really awesome makeup sex. Now va-moose.

Peaches vamoosed.

Wondering what to say, I walked up to Paul. Nothing brilliant came to mind. I'd have to wing it. I cleared my throat, then nudged his knee with my toe. "Heya, sweetie. Wakey wakey."

He opened his eyes. I watched a series of emotions play out on his face, but the one he settled on was confusion. "Yes?"

"Paul, it's me. Jesse."

His brow furrowed as his gaze searched my face. "Jesse? Do I know you?"

The words sliced into my heart.

Next to him, Tracy stirred, stretched. She blinked sleepy eyes at me, then glanced at Paul, and back at me, all traces of sleep shed like snakeskin. A smile glued on her face, she sat straighter against Paul's body, her tiny breasts thrust out like weapons beneath her shirt, one hand resting lightly on Paul's lap. Everything about her body language shouted *hands off*. She had never met me before, but somewhere deep inside she knew me, knew what I was.

Knew what I meant to do.

"Don't you remember me?" I tried to smile, to show that ha-ha, we all forget things like the loves of our lives, but my mouth kept slipping and my chest felt too tight.

He was looking at me, focusing on my face. "You look so damn familiar, but I just can't place it."

"We met at South Station," I said, remembering that morning when we'd first met, "took a train together to New York City."

He tilted his head to the side, considering. "Really? I haven't been to Boston for a long time."

"Sweetheart, what're you talking about?" Tracy looked up at Paul, her mouth set in a moue. Her voice was deeper than I would have imagined. "We're in Boston now."

"We are?" He smiled at her, bemused. "Looks more like New York City to me. See? There's the Fifth Avenue Arch."

A sheen of panic glinted in Tracy's eyes before she blinked it away. Interesting. Smiling big and fake, she said, "Who's your friend?"

"I'm trying to figure that out. Jesse, right?"

I nodded.

"Well, pleased to meet you, even if I don't remember you." He laughed, a wonderful rich rumble from his chest. Tracy must have felt that sound vibrate against her back. Jealousy wormed its way through me, turned my stomach to acid. "This is Tracy."

"Paul's fiancée," she said, honey dripping off the words.

"Hey, that's great." My words were as phony as Tracy's smile. "Congratulations."

"Thanks." Maybe sensing my unease, Tracy settled back against Paul, smile still in place. First blood, Tracy. Bitch. She said, "It's been a long time coming."

"Will the big day be here or in Boston?" I asked, trying to figure out what to do. How could I make Paul remember me?

"Boston," Tracy said over Paul insisting "Here." They looked at each other, shared a laugh in the easy way that lovers do. It made me want to claw her eyes out and suck on them until they popped between my teeth.

"We're figuring it out," Paul said, chuckling.

"Nice meeting you." Tracy snuggled deeper into Paul's lap, dismissing me.

Fuck that. "Paul, you really don't remember me?" I squatted on my heels, looked into the stormy depths of his eyes. "Hotel New York? Belles?"

Something moved over his face—a spark of recognition. "Belles. The gentlemen's club, right? I heard that place was shut down."

Tracy clucked her tongue, drawing the attention back to her. "What do you know about those kinds of places?" she asked, playfully slapping his arm, then shooting me a look that should have flayed the skin from my bones.

"Research," Paul said to her, waggling his brows.

She giggled, a lighthearted titter behind a delicate hand, all the while murdering me with her eyes. For someone who was the prior light of Paul's life, she was downright evil. Maybe love brought out the best in her.

Oblivious to her look of pure hatred, Paul smiled at me. "I'm a vice cop."

"I know." I reached out, stroked his cheek. Instead of balking from the familiar touch, he leaned into it, his body remembering what his mind had forgotten.

In his lap, Tracy stiffened. "Hey. Do you mind?"

"I know a lot about you," I said, willing him to remember me. "I know how you got that tiny scar beneath your left eye. I know how you love Chinese food and hate anything with curry. I know how you love Eighties music but would rather get a root canal than go out dancing. I know how you have to save the world at least once a day before coming home."

As I spoke, his eyes flashed between concern and distress, now blue, now green, now settling into hazel. Voice thick, he asked, "How do you know all this?"

"I know *you*," I said. "You're my White Knight."

The moniker clicked; I saw it in his eyes.

"You've got some nerve," Tracy huffed, but Paul shushed her with a touch on her shoulder. She quieted, but her body radiated poison. Silently, she skewered me alive, watched me bleed, and gleefully tap danced on my carcass.

If Paul sensed her ire, he ignored it. To me he asked, "Who *are* you?"

"I'm the one you saved from Hell. I'm the one you taught how to truly love. I'm the one who returned to Hell to save you. I'm Jesse," I said, pouring my soul into the name. Then I kissed him.

Our lips barely touched before small hands shoved me back, pushed me away. But that instant had been enough—a force had moved through us, lightning quick, connecting us stronger than any magic.

"How dare you," Tracy screamed. "Who do you think you are?"

"Jesse," Paul whispered, touching his lips. A grin broke across his face, and he reached out to me. "Jesse!"

My fingers entwined in his. "I told you I'd come for you," I whispered, smiling through sudden tears.

"Paul Matthew Hamilton," Tracy said, her tone cold enough to freeze over the Sahara Desert. "What on Earth is going on?"

Paul's eyes widened. He looked down at Tracy, then over at me. "Well," he said, "this is a little awkward."

"**G**et out of here," Tracy yelled at me. "Just go away!"

"Not without him," I said, a growl sounding in my throat.

"Okay, ladies, hang on a second." Paul had untangled his hand from mine, had set Tracy next to him instead of on his lap. The three of us were sitting in a semicircle, Paul sandwiched between Tracy and me. Normally, the thought of a *ménage-a-trois* would have made me all sorts of happy. But the idea of Tracy fucking Paul turned my stomach to putty.

Oblivious to our metaphysical soap opera, the other people in the park went about their business. Off to the side, the guitar player switched to a different Beatles tune, strummed the opening chords to "We Can Work It Out." Terrific. Our own Greek chorus.

Paul said, "Let's talk this through."

"There's nothing to talk about." Tracy crossed her arms over her chest. "She's trying to steal you from me!"

"You're dead," I told her.

"What's that got to do with anything?" she snarled. "So're you! So's he!"

Pretty intuitive for part of a soul's fantasy.

"I'm not dead," Paul said.

"Yes you are," Tracy and I said together, then glared at each other.

"Really?" Paul touched his face, his chest. "I don't feel dead."

I said, "A demon seduced you and stole your soul. I'm here to bring you back."

"You're the demon," Tracy shouted, pointing at me. "You're the one stealing him from me!"

Hmmm. The girl sort of had a point.

"Jesse's no demon," Paul said to her.

I thought of how I'd tried to tell him the truth Above, how he'd scoffed, refused to believe me. How he wanted me to be something I wasn't. Swallowing the lump that had formed in my throat, I said, "Yes, sweetie. I am." With my silent command, my costume slid off my skin, pooled to the ground.

Tracy stifled a scream and slunk backward, seeking shelter behind the base of the sycamore tree. I didn't care about her; my eyes were focused on my love.

Paul stared at me, wide-eyed, his mouth open in an *O*. I heard his heartbeat slamming in his chest, smelled the fear wafting from him like strong aftershave. Once, that smell from him would have been an aphrodisiac, would have inspired visions of me seducing the terror away from him. Now it just made me sad.

"This is me," I said, my voice soft, imploring. "The demon Jezebel. I ran away from Hell, pretended to be a human. Then I met you and fell in love with you. I almost died for you. I earned a soul because of you."

His adam's apple bobbed in his throat as he swallowed, staring at me. The fear in his eyes dimmed, and he squinted, stared through me. "This is how you see yourself?"

"This is who I really am."

"She's evil," Tracy cried from behind the tree. "Get away from her!"

Paul's gaze softened, and a smile blossomed on his lips. "Oh, Jess. You really have no idea, do you?"

I felt my brow furrow. "No idea about what?"

He reached out and clasped my hand. "Who you really are. I see it, like a glow around you."

Did he see my soul beneath my demon's guise? Had he pierced Angel's magic to glimpse the truth? In my mind, I saw Daun's awed face, Angel's look of amazement.

You may call Me sire, if you wish.

Unholy Hell, what was I?

"What do you see?" I asked Paul, dreading the answer.

"I see you." He squeezed my hand. "God, you're so beautiful."

I blushed from the top of my bald head down to my hooves. "Flatterer."

"It's a lie." I couldn't see Tracy's face, but I heard the sulk in her voice. "She's trying to take you away from me."

The sour taste of truth on my tongue, I said to Paul, "She's right, you know. I *am* trying to take you away. This is Hell, sweetie. You don't belong here."

"No!" Tracy emerged from the safety of the tree, claimed Paul's other hand. "She's wrong, she's lying. This isn't Hell, this is Heaven! Here with you, this is Paradise."

"If this were Heaven, love," I said to Paul, "I wouldn't be here. Whatever you think of me, I *am* a demon. And demons can never know Paradise."

Tracy said, "Please, sweetheart, don't listen to her. Just tell her to go away. You can do that. This is your Paradise, here with me."

Paul looked from me to Tracy, and back again, like a kitten watching a tennis match.

"Paul," I said to him, "if anyone's meant for Heaven, it's you."

"Yes," Tracy said, nodding. "That's right. Paul's meant for Heaven. So go away, leave us alone."

Frowning, Paul looked at her, peered through her. "If this were Heaven, why would Jesse try to lure me away?"

Tracy's mouth opened, closed.

"There's no temptation in Heaven," he said.

Or wild parties, from what I heard. I decided to keep my mouth shut.

"Please," Tracy whispered, "stay here with me."

Paul's hand slipped out of my grasp, and my stomach dropped to my knees.

He touched Tracy's pale cheek. Tears sparkled in her eyes, and she smiled at him—a good smile, one full of love.

"I love you, Tracy," he said softly. "And if I'm meant for Heaven, surely you are too."

Her smile froze.

"Jesse's right. This isn't Heaven. And my Tracy is in Heaven."

"Paul," she whispered, "please . . ."

He nudged her away. "Go," he said. "You're not my Tracy."

She gasped, her eyes huge and hurt. "I am. Paul . . . please, sweetheart, it's me . . ."

Paul looked at me. "Can you lead a White Knight away from temptation?"

"Let's find out together." I reached out to him, and he took my hand. Together, we climbed to our feet. I buried my head in his chest, delighting in the feel of the soft curls of hair on his torso. I breathed him in, took his unique scent deep inside of me. "Bless me, Paul, I thought I'd lost you."

"You did," he said, wrapping his arms around me. "But then you found me again."

Covering her mouth with her hand, Tracy scrambled to her feet. She called his name, the sound muffled by her fingers.

His back to her, he didn't reply, but his arms around my waist trembled. I placed my hands over them, easing their quakes.

With a sob, Tracy turned and fled. I watched her leap through the sycamore tree.

Not a false vision, not a temptation: the ghost of Paul's dead fiancée, trapped for eternity here in the Endless Caverns.

Tracy wasn't meant for Heaven after all. But far be it from me to tell Paul that.

Long since stepping through the door and then the mirror, Paul and I wandered around the Endless Caverns. I'd created flashlights so that we could see our way, but that being said, there wasn't anything to see but rocks, rocks, and rocks. Some were enormous and many were tiny, and a handful served as treasure chests of precious gems in the rough. But at the end of the day, they were just rocks. Lots of them.

"You know," Paul said, "I'm starting to believe I'm really dead. We would have run out of air a long time ago."

"Yeah, the not breathing thing has its perks."

"So why am I sweating?"

I shrugged. I had no idea why I could still feel my heartbeat when I had no heart in this form. "Chalk one up in the Mysterious Ways column."

He said, "Tell me again that you know how to get out of here."

"I know how to get out of here," I lied.

"Because maybe I'm crazy, but it seems like we're lost."

I stopped walking and jabbed a finger at his chest. "We're not lost. These are the Endless Caverns. That means the path goes on for a long, long time. If the path was short, don't you think they'd be called the Not So Endless Caverns?"

"I'm just saying."

I put my fists on my hips. "You know, in Hell we take the naming thing seriously."

He held his hands up in a "my bad" gesture. "Okay, sorry."

"Besides," I grumbled, "I don't hear you coming up with a better idea."

"Better than what, walking forever and ever?"

I glared at him. "Are you complaining?"

"Me? Never."

"Good."

"I'm just wondering if maybe next time you rescue me from Hell, you could get directions."

I frowned. "Are you *sure* you're a man?"

"Hey, real men know when they're lost, they better get directions. Or a map. You have a map?"

"I must have left it in my other demonic catsuit."

"Jess."

"Yeah."

"I love you."

I smiled. "Yeah. Me too."

We walked.

And walked.

Finally, even I had to admit that we were going nowhere fast. Crap. I'd been hoping that we could just stroll out of the Caverns, and then I could poof him back Above. But even though I still had my demonic powers (and no way was I looking a gift hellhound in the mouth), I couldn't just bamf us out of the cave. (I'd tried. It had given me a killer headache and a mad desire to burst into showtunes, but it hadn't gotten us out of the cavern.)

Time for Plan B.

After changing my flashlight into a kerosene lantern and placing it on a large rock, I slid the bracelet off my wrist and offered it to Paul.

He eyed it skeptically. "It doesn't really go with my outfit."

"Take it," I said. "It's the Rope of Hecate you bought for me. It'll get you back home."

He blinked once, twice, then said, "Once more, for those of us slow on the uptake."

I explained about Caitlin and the peddler, and how the Hecate was watching me. "The witch wanted me to have the bracelet," I concluded, "and went out of her way to explain how it was a tie to life. Put it on, sweetie, so you can go home."

After a pregnant pause, he said, "You're kidding, right?"

"*Paul . . .*"

He shook his head. "Even if I believed that your jewelry would be an express train out of here, if you think I'm abandoning you, you're insane."

He was the third person (well, entity) to call me crazy in the span of a few hours. It was starting to piss me off. "It's not like you'd be leaving me in the middle of nowhere. This is my stomping ground. I was raised on stuff like this."

"Yeah, and I grew up playing Dungeons and Dragons, so I know a thing or two about underground passages. I'm not leaving you, period."

I frowned at him. "Will you quit the White Knight thing already?"

"In D&D, we were called paladins."

"Damn it all," I said, stomping my hoof, "I'm not joking."

"No, but you're cute when you pitch a fit. Even when you look like something out of *Paradise Lost*."

I counted to ten, decided not to morph him into a salamander. "I can get my way out of here and find my way back home. But I can't do that if I'm also looking out for you."

"So this whole time we've been walking in the dark," he said, doing an impressive Bambi Eyes, "that was you looking out for me?"

I stomped my hoof again. He had no business poking fun at me when I was trying to be all self-sacrificing. It ruined the mood. "What do I have to do to get you to trust me?"

He pulled me close, stared into my green cat's eyes. "Hon, this isn't about trust. You're asking me to leave you here, in the dark, alone. How can I do that? I'm supposed to protect you."

"There's no *supposed to* here, love." I plucked the flashlight from his grasp and tossed it to the rock-strewn ground. Taking his hands in mine, I said, "You're not a cop here. You're not even my lover here. Here, you're just another soul. Take the bracelet and go back to the real world, where you're my man. Go back, and wait for me."

"No."

"Please! Paul, I'm begging you." I dropped to my knees, pleading with my body and my words. "Do this for me."

"Get up, Jess." He gently pulled me to my hooves. "Hon, I can't leave you. It's not right. I'm sorry, but I won't do it."

"For once in your stubborn life, don't be a White Knight. Don't do the right thing. Do the best thing, for you and for us. Please," I said, "trust me."

"I do trust you, Jess." He traced his fingers down my cheek, his calloused fingers soft against the leather of my flesh. "I do. More than ever. You came to Hell to free me. How can you think even for a minute that I would do anything less? I'm not leaving you here, Jesse."

I blew out a frustrated sigh. "You are so damn infuriating."

"This from the woman who went out to a strip club after I asked her not to."

"You didn't ask, you told. And don't change the subject." I rested my head against his chest, and he wrapped his arms around my shoulders. "I was going to move out, you know," I whispered. "After our fight, I thought we were done."

He said nothing for a moment, just held me close as he stroked my shoulder. It felt nice. I closed my eyes, listened to his heart beating in his chest, the sound working its music into my body.

"I'm so sorry about that," he said, breaking the silence. "God, it feels like forever ago. It was stupid, Jess. I'm sorry I hurt you."

"Me too, love." I hugged him tight. "Me too."

"Is this the part where we kiss and make up?"

I looked up at him, saw the love sparkling in his eyes. Bless me, I felt like I could fly. "You bet. Wait, hang on a sec." I let my power wash over me, turning me once again into Jesse Harris, human, sister of a rather annoying know-it-all witch.

"Stop."

"What's wrong?"

"You don't have to do that." He motioned to my face, my body. My human shell. "You don't have to hide what you think you are."

I smiled, feeling melancholy and proud and so much in love. "Sweetie, you've been through a lot today. I mean, we broke up, you got seduced and killed, then you went to Hell. Now you're coming to grips with your girlfriend being a bona fide demon. Ex-demon. Whatever I am. Too much shock is bad for you."

"What's it going to do, kill me?" He smiled, squeezed my shoulder. "Jess, I love you, whatever you look like. You don't have to hide yourself from me."

I wanted to cheer and cry and laugh all at once. "I'm not, love. Think of it as me playing dress-up."

"Jess . . ."

I shushed him with a kiss. His mouth parted, and our tongues touched, connected, rolled together. I gripped him tightly, pulled his torso against my breasts as the kiss deepened. His hands roamed down my back, tripped down my spine and cupped my ass, squeezed. Yum.

He broke the kiss, whispered in my ear: "Please tell me that there's nothing chasing us, that we're really alone and have all the time in the world."

"Endless Caverns," I said, "remember? All we have is time."

"Just checking."

Then his mouth was on my earlobe, sucking the sensitive skin until I moaned. He worked his way down my neck, traced the outline of my collarbone with his tongue. I took his head in my hands, lifted him back up to kiss him again, mashing his lips against mine, showing him with my mouth how much I wanted him inside of me. His rod pushed against his jeans, pressed against my belly, thick with need, announcing his want for me in return.

We moved together, our bodies finding a shared rhythm as our hips danced in slow circles. My fingers trailed down his chest, found his nipples and rubbed them, flicked them until they were erect beneath my touch. He *ummmed*, the sound muffled by our tongues and teeth.

Yes, love. I know.

My hands moved down his torso, brushing over his firm stomach, pausing at his jeans. Even with thousands of years of experience under my belt, I still needed two hands to unfasten his pants and yank them and his underwear down his thighs. His cock saluted my efforts.

Ooh. Ten hut, soldier.

I ran my hand over the thatch of kinky hair just above his engorged penis, traced the V of his groin. Then my fingers danced over his tip, and he quivered beneath my touch. Feeling him want me so much nearly brought me to orgasm by itself— bless me, I loved making him feel so good. Speaking of which . . .

Taking his erection in my hand, I squeezed gently, feeling him throb. Paul moaned into my mouth as I kissed him harder. I stroked him slowly, up to his tip and down to his pubic hair, and back again, rocking my hips with the movement.

One of his hands left my ass, reached behind and under me. Between my legs he found me hot and moist, ready for him. He pressed inside of me, and I gasped as he stroked my nub. My body tensed, a coil ready to spring. Wait, not yet . . .

Biting my lip, I moved his hand away from my lips, stopped stroking his shaft.

"Love?" His breath tickled my neck. "Everything okay?"

"Yes, just have to . . ."

I stopped speaking and instead threw my concentration into creating a futon mattress resting over the jagged ground. Couldn't have the rocks slicing our tender mortal flesh. Once the makeshift bed was in place, we tumbled onto it, our hands already latching onto each other's sex. I rolled him onto his back, then slid my body down his. His erection rubbed against my belly, between my boobs, against my lips. Opening wide, I swallowed him down.

His hands clamped down on my head, but I didn't need his direction to know he wanted me to go faster. And I did, sucking him, pressing my tongue against his cock and fondling his balls with my hand. His groans grew louder, encouraging me to take him even deeper. Yes, love, yes—all for you . . .

Then he moaned, "Stop, please, I want us to come together."

As my White Knight commanded.

With one last kiss on the tip of his shaft, I crawled up the length of his body and mounted him. He thrust himself inside of me, speared me, pierced my core. Limbs entwined, we pumped, me riding him and him bucking up to meet me, our bodies slapping time. Heat pulsed in my groin, my breasts, my thighs; I moved faster, took him deeper, felt liquid fire coursing through my blood as my body tightened, *tightened*—

Paul cried out, his body arching up and up—

—and I screamed in pure pleasure as the orgasm crashed through me—

—and he ejaculated inside of me, our juices mixing like a sex cocktail.

Tangled together, we murmured thank yous and whispered words known only by lovers sharing a climax. Basking in the afterglow of sex, I ran my hands through Paul's hair, enjoying the feel of the curling strands around my fingers. He stretched out beside me, luxuriating in my touch and making contented sounds as I played. Eyes closed, he smiled at me.

I loved his sounds. I loved making him feel good.

I loved him.

Soon his head nodded to the side. The long day of death and afterlife had finally caught up with him. Good. He needed rest. I watched him until I was sure he was truly asleep. Then I slowly unclasped the golden bracelet from my wrist.

A sad smile on my face, I gently lifted Paul's arm and wrapped the jewelry around his wrist. His eyelids fluttered open just as I lined up the clasp.

I kissed his lips, then whispered, "Goodbye, love. I'll see you soon."

His mouth opened, probably to protest. I snapped the clasp closed before he could speak.

The Rope of Hecate glowed—and Paul vanished, his voice calling my name. It echoed in the empty passage of the Endless Caverns until it, like Paul, disappeared.

Chapter 19

Hell

One down.

I stood, shaking off the post-lovemaking soporific dregs. As much as I wanted to curl up and sleep, I didn't have the luxury. Despite what I'd told Paul, there was a Big Bad Evil out there, waiting for me. Every second I delayed was another that Lillith would use to plot something particularly spiteful and nasty. My own fault; I should have listened to Daun and killed her.

You're not a killer, Jesse. Even when you were a demon, you weren't all about death, doom, and damnation.

Well, maybe the damnation part. And, you know, the death thing.

I felt Peaches shrug. *Semantics. You've always cared for others, even here in Hell. That's why you actually have friends, here in the place where friendship is scorned.*

I also seem to have a growing list of enemies.

One that will keep getting longer if you don't start culling the list, one way or another.

What, so you're encouraging me to be all about the vengeance?

If not you, then someone. Otherwise, you may have a very short ride on the mortal coil.

Dandy. My conscience wanted me to hire my very own demon killers.

Hey, Peaches said, *at least one of us should be thinking about your continued survival.*

So, what, should I place a personal ad? Wanted: Demon Hunter? Maybe take a stroll into Van Helsings R Us?

Peaches muttered a slew of curses that nearly set my hair on fire.

Running my hands over my body, I worked my magic to clothe myself in the outfit from my fantasy, enjoying the feeling of the silk wrapping itself around me, girding me, hiding yet flaunting my body. My human body. Whatever I once had been, now I was a mortal. And it was as a mortal that I would help free Meg.

You're insane.

I sighed. *Et tu*, Peaches?

Meg's a Fury. You really think she could be forced into doing anything she doesn't want to do?

She has a warped sense of duty. If she thinks she deserves punishment, she'll allow herself to be punished.

So maybe you should leave it alone. If it's what she wants, who are you to tell her otherwise?

I'm her friend.

She left you to die.

I know. But I love her still.

Humans, Peaches snorted, disgusted. *You guys are really fucked up in the head.*

I knew that too. Sighing, I pinched the bridge of my nose, wondering if the knocking in my brain was Peaches throwing a temper tantrum or if I was on the verge of a migraine. I lowered my hand and lifted my chin. Enough of the mental Damned If You Do thing. Time to get moving, before I lost my nerve.

What I'd said to Paul before was true: in Hell, we take our names seriously. If someone speaks the name of an entity residing in Hell, that entity will hear the speaker, even if it's just a background voice nearly lost in the flotsam of nefarious whisperings. Whether that entity would choose to address (or torture) the speaker was another story. Three times, I decided: speaking her name three times would be enough to get her attention.

"Alecto Erinyes," I called out. "You asked me to go to Hell to save your sister. Alecto Erinyes, I'm here, in Hell. Alecto Erinyes, she who was Jezebel is waiting for you."

In my mind, a presence stirred, a serpent uncoiling. *Jesse Harris. Jezebel. You've come to do as I've asked?*

Yes.

You've come freely, and of your own will?

Yes.

You've come to free Megaera?

Yes.

Then come to me.

The Endless Caverns winked out, and in a blink I was somewhere else. I immediately shielded my face, but not before the brightest of lights dazzled my eyes, momentarily blinding me. Hazard of being summoned by one of the seven most powerful entities in the Universe: sometimes that power shone through, dwarfing everything else.

Crap. I hated dealing with über-powerful entities without my sunglasses.

"You who were the demon Jezebel," Alecto said, her voice deceptively light, almost girlish, "open your eyes."

Licking my lips, I lowered my arm from my face and opened my eyes to stare at a wall of small television screens, stacked like bricks, one atop another—all on, the volume just north of inaudible, and all set to different channels. My vision blurred as I took in the thousands of programs: newscasts and talk shows and political commentary and stand-up routines. I distinctly felt my mind lurch. During the best of times, with Paul lying next to me on the lumpy sofa in his living room, I had trouble trying to follow the text crawler at the bottom of the 24-hour news network while paying attention to the pretty anchors. Trying to focus on even one of Alecto's television screens now was like trying to read every word in the dictionary at once while singing "The Star-Spangled Banner" in five languages simultaneously, in harmony with myself.

Gah.

My head throbbing, I turned away from the television wall to see a collage of thumbnail photographs—hundreds of thousands of them, colorful stills of people in mug shots and glamour poses, in candids and in formals, tacked to the adjacent wall. Each photo had a series of words printed beneath it. Names, I realized: for every photo, a name. Next to that came the bookshelves, teeming with books and tomes and magazines, words crammed into pages, those pages squished into covers, those covers squeezed onto thousands of shelves.

And then there were the maps. Hundreds of them, spread over every spare portion of wall not claimed by a picture or a television screen or a bookshelf: here a section detailing the villas in France; there, topographical drawings of the Australian Outback. From Darfur to Detroit, from Hong Kong to Helsinki, maps and plans and sketches of the corners of the world. If there was a color to the walls, it was long buried beneath televisual and static information. Data as wallpaper.

A ringing sounded in my ears, and my stomach threatened to revolt. Rather than explaining to my body that I couldn't vomit—I was dead, a soul without the need for food—I turned away from the televisions and pictures to focus on the one piece of furniture in the room.

In the center of the floor sprawled a desk easily the size of a pregnant whale. Maybe it was a dining room table and not a desk—it was impossible to tell by its surface, which was completely littered with computers, books, and stacks of paper. Suspended behind the table, floating on nothing, was an enormous whiteboard. On it, in red, was a list. The first three items had check marks to the left of their entries.

√ Kingdom v. Kingdom
√ Nation v. Nation
√ Doctrines of Devils
Tribulation
Famine
Abomination
Earthquakes
Eternal Damnation = Salvation

I had a sinking suspicion these weren't new lyrics to INXS's "Mediate."

Amid the laptops and piles of books, the desk spoke. "I didn't think you were coming."

Standing on my toes, I tried to peer over the mountains of electronics and hardcovers. "Alecto? Erinyes, are you here?"

Mounds of papers were shoved aside, and a stack of books crashed to the hardwood floor, revealing a woman in her mid-thirties, her black hair coiled around her head in elaborate braids. Her exposed skin gleamed like olive oil beneath her rumpled white peasant blouse. A black scarf wrapped around her neck, its pattern mimicking snakeskin. Her lips pressed pencil thin, she stared at me, her large blue eyes so bloodshot that they nearly glowed. Exhaustion clouded her like perfume. I couldn't blame her; I was exhausted just looking around the office.

"Bless me," I said before I could stop myself, "you look horrible."

She smiled tightly. "I think I preferred you completely terrified and polite."

Whoops. I thought about falling to my knees and begging forgiveness, but I couldn't summon the fear to drive me. "I've come too far to be properly frightened, Erinyes."

That earned me a quiet laugh. "Death will do that, I suppose."

"It's a temporary condition."

"Perhaps." She shrugged, her bony shoulders jutting beneath the large shirt. "You're right. I look like shit. You try keeping tabs on all of Hell and most of Earth, see if you get any rest."

"What are you," I asked, "His secretary?"

She opened a desk drawer and tapped in a code, and all the television screens muted. "Majordomo, actually."

The epitome of never-ending fury, trapped behind a desk. I shook my head, marveling at this display of chutzpah on the King's part. Then again, I had to admit, however grudgingly, that it was a particularly smart move. If I were in charge, I couldn't think of a better creature to be my go-to person. The

Erinyes all had an affinity for seeing the truth of things and for predicting the most likely future. Add to that their nearly un-limited power and how almost every creature in existence was completely terrified of them, and you had at your disposal the most important players in all of Creation, save the Devil and the Almighty. And that last was a toss-up; it was rumored that even God Himself gave the Furies a wide berth.

I said, "Your Queen must be thrilled." Lyssa, the bird-woman goddess of madness, wasn't exactly known for her gen-erous spirit; she guarded her role as Queen of the Furies with a mad conceit that made the Arrogant look positively humble.

Alecto grimaced. "Her name isn't spoken here."

Ooh, dirt. "Problems?"

"That isn't your concern." She sighed, closed the cover of the laptop closest to her. "Blessed thing's giving me eyestrain."

"Why don't you change forms, switch into something with stronger eyesight?" Maybe the rabbit from *Monty Python and the Holy Grail.*

Her mouth twisted into a sneer. "Dress code. The King in-sists on human attire when in the office."

"Ah." Workplace rules could be such a bitch. "So, major-domo of the Underworld. Not too shabby. It would look nice on a business card."

She leaned back in her chair, watching me. "I can't decide if your glibness is refreshing or annoying."

"I have that effect on people." One thing about being pushed beyond the limits of my endurance: I got very stupid. Next thing you know, I'd be chasing after the Minotaur, wav-ing a red hat and singing "Raspberry Beret."

But it wasn't just me pushing my luck with the Fury. If I stopped to think about what I was doing, what I intended to do, it would paralyze me. How was I supposed to free Meg from a punishment she believed to be just? So I stalled, hoping that I'd get struck by a brilliant idea. I asked Alecto, "Do the thirteen Kings answer to you?"

"Eleven Kings. And no."

I blinked. "Eleven? But there are thirteen Kings of Sin and Land . . ."

"There've been some changes here in the past month." She leaned forward, closed another computer. "Some larger than others."

Thinking of the ruined Wall and the softening borders between Sins, I shivered. "So I've heard."

"Different rulers have different styles, of course," she said, her elbow resting on the desk and her fist cupping her chin. "He is not the Light Bringer. And some here appreciate that. Boiling down the Ten Great Rules into One, well, some would say that's genius."

"Some would say that's the sign of a megalomaniac."

"Careful," she said.

It was too late for caution. "'Obey your King, or be destroyed.' King Lucifer never had to spell out such threats."

"As I said, times are changing." She glanced at the silent wall of televisions. "Times have to change. The dance for the Devil has gotten more complicated."

"I've heard about some of your changes," I said, remembering the words of the Arrogant after he failed to entice Circe to suicide. "Demons actively encouraging people to sin, instead of waiting until they actually sin before claiming them for Hell. It's wrong."

She shrugged. "Right and wrong, Good and Evil. Black and white. It doesn't work like that. What it all comes down to is survival. The Almighty wants the world and its peoples to survive. And that means keeping the Devil distracted, no matter what the method."

"I've noticed." I motioned to the televisions. "The news is full of goodies about genocide, homicide, patricide. A billion ides. Your doing?"

"To a degree. Humans have always excelled at evil. Now we influence that evil, help it along. Get them here that much quicker."

The irrationality behind the statement was enough to make my head spin. "Didn't it occur to you guys that the worse the mortals are on Earth, the more that will incite the Nameless One to watch Earth, to forget about the tortures of Hell?"

She stared at her hands. "All I can do is advise. I do not make the rules."

"The Rule," I said.

"Right." She paused, drumming her fingers on a stack of books. "He's still new to His role. With time, I think He would do an excellent job. There's a bloodlust to Him that even He hasn't acknowledged."

You are too soft.

Even now, that judgment cut me to the quick.

"But there isn't time." Alecto sighed, leaned back in her chair. "For all of His changes, for all His decrees, it isn't enough. The Nameless One grows bored. You've seen it in the headlines Above. Our influence is nothing compared to that of the Devil."

"So stop fucking around," I said. "Stop enticing people to sin. Save the creativity for Hell itself. Make this place a beacon for Evil, not a shadow of the mortal coil."

Something passed over her face, a string of emotions too quick to follow. Grimacing, she said, "My hands are tied."

"Bullshit. You're one of the most powerful entities in all of Creation. No one can tell you to do anything."

A smile quirked her lips: sour, devoid of mirth. "There are always rules, you who were Jezebel. Just because you broke them, don't think that others can blithely walk that path."

"Why can't you?"

Tears of blood seeped from her eyes, stained her cheeks. "We all do what we must."

Meg's words, Alecto's voice. I wrapped my arms around myself to keep from shivering. "So I've heard."

"I obey the King of Hell. That is the right thing."

My voice soft, I asked, "Is the right thing always the best thing?"

She stared at me, her eyes bleeding. Finally she said, "It's moot. Things are coming to a boil, far quicker than any had anticipated. At this rate, humans will destroy themselves in a matter of years rather than millennia." Alecto glanced at the checklist on the whiteboard.

Tasting bile on my tongue, I said, "If He's not up to the job, get another King."

"Sure," she said, a grim smile on her face. "Are you planning on telling the Almighty that He made a mistake when He reassigned the Light Bringer?"

Thinking about how Earth had morphed into a reflection of the Abyss, of how murder had become entertainment and other people's pain was a catharsis, I said, "I'm not even sure God exists anymore."

And to my surprise, Alecto nodded. "You and me both."

We looked at each other, a Fury chained to a desk and an ex-succubus chained to a soul. "You could always leave," I said.

She closed her eyes, a smile spreading across her face. "You had that choice. I do not. I have my duty."

We all do what we must.

I said, "That seems to be a nasty trait in your family."

"Perhaps." She opened her eyes, pierced me with her gaze. "Why did you decide to help me?"

"Because no matter how much Meg hurt me, I still love her." I opened my arms wide, palms up, trying to express with my hands why I had to act on that love. "She's my friend. I have to help her."

Pursing her lips, Alecto nodded. "Come," she said, rising to her feet. "I'll take you to her."

I frowned, waiting for the rest. This was where she would tell me about the bad-tempered dragon guarding her, or the roomful of lasers that I had to cross. Finally I said, "Just like that?"

Her bloody gaze meeting my eyes, she nodded again. "Just like that. My sister is in the next room."

We materialized somewhere else, and I teetered for a moment before I found my balance. I hated it when entities bamfed me around without any warning. It was murder on the inner ear.

Alecto's office had been lit by the television screens and a few standing halogen lamps; this room blazed from ten crystal candelabras dangling from the vaulted ceiling like a string of diamonds. Elaborate silver sconces dotted the walls, stuffed with fat white candles, the wicks glowing softly, their light mixing with that of the chandeliers: electric candlelight. At the peak of the rounded ceiling was a speck of red sky—a window, perhaps, or a skyway entrance into the chamber.

Vertigo washed over me, so I tore my gaze away from that tiny skylight, focused instead on what was eye-level. Two tiers of rectangular mirrors decorated with ivory thorns lined the long walls, stretching the huge room—easily fifteen meters all around—into something gargantuan. The marble floor and walls reflected the light, casting the entire room in a pearl opulence. I swallowed, uneasy. White had never been my favorite color.

The elite weren't big on furniture, I noticed. Here, as in Alecto's office, there was exactly one piece of furniture: directly before me stood a dais, three steps swathed in red velvet. On the top step sat a large marble chair, high-backed and wide, its arms and edges carved with the faces of lions snarling in attack, of bulls charging, of eagles with open beaks and talons, ready to do violence.

The throne of Hell. It looked as uncomfortable as I felt.

Above it, fastened to the wall directly over the seat of the Abyss . . .

. . . was Megaera.

Staring at the ruined form of my friend, I bit back a cry. She hung, spread-eagled, manacled to the wall by her wrists and ankles. Her body drooped from the weight of chains wrapping her limbs and torso like iron vipers. The small flashes of exposed skin on her arms and legs were charred, blackened with glimpses of oozing red. Her head hung low, her long brown hair a tangled curtain hiding her features. Only her aura—pale blue, pulsing weakly—proved her to be Meg, my Meg, a creature of patience and terror, of passion and steadfast duty.

My hand by my mouth, I whispered, "Meg."

She lifted her head, and this time I did cry out. Blood streaked from the holes where her eyes had been. Fixing those empty sockets on me, Meg spoke, her voice a harsh rasp. "Jezzie."

"Oh, you stupid thing," I said, running up to her, "what did you let Him do to you?" I strode up the dais, climbed onto the marble throne and reached up, touched her bare foot hanging over my head. The toenails had been plucked out, and spikes had been driven into her feet. Overkill, I thought numbly— the manacles were enough to fasten her body to the wall. The only purpose of the nails had been to inflict even more pain.

How long had she subjected herself to torture, all because of me?

Meg spoke again, her words lacerating me like hot blades. "You shouldn't have come."

"I know," I said, wondering if Angel could heal Meg's wounds, soothe her spirit. "After what you did to me, I should have left you here to rot."

She sighed, a sound of defeat. "No. You shouldn't have come because it's a trap."

Chapter 20

The Throne Room

I frowned up at Meg, hanging like a piece of performance art. "Be quiet. I'm here to rescue you."

"Jezzie," she said. "I'm so sorry."

"Hush. I need to think." It hit me then that I had no idea how I was supposed to free her, let alone return to the mortal coil. Mental note: Finish planning the rescue before executing it.

Meg said, "Please, go. Go before He comes."

"I'm not leaving you. Now shut up." What would my White Knight do? I reached out with my power, tried to unlock the chains, but something slapped me away like a metaphysical demon swatter.

Crap.

"Sire," Alecto said from behind me, "she is here, as promised."

YES.

The voice exploded in my mind, tore through me like shrapnel. I fell backward, barely felt the impact of crashing to the floor. My hands fisted against my head, tried to muffle the reverberating sound.

I AM COMING.

Those words thundered, building in my mind until they were the roar of stars colliding, bursting in a supernova to rock the rim of Creation. Curled like a fetus, I chewed my lip to keep from shrieking.

Fuuuuuck.

His words echoed, then gradually faded, but the air remained charged from their power—the fine hairs on my body stood on end and electricity kissed my body, crackling softly as it traveled up my spine, my skull. Arms wrapped over my head, I shook with aftershocks of agony. Unholy Hell, I hurt all over. It felt like my brain was about to rupture. Fine with me, just please do it fast.

Through the lingering pain, I distinctly heard Alecto sigh. "He has a tendency to overcompensate."

I couldn't answer her; I was too busy trying to keep my brains from leaking out of my ears.

Above me, Meg whispered, "Perhaps you should tell Him that."

Alecto sniffed. "He already has one wall hanging. I'm not eager to add to His art collection."

"Jezzie, please. Run."

"Too late," Alecto said. "From the moment she first ran, it was too late."

Grinding my teeth to keep from screaming, I stared up at Alecto. Nothing on her face registered any guilt. "You asked me to save your sister." My voice was a raw wound, seeping with hurt, both physical and emotional. How could she have betrayed me?

"I asked many things." Blood gleamed in her blue eyes, turning her gaze a royal purple. "I asked Daunuan to entice you back, and he was all too happy to agree. I asked Lillith to force you back, and once I healed her, she swore on her name to do whatever it took. Between the three of us, I knew you would once again return to Hell."

Black spots swam in the edges of my vision, and I felt my heart shrivel. They'd played me. All of them. Daun and Lillith, I could understand—whether lust for sex or lust for revenge, I could understand obsessive desire. But Alecto? "Why?"

"I promised our sovereign ruler that I would deliver you to

Him, Jesse Harris, willingly, in exchange for my sister's freedom."

My throat tight, I asked again, "Why?"

The Fury smiled grimly. "While you are here, at His mercy, He will be distracted. And then I can do His job, far better than He. I can put Hell back to where it needs to be."

A gust of icy wind swirled around me, chilling me, freezing my pain. My teeth chattered, and when I ground them closed my body shook violently. I doubled over as the wintry gale teased my flesh with goosebumps. Pit swallow me, it really was a cold day in Hell.

Over the sounds of my shivering: the sound of wings slapping the air.

I looked up to the skyway above, my hair swirling around my face, stinging my eyes. Against the dot of red sky, a white speck winked. As I watched it grew larger, soon taking the outline of a man with bird's wings. I felt His presence—power, sweet Sin, such raw power!—long before I saw His face. The frosty air that surrounded me was nothing compared with the tendrils of cold fear that worked their way up my body, icing my heart, chilling my courage.

"Too late," Meg said like a sob. "Jezzie, I'm so sorry."

The shape slowly approached from above, the powerful wings beating the air as if it were insignificant. Now I saw His features: the frozen beauty of a winter sunrise, the threatening power of a snow-capped precipice a breath away from an avalanche. It wasn't so much that He glowed; He was the epitome of light, captured in flesh—alabaster, pure, a living statue of ivory. From His dove's wings to the thick wavy locks crowning His head, He was white—save for His eyes, which blazed with emerald fire.

I'd seen those eyes before, set in another's face, but on Lucifer, they had brimmed with bitterness and sorrow, had glinted with dying hope. On the creature hovering above me, those green eyes burned with cold fury.

His bare feet touched the dais, stark white against the bloody red velvet. His wings beat once more, then folded against His back, poised to strike, weapons even at rest. He wore beauty like a garment cut from expensive cloth; His naked body was too perfect to be handsome, far too cold to ever suggest the warmth of desire. He stared down at me, those green eyes weighing me, finding me wanting.

Michael, Archangel, King of Hell.

Cowering on the floor, my limbs half-frozen, I tore my gaze away and touched my forehead to the ground. Always show respect to those who could destroy you on a whim.

"Alecto Erinyes," He said, His voice as soft as falling snow. My heart jackhammered so loudly that I almost didn't catch the words. "You have succeeded where your sister failed."

"Yes, Sire," the Fury said—not smug, not proud. She spoke simply, as if she'd confirmed that yes, she did place the order for lunch. Nothing about her tone conveyed that she, like her sister before her, had betrayed me.

Mental note: Stop trusting the Erinyes.

Mental note, part two: Learn important lessons before imminent death.

I wondered what dying felt like when you were already dead.

"So," Michael said, "this is the tempter who thought she could outwit Hell." Something nudged my ribs—His foot. I hadn't heard him approach. Paralyzed from fear and cold, I remained prone, hiding my face. "She doesn't look like much."

"The Light Bringer held her in high regard, Sire," Alecto said. "His kiss is still visible on her lips."

He did? It was?

Lillith's voice, snide, mocking: *He would ask about you.*

That did it: all female residents of the Abyss were utterly insane. If I weren't beside myself with terror, I would have told Alecto that her mother obviously had dropped her on the head one too many times. (Not that she actually had a mother.)

The prod jabbed into a sudden kick, and I grunted.

"You constantly remind Me that the Light Bringer had done this, or the Light Bringer had done that," Michael said, His voice like frostbite. "I grow sick of such constant reminders,

Fury. What do *I* care for what the Light Bringer has done? His reign is over."

"Sire, I meant no disrespect."

"I grow sick of you, Alecto, you and your sister both. Perhaps Tisiphone would serve Me better as an advisor."

Tension hummed in the air like a diamondback's rattle before Alecto spoke. "I'm sure our other sister would be honored, Sire."

"I will think on it." The voice moved away from me, but my body felt even colder than before, as if His kick had laced me with ice. "Tell Me, you who were Jezebel. What was it that finally brought you back to Hell freely of your own accord? How did the Fury convince you?"

"She didn't, Lord." My words were a bare squeak. As mind-numbingly frightened as I was, I couldn't bring myself to call Him "sire." For me, there would be only one true Sire of Hell.

"No?" Amusement tempered the chill of His voice. "What, then?"

I swallowed hard before I answered. "Lillith stole the soul of my love."

"Did she now?" Frost, hinting of an impending blizzard.

"He was innocent, Lord," I said through clenched teeth. He could destroy me only once; I had little to lose by venting my anger. "She had no right to claim him for Hell."

"You don't say. Tell Me how your former Queen stole the soul of your love."

"I heard sounds from his apartment. When I entered, I saw Lillith seducing him. She had taken my shape, tricked him into thinking she was me." My voice wavered as my mind flashed on Paul bucking beneath Lillith, her hips on his, her eyes on mine. "And then she killed him and took his soul, abandoned it in the Endless Caverns."

"And how do you know this?"

"I returned to Hell to save him, and she attacked me. When I bested her, she admitted to me where he was."

"How do you know she did not lie?"

"I found him, Lord." The words fell from my lips, and as I

spoke, something tightened in my chest: Anticipation. "I saved him from the Caverns. He's Above. Safe."

A long pause, and then He said, "So the one-time Queen thinks she can ignore My rule?"

I felt something icy brush past my mind, an arctic gust riding the air, but I couldn't make out the words behind the power. A command from the King of Hell, but not for my ears. And then a rending sound, as if the air itself were being torn asunder: a door opening like a scream. With the scream came smells—garlic, raw and overpowering; new money, crisp and heady; burned coffee and old sweat; roses; sautéed onions. Beneath those odors, weaving them together, was the cloying stench of wet dog covered with dirt. The sound of footfalls on marble, the palpable feeling of hatred and cold certainty of terror—the crushing sense of a sudden throng.

Despite myself, I looked up. And then ducked my head, wanting desperately to be anywhere else, even at the bottom of the Lake of Fire.

They lined the walls of the throne room, four rows thick, wearing human forms and radiating malefic ire—the demon lords, the principals and dukes, entourages to the most powerful of the nefarious. Prone on the ground, their heads touching the floor, they waited, an undeniable anxiety working its way through them, bordering on panic. Bowing before the throne, ten figures offered supplication: the great Kings of Sin and Land.

This, I thought bleakly, was really bad.

"My Court." Michael's voice filled the room with ice. "I have summoned you here to witness My judgment on one of your own."

A sudden smell: a splash of scented oil. Then a startled squawk and a gasp.

I glanced up again, and this time my gaze held. In the center of the chamber, Lillith and Asmodai hastened to untangle their sweaty limbs, the smell of their sex play wafting over them. Together, naked, they fell before the throne, displaying absolute reverence.

"Lillith, First Woman. I know you of old," Michael said. "With the Almighty's command, I cast you from the Garden."

Her body folded over itself, Lillith showed no reaction. She was much braver than me; if His voice had been lacerating me like that, I would have pissed myself.

He said, "You have come far. You have prostituted yourself since the dawn of Creation, offered yourself to whoever could increase your power. You were a Queen of Hell."

I saw a shiver work its way down her back.

"You have ambition," He said. "You wish to sit by My side, to have My ear. You wish to be My mate."

Next to her, Asmodai stirred but said nothing.

Michael said, "Your ambition ends here."

She looked up. Because I was sprawled before the throne, I saw her face clearly, her beautiful, malleable features stamped with abject terror.

"You are charged with stealing the soul of an innocent, with abandoning it in the Endless Caverns for eternal damnation." He spoke without passion, almost as if bored. "How do you answer this charge?"

"Sire," she whispered, "please, let me explain—"

He said again, "How do you answer this charge?"

She swallowed, averted her eyes. "Not guilty, Sire."

"You lie. Your guilt stains you like a pox."

Tears glinted in her eyes. "Sire, please. Mercy."

"No."

Smoke drifted up beneath her, and a look of horror crossed her face. My nostrils pinched with the stink of burning meat. Biting my lip, I stared at her wide-eyed as Michael passed judgment.

The flesh of her legs bubbled, flowed off her like oil, and the muscles slid away from the bones. She screamed, reached out, begging forgiveness as her body slowly melted. She screamed as her legs disappeared, as her spine peeled away from her back, as her breasts flapped off like discarded wrapping paper. She screamed until her tongue fell from her mouth and her face slid off her skull. Her skeleton reached out once more, then crashed to the marble floor. There it, too, melted, until all that was left of her was a pool of shifting liquid, now bronze, now golden, winking with all the colors of every race of man.

Lillith, once the Queen of the Succubi, was gone.

Oh fuck.

"**A**smodai, King of Lust."

The incubus was staring so intently at the bubbling liquid that had been his lover that at first he didn't respond. His dusky skin had gone pale, and his handsome face was drawn into an ugly grimace. Then he shook his head. Blinking shocked eyes, he turned to face Michael. "Sire?"

"Your Queen insulted Me with her action."

Sweat beaded on Asmodai's brow. "Sire, she acted without my authority. I had no idea she was seducing the innocent—"

"Indeed. And what else are you unaware of, little King?"

Asmodai's mouth clicked shut. Rivulets of sweat meandered down the sides of his face.

I watched, horrified and fascinated, like it was an oncoming car crash. I knew what was about to happen and I was powerless to stop it.

"You allowed yourself to be blinded by your Queen." Michael shook His head, a parent disappointed with its progeny. "You are a fool, Asmodai. And I do not suffer the presence of fools."

"Sire—"

Michael said nothing. He didn't move, didn't narrow His eyes—didn't show any reaction. But Asmodai's voice gave way to a tortured scream, and even before his flesh began to bubble off his frame, it was clear that once again, the King of Hell had passed judgment.

Smelling Asmodai's slow death, I turned away, forced the bile back down my throat.

An indeterminable amount of time passed, punctuated with the sizzle of frying meat. Finally, Michael said, "My Court. You have witnessed My judgment. Learn well from this lesson. Especially you, Pan. You are now King of the Seducers. I encourage you to do better than your predecessor."

I didn't see the satyr god, but I heard him mumble something that was either a thanks or a curse. Maybe both.

"We shall discuss your coronation later. For now, you are all dismissed. Go."

At Michael's command, the demons vanished, only their lingering stench marking where they had been. I stared hard at the spreading stains on the floor, the reddish brown marring the perfect white of the marble. I had despised Lillith more than anything in all of Creation, had wished for her annihilation too many times to count. But I hadn't wanted her to die like this.

I didn't want to be the cause of her death.

Bless me, I was such a sorry excuse of an ex-demon.

"Now then," Michael said. "Whatever shall I do with you, little whore?"

Eep.

Alecto cleared her throat. "Sire, now that You have the runaway, I most humbly request that You release my sister into my care."

"Denied."

Something cracked on Alecto's impassive face—the slightest pull of her lips, the barest hint of anger flashing in her eyes. "Sire, You promised . . ."

"I am beyond such limitations, Erinyes."

All living beings have a breaking point, that fabled point of no return, when absolutely nothing can faze them. In the past twenty-four hours, I'd been manipulated, threatened, broken up with, betrayed, assaulted, seduced, killed, terrified, and tempted. I'd run the full gamut of emotion. I was done. Finished. Nothing could scare me beyond where I'd been—I thought that nothing could shock me further. But Michael so blatantly breaking His word pushed me past that breaking point. Demons lie, but Kings are supposed to rule. If Kings lied, their rules are meaningless.

King Lucifer had never lied, not in all the thousands of years I had known Him.

Alecto's mouth opened, possibly to beg for her sister's pardon, possibly to insist on it; I'd never know. Because that was when I said, "Let her go, Lord."

A heavy pause, then: "Who are you, to demand anything of Me?"

I sat up, held my chin high. Michael was leaning back in the marble throne, brooding. As I dared to meet His gaze, His green eyes narrowed, and His hands gripped the armrests tightly.

"Her friend, Lord," I said. "Let her go."

"Would you take her place?"

Shit. "Yes, Lord."

From above: "No."

I glanced up at Meg, saw something close to horror on the ruins of her face. "That is not acceptable," she whispered. "The punishment is mine, not hers."

A cold smile blew across His white lips. "And you agree with your punishment, Megaera, don't you?"

"With mine, Sire, yes. But it is mine alone."

"Indeed." He stared at me, that blessed smile playing on his face. "I won't let her go."

By my side, my fists shook. In one word, I expressed my disgust, my despair: "Why?"

"I could tell you it is because her sister tries My patience, continues to push Me in directions I do not wish to go. I could tell you that I wish to continue punishing her for failing to retrieve you when you ran away." Michael's eyes gleamed, brightened, and the smile melted from his mouth. "In truth, it is because you balked My authority. You, a minor succubus. And so I keep Megaera here, serving as a reminder to all that if they, too, choose to balk My authority, they will pay a price."

"Take me instead." My voice cracked and my lip trembled, but my gaze never wavered. "I'm the one who embarrassed You. Let her go. Hang me upon Your wall, use me as a Christmas tree ornament, whatever You wish. But let her go."

He watched me for a moment before He said, "You love her, don't you?"

"Yes, Lord."

"Love. How quaint." Michael shrugged. "If she really wished to leave, even I couldn't stop her. Megaera suffers because that is what she wants."

My mouth dropped open. Staring up at Meg, I asked, "Is this true?"

Hiding herself behind her curtain of matted hair, she didn't answer.

"Bless me, Meg," I cried, "I forgive you."

Her voice soft, she said, "But I don't forgive myself."

Chapter 21

The Throne Room

"**F**orgiveness," Michael said. "Another charming concept."

"Charming?" I looked away from Meg to see Michael smiling tightly, the look almost a smirk. That condescending sneer transformed His wintry beauty into something bordering on repulsive—rot creeping beneath the petals of a peace lily. I said, "You of all beings should know that it's all about forgiveness."

The smirk froze into place. "You dare . . . ?"

"You insult friendship. Fine. That I understand—this is Hell, and Hell has no patience for any loyalty other than to itself. But forgiveness?" I spread my arms wide, taking in all of the Abyss. "If not for forgiveness, how could the damned be redeemed?"

He smiled again, bemused. "Who said anything about redemption, little whore?"

That hit me like a sucker punch in the gut.

"Times are changing," Alecto said from behind me, her girlish voice strained, tired. "Times must change. The damned no longer have any hope for Heaven. They remain here, for the eternal amusement of the Nameless Evil."

A shudder worked its way up my spine. I wrapped my arms around my stomach, but I couldn't stop from shivering. "But King Lucifer said the entire reason for Hell was to make mortal souls worthy of Heaven. That's our purpose."

Michael shouted, "*He* is no longer your King!" He pointed at me, His alabaster finger threatening to shoot me into oblivion. "You will not compare Me to Him! Do you hear Me, slut?"

Biting my lip, my eyes fastened on His feverish green gaze. In my mind, my Sire's voice whispered: *Listen*.

"I hear You," I said, either to Lucifer or to Michael—one King or another, it didn't matter. I listened as Michael spoke . . .

"I am sick of always hearing His name. His reign is done. He has been removed from here by the Almighty. I am King of Hell, not Him. No one has the authority to refuse Me."

And through the growl of cosmic power, over the undertone of rage, I heard the insecurity in His voice, the sheer frustration that danced along the edge of dejection.

Bless me, He was just a little boy. The oldest of little boys, and almost on par with God in terms of power, but just a child needing to be praised.

Listen.

I thought of Ranger from Spice, of all my customers in the Champagne Room who begin so nervously, who think they have to prove something before they can get what they want. Most of my clients think they want me to dance for them, think that the fantasy of flesh is what they crave. Even they don't know that usually most of them want to talk, to have a sympathetic ear, to be told that their small lives are important.

That they matter.

"It must be hard," I said to Michael.

His eyes glinted, jade sparkling in an ivory frame. "What is?"

"Having Your subjects think of Him when they hear Your words. Always being compared with someone else."

He stared at me, hard, His eyes drilling into me, seeking the truth behind my words. "Alecto," He said. "Leave us."

"Yes, Sire." A tickle of sulfur, and she was gone. Suspended above, Megaera said nothing, faded into the background like a shredded painting.

"You who were Jezebel," Michael said. "You speak as though you understand Me. You can never understand Me."

"Of course not, Lord." I bowed my head slightly, a token of deference. "I can only try to imagine what it must be like. You've been appointed to this most important of roles, and instead of seeing You, those around You continue to see the One who was here before. It must be infuriating."

"You have no idea," He said, leaning back in the throne as if seeking refuge. "To finally be rewarded as I should have been from the first, only to have His name constantly shoved at Me . . ." He bared His teeth, which shone as whitely as His naked skin. "What must I do to be free of Him?"

For an Archangel, he radiated sin—envy, pride, jealousy . . . even lust: a lust for acknowledgement, a consuming hunger for self-fulfillment. I said, "Only Your best, Lord."

His gaze sizzled green fire. "I am. But even so, all I get is criticism. From Alecto with her comparisons that sting worse than scorpions. From the Kings, yammering with their quiet demands, their enormous ambitions. From everyone."

"It must be difficult to be so patient," I said, thinking of how He had destroyed Asmodai for being a fool. No, stop— don't be a hypocrite. Believe your words. "No one could possibly understand the pressure of being King of Hell."

"No one," He agreed.

"You were appointed for a reason," I said. "Surely, what other creatures do or think doesn't matter, when compared with the Almighty's belief in Your ability."

"The Almighty." He covered His eyes with a pale hand. "The Almighty won't speak with Me, won't offer either guidance or praise. He doesn't even voice any criticism. He threw Me here in Hell and abandoned Me."

Frowning, I said, "Lord, I don't understand. You said that You were finally rewarded as You should have been long ago. Don't You want to be King of the Pit?"

"Want? I want what I have ever wanted. I want the Almighty to recognize all that I have done for Him."

"Lord?"

"*I* convinced Abraham to sacrifice a ram instead of his son, and *I* saved his grandson not once but twice. *I* taught Adam to farm and Moses the Law. *I* was the first of the angels to bow before humans," He said, snarling, "to accept the Almighty's decree that humans are our superiors because they can act for themselves. I am Saint Michael the Archangel, Viceroy of Heaven."

His voice echoed in the chamber as I absorbed His words. I had to admit, He had a damn impressive résumé. And enough personal issues to keep a therapist in business for at least three lifetimes.

"All I ever wanted," Michael said, "was His love. But the Almighty saved that love for one other, had none left for Me."

"Perhaps He showed you His love in other ways," I said. "He did appoint you King of Hell, after all."

"Yes, at the Almighty's word, We switched roles. Now the Morning Star is a psychopomp, the overseer of death, and I am King of the damned." He laughed, a bitter sound that reminded me so much of Lucifer. "I am an Archangel. What do I know of damnation?"

Maybe it was the laugh that struck a chord; maybe it was His words. Maybe it was the memory of Lucifer's advice. Whatever the reason, I suddenly understood what I needed to do.

I rose to my feet, took a step toward the dais. "You are learning, Lord. Things take time."

"Time that I don't have." He sighed, a mournful note in the chill air of the throne room. "Alecto told you her latest projections, did she not? The Nameless One stirs. No matter what I do, it is not enough."

My foot touched the bottom of the dais. "Lord, You are still new to the role. You are exploring new options, doing things that Your predecessor had never imagined." Like softening the boundaries of Sin. Like replacing Seducers with virginal holiness. As horrific as those actions were to the denizens of Hell, at least He'd tried to do something different. The old way had no longer been enough; if it were, then Lucifer would still be King of Hell.

Times had to change, as Alecto said. And Michael, whatever else He was, brought with Him vast change.

Maybe it would be enough to tempt the Devil and save the world.

As if He had read my mind, Michael said, "It is not enough."

"No," I agreed. "Not yet. But Lord, Alecto said to me that she thinks you will do an excellent job."

He lowered His hand to peer at me. "You are not lying. I see that clearly. The Erinyes really said that to you." His voice trailed off, sounding lost.

"She did, Lord. Sire," I said, swallowing, testing the word on my tongue as I walked up the dais steps. "You can be a superb ruler of the Abyss. You can keep the Devil Itself from destroying the mortal coil. You can do this, Sire."

He looked at me, standing at the foot of His throne. "How do you know this? How *can* you know this?"

I reached out, touched His hand, its flesh so cold that it burned. "I don't know, Sire. But I believe. You stand just beneath the Almighty in power. Nothing is beyond You. All You have to do is want to rule well, Sire. Want it," I said, moving to the side of the throne, "and it will happen."

"Want," He said, staring at my hand on His. "And what do you know of want, you who were Jezebel?"

Remember, Lucifer had said, *even the butcher may turn piper.*

Standing next to where He sat, I stroked Michael's cheek, so cold, so perfect—so needing to be warmed with another's touch. "If there's one thing I do know, Sire, it's want."

Before He could say anything else, I leaned forward and kissed Him. I opened my mouth, ran my tongue over those frosty lips. He made a sound, but I swallowed the gasp of surprise. His mouth opened and I reached in, touched His tongue with mine, shared my heat as I moved in slow circles in His mouth. He tasted like falling snow.

Leaning against Him as I deepened the kiss, my breasts pressed against his cold flesh, and my nipples pebbled from the contact.

Let me melt You, show You that someone understands . . .

I was so lost in the kiss that I didn't realize something was wrong until I couldn't feel my lips.

My eyelids fluttered, but refused to open; my tongue was a sheet of ice. Numbness spread across my face, lacerating my flesh with threads of frost. I forced my eyelids open, felt the yank of my lashes pulling free. Tears welled up and chilled over, stealing my sight. My lids throbbing, I blinked away the ice until it softened and thawed, finally meandering down my cheeks. When my vision cleared, I saw the pure white of Michael's face, the bright green of his hungry eyes as He devoured my kiss.

With a cry I pulled myself away, then shrieked from the searing pain at the base of my throat. Blood gushed from my mouth. I clasped my hands over my stinging lips, felt the hot liquid seep between my fingers, the thick heat sliding down the raw wound until I coughed, choking.

Michael grinned, my frozen tongue dangling from His red-stained mouth before He opened wide and sucked it in. Chewing, He smiled at me, working His jaws and grinding His teeth before He swallowed.

"You taste divine," He said.

In that one moment, all I could think of was attacking Him, destroying Him. And in my agony and my rage, I summoned my power and cocked my fist back, a breath away from releasing it. I couldn't win against an Archangel, let alone one on par with King Lucifer. It would be the last thing I ever did. I would be annihilated. But maybe, just maybe, I'd take Him with me.

Come on, You holy bastard. Let's dance.

"Stop."

Meg's voice froze me where I stood. My muscles quivered, crying for movement; my magic sizzled through my body, begging to be released. But the Fury had commanded me to stop. And so, I was stopped.

I was really starting to hate it when other entities forced me to their will. Being a demonic Barbie doll really sucked.

From above, the sound of iron against iron. The chains fell to the floor with an enormous crash, followed by the clang of four spikes.

"Megaera," Michael growled, "this does not concern you."

She floated down, landed before me, her back facing me.

Reaching back to place one hand on my shoulder, she said, "It does, Sire. She would not be here, if not for me. That responsibility is mine."

"And you are here because of her," He said.

"Not any more, Sire." Power flowed through her, hummed beneath her hand and worked its way through my body. My blood sang with magic, coursed through me, soothing my hurt and easing my pain. Healing me. It bubbled over the tear in my mouth, sealed it. And then it slowly knit me a new tongue.

It hurt like a motherfucker, and when it finally was done I wanted to crawl under a rock and bury my head until the pain ebbed away. Instead I stared at the King of Hell, my face impassive, seething inside with such rage that the Berserkers would have mistaken me for one of their own.

To Meg I said, "Thank you."

"You're welcome, Jez." She squeezed my shoulder, and I pulled my murderous gaze from Michael to look at her. Meg turned and smiled—a pale shadow of her usual easygoing grin, but a real smile all the same—and winked one of her sky-blue eyes. All signs of her torture, gone in a flash of power. It was good to be one of the mightiest entities in all of Creation.

Of course, one of the other ones was squatting on the marble throne across from us.

"I never meant for my sentence to be bait, to get you to return to Hell willingly. But you did." She arched an eyebrow. "Even if it wasn't for me at first."

"I was sort of pissed off at you."

Her smile stretched into a grin. The devil-may-care attitude looked good on her. "Have I told you that I'm glad you weren't obliterated? No one else speaks to me like one of the girls. I would have missed that."

"Erinyes," Michael said softly, dangerously. "I did not permit you to end your punishment."

The humor disintegrated from her face as she turned to face Him. "I did not need Your permission, Sire. My punishment is done." She was polite, but a sex-crazed rhesus monkey would have shown more deference. Everything from her tone to her stance suggested that she was speaking to an equal. In terms of sheer power, she was. "I have been forgiven by the one I had wronged."

His eyes narrowed. "You wronged Me, when you failed in your duty."

"There are some bonds stronger than those of duty." She squeezed me once more, then released my shoulder. "By Your leave, Sire."

Eek! "You're leaving me? Now? Here with Him?"

She nodded. "I have to speak to Alecto. She and I need to have a little understanding."

"Couldn't you pick a more convenient time to do the talk show make-up thing?"

"We all do what we must, Jezzie. Besides," she added with an innocent smile, "I know how this all plays out."

I hissed, "For those of us who aren't cursed with foresight, could you maybe offer a hint?"

Her smile broadened. "No. You'll have to get there on your own."

For a best friend, she could be such a bitch.

She bowed to Michael and repeated, "By Your leave, Sire."

He nodded, once, His eyes flashing.

Meg raised her arms and took flight. I watched her soar up and up, until she was a dot against the red skyway far above. And then she flew out of sight.

"Now then," the King of Hell said, "where were we? Oh, yes. I was about to destroy you."

Crap.

"**Y**ou think you can kiss Me and charm Me, that you can touch Me as if there were a connection between us." He smiled His contempt. "I will not be tempted by one such as you."

As if that explained why he'd ripped my tongue out with His teeth. I lifted my chin high. "It wasn't meant to be temptation."

"No? What then, little whore?"

"It was a mistake. I thought that I understood You, understood having to be something You're not."

"You understand *nothing*."

No shit, Sherlock. Now that I had a new tongue, I wasn't that eager to get it ripped out again, so I said nothing while He ranted.

"Before, you spoke so easily of want. I don't want Hell. I don't want any of Lucifer's leftovers." That last word He emphasized with a pointed sniff at me.

Fuck you, too, you self-righteous asswipe.

"But wants don't matter," He said. "I am the King of Hell. I have no choice. Except, perhaps, on whether I will eat another of your body parts. Maybe this time, I'll chew on your heart."

I was too enraged to be terrified by His threat. Either He'd eat me alive and kill me dead, or He wouldn't. But I wasn't going to stand there and listen to how He had no choice but to be King, poor thing—and no alternative but to destroy everything Hell had been. "You *do* have a choice. All creatures have choices, even if they don't want to make them."

"It has nothing to do with *want*!" The words echoed in the cold air. He clenched His teeth, gripped the armrests of the throne until His arms shook. "Only those with free will may choose. Only humans. For the celestial and the nefarious, there are only roles. There is no choice."

"I made a choice before I became human." I offered him my most innocent smile, one that had won over six American presidents and three European kings. "If a minor succubus can do it, You certainly can."

He shouted, "What *I* can do is torture you for eternity! I can string you up before the legions of Hell and have you drawn and quartered!"

I should have been on my knees, begging for mercy, terrified down to my core. I should have felt something other than scooped out, hollow. But I was beyond fear, beyond rage: clear-headed, and so very cold inside.

I preferred the heat of fury.

"I can crucify you every sunrise," He said, getting into the rhythm of intimidation, "and bury you alive every nightfall!"

As Michael voiced His threats, it hit me that if He had intended to do any of that, He would have already done so. He was full of bluster, spouting Shakespearean sound and fury.

The King couldn't hurt me, not any more than He already had.

He said, "I will rip your head from your body and fly it up to the top of Abaddon itself. I will place it there on a spike, as a warning to any who think they could defy Me!"

"No, Lord." My voice was steady, calm. "You will do no such thing."

"You dare speak that way to Me?" He riddled me with His gaze, green as Envy incarnate. "Who are you, little whore, to tell Me what I will not do?"

I smiled, thinking of my Sire, of the only King I would ever willingly follow. "I'll tell you who I'm not. I'm not the demon Jezebel, not anymore. Your problem was with her. Your contract was on her head, not mine. And Lucifer Himself said that contract was null and void, thanks to my human soul. My clean human soul."

If it hadn't already been an icebox in the throne room, His look would have dropped the temperature by twenty degrees.

"That's right, Lord," I said, fueled by His unspoken ire. "The innocent can't go to Hell, not unless You mean to steal them away from Heaven. And while that might be damn amusing to the Devil, I have a feeling Your boss won't cotton to it."

"And now you profess to know the will of the Almighty?" He smiled thinly. "If that's not pride, I don't know what is."

"No, Lord, not pride. Simple fact: Hell was outsourced to Heaven, not the other way around." Something clicked into place. "That's why You punished Lillith, isn't it? She did the one thing that even You would be answerable for in the eyes of the Almighty. You can't punish the innocent." Not for long, anyway.

He said, "Innocence is subjective."

"Not when it comes down to the soul. Paul was innocent.

And I've done nothing wrong that would land me here permanently."

"You chose to be here."

"I was manipulated into making the choice."

Michael stared at me, dark thoughts flashing behind those emerald eyes. "You are a slut who tempts mortals with lust."

And He was an egotistical schmuck, but I didn't say so. Look at that—I had better manners than the King of Hell. Wonders would never cease. "My entertainment keeps mortals from acting on that lust, Lord. And You know it. You can't judge humanity by its dreams. You can't condemn them for their fantasies. Only their actions, Lord."

"Intentions matter, little whore."

"Maybe," I said. "But actions matter more."

He sniffed his derision. "Your actions speak for you. You ran away."

"I couldn't stay here as a Nightmare," I replied, "scaring mortals with no greater purpose."

"It was your role."

"It wasn't the right one. I was meant to be a Seducer, not a Frightener."

He looked at me the way a Bengal tiger watches a deer. "And *I* was meant for greater things than the Abyss, little whore. Yet here I am."

Oh, spare me the pity parade. I folded my arms across my chest. "I'm sorry that your feathers got singed. Maybe You're content to sit back and sulk about it. Me, I couldn't be shoehorned into doing something for all time that I despised." Thinking of how Meg had allowed herself to be punished, I said, "Some, when given a choice, will choose duty over desire. But some won't. I chose not to. If You choose to stay in a role You despise, don't blame anyone but Yourself for it."

"Blame." A smile flitted across those red-stained lips—bruised cherries on bone china. "Perhaps I blame you for embarrassing Me."

"You can't hurt me any worse than You already have. My soul is clean. You have to let me go," I said, the realization breaking over me like the sunrise. "You have to send me back."

Our gazes locked, green on green. Hatred sparkled in His eyes, as pure as His white flesh. "I will see you here, half-breed. Mark my words. We're not finished, you and I. Now get out of My realm."

With that, Michael banished me from Hell.

Chapter 22

Limbo/Paul's Apartment

Through the grayness of nothing: "Jezebel."

Sire?

"I know you listened."

I tried, Sire. But I heard something that He didn't say.

"No, Jezebel. You heard what He wanted to say, but couldn't."

I tried to play the piper, Sire. But He didn't dance.

Laughter, and the feeling of a hand stroking my cheek.

"No, Jezebel. It was He who was the piper, although He didn't know it. When the wolf plays piper for the lamb, the dog will hear the music and will chase the wolf away."

You knew that Meg would save me, Sire?

"And what makes you think that you did not save yourself?"

I couldn't think of a blessed thing to say to that.

A feathery kiss upon my brow. And then: "I don't intend on seeing you again until it's the proper time."

Yes, Sire.

"Farewell, Jezebel."

The gray gave way to swirls of color—

—and I opened my eyes to find myself staring up at Angel's upside-down face. She frowned at me, which was really a smile, and her warm voice announced, "She is here."

She? Oh. That would be me. The former demon, former living, former dead . . .

Oh, fuck it. I was who I was. Whether Jezebel or Jesse Harris, I was me.

Whatever that meant.

Sounds of scuffling, then Daun's face peered over Angel's shoulder, his golden eyes gleaming. "Look at that, a mortal of her word. Welcome back, babes."

Someone took my hand, and even though I couldn't see him from this angle, I knew that Paul was holding me tight. "Love," he said, his voice brimming with joy, "you've really come back. You've come home."

I smiled at him, at all of them. "Hi."

Mental note: Work on better opening lines.

When I tried to sit up, Angel pressed her hands down on my shoulders, kept me pinned. I said, "Let me up, will you?"

"You need to take it slow," she said. "You've been dead for hours. That's going to take a while to shake off."

"I'll take vitamins in the morning. Please, let me up."

Sighing, she helped prop me up. Then Paul scooped me into his strong arms, crushed me in an embrace. Hugging him back, I breathed in his smell—oh, bless me, it was so nice to be breathing again—taking in the heady mix of musk and sweat and gunmetal that was all Paul.

My love.

"Thank God you've come back," he whispered.

I didn't think God had anything to do with it, but far be it from me to ruin the moment. "I told you I'd see you soon."

Gripping my shoulders, he broke the embrace, gently pushing me away from his body to glare at me. "You had some damn nerve doing what you did."

"Which part?"

"All of them. Especially seducing me, then slipping your magic bracelet on me when my guard was down." He lifted his hand, showed me the golden Rope clinging to his wrist.

"If I remember correctly," I said, "you were the one who asked if it was time for us to kiss and make up."

"That was because you worked your wiles on me. And not

just any wiles. Demon wiles. What's a mortal supposed to do in the face of demon wiles?"

More than the smile on his lips, I saw his love for me shining in his eyes, stars swimming in the ocean. "So now you believe that I really was a succubus?"

"Well," he said dryly, "seeing you with hooves and red skin was a hell of an argument."

Heh. "And you're okay with that?"

"Let me think for a minute. Yes." He lifted my chin in his hand, stared deep into my eyes. "I love you, Jesse Harris. Jezebel. Whatever name you want. We can figure out the whole difference in religion thing as we go."

"You know," I said, "I don't really have a religion."

"Jess."

"More like a world view."

"Jess."

"But it's pretty adaptable . . ."

"Jess. Now would be a good time to kiss me."

"You bet."

We sealed our lips together and kissed as if our souls depended on it.

"Hey," Daun said, "bets on whether the foreplay's longer than the actual fucking?"

Angel cleared her throat. "My Lord, perhaps we should let them be?"

"Be what? Hot and bothered? Me, I want to watch."

Sighing, Paul ended the kiss. "More later."

"Aw," Daun said, "what's the matter, Shoulders? You're not into exhibitionism?"

Paul shot Daun a look. "Last I heard, this was my apartment. Why don't you give us a little privacy?"

"You're the one about to ravage her on the sofa," Daun said with a shrug. "If you were a gentleman, you'd take her to the bedroom. If you're going to do her here, least you can do is let us watch."

Hold the phone. I said to Paul, "You can see Daun?" In his true form, the incubus should have been invisible to Paul, his words nothing more than a tickle in Paul's mind.

"If he's the thing that looks like a satyr," said Paul, "then yeah, I see him."

"'Thing,'" Daun said, grinning. "I like that. You trying to butter me up, Shoulders?"

Crap, crap, crap. I could handle the paranormal shit; seeing auras (sometimes) and being threatened by malefic entities (frequently) sort of went with the territory. But Paul was human. Normal. A mouth breather. He wasn't supposed to get hit with stuff like this. My head started an impromptu bongo jam session, so I rubbed the bridge of my nose. No help. Welcome to Migraine Country.

"And I see there's something different about the blonde next to you," Paul said.

I glanced at the cherub, who was blinking prettily. Even utterly confused, she was stunning. Bitch. I said, "You mean, besides how her legs basically start at her chin?"

"Jesse Harris," Angel said primly, "my limbs are all proportioned quite evenly."

Bless me, at least she was still stupid. That made me grin.

"And I see the sorority girl," Paul said, "sitting in the easy chair in the corner."

Sorority girl?

Following where Paul pointed, I saw Meg curled up in the overstuffed chair, her legs tucked daintily beneath her, her white toga resplendent. Her long brown hair framed her face in ringlets. She blew me a kiss, then grinned wickedly.

"Really," Meg said, batting her lashes. "Don't let us stop you. Pretend we're not here."

Daun waggled his brows. "Better yet, you guys take requests?"

Next to me on the sofa, Angel blushed.

"Right," I said, my head throbbing. "Anyone want a drink?"

There's something rather surreal about having coffee with someone powerful enough to erase your existence with a thought.

"Milk?"

Meg made a face.

"Yeah," I said, "I know. Me too. But the humans seem to like it."

"Now, if you were stocked up on the blood of innocents, then I'd take you up on it."

"Sorry, fresh out. I think you need to get that at a health food store."

From the living room we heard Daun guffaw. "Sure," the incubus said, "you could make her meow. But did you really turn her into a cat? *I* can do that."

"You know," Paul said with a sigh, "I was quoting from a movie."

"What, so now there was no girl? Or no cat?"

Meg and I exchanged a look. She said, "Should we tell the angel to join us?"

Shaking my head, I stirred more sugar into my coffee. "Someone's got to keep those two from pissing on the carpet."

"Do men really do that?"

I shrugged. "Depends on how much they want to out-testosterone each other . . . "

There was a muffled thump from the other room, then a tinkling sound.

"Sorry," Daun said.

Paul shouted, "You sure you're a satyr and not a bull in a china shop?"

"Hey, no need to insult my parentage."

"I can fix it," Angel said quickly.

Meg and I ducked our heads low.

"So," I asked, tuning out the male grumbles from the other room, "how'd it go with your sister?"

She frowned, and for a moment her baby blue aura spiked with orange slashes: a grudge from long ago, unceasing anger. An argument with no resolution and too many hurt feelings to ever reconcile. "Not so good," Meg admitted. "We don't see eye-to-eye on some things."

My head slammed into overdrive, and the aura winked out. Rubbing my temple, I said, "Like on how your King is a—"

"Don't say it."

I smiled sheepishly. "I was going to say, a conflicted individual."

"Liar." She sighed. "Ally and I got into a fight a long, long time ago. Never really healed the rift between us."

"Still," I said, "she tried to help you. If not for her, you'd still be hanging on His throne room wall."

"Yeah. She was a big help." She paused. "She was quite keen on sacrificing you for me."

I took a sip of coffee as I mulled that over. "She doesn't like me, does she?"

"Not one whit."

"Just because you and I are friends?"

"You know how Hell is on that sort of thing."

Humph. "Some entities have no taste."

"And some humans push their damn luck," she said, shooting me a look. "What on Earth were you thinking, kissing Him like that?"

I felt my cheeks flame, as if to fend off the ice from His lips. "I don't know, I just . . . bless me, Meg, I felt sorry for Him. I thought I understood Him, wanted to show Him that I understood what it's like to try to be something you're not."

Meg pinned me with her gaze. "Two things, Jez. One, never, ever, feel anything for an Archangel but awe and dread. And two, you have to start showing your understanding in other ways than sucking their faces off. Your man won't like it if you start kissing every creature you think is in poor spirits."

"Hey," I said, affronted. "He was the one who tried to eat my face. I just wanted to be nice. Why're you yelling at *me*?"

"Because what you did was stupid." She sighed, sloshed her coffee in her cup. "No matter what you may think, Archangels are dangerous. They don't have emotions the way humans do. They're all ego. And they're concerned only with themselves."

"Not all of them," I said, thinking of Lucifer.

Meg frowned at me. "*All* of them, Jez. Some may change over time. But no matter their words, no matter their form, they're still Archangels, the first creations of the Almighty. You should stay far away from them."

I blew out a sigh, lifting my bangs off my brow. "No worries there. The only two I know personally are in dimensions other than mine. And I'm planning on staying here for the rest of my life."

"He's not going to let you live your life unaffected by Hell," she said quietly. "If you think you can just bury your head in mortal sand, you're mistaken. You need to be on your guard. He has a long memory."

My voice tight, I asked, "Why does He hate me so much?"

Meg stared at me, her unreadable blue eyes searching for something I couldn't name. Finally she said, "You offended Him."

"By running?"

"No. That was an affront that He probably would have overlooked after time had passed."

"Then what?"

She took a sip of coffee before she replied. "You have a way of flaunting your free will as if it's the latest fashion."

"Oh please," I said, "not you too. It's not a question of free will. It's about choice. You guys make it sound like the nefarious and the celestials really can't think for themselves, which is utter bullshit. I made my choice, and I'm just as much a creature of the Pit as you, or as Him."

"Jezzie," Meg sighed, "you're wrong."

"About what?"

"Whether from Hell or Heaven, supernatural entities aren't meant to choose things. They have a role, and they complete that role to the best, or worst, of their abilities. But not you." She paused, stared into her cup as if trying to read the future. "If you don't like something, you change it. You act. You don't realize just how rare that ability for action really is."

I shook my head. "Choice is all around me. For Hell's sake, Meg, *you* gave me a choice." She looked up at me, and I met her unflinching gaze. "A month ago, you came after me, were going to drag me back to the Underworld. But you didn't take me. You asked if I'd return with you."

"And you said no," she said.

"And I said no."

"And then I led you to your death." Her face paled, and she

looked like she was about to vomit. "That was one of the hardest things I ever did, in all of my existence."

My voice soft, I asked, "Why did you give me the choice, Meg?"

She didn't answer right away. I waited, sipping my coffee, my heart racing from caffeine and anticipation. Finally, she said, "Maybe you have a way of influencing those around you. Or maybe we've always had choices, but we didn't know that we did. And maybe, knowing that we do have free will, maybe some of us aren't strong enough to handle that." Frowning, she looked away.

"Hey," I said, "you're one of the strongest creatures I know." I reached out and patted her hand. "And I don't mean in the unimaginable might kind of way. You can handle anything."

She smiled, looking sad and hopeful all at once. "You think so?"

"I know so."

"And Jezzie knows all, huh?" She laughed softly, stared at my hand on hers.

"Sweetie, I'm not going to argue that point." I lifted my cup for another sip.

She said, "I'm going away for a bit. I need to think things through. Should be back in a couple of years."

I nearly splurted my coffee over the tabletop. Bless me, non sequiturs should come with warnings about hot beverages. "Years? You're leaving your role as a Fury?"

"More like taking a long-deserved vacation. Be good, Jez." She winked at me. "Or, if you're going to be evil, don't get caught. Bye."

I spluttered, "Wait!"

She waited.

"You don't mean you're leaving now, right this second, do you?"

"Why not?" she asked, shrugging. "There's nothing good on television."

"But . . ." I floundered, trying to think of how to make her stay. Now that I had my friend back, the last thing I wanted to do was tell her goodbye. "We've got to go shopping, get you some decent traveling clothes. The toga look is so BCE."

"Thanks," she said, "but no. New York City's too expensive."

"Boston, then."

"Sorry, Jez."

"You can't go yet," I said, racking my brain for anything that would delay her impromptu trip. "I haven't asked you any of the questions I have."

She smiled, shook her head ruefully. "You're a piece of work, I'll say that for you. Tell you what—I'll answer you one question. Just one. But then no more stalling, girl. I've got an interdimensional plane to catch."

Just one? Crap. I had only about a million of them. I bit my lip, thinking. Why was the Hecate watching me? What was the deal with the auras? Why was Paul able to see supernatural entities? Daun bonded my soul once—was I free of his influence? Would I see Lucifer again?

Those were just some of the personal questions, which didn't even graze the surface of the big-ticket items. Was Michael the worst thing for the Underworld, or would He prove to be its redeemer? Or Alecto?

And what about God—so silent and yet, if I listened to Michael, so judgmental—why was He not intervening to save His favorite creation? Was the Devil going to destroy everything?

Whose side was Hell really on?

"There's a time limit on this offer."

"Okay," I said, flipping through the myriad questions and grabbing one. "In Hell, the Rhymers and the King both called me 'half-breed.' What's that about?"

Meg smiled. "You should ask your sire."

"Hey, no fair being mysterious. That's not an answer."

"Yes it is. It's just not the one you want to hear."

She had a point. Thinking of Lucifer, I touched my brow, felt His kiss—so simple, so gentle. So warm.

Even the butcher may turn piper.

I said, "Maybe I will ask Him about that." And about His affinity for Aesop.

The sounds of Daun and Paul arguing drifted into the kitchen, and Angel very clearly uttered a curse. Cool.

Then something went boom.

I rolled my eyes. "But at the moment, I've got too many other males on my plate."

Meg laughed. "That you do. See you."

"Meg?"

"Yeah."

"You take care of yourself."

"I will, Jez. And I promise, I'll send you some postcards."

Megaera, one of the Three Erinyes and my best friend, blew me a kiss. Then she disappeared. I tasted peppermint and old parchment on my lips—her kiss, lingering for a moment, then fading to a memory.

"Bye," I whispered, hoping she would find whatever answers she sought.

Barring that, I hoped she'd at least go on a mad shopping spree. The ancient Greek thing really was so Zeroeth Century.

One thing about dealing with supernatural houseguests: it's a bitch trying to kick them out.

"Maybe one day I'll earn my halo," Angel said, sighing. She was clutching a Luther Vandross CD to her chest, fat tears rolling down her cheeks. We'd learned the hard way that apple juice acted like hundred-proof alcohol in her system. It had taken Paul and me fifteen minutes to coax her down from the ceiling; she'd been convinced that if she stopped clutching the light fixture, the entire room would spin away. Daun had been no help—he'd been too busy puking up a lung from laughter. He was still chuckling, leaning against the wall and watching Angel with sinfully gleeful eyes.

"One day," I agreed, trying to figure out what would sober up a drunken celestial. Maybe some cough medicine? At the very least, that might knock her out . . .

"I'll earn my halo and will sing with the Seraphim," she said, a happy smile on her lips. "And I'll get my name, and it can be anything I want it to be."

Except Elektra, Peaches said. *That one's mine.*

I told my conscience it should consider sharing the name. She raspberried me and skulked away into the corner of my mind.

Angel started singsonging the Psalm of David.

Gah! "We've got to do something," I said, desperate.

"Maybe coffee?" Paul suggested.

"Didn't work before." Angel had finished the pot, with no effect other than being a wide-awake drunk. "I'm thinking cough syrup."

"I'll get it."

I watched him scoot down the hall. Bless me, his ass looked so good in those jeans . . .

"So, babes," Daun said. "You going to tell your meat pie?"

I glanced at him, my guard immediately up. "Tell him what?"

"Why, about us," he said, a lazy smile on his face. "You begging me to fuck you so that you could go rescue him. You coming twice, thanks to my touch. You dying with my name on those sweet lips."

My heart froze.

"Damn," he said, shaking his head. "I do so love that look. No worries, babes. Mum's the word. If there's one thing that demons are good at, it's hording dark secrets. Just remember that you and I both know the truth."

"The truth," I said coldly, "is that I did what I had to do to rescue him."

"Right," he said, staring at me from across the room. "So my touch means nothing to you now."

Invisible fingers slid down my shirt, cradled my left breast. Tingles ran up the backs of my legs as those fingers danced over my curves.

Swallowing thickly, I whispered, "Stop that."

"Stop what?"

The hand moved down, touched me between my legs, pressed. I gasped, rocked my hips as those fingers stroked my nub. "That," I panted. "Stop that."

A finger slipped inside me, flicked my core. I bit my lip to keep from crying out as I came.

"Stopped," Daun said, licking his finger. "Sticky sweet."

Fuck. My panties were completely soaked. "You are such a bastard."

Invisible fingers pinched my ass. I squealed, jumping about a foot in the air.

"Smile when you say that, babes."

"Here we go," Paul said as he walked up the hall, holding a bottle of over-the-counter relief. "It's the evil green liquid, I forgot to buy the caplets . . ." He stopped, looked first at me, then at Daun, who was still sucking his finger. "Did I miss something?"

"Nothing important," I said, flaying Daun from head to hoof with my gaze.

"Not on the level of, say, the Announcement," Daun said between sucks.

Paul looked at me. "Announcement?"

Daun smiled.

I took a deep breath. "Sweetie, I can't tell you. It was from before, and it's officially filed under Off Limits. I'm sorry."

"You had to be there," Daun said. "It was the biggest thing Hell had ever seen."

"Daun, stop being such a dick."

The smile morphed into something evil. "You want me to be a dick, Jez? Just say the word."

Hooboy.

"It's okay, Jesse," Paul said, emphasizing the name. "You can't tell me. I got it. I'm okay with that."

I could have slurped him up like hot chocolate. "Really?"

He cast Daun an unreadable look. "How's it go? There are more things in Heaven and Earth than are dreamed of in your philosophy."

"You're murdering Shakespeare," Daun said.

"And yet, somehow, I'm able to live with myself." Paul stared hard at the incubus. "Jesse can't tell me some things about her past. I'm okay with that. Hell, I'm okay with her wanting to keep on dancing."

"*Really?*" I said, stunned. "But I thought . . ."

He turned to face me. "I don't like other guys seeing you naked and fantasizing about sleeping with you. But if that's what you want to do, if that's what makes you happy, then I'll come to grips with it. I don't have to like it, but I'll deal." He shrugged. "Could be worse. I'm just glad you changed careers in the first place."

I ran up to him and squeezed him until I heard his bones creak. "I love you, you big goof."

He embraced me, held me tight. "I love you too, Jess."

"Excuse me while I vomit from all the love in the air," Daun said, then proceeded to make puking sounds.

I ignored the incubus. "Sweetie, I don't want to make you unhappy. If my dancing really bothers you that much, I'll stop."

"We'll talk about it later," he said.

"I know," Angel said, sitting cross-legged on the carpet in front of the stereo. "You can teach other angels how to be seductive!"

I stared at her. "Say what?"

"You know, for those of us stuck being Seducers. Damn me, what do angels know about seduction? It's a. It's a. You know."

I said, "A sin?"

She snapped her fingers. "Exactly. A sin. We're not supposed to do sin. But now we do. And we're terrible at it."

"She's right," Daun said. "They are."

"So you could teach us!" Angel's eyes lit with passion.

"Brilliant idea. Here," Paul said, handing her a capful of evil green liquid. "Why don't you toast Jesse's new career move?"

"Ooh, green," she said. "Pretty. Like Jesse Harris's eyes." She quaffed the medicine, then gagged. "Damn me, what is that? It's horrible!"

"It'll help you sober up," Paul said. "Maybe."

"We hope," I said.

"Blech." She wiped her tongue on her arm. "Look, Jesse Harris. I'm like you kissing."

I blinked. "Excuse me?"

"She sticks her tongue out when she kisses me," she confided to Paul. "It's sort of disgusting. But I didn't tell her that. You know. Didn't want to hurt her feelings."

Paul and Daun both stared at me. I said, "What? I was proving a point."

The two males exchanged a look.

"I don't want to know," Paul said.

"I do. You sucked face with the angel here, and you didn't tell me? Babes, I would have paid good money to see that. I would have forfeited a week's soul quota to see that. You and the angel? Really?"

"She said I tasted like gold," Angel said, then hiccoughed.

"So, what does gold taste like?" Paul asked me.

I shrugged. "Angels."

"She'd be such a good teacher," Angel said, yawning. "Except for the kissing part." Then she snuggled against Paul and fell asleep. Even her snores were gorgeous.

I sighed. For an utter bitch, she was sort of cute. Like a puppy. A baby hellhound. A hellpuppy?

"I'll take her," Daun said to Paul, grabbing the cherub and cradling her to his chest. "She can sleep it off in Pandemonium."

"No taking advantage of the unconscious celestial," I said.

"Right, as if. She's just a frigid bitch."

Thinking of Michael's arctic kiss, I shivered.

"You two lovebirds have fun." Daun smiled at me. "And no worries, Jezzie. I won't come calling. You and I, we're quits."

"Really," I said, not believing him.

"You're too human for me, babes. I have different standards."

Before he bamfed away in a puff of sulfur with the snoring angel, I caught a glimpse of his aura: red and green, like Christmas for the damned. And I knew that he was lying. I wasn't too human for him—far from it. But hey, demons were made for lying.

I'd be seeing Daunuan again. I'd bet my soul on it.

On second thought, I wouldn't. This soul cost me a Hell of a lot. I think I'll keep it.

"Love," I said to Paul, "this is the part where we kiss."

He walked up to me, took my hand. "And have wild animal sex?"

I smiled just thinking about it. "Only if you ask nicely."

Please turn the page for an exciting sneak peek at
Jackie Kessler's next book in the *Hell on Earth* series:
the incubus Daunuan's story,
HOTTER THAN HELL,
coming August 2008!

Chapter 1

Coitus Interruptus

Anyone in my position would've thought the buzzing in my head was anticipation. Five minutes to go, then the client would be eating from my hand. Literally. I had the grapes ready and waiting in the ice bucket, chilling. She liked it when I let the cluster dangle over her lips—she'd poke her tongue out, sinewy and slick against the ripe fruit, darting pink flesh over purple. Sweetness on sweetness, both begging to be sucked. Plucked. My blood pounded through me, boom *boom*, boom *boom*, sending happy signals to my brain and my balls, getting my body primed. T minus five minutes, and counting. Small talk until then—light touches here, knowing smiles there, lying about her job and mine. Thinking about sex. Killing time.

So it sort of wasn't my fault that I didn't sense the demon approaching.

The client had moved some things around in the bedroom since my last visit. Now her wedding photo was missing ("Getting it reframed") and the threadbare pink comforter had been replaced with one that was red and advertised sin. We sprawled on the bed, clothing still on, intentions thick in the air. She was decked out in a white silk sheath and pearls and lacy thigh-highs. I was a study of blacks. A bit cliché, but Tall, Dark, and Handsome was all the rage. She liked it, and I aimed to please.

"I got a new perfume," my client said. "Envy Me."

"I'd prefer to ravish you."

Her smile pulled into a grin—white teeth flashing in a lip-stick sea of red. "The perfume, I mean. It's Gucci." She leaned forward, offering me her neck as she pressed her breasts against my chest and rubbed. Looking for a quick feel through the silk. My kind of woman. She purred, "Like it, baby?"

Inhaling deeply, I took in the peony and jasmine and other scents blending together with her eager sweat, her underlying smell of female in heat. "Nice," I lied. Me, I preferred the musk of her sex alone, without the cloying flowery scent over it. "You smell good enough to eat." No lie there.

"Yeah?" She was playful, almost kittenish. "You going to . . . eat me?"

Heh. Sex kittenish. "Oh yeah, doll. Eat you alive." Among other things.

"My big bad wolf."

That made me chuckle. Brushing her hair away from her face, I said, "You my little red riding hood?"

"Depends, baby. You want me to ride you?"

I smiled, wistful. "Like you would not believe."

My head buzzed, hummed as she oozed sex, her body prac-tically begging me to climb on top of her. Soon, doll. Soon. She jiggled against me once more, reached her hand out to-ward my thigh—stroked once, lushly, then pulled back. She knew the dance by now: only teasing at first, quick-fingered taunts. Nothing overt. Not yet.

Seduction, after all, had its rules. Date Number One had been all about getting her to kiss me. Number Two had been pleasing her like no other man or woman ever had before. Three had been making her want me more than anything else. (One thing about us Seducers: we always put our clients' de-sires ahead of our own. If not for the rules, I would've fucked her silly after I introduced myself.)

Here we were at Date Number Four: D-Day, the Big One. My Turn. Otherwise known as The Payoff. It set my blood to boil just thinking about it.

But first things first: I had to get her revving, ready, steady go on the first real touch. Thus a five-minute warmup of sex-ual tension. Seduction 101. Child's play. And never mind how that single stroke of hers on my leg had rippled up my back, settled into my stomach. I shifted; the front of my pants was too damn tight.

Sometimes the rules really sucked.

"Don," she said, her voice a low purr that went straight to my crotch. That's all she said: my name, or her version of my name. That's all she needed to say. Her hand again, now on my stomach. I wagged a no-no-no with my finger as I grinned, thinking about how she'd taste like candy. Thinking about how she'd call my name.

Mmm. Shivers.

"I've been waiting for this all week," she whispered.

"Me too."

"I couldn't stop thinking about you." She dropped her gaze to my fly, where she saw just how much I was thinking about her. Her desire filled the air, thick and pungent, as she begged me to come on, baby, let's get started already.

But damn, how I wanted to. Oh, the things I wanted to do. Would do. Four minutes—no, less now. Three and counting. I said her name, put just the right amount of foreplay into my voice.

She looked up at me through her makeup-crusted lashes, slowly ran her tongue over her fuck-me lips. Bedroom eyes; blowjob mouth. Intoxicating. Boom *boom*, boom *boom*.

"Now, baby," she said, her voice a throaty growl. The woman was giving way to the animal, to the instinct that tingled deep inside her. Giving way to lust. And all with no nudging from me. *Sweet*. She said again: "Now." Insistent. Demanding.

A hum again, this time strong enough to make me sit up. Frowning, I felt the buzz resonate through me, pitched high in warning. No this wasn't just anticipation. This was—

—her mouth on mine, her tongue jabbing through my lips and running against my teeth. My momentary caution faded into bemused surprise. She usually wasn't so direct, but who gave a damn? Screw the countdown to bliss. She was ready. Steady.

Go.

Heat rolled over me, bathed me in fire from head to toe. I

opened my mouth to hers, pushed that heat into her. She said "Mmmmmm," melted into the kiss like chocolate over flame. I washed my hands over the silk of her body, and the buzzing in my head sputtered, died.

Oh, doll, how I'm going to make you scream . . .

She groaned against me, and my tongue lapped up the sound. I left her mouth to kiss up the length of her jaw, now playing by the lobe of her ear. She squirmed against me, all soft and delicious, delectable, making contented sounds that told me I hit one of her sweet spots. Her hand clenched on my shoulder, then pushed. With a hungry "Rrrr," she rolled me onto my back, straddled my hips. The hem of her dress rode up, exposing the fullness of her upper thighs, the flash of white satin panties.

Boom *boom.*

"This is different," I murmured, my hands on her waist.

"You're always so good to me, baby." Her voice was thick with need, her eyes dark and brimming. Leaning down, she poured herself over me to whisper in my ear, "I want to ride you. Now."

Maybe I ditched the countdown, but other rules had to stay in place. Clients first, even on D-Day. That was ever the rule. So I ignored the ache in my groin and said, "Ladies first, doll."

"Don . . ."

"Maybe I'll take the grapes, run them over your naked body. Nibble them off your skin."

"I don't want grapes. I want you."

"You got me."

"No I don't. You never let me do you, bring you there." She gyrated over my crotch, a slow dry hump that did maddening things to me. "It's always been about me."

"I'm a giving sort of guy," I said, my voice husky.

"Your turn, baby," she said, punctuating her promise with wet kisses down my neck. Her fingers played by my crotch, and over the buzzing in my head and the pounding of my heart, I heard her unzip my fly. "I'm going to love you so fine," she said, "you're going to sing my name. I'm going to make you explode."

Down she kissed, down my chest, my stomach, my—

Wa-*hoo*.

Okay, maybe the customer was always right . . .

In the midst of mind-blowing pleasure, a deafening crash, followed by a man's shout: "What the fuck're you doing with my wife?"

Uh oh.

Louder than the man's words, the buzzing screamed its warning in my head.

Shit.

Getting interrupted in the middle of sex is bad enough. Worse is when the cause of *coitus interruptus* is a demon.

A glance told me all I needed to know: he was obscenely muscled, and his eyes glowed with malefic presence. Definitely not a Seducer; I would've felt the psychic connection. Sloth was out of the question. Pride, maybe, or Envy . . .

Between my legs, the client was still going to town. Side effect of entrancing the clientele over the course of four dates: they wound up being a bit one-track minded. Usually it was anything but a problem; at the moment, though, the pleasure was a tad . . . distracting. Not that I was complaining.

Because my client didn't seem to be one to talk with her mouth full, I put on my charming face and said to her husband, "Your wife's told me so much about you."

He roared, a wordless cry of pure rage. Terrific—one of the Berserkers was riding his body. They weren't exactly known for their reasoning skills. How was I supposed to convince a demon of Wrath that the client was mine? Hell knew I had all the paperwork to prove it . . .

The husband cocked back a fist. The flesh burned red, and energy sizzled off his skin.

Whoops. I grabbed my client by her shoulders and pulled her off of me, then rolled with her to the floor. She landed on top of me, her mouth working like a landed fish. Sandwiched between the wall and the bed, we were trapped. Last Stand at the Sealy Corral.

From the other side of the bed: "I'll kill the both of you!"

The haze of passion began to clear from my client's eyes. Before the fear took hold, I ran a finger over her brow, pushing a command into her mind. She crumpled on my chest, dead asleep. I nudged her to the ground. Back in a second, doll.

Far over my head, a bolt of magic slammed into the wall. Smoking plaster fluttered down, singeing my face with tiny kisses. Maybe the man was possessed, but he was also a lousy shot.

He bellowed, "Think you can sleep with my wife?"

"Actually," I called back, "sleeping wasn't what I had in mind."

He screamed his fury, then the wall behind me exploded. I threw myself over the unconscious woman, shielding her from the smoking debris. I'd be blessed if I let another demon claim her. I'd been on her case for a month; she didn't die until I said so.

Sometimes, I was as possessive as a Coveter.

Pieces of the ruined wall crashed on me and around me, covered me in filth and soot. Dust made me sneeze, and sneezing during a fight was both dangerous and rather lame, so I stopped breathing. The stench of smoke lingered in my nostrils. Nice. Reminded me of home. Not including the part about getting buried by a falling wall. The wreckage hadn't killed me—when I was on a collection, the only thing human about me was my appearance—but getting slammed with it hurt like a bastard. My own fault; I should have known better than to taunt a Berserker.

Over the sound of the settling rubble, he shouted, "You dead yet, asshole?"

"Hate to break it to you, chuckles, but you missed."

Couldn't help it. For demons, Berserkers were just so fucking stupid.

"Seducer!" The man's voice deepened to that of a constipated buffalo's bellow. "I'm going to rip you apart!"

"Some nefarious just talk, talk, talk." I shot my arm out and leveled a blast overhead. The light fixture shattered and crashed down to the ground. I heard the man jump clear and land heavily in the far end of the room. Recharging my power as the man regained his footing, I reviewed the possibilities. It came down to three options.

One: I could kill the possessed human.

No, the paperwork involved in the accidental slaying of a mortal would kill my sex drive for the better part of a decade.

Two: I could run.

Hah, as if.

Three: I could banish the demon, leave the human alive.

Ding ding ding, we have a winner. Banishing, *sans* killing. That meant attacking him directly with my magic was right out. And *that* meant I had to figure out what his weakness was and kick-start the exorcism.

It occurred to me that priests had other uses besides between meal snacks. Live and learn.

The sound of clumping footfalls, along with labored breathing. Some mortals just couldn't take a hint. I scrambled to the foot of the bed and yanked on the baseboard until I pried the wood free. Shouting to do the Banshees proud, I leapt up and hurled the makeshift weapon at the human.

And . . . bullseye! The wood splintered against his torso with a satisfying crack. He staggered back three steps, blinked stupidly at the slivers embedded in his flesh. Then he snarled something about my parentage and aimed another blast my way. I hit the carpet two seconds before it rained plaster again.

Wood was a big no. What else? I didn't have any iron on hand . . .

He shouted, "Come out and fight like a man!"

"I'm not a man." I reached out blindly, found the ice bucket, heavy with grapes and melted ice. The rim and handle on the black lacquered wood gleamed with a silver sheen. Yes, maybe silver would do the trick. Come a little closer, chuckles. Give me a hug.

"Fight me!" Two voices spoke the same command—the mortal's ire blending with the demon's innate Wrath.

I gripped the bucket, getting ready for the windup. "Don't you think two on one is a bit unfair?"

"Fight me!"

"Come here and make me."

He shrieked his unholy rage, and then I heard him stomp toward me. Charge of the Dark Brigade. I popped up and pitched the ice bucket at the ballistic human, catching him full in the face. The silver handle bonked him about a second before the melted ice and chilled fruit splattered on his skin . . . skin that immediately bubbled and smoked. He roared in either fury or agony, and then he swatted madly at his face.

Gotcha.

I took a moment to zip up my fly. Then I stepped around the wreckage strewn almost artfully through the ruins of the bedroom to approach the wounded demon. Under my feet, a collage of shattered glass sparkled amid the chunks of smoking plaster and plywood. Love really was a battlefield.

The man had fallen to the floor, clutching at his steaming face and gibbering in pain. Interesting. The silver handle was nowhere near him, yet he was still reacting so strongly . . . Ah. Smiling, I scooped up a handful of stray ice cubes. Allergic to water, my my. If I had any feelings, I would have felt sorry for the creature; having such an Elemental sensitivity would crimp any demon's style. But I've never been accused of being compassionate.

Water pooling in my hand, I squatted over the squirming form. "Need a towel?"

Beneath his clawed fingers, the flesh of the man's face looked rather spongy. Hmm. Hope that's not permanent. I didn't think the human would be long on the mortal coil with his face slipping off his skull. The thought of all the red tape associated with accidental slaughter made my stomach roil. Damned bureaucracy would be the death of me.

He snarled, "Bless yourself, asshole!"

"Don't suppose it'll help to tell you there's been a mix-up," I said, juggling the ice from hand to hand.

Lowering his fingers, the Berserker glared up at me through the human's red-rimmed eyes. "No mix up, whoremaster."

"That's 'Mister Whoremaster' to you."

He spat at me, but the thick glob sizzled and vanished before it touched my skin. Company perk: adjustable heat aura.

"Bastard!"

"Now, now," I said, dangling a sweating cube over his face. "Play nice, kitty, or you get a bath. What do you mean, no mix-up?"

For a long moment, he stared his hatred at me, charged the air with fury so brutally raw that my flesh should have been flayed from my bones. Finally he said, "I was sent on purpose."

"A snafu, then. I've got all the paperwork. She's mine, chuck-les."

"No snafu."

Oh really? "Explain yourself."

"Killers, the man and woman both."

I'd known about the woman; there was a reason she was a client, after all. The man, though, was a surprise. Then again, I hadn't bothered to research him. He wasn't the one I was supposed to fuck to death. "What, they get off on murder?"

"Thrill of the bloodshed." His eyes gleamed, and a smile unfurled on his softening face. "The gospel of butchery. The ecstasy of violence."

"Uh huh." I'd heard the Wrath party line before. "That's lovely. But she's still mine."

"No, whoremonger." He bared his teeth in a parody of a grin. "The flesh puppets, they were to kill you."

Jaw clenched, I said, "Kill *me*?" Humans, attacking a demon? Outside of some wildly popular television shows, that was un-heard of. There had to have been a mistake.

"They were to bathe in your blood," he said with a sigh of pleasure. "Then I was to slit their throats, claim them both for Wrath."

Blinking, I repeated, "For *Wrath*?"

"Want I should speak in smaller words, rake?"

I didn't know which was more insulting—that the humans wanted to kill me, or that a Berserker was insinuating I was stupid. A snarl on my lips, I crushed the ice in one of my hands and wiped it over the remains of his forehead. His squeal of pain was almost worth the mess of melted flesh on my fingers.

After his screeching faded, I said, "Why me?"

Arms wrapped over his head, I almost didn't hear his muffled reply. "Would be telling."

I still couldn't grasp that the mortals had wanted to slice and dice me. *Me.* That wasn't in the Demon Playbook. Not that we had a playbook, but still . . . "She was *my* target," I insisted.

"Murder is murder. The more, the better." Panting, he peered out from his barricade of arms. "Kill two humans, kill one Seducer. All the same to Wrath. But destroying you, that would have given me pleasure." He chuckled wetly. "You understand pleasure, no?"

I sat heavily on my haunches. Well, this just sucked angel feathers. Where did humans get off, thinking they could actually take down a demon? Next thing you knew, they'd be shooting me with silver bullets and flinging Holy Water on me. Idiots.

No, my client couldn't have known I was a demon. To her and her husband—before he'd been possessed—I'd been just another flesh puppet, one whom they could play with and prey on. No more.

The man's breathing took on a burbling sound. I said, "You dying on me, chuckles?"

"You Seducers . . . all the same," the demon whispered. "Clap-carrying . . . sluts . . . suck the fight . . . out of a body."

Could I help it if I was a lover, not a fighter?

"Paperwork . . . keep you bound . . . for eons."

"Ah, go to Hell." I dropped the rest of the melting ice on him.

"**O**pen your eyes, doll."

My client's eyelids fluttered, then opened. The confusion I saw staring back at me was like a shot of whisky burning the back of my throat. Mmmm. Straddling her hips, I rubbed against her, just once, just enough to send her body signals her brain was still too fuzzy to interpret. Beneath us, the ruined bed protested but still held. I was planning on breaking it within ten minutes. Anticipation . . .

She blinked, tried to open her mouth. Then she tried to move her body. No dice; she was frozen on her back, her arms by her sides, her virginal white silk dress covering her from knockers to knees. Confusion sparked into fear. I inhaled deeply, took in the scent of her growing terror.

Boom *boom*.

"You're wondering why you can't move." I smiled, picturing all the things I was about to do to her. "You're wondering what happened. I'll recap."

I stretched over her, ran my hand from her cheek down to her chin, her neck, her breast, her belly. "You were going down on me when your loving husband came tearing into the room." I reached behind me until my hand found her crotch. Sliding between her legs, I ran two fingers over the whisper softness of her satin panties, felt the lips of her vulva quiver. "He was going to kill me, with help from you."

She stiffened beneath me.

Grinning, I said, "That's him on the floor. Had the audacity to die and not remove himself after. I'm afraid he's going to stink up the place in another day or so."

Her eyes slipped closed, and tears leaked through her lids. How touching. I pushed her underwear to the side and stroked my fingers over her clitoral hood, then pressed gently. Stroke, press.

"No worries, doll," I said. "You won't miss him for long."

Stroke. I heard her breath catch in her throat, and I grinned as I pressed, lingering. Now her inner muscles tensed with my touch, seemed to reach for my fingers as I moved them away. Passion in the depths of despair. Sin at its sweetest. The smell of her fear was now spiced with desire. Demonic aromatherapy.

"I have a question for you. I'll go easier on you if you tell me the truth. And believe me, I can smell the truth on you." I rubbed her sex harder. "You do believe me, don't you? Go ahead, doll. Speak."

"Yes," she said thickly.

"Good. Now then, tell me why you and Loving Husband didn't try to kill me on our first Date."

Shuddering from my touch, she said, "You were a surprise. We always pick our takes together. But you, you came on to me. He was out of town, and you picked me up . . ." Her voice turned into a moan as I reached inside her, nudging her toward bliss.

"So your man was away, and you decided to play?"

"You kissed me," she breathed, "and nothing else mattered . . ."

Have to love the demon gigolo mojo. Gigolojo at its best.

"Actually, doll, you kissed me." I slid my fingers out of her, then moved my hand up and down her inner thigh, tickling her flesh with her own wetness. She reeked of passion and panic. Mmmm. Soon, soon, soon. "That's how it works. You kiss me willingly, and then boom. Magic. But the fun starts when you call my name."

She opened her eyes, looked at me as those fat tears kept winding down her cheeks. "Please," she said. "I wasn't going to hurt you, not you . . ."

"Uh, uh, uh. That's a lie. Shame. Here you were doing so well until now." I pressed the nails of my fingers harder against her plump thigh. "You and hubby, you were going to kill me good and dead, then do whatever it is serial killers do to celebrate. Champagne, maybe? A blood bath? Tell me true."

"Sex," she whispered. "We have sex. We're already sticky with your blood, and we kiss, tasting you on us . . ."

"Why, doll, that's positively perverted. How impressive!" With my other hand, I cupped her full breast, feeling the hardness of her nipple poking through the silk of her dress. "How many have you killed? I'm just curious."

"Seven . . ."

"A powerful number. So they say." Now I had her other breast in hand, rolling the mound in my fingers, teasing her until the nipple was fully erect, begging me to have a taste.

"Please . . . why can't I move?"

I leaned down to whisper in her ear. "That would be because I commanded you not to move. Boom. Magic."

She bit her lip—a nervous tic that reminded me of someone else. "You a magician?"

A quick suck on her earlobe, then a sharp nip. "I eat magicians for breakfast."

She squeaked: a tiny, terrified sound. I nearly exploded in my pants.

"I'm an incubus," I said, stretching the last *S*. "And do you know what an incubus does to fragile human dolls like you?"

Stinking of terror, she whispered, "No . . ."

I leaned over her until my mouth was bare inches away from hers. "An incubus sucks the life from you. An incubus fucks you and kills you, then takes your soul to Hell."

"*No* . . ."

A quick kiss on her dry lips, wetting her mouth with mine. "So here's where we are, doll. Your man is dead. Your life was already forfeit. Now it's going to happen a bit sooner than I'd planned."

"Please . . ."

I loved it when they begged. "Tell you what, my little murderess. I'll give you a chance. All you have to do is not call my full name when I make you climax. If you can do that, I won't fuck you to death." I'd break her neck. But what was the point of telling her that? "What do you think? Tell me true."

"I . . ." She swallowed, said, "I don't know your full name."

"But you do." I licked the hollow of her throat, kissed the sensitive flesh. "In their souls, all humans know the nefarious. What do you say, doll? I'll screw you so hard you'll see stars." Between her legs, my fingers danced over her slit. She groaned, tried to move, groaned harder when I pressed down. "Think you can keep from calling my name when you come?"

Gasping, she said, "Yes."

"Wonderful." I kissed her neck, worked my way down to her breast. Debating whether I should let her move beneath me, I gave her fifty-fifty on being able not to call my name. She was evil down to the core. I had to admire that in a human.

She was mine three minutes and forty-nine seconds later.